DGAR ALLAN POE may be long beyond this world, but the themes of his terrifying works live on in modern fiction for young adults. And with this collection, a host of some of today's most beloved authors come together to reimagine Poe's most terrifying, thrilling tales in new and unexpected ways.

Whether Poe's stories are already familiar or discovered here for the first time, readers will revel in the errors and thrills of his classic tales and how they've been brought to life in thirteen utterly unforgettable ways.

gamut from futuristic to gothic to lots in between. Diversity in race, gender identity, and sexuality is well represented. Poe's ghost happily haunts this fresh, delightfully dark collection."

—*Kirkus Reviews* (starred review)

"While we love Edgar Allan Poe—the original sadboi and Halloween's unofficial literary mascot—we have to admit that his 150-year-old stories could use a 2019-worthy glow-up. The story collection *His Hideous Heart* takes that challenge and *runs* with it. Each of the anthology's contributors revamps or totally reinvents thirteen of Poe's best-known stories and poems, imbuing most of them with a much-needed dose of feminism, LGBTQ representation, and racial diversity."

—*HelloGiggles*

"Thirteen authors reshape short stories by Edgar Allan Poe in a collection that practically pulses with curricular potential. Both well-known works and lesser-known stories are reimagined here, and the retellings echo the suspense, wit, and undeniable sadness that move through the original pieces. Poe's original short stories are all provided in the second half of the book, and any fan of the writer will appreciate these modern takes on the morbid and macabre."

—*The Bulletin of the Center for Children's Books*

"In Adler's inclusive anthology, thirteen YA authors honor Edgar Allan Poe's pioneering work in mystery, horror, and science fiction with retellings that emphasize diverse characters, settings, and genres. Poe fans new and old will find stories to appreciate here."

—*Booklist*

HIS HIDEOUS HEART

*Thirteen of Edgar Allan Poe's
Most Unsettling Tales
Reimagined*

Edited by
Dahlia Adler

FLATIRON
BOOKS
NEW YORK

To Jaclyn, for her generous heart, and of course, to the man himself

HIS HIDEOUS HEART. Copyright © 2019 by Dahlia Adler. All rights reserved. Printed in the United States of America. For information, address Flatiron Books, 120 Broadway, New York, NY 10271.

www.flatironbooks.com

"She Rode a Horse of Fire" copyright © 2019 by Kendare Blake. "It's Carnival!" copyright © 2019 by Tiffany D. Jackson. "Night-Tide" copyright © 2019 by Tessa Gratton. "The Glittering Death" copyright © 2019 by Caleb Roehrig. "A Drop of Stolen Ink" copyright © 2019 by Emily Lloyd-Jones. "Happy Days, Sweetheart" copyright © 2019 by Stephanie Kuehn. "The Raven (remix)" copyright © 2019 by amanda lovelace. "Changeling" copyright © 2019 by Marieke Nijkamp. "The Oval Filter" copyright © 2019 by Lamar Giles. "Red" copyright © 2019 by Hillary Monahan. "Lygia" copyright © 2019 by Dahlia Adler. "The Fall of the Bank of Usher" copyright © 2019 by Fran Wilde. "The Murders in the Rue Apartelle, Boracay" copyright © 2019 by Rin Chupeco.

Grateful acknowledgment is made to reproduce from Project Gutenberg.

Frontispiece and illustrations by Jon Contino

Designed by Devan Norman

The Library of Congress has cataloged the hardcover edition as follows:

Names: Adler, Dahlia, editor. | Poe, Edgar Allan, 1809–1849.
Title: His hideous heart : thirteen of Edgar Allan Poe's most unsettling tales reimagined / edited by Dahlia Adler.
Description: First edition. | New York : Flatiron Books, 2019.
Identifiers: LCCN 2019286687 | ISBN 9781250302779 (hardcover) | ISBN 9781250302786 (ebook)
Subjects: LCSH: Horror tales, American. | Short stories, American. | Young adult fiction, American.
Classification: LCC PZ5 .H638 2019 | DDC 813.0087380806
LC record available at https://lccn.loc.gov/2019286687

ISBN 978-1-250-30279-3 (trade paperback)

Our books may be purchased in bulk for promotional, educational, or business use. Please contact your local bookseller or the Macmillan Corporate and Premium Sales Department at 1-800-221-7945, extension 5442, or by email at MacmillanSpecialMarkets@macmillan.com.

First Flatiron Books Paperback Edition: 2021

10 9 8 7 6 5 4 3 2 1

Contents

Introduction   1

The Tales Retold

"She Rode a Horse of Fire" by Kendare Blake   5

"It's Carnival!" by Tiffany D. Jackson   21

"Night-Tide" by Tessa Gratton   32

"The Glittering Death" by Caleb Roehrig   49

"A Drop of Stolen Ink" by Emily Lloyd-Jones   83

"Happy Days, Sweetheart" by Stephanie Kuehn   110

"The Raven (Remix)" by amanda lovelace   124

"Changeling" by Marieke Nijkamp   132

"The Oval Filter" by Lamar Giles   151

"Red" by Hillary Monahan   170

"Lygia" by Dahlia Adler 182

"The Fall of the Bank of Usher" by Fran Wilde 193

"The Murders in the Rue Apartelle, Boracay" by

 Rin Chupeco 231

About the Authors 253

Acknowledgments 259

The Original Tales

"Metzengerstein" 265

"The Cask of Amontillado" 277

"Annabel Lee" (poem) 286

"The Pit and the Pendulum" 289

"The Purloined Letter" 309

"The Tell-Tale Heart" 334

"The Raven" (poem) 341

"Hop-Frog" 349

"The Oval Portrait" 362

"The Masque of the Red Death" 367

"Ligeia" 376

"The Fall of the House of Usher" 397

"The Murders in the Rue Morgue" 423

Introduction

Love and loss. Grief and death. Rivalry and revenge. The themes of Edgar Allan Poe's work have eternal relevance, but what I remember most about learning it in school was that it just seemed so much cooler than everything else. He turned my skin cold and damp while I read about the catacombs in "The Cask of Amontillado" and slowly crumbled my heart with "Annabel Lee." He set my entire body on edge through "The Tell-Tale Heart" and stole my breath with "The Pit and the Pendulum." He made me mourn for women I'd never met and cheer for retribution I didn't even completely understand, and all I knew was that he was the first person I'd been assigned to read who made me marvel at what an author could do, where an author could place you, what he could make you physically feel.

It's a tall order, running off of those feelings, those memories, and trying to both recapture them and reimagine them into something new. This collection is a way to honor the work of Edgar Allan Poe, but it's also a way to view it through different gazes, to take classic literature with its relatively homogeneous perspectives and settings and give them new life.

What I learned while editing this collection was how much changing those aspects of a story can affect the greater picture, how you can maintain so many of a story's themes but find entirely new motivations by centering characters from society's margins, characters who seldom got to be Poe's heroes.

We all have our dark sides, and we all have our tragedies.

So many of us have seen them through his eyes.

Now I hope you enjoy reading them through ours.

—*Dahlia Adler*

The
Tales
Retold

She Rode a Horse of Fire

»»»» Kendare Blake «««

inspired by "Metzengerstein"

The night the stables burned, the air turned cold and still as in the dead of winter. They had caught not long past 10:00 p.m., but ours was a quiet estate, none of the staff known to keep late hours, and each of us tired into our bones after that evening's revelry. So by the time the main house wakened to the fire, it had gone too far to be stopped. Flames shot up some twenty meters into that still sky as the doors and walls were eaten away and caved in. They said it was a blessing, the still of that night; that it kept the fire from jumping into the trees and making its way to the manor house. But it seemed no blessing to us gathered in the cold, dressed hastily in boots and bedclothes, our horrified faces turned orange by the glare, listening to the shrieks of the horses and men still trapped inside. A violent wind would have been most welcome, if it could have covered that sound.

By morning, all that was left of the stable was a smoking ruin. Someone said later that one of the grooms found the remains of a doorknob, melted and warped. He held it up to his face and laughed at the strangeness just before he burst into tears. Twelve horses and two stablehands perished in the blaze. Good and loyal servants, all. Twelve horses, two stablehands, and one new maid, who had no business in the world being there.

They found her amidst the caved-in rafters, her body nestled beneath a fallen pile of planks. They said her dress was torn and there was blood upon her cheek, but the rest of her was not badly burned. Nearly untouched by the fire. As if her youth and beauty had protected her from it. I can't attest to the veracity of these statements. I lacked the heart to go and see. I didn't want to face the steaming carnage of the others lost, those men and gentle horses whose youth and beauty had not been near protection enough.

After the fire, cleanup at Baron Park was, as ever, fast and thorough. We'd certainly had enough practice, even before Friedrich came into his inheritance and seemed fit to press the limits of debauchery. His parents had been no strangers to balls and soirees, and in summer the grounds were often crowded with guests, stuffed into every room and tucked into every alcove. Their shrieks of laughter kept us awake long into the night—a night we had illuminated for them with hanging lanterns—and in the morning they would snap at us if their empty cocktail glasses clinked together as we cleared them.

They were all the same. Except for Friedrich. Friedrich

never yelled at us, or kicked over our mop buckets when they were in the hall. And if we were late, or slow, or the tables in the billiards room hadn't been cleared of cigar ash, he would only smile and shrug, tug at his sleeves and find another room to lounge in. After his parents died, cruel rumors abounded in the city: rumors of excess, of nights of drinking until dawn, gambling and deep debts. They said he drove his car at speeds that were downright reckless for the twisting, pine-lined roads along the cliffs. But he was only eighteen. Parents dead in a boating accident. He was newly alone and with so much money. It could be argued that given the circumstances his behavior was rather restrained.

But he was still the reason that maid died in the stables.

I saw them go in together, you see. Just past dusk, in that soft light, so the curve of Friedrich's devious smile was still visible along with the unbuttoned collar of his shirt. He had an open bottle of champagne in one hand and was leading her forward with the other. He had already taken her hair down out of its pretty golden twist.

She was a terrible maid. Didn't even know how to dust properly and looked aghast when someone suggested she scrape the dishes clean or empty a trash bin. She had been with us nearly two weeks before we gave up and let her do nothing but fold the laundry. What did it matter? Anyone with eyes knew what she had been hired for. Friedrich's first addition to the staff since the loss of his parents, and it was hard to miss her lovely face, and the way her curves filled out the uniform.

The day after the fire, Friedrich found me as I was reordering a bookshelf that did not need to be reordered, hiding in a deeply interior room away from the scent of smoke and ashes, the horrific smells of burnt flesh lingering underneath. He looked nearly lost, still in the same trousers from the night before and his white shirt misbuttoned and streaked with black soot and a little blood. No doubt he had been combing through the wreckage of the stables.

"Friedrich," I said to him as I stepped off of the ladder, and his eyes snapped to my face almost angrily, as if surprised to see me standing there, though he would not have been able to miss me when he came into the room. At once, his expression calmed, then crumpled, and he ran his hand roughly across his mouth.

"Eliza," he said to me. "Of course. Who else would I find now but my Eliza, still working amidst all this madness."

"Have you slept?"

"Not a bit."

"You must then. There's still a few hours before supper." I patted the sofa and pulled a soft blanket off a shelf, and he came slouching toward me obediently. He grumbled all the while as I laid him down, covered him over, and smoothed his hair away from his brow.

"There will be questions," he said. "Arrangements to be made. Insurance forms for the attorneys."

"Later. Later."

He grasped my wrist. His fingers, though covered with ash, were ice cold. "She was no older than you or I," he whispered, though I'd taken her for at least a year younger. Seventeen. Perhaps sixteen.

"A great tragedy," I said as his eyes slipped shut and he began to murmur.

"My father's roadster. Irreplaceable."

Weeks earlier, Friedrich had ordered the annexation of part of the stables for his growing collection of cars. Half of the horses were moved out and many were sold, in order to make room. The grooms who had quietly cursed the decision loudly sang his praises after the fire, for the loss of their beloved horseflesh would have been much worse.

I will admit that I stayed with Friedrich after he fell asleep. Too long, perhaps, stroking his hair and making sure he didn't stir from some horrible nightmare. But I didn't curl up beside him like they would later say I did. And no one found us in the evening in a state of disarray, my uniform unbuttoned and his arm thrown about my waist. Gossip, as they say, is feathers torn from a pillow and set upon the wind: ridiculous and impossible to gather up.

In the days that followed, Friedrich seemed completely re-covered. Cleaning of the burnt and blackened stables contin-ued, and though he had to pass directly by the charred and stinking husk on his way to his car, he simply did not acknowl-edge it. He would not even look at it. The only hint we had that he was even aware of the chopping and shoveling, the removal of carcasses, was a tightening of his right cheek that would not release until he reached the shadow of the manor house.

Indeed, all might have returned to normal had it not been for the man in the long silver sedan who arrived with a brief-case late in the evening. He made his way into the house and demanded a brandy, and for the fire in the drawing room to be stoked. We did as we were bid, not knowing any other way, but it was a great affront, as we had never laid eyes upon him before! Once settled comfortably with his brandy in hand, he bade us to summon our employer.

All of this now I tell to you secondhand, as I was not one of the poor maids serving in the drawing room that night. That maid, and other maids, recounted it to me, the state of poor Friedrich when he was summoned, found in the billiard room and already heartily drunk. He'd not had another girl since the night of the fire, and a lack of girls always put him in a dark mood.

When Friedrich went to the drawing room, he closed the door and there was some quiet talk inside. It was not five minutes before the voices rose to shouting, and he burst back through the door. The man with the briefcase followed him into the hall, and grasped him very fiercely just above the wrist (and this I can tell you as I was quite startled by the noise and came down to find what was the matter). He whispered urgently into Friedrich's ear, until Friedrich pulled free and shouted, "I didn't know who she was, and I don't care!"

Then he was gone, down the darkened corridor. And so the man left as well, with nary a glance at any of us.

The other servants went back to their work with raised eyebrows and a shrug. I followed Friedrich through the halls.

I won't hesitate to say that Baron Hall is a fearsome place at night; built nearly a century ago and then improved upon and expanded by every subsequent Baron inheritor, each with different taste so that style and decor can change rapidly from one step to the next. Wood gives way to stone gives way to brick or tile. So many twisting hallways that they have begun to double back on one another. Useless passageways leading to nowhere.

Some of the sillier girls are too afraid to go roaming after dark. They say the ghosts creep out of the family portraits and go creaking through the rooms. All nonsense, of course. Though there is bad history within the Baron walls. It would be strange if there were not, after so many generations of wealth, so many souls driven to excess and wicked sins sunk into the shadows.

I found Friedrich in the stone wing, the oldest part of Baron Hall, shut up in a small circular room, an odd room, hung with tapestries that smelled like mold and with what seemed to be a child's bed against one wall. I do not know how he found himself inside. We'd grown up together at Baron—he the privileged heir and me the orphaned daughter of a beloved chambermaid who died of fever—but I had never before been inside that room.

"Eliza," he said when he saw me, then came and took me by the shoulders. "He said she was a Berlifitzing!"

"Who was a Berlifitzing?" I asked, for the family, now dwindling, had only seven or eight living members, and all seven or eight could be said to hate Friedrich Baron, and all Barons, with a great passion. Not for anything he had done, mind you, but for some old wrong carried down through years.

"They will blame me now, for sure," Friedrich exclaimed, and released me to put his head in his hands.

"Who will blame you? And for what?"

"She was a Berlifitzing! Not a maid! The girl who died in the fire, the girl I took up to the hayloft, was Hazel Berlifitzing!"

I stared in shock. Hazel Berlifitzing. I recalled her then, from the edges of garden parties the previous summer, one of those brief, shining times when the Barons and Berlifitzings had tried to make peace. That was her face, to be sure, the same face I had seen again and again during her short and ill-fated stint as a housemaid.

"But you did not recognize her, Friedrich?"

"I didn't. I swear." He pointed a firm finger in my face. "And you didn't either, Eliza. I know you were watching last year, when she came around." He lowered his hand and looked at me, aghast. "You didn't, Eliza, did you?"

"Who would have thought it," I said. "As old an aristocratic family as the Berlifitzings, and one of them pretending to be a maid? Putting on that uniform was akin to putting on a mask!"

Friedrich nodded. He touched my arm and guided me toward the door.

"I just need a moment, Eliza, you understand," he said. "A moment alone, to think."

I went into the hall and the door closed behind me. I heard a key turn in the lock.

The next morning the house was buzzing with news and rumor. I could not walk a step without hearing the whisper of "Hazel" or seeing a pair of darting eyes.

And Friedrich was nowhere to be found.

"What could she have been thinking?" Cook asked as she and the kitchen staff prepared an afternoon tea. "A rich girl like that, pretending to be a maid. It isn't right. Bad enough having to watch out for the Barons' vile tempers without thinking some rich folk is turning a spy right in our midst."

"Having some adventure, no doubt," said one as she cut the crust from a loaf of bread.

"She was thinking the same thing all the girls think when they look at our young master Baron," said another, and the three of them laughed.

When the food was ready, I volunteered to take the tray to Friedrich, and since none of them knew where he was, none objected. I searched his usual haunts in vain before resigning myself and returning to the small, strange room of tapestries I'd found him in the night before.

He was in quite a state. It took several knocks before he would open the door, and when I entered he returned immediately to the spot he'd come from: seated on the child-size bed, staring at a tapestry hanging on the wall.

"Tea," I said. And when he didn't reply, "Friedrich, you should eat something."

"Yes, yes. But you eat it for now, Eliza. You look frightfully thin."

I set the tray down beside him on the bed. He gestured to the tapestry.

"Extraordinary, isn't it?"

I looked. It was faded and ragged in places around the edges. There was not much in color or freshness to distinguish it from the other aged and moldering pieces hung around the room. But something about that one had drawn his eye.

"What is it?" I asked.

"Don't you see? It's a depiction of a duel. The girl in the foreground has arrived too late, and that man there has just killed her lover. See how he lies prostrate, with the blood on his chest and running out onto the ground."

He seemed quite adamant, so I did my best to discern what I could of the faded shapes. There indeed was the body of a young man, and his attacker standing over him in triumph. The girl, however, was much more vivid. She was very beautiful, though there was something rather cold about her eyes, and they were an unnatural color. The lavender of a dried flower. But perhaps the colors were simply off from years of sun. The horse she rode was also strangely colored: a hideous red-orange that almost seemed to glow.

As I studied the tapestry, Friedrich suddenly gave a start, and shuddered all over.

"Friedrich? Are you all right?"

"She moved!"

"Who moved?"

"The girl!" He pointed to the tapestry with a shaking finger, and I looked back at the weaving, which was of course, just as it had been when I had walked into the room. "Eliza, look at it, and tell me what you see. Is her horse there, is it facing us? Is she looking at us?"

"She's facing us on her horse, just as she was when I came in," I said.

"But she wasn't," he insisted. "She was turned and facing the duel. Her horse had his neck outstretched toward the fallen man as if in mourning!"

"Friedrich—" I reached out, perhaps to tell him he needed to sleep. I could see that he hadn't, rumpled as he was and still in yesterday's clothing. But to my surprise, he grasped me and in my shocked state we struggled, locked together as his hands formed claws and dug into my shoulders. I do not know what he intended to do, because when he turned toward the tapestry once more he gasped and froze.

"Friedrich?" I twisted in his arms to look upon it myself, and indeed I saw the oddest thing: our shadows had twined together and been cast upon the scene, projected onto the very spot where the girl's lover had lain dead. Only our shadow had formed in such a fashion as to appear to be her attacker, leering over her with outstretched arms and hooked fingers.

"It's only a shadow, Friedrich."

"Go, Eliza," he said, and released me, shoving me lightly toward the door. "I need to be alone."

So I left, and the key turned in the lock.

For two solid days, he rarely left that room. And when he did it was only for moments: to shower and for a fresh change of clothes. To eat a hastily made supper hunched over the table in the kitchen. Questions were answered with terse nods or grunts. And as soon as he was finished, he would dash off again, and the key would turn in the lock.

Until her car stalled at the end of our road.

It took three of our men to push it up the long paved drive with her sitting inside it, keeping the wheel straight. They stopped just outside the closed gate. When Friedrich appeared at the door, he seemed no different than he had been since learning the identity of the maid: his fine hair unkempt, his shirt half buttoned and baring his torso. But when his eyes set upon the car and the girl inside, he seemed to calm. He drew himself up and fixed his clothes as the men advised him of what they had found.

I heard the exchange from afar.

"She was stranded near the side of the road when we returned from town this afternoon," one said. "Just standing there, leaning against her door with one hand in the air, signaling us."

"Who is she?"

"None can say. And I didn't ask. She has the look of society, but I've never seen her or her car before."

"It is a fine car," said Friedrich. "Most unusual."

The car itself was most unusual, though I found it monstrous from the start; it was hulking and mean looking, with a razor-sharp grille cleaned to a high silver shine. And the color! The color was difficult to define. Not quite red and not quite orange, shifting yellow in the light.

"We thought," one of the men said, "with your permission, sir, we thought we might push it into the garage? We could find the source of the trouble before nightfall, and call the young lady a cab to take her home?"

"No," Friedrich replied, buttoning the cuffs of his sleeves. "I'll take care of it."

He ran down the drive and through the gate. The girl took to him immediately, leaning toward him and laughing. She was nearly as tall as he was and clearly very rich. She held a pair of driving gloves in one hand and had a pale gray scarf wrapped around her neck and covering her hair. Her eyes were hidden behind dark glasses, but there was something oddly familiar about her just the same.

I watched Friedrich run his hands over the hood. She popped it for him, and he looked inside. Whatever the trouble was, it couldn't have been much, because a few moments later the engine roared to life, and he climbed into the passenger seat. Rocks pinged against the gate as the wheels spun and they sped off together.

After that, he and the girl became inseparable. Gone were the lavish parties that carried on late into the night. Gone were the halls full of guests. Dinners made and set out went cold and were tossed away untouched. His own beloved and coveted collection of automobiles gathered dust as he and the girl drove up and down the coasts, flying along the curving forest roads. They said the girl drove as if behind the wheel of a race car, that she drove faster and with more daring than seemed possible.

As weeks passed, former friends and acquaintances came round to inquire after the Baron heir. What had become of him? Would they never again be invited to the famous Baron Hall? Eventually even Isabelle Marbury, with whom Friedrich had had a whirlwind romance two summers ago before he dropped her in the autumn, deigned to knock on our door one cloudy afternoon.

"He is never here," I finally told her after she had waited with the same cup of tea for nearly two hours. "He is almost never at home anymore."

"Never?" she asked. "So it's really true then, what they're saying. Someone has finally come and won his heart." She regarded me pitifully from beneath her sleek, styled bob, large eyes half vengeful and half wobbling near to tears. "They say he's going to marry her. But no one knows a thing about who she is or where she came from. Do you know?"

I shook my head. She had been to the house and even stayed inside it, but rarely spoke in front of any of us. Except for laughter. Bubbling laughter, behind her hand.

Once, on one of their rare nights at Baron, I stole into the garage with a light and looked upon the car. How it shone, under the light, the unnatural color swimming in and out of shadow. A fine automobile. Everyone who saw it said so. But I couldn't bring myself to touch it.

"Isn't there anything stronger to drink besides tea?" Isabelle asked me, and I brought her some of Friedrich's whiskey. I poured some for her, but she turned over another teacup and poured some more, then pushed it toward me.

"It's a hell of a thing, isn't it?" she asked. "He used me two summers ago. He used every girl in the county over the course of a few years. He probably used you, too. But even you had more of a claim to him than she does—at least you put in the time. And I was a catch, a fitting match. But he dumped me and now he's going to marry a girl from nowhere. After a few weeks of knowing her." She laughed. "It's a real bitch."

Isabelle left soon after that, and it was a relief. I hated it when girls of her ilk spoke to me like that, like we were friends or equals. When there are things that a girl like me could never say to a girl like her without losing everything. When girls like her are never to be trusted.

It was bad enough listening to the other servants gossip and wonder about what it would be like to have a young mistress at Baron Park. Would she be harsh or easy to please? Would she fire the lot of us and bring in new staff?

"He's rushing into it, you ask me," Cook said one evening over the soup pot. "Trying to run away from the rumors, and the fire, and the damned Berlifitzings."

"I don't know," said another. "He seems happy enough when he's here. Almost like he's forgotten that the fire even happened. Besides, the Berlifitzings are covering all that up themselves. Even they want to forget that one of theirs died while posing as a maid."

They laughed and they conjectured, speculating on the master's life as servants do, as if their lives are so much more important than ours that they are all we can think of even in the hours that are our own. I avoided all of it, as I avoided Friedrich, though that was not hard, as when he was not with her he was locked in the small room of tapestries. I had not seen him at all in several days, until one night, when his voice woke me in the dark.

It was a sudden sound, and I was suddenly awake. I could feel his breath at my ear and, though I could not see him, I was able to glean a distinct impression of him in the dark. He was crouched beside my bed and seemed somehow gaunt. His lips pulled back from his teeth as he spoke and in the shadows they appeared elongated, as though his gums had receded, or they had grown.

"How did the lamp overturn in the straw?" he asked in a hissing whisper. "How did the lamp overturn in the straw?"

He asked it once more. Then twice. Then over and over until I clutched the blankets to my chin. I squeezed my eyes closed and felt the movement of air across my cheek, and when I opened them again, he was gone.

That was the last time I spoke to Friedrich. Two days later they found him before our front gate, his body crushed as though by a great weight and his bones snapped from a heavy impact. The tire marks suggested that he had been run down and pinned against the gate without braking. The authorities questioned us, but no one heard anything, not the car, nor his screams. They questioned the Berlifitzings, and even Isabelle Marbury. But we all knew who had done it. The girl in the hideous red-orange car had not been seen since.

In the aftermath of Friedrich's passing, Baron Park and its staff carried on as if nothing had happened, chattering all the while about what would become of us and the grand old house. Friedrich, being young and seemingly immortal, had left no will and testament, no hint of his wishes. He was the last of the Baron line, and to the Berlifitzings' great joy the house and everything in it would likely be auctioned off piecemeal.

But I can't abide that. Since Friedrich's death I have been

plagued by strange dreams, dreams of locked doors with laughter behind them. In the dreams I ascend the stone staircase with a lamp in my hand, drawn to the laughter and the closed wooden door. Except the door will never open, and the lamp is never brighter than the headlights that come racing up behind me.

Something has gone wrong in this house. Perhaps too much, over the years, but it has been my home, and after it is gone there will be nothing left for me. I have brought the lamp deep into the interior, to the small room full of tapestries that ensnared my poor Friedrich. It has not changed since the day he let me inside it: the walls are still hung with faded weavings and there is still the small bed pushed up against the wall. It still reeks of mold, even above the gasoline.

I face the east wall, and the tapestry of the duel that held Friedrich so rapt. The girl's lover is still dead, his life bled out in faded red thread. I never noticed before that her eyes were the same shade of lavender as Friedrich's girl's eyes. How strange.

I throw the lamp against that part first—her face, watchful and oddly expressionless—and the flames burst across the tapestry. Fueled by the gasoline, they race around the room in seconds, and my skin starts to blister even as I stand near the door. I will not leave until every last thread is ablaze. Until every inch of her is consumed and shriveled, and the unnatural red of her horse is charred to black.

I wait, as the smoke stings my eyes and the edge of my uniform catches fire. I wait, as the blisters pop and run down my arms. I wait, and still that damned red horse leers back at me through the orange light, refusing to burn.

It's Carnival!

>>>>> Tiffany D. Jackson <<<<<

inspired by "The Cask of Amontillado"

y J'ouvert morning, when the baby powder dust settled and the splashes of paint dried on arms beating steel calypso pans, I decided that I had suffered enough insults from Darrell Singleton to last a lifetime.

Ting ting ting ting ting ting ting

Sticks rapidly slapped on cowbells. Eastern Parkway was flooded with thousands of human birds, sparkling on floats carrying giant speakers in the hot sun. The yearly Brooklyn West Indian Day Carnival mixed Caribbean islands in a bowl of coconut juice. The sounds of Haiti, Barbados, Trinidad, and Jamaica clashed and bounced off streets lined with apartments. An endless field of costumes, men dancing on stilts, corn roasting on grills, chicken jerking in pots on the corner.

That was where I found him. On the corner of Bedford Avenue, his face still wet with streaks of black paint, bare chest, winding up on a gyal dressed in glittery gold and fire-red feathers. A flock of his friends surrounded him, passing around a small canteen, cackling over the music. Darrell stumbled, but his drunken wobbly legs did nothing to stop his revelry. He pulled a mini air horn from his pocket, clicking it at the sky.

He will be thirsty soon, I thought as I made my way through the crowd. The girl's feathers grazed against my cheek as I tapped him on the shoulder.

"Cindy!" he shrieked, eyes bulging, pushing the young girl out of his way. "What are you doing here?"

His rum-soaked words made his accent thick like banana porridge.

I chuckled. "It's carnival!"

"I know, but . . . you never hit the parkway. And never dressed like *this*."

He stared down at my breasts snuggled up to my neck, cradled in a gold bikini top covered with gemstones and pink and orange feathers that tickled my ears. I felt damn near naked, but I had picked out the costume especially for him.

"Maybe you've never noticed. But I was just thinking of you."

"Of me?" He smiled, and I had his full attention. "What for?"

"I was talking to DeMarco about my daddy's sorrel. He says you love sorrel."

Darrell squinted. "Your fadda makes sorrel?"

"Yes. He got the recipe from my grandmother. Been called the best."

He raised an eyebrow. "Eh. What does your *American* fadda know about sorrel?"

Patience. My father taught me patience. As much as I wanted to crack a glass bottle on the curb and shove it in Darrell's eye for the disrespectful ribbing . . . I had to be patient.

Something sweeter was coming.

I cleared my throat over the music. "Knows enough. DeMarco is stopping by to pick some up to mix in his rum punch for tonight's bashment."

"No! He using your fadda sorrel? Nah nah nah. DeMarco knows nothing about sorrel. What if it taste too sour and break up the party? I'm a connoisseur, I know what's best."

"Well . . . do you want to try some?"

The crowd thickened around us as one of the Trinidad floats approached the intersection. We blended into a sea of red and white feathers.

"What? Right now?"

"Why not? I live right here." I jutted my lips at the apartment behind him. "It will only take a second. It's nice and cool. Aren't you thirsty? Dancing in all this heat."

I flicked my tongue ever so slightly, and he licked his lips.

"Yes, but—"

"What? Are you scared?" I teased, rolling my shoulders back, my gold top twinkling in the sun.

"Me? Scared? No, mon!"

"Then come on."

He stared at me for a moment, the decision churning in his head, before turning to his friends. "Fellas, I'll be back! Cindy plans to show me a *likkle* something!"

His friends didn't hear him over the roaring music, and it

didn't bother me that he had insinuated much more than an offer of a refreshing drink. He'd never see them again anyway.

Ting ting ting ting ting ting ting

We entered the lobby of the old prewar building, the place near empty with everyone partying outside, just as I'd suspected. Music bounced off the marble tiles through the hallways. The elevator door rattled closed behind us as I stuck in the key and pressed *B* for basement.

"Eh. Where are we going?" he asked with a frown. "Thought we were heading to your place?"

"Daddy keeps the sorrel in a fridge in the basement. He gave me the keys."

Darrell took a swig out of his canteen. "Why your fadda has keys to the basement?"

"He's the super."

"Ha! I see. So, he cleans up after people's shit?"

It took all my willpower not to slice his tongue out of his mouth with my keys. I imagined throwing it on the floor, stomping it into ground meat, making him sorry for every blasted word he had ever uttered about my family.

I bit my tongue. Patience. "He's renovating the building."

Darrell grinned and stepped closer to corner me in the cramped box, placing his arms on either side of me.

"So. What do you *Americans* know about sorrel?"

Americans sounded like a curse word in his mouth, and I wanted to rip his teeth out. Just the sound of his voice made my pulse sharpen as I imagined committing unspeakable violence. But violence is ugly and messy. I had something better in mind.

"He's not American," I said through clenched teeth, keeping my eyes soft. "He was just born here."

He sniffed my neck. "So, he's only partial Bajan. Like you. Not a true one."

I stiffened, if only to keep myself from striking him. His stench was revolting. If I'd had any second thoughts, he erased them, making my next steps too easy.

"You'll see it won't matter when it comes to sorrel."

The elevator jolted to a stop. I slipped under his arms and pushed open the door.

"This way."

The chilly, damp tunnel provided relief from the late summer sun beating on our shoulders. Darrell stumbled in through the darkness, tripping over brick crumbles.

"Dah! Your fadda nah put light down here," he slurred, rum sloshing out of his canteen.

The lies poured out of my mouth smooth as water. "They're broken. Electrical problems. Come on, over here."

We reached the far end of the basement and entered a super's old workshop, covered with a thick layer of gray dust. Tools, building materials, and cinder blocks were scattered throughout, the room lit by a small cellar window, covered in soot and cobwebs that dulled the sun. Shadows of carnival lovers outside danced on the floor.

"Hm. He ain't so good at cleaning, is he?" Darrell said, his body swaying as he picked up a red-handled trowel off the workman's bench.

My stomach clenched tight as I gulped, wondering if he noticed how fresh it was compared to everything else in the room, or the price tag I'd forgotten to peel off.

"He's . . . been busy . . . with this," I said, motioning to the giant gaping hole in the cement wall. To its left was an old white freezer, shaped like a perfect cube, that buzzed and shook with age. I lifted the top, revealing a bevy of reused rum bottles filled with dark purple sorrel.

He popped open a bottle and sniffed. "Hm."

He took a quick swig, and his eyes lit up. "Whooooooa. This *is* good!" He tossed the trowel and poured some into his canteen, mixing the liquid together with another sip. "Mmm! Perfect! Let me take a seat, rest my feet for a few."

"Of course. Go right ahead."

He plopped down on the stack of dry concrete bags strategically placed at the mouth of the gaping recess, not noticing the wheelbarrow filled with premixed concrete in the corner behind him. I grabbed a bottle for myself, taking a sip to cool my nerves. It was sweet and tart, not perfect like Daddy makes it around Christmas, but close enough. Music slipped through the bars on the window, calling us outside.

Ting ting ting ting ting ting ting

"This is quite good," he said, wiping his mouth with the back of his hand. "Why your fadda make so much?"

"He planned to sell them around the parade route, but he had an emergency."

"Hm. How your fadda the super and can't fix electrical? What does he know how to do?"

"Construction." I motioned to the hole. "Management asked him to patch up this wall. Broke it open to fix the plumbing." I held my breath for five seconds, watching Darrell try to drown himself in sorrel. "You should see inside."

"What? Inside this hole here?"

"Yeah."

Darrell stuck his head in and gasped. "Ohhh!"

Inside were the remnants of an old sleep shed. A wooden chair and a low cot with fresh sheets. He stepped in, turning back to me.

"Ha! So . . . this why you brought me down here? To be *alone*?"

I smiled with a small shrug, joining him. "Maybe."

He smirked. "Ha! Boi, Cindy. Yuh full of surprises today," he said, stepping in farther to investigate the bed.

That was when I swiftly clicked closed the waiting handcuff around his ankle and jumped back out the hole.

Darrell looked down at his foot, now chained to one of the cinder blocks sealed to the wall, almost amused.

"Heh. What's this?" He kicked and the short chain jingled. "Cindy, I didn't know you were into freaky shit."

I held a stare with him. He had no idea what was about to happen. That made the moment all the more satisfying.

"You know, my grandfather—from Bridgetown, *Barbados*—used to build houses using these blocks," I said, motioning to the stack in the corner. "He was good with his hands. He taught my daddy, who then taught me."

I wheeled the fresh concrete mix closer to the hole. Darrell blinked, his smile slowly fading. He tried walking toward me, but the chain snapped him back, keeping him a hair away from freedom.

He chuckled, nervousness caught in his voice. "Cindy, come now, quit playing around."

"These blocks can be so heavy," I continued, lifting one off the stack and setting it in place at the bottom of the hole. "But not too heavy for me to manage."

I set down three blocks and grabbed the tossed trowel,

holding it up like a knife ready to slice a cake. Darrell wiggled, his eyes growing wider.

"He had a rhyme for it," I said. "He would say, 'Scrap, slap, brick, pat.' Watch me?"

I scraped a large chunk of wet cement, slapped it on the bricks, then laid another brick on top and patted it in place . . . just like Daddy taught me.

"See?" I asked, watching the realization dawn on him. "This shouldn't take long."

"Ha ha ha! Very funny, Cindy. Who put you up to this? DeMarco? Ah, I'll get him good for this." Darrell pulled at his chain, quickly sobering. "Okay now, Cindy. This isn't funny anymore. This thing is starting to hurt my ankle."

I focused on smoothing the cement, keeping the blocks nice and even so I could patch the hole without anyone noticing the mix of bricks.

"Okay, stop it, Cindy," Darrell snapped. "What? You're gonna bury me in here? You can't!"

But I was already at the third layer. I always moved quickly under pressure.

"Cindy! Cindy, quit playing! Stop!"

I ignored his cries as he grew more frantic.

"You can't be serious! This is crazy!" he hollered. "My friends! The ones who saw us! They'll be looking for me!"

"No one saw us come in here," I said with a laugh. "Every-one is out enjoying the bacchanal."

Darrell froze, his lips trembling.

"HEEELP!" he screamed toward the window. *"HELP ME!"*

I laughed. "Boy, no one can hear you. See?"

We fell silent, listening to the roaring crowd outside, cheering at the passing floats, waving flags as the pans played.

Ting ting ting ting ting ting ting

"No! No!" Darrell yanked harder at his chain. *"HELP!"*

Scrap, slap, brick, pat. Scrap, slap, brick, pat.

"DeMarco! You said he'll be coming by! He'll see what you did here!"

I chuckled. "You really fell for that? I don't even live in this building."

Darrell shuddered, pulling on the handcuff, desperate to break free. Suddenly, he snapped his fingers and dug in his pocket, retrieving his air horn. With a smirk, he tooted it towards the window and screamed.

I paused to watch him, wondering if he knew his air horn was indistinguishable from the dozens of other air horns on the road, or that no one could hear his screams through the blasting music. The hope the air horn spurred in him was useless, but it was hard telling anyone that when freedom was just a short distance away. He wore himself out trying, and I continued on.

Scrap, slap, brick, pat. Scrap, slap, brick, pat.

"Okay, Cindy, what do you want?" he gasped, out of breath. "Money? I can give you money!"

"Money can't fix everything."

"Fix what? What I ever do to you?"

I narrowed my eyes at him. "What didn't you do?"

"Nothing! I did nothing!"

"Hey, flat-back American gyal!" I said, mimicking his accent. *"Flat-back, big-belly gyal!* That was what you called me, right? How many other names did you and your stupid friends make

up about parts of my body? How many times did you talk about my father? My mother? I lost count."

"But . . . but . . . meh only teased you!" he wailed. "Not enough for all this!"

My stomach rumbled. A part of me wanted to believe him. Perhaps I was taking this too far. Perhaps not.

Scrap, slap, brick, pat. Scrap, slap, brick, pat.

The wall was nearly complete. Only a few smaller bricks left, and enough time to enjoy the rest of the parade.

Darrell worked himself up into a sweat, honking the horn until it only sputtered out a squeak. The hole grew darker and darker. He collapsed on the ground, sobbing.

"I can't breathe, Cindy. I can't. Please!" he cried. "Please. I'm sorry. Please let me go!"

Ting ting ting ting ting ting ting

"Ah . . . finally. The last block," I said, and peeped through the remaining hole, squinting in the darkness. Darrell's glassy eyes stared back at me, straining.

"Jesus, Cindy! PLEASE! *PLEEEEEEASE!*"

I mocked his cries and slapped on the last of the concrete, wiggling the brick into place. I dusted my hands and took a step back to admire my work.

Silence. Not even a whimper.

"Darrell?" I whispered softly.

A weak horn blew from the other side of the wall. I had thought about taking it from him, but the horn would be out of air before Carnival was over.

As the elevator hummed back up to the lobby, my stomach twisted, tying itself in tiny knots. *Food, that's all it is,* I thought. *I just need something to eat and drink after all that work.* I tossed the left-over materials in the trash outside and headed for the jerk pots.

∽∽

I bet you're wondering why I'm telling you this story, after so many years of silence. I bet you're wondering if I still feel that clawing at my insides. Was that a form of guilt? Do I feel sorry for what I've done?

No. I feel nothing. I don't feel the least bit guilty.

I'm telling you this because it brings me great amusement knowing he's still down there, propped up on the bed, horn rusted to his bones, listening to Carnival pass him by every year.

Night-Tide

Tessa Gratton

inspired by "Annabel Lee"

No one will tell me how she died. Not exactly.

The cold ocean slips up my ankles, to the ruffled cuff of my bloomers, grasping at my skin. Beneath my back the sand is cold, too, but I've made a cradle for myself under this beaming moon. As the night progresses, the water will rise.

This is Kingdom by the Sea, a resort hotel only a decade old, perched on the grassy bluff overlooking this bright blue bay. Black-winged cormorants soar against the pristine afternoon sky, distracted only by loud seagulls. Sandpipers rush like packs of eager kittens toward the surf to bob their long beaks into the sand, then scatter for oncoming waves. Colorful umbrellas dot the creamy beach; under them, wealthy ladies pretend to enjoy the sun while their husbands, sons, and young daughters romp with kites or swim the shallows in their sleeveless bathing suits. We girls unfortunate enough to be too old for play but too young to make our own lives sip cordials beside our mothers, sneaking a hand out of the shade if we dare, reading poetry or discussing gossip or playing word games. Mornings we walk arm in arm with other girls for exercise, allowed to go unsupervised if there are three or more of us. And we remember to wear our virgin-white straw hats. If the wind blows too harshly or rain drifts in off the Atlantic, we gossip and pretend to enjoy the tea in one of the sitting rooms, watching the different beauty of bad weather through tall, narrow windows. In the formal dining room for the evening meal we behave as though we're still in New York or Baltimore or Philadelphia—whichever city we reside in during the rest of the year. The silver and fine linens are arranged, and every course is served by maids in pressed aprons.

Last year, Mother allowed me a single glass of wine with dinner.

Perhaps it signaled something to me, that I was nearly an adult, that I was *ready*. For what I could not have said, nor would I try to explain now. But Annabel had a glass of wine with her dinner, too, and it put a flush in her cheeks. Mr. Crane Fitzwarren said to my father that it reminded him where she'd come from. They did not think I was listening.

I knew, of course, the rumor that Annabel's grandmother had not been a lady, but one of the family's maids. Fortunately,

Annabel was so pretty—her mouth a dark pink bow, her eyes light and her pale skin soft, unblemished—and she was so sweet tempered, she'd clearly not been tainted, regardless of the truth. And I adored her freckles. Annabel told me it happened so long ago it didn't matter, but I wonder, now: if not for that scandal, would they have looked so hard for ours?

We arrived a week late this year, and I was ill with eagerness, light-headed with the thought of Annabel Lee.

People turned from me, glanced away—as if I'd not buttoned my collar up my neck, or wore scarlet paint on my lips. There were no whispers yet. Those grew like a tide over the first twenty-four hours. I searched for her, expecting her to find me first as she had every previous year, with a new ribbon for me to match hers, and together we would scamper off to one of the cushioned benches in the lobby so Annabel could rebraid my hair with it.

She did not manifest. I looked a question at Sally, one of the lobby attendants, but her mouth bowed in sorrow and she glanced away. She ought not be seen speaking to me here, when there were men and guests in need. I shouldn't glance too warm at her either, or I'd get her in trouble with the concierge. It wasn't until my family had been shown into our suite and I swore I'd unpacked well, not in the whirlwind it seemed, that Mother gave me permission to visit the Lees.

Smoothing the pale blue of my skirts, I went to find Annabel Lee, polished shoes sinking into the thick carpets of the elegant hallway. I pinched my cheeks for color, laughing at myself, but I wanted her to be struck by how I'd matured. I was sixteen now, and my mother allowed me a day dress with darker trim, instead of childish pastel. My breasts were grown and fit nicely flat beneath the modest bodice, my hips just round enough to provide a curve to the fall of my skirts. Beneath, my legs were strong, for I ran when I could and joined my brothers in calisthenics when we were home.

I arrived at the Lee suite and knocked just beneath the golden *Room 107* painted on the wood.

A stranger answered; I apologized, gape mouthed, and asked after the Lees.

They'd changed rooms this year, the young man told me. I continued to stare. He was obviously a guest, and leaned his shoulder against the doorframe, hands in the pockets of his pressed slacks. He said quietly, "They did not wish to be reminded too directly of their loss."

"Do you know the room?" I asked, breathless at the word *loss*.

The young man did not answer immediately but watched me, his smile curving with a hook of flirtation. "Just above us, I believe. If their daughter was as pretty as you, I'd be more inclined to remember."

It was easy to turn and leave stiffly, my ears ringing dull with the word again and again, *loss loss loss*. I nearly unbalanced, feet unstable against the stairs, and brushed my fingers against the cold wall for support.

I paused. I shuddered. I whispered her name, just to taste it again before I knew.

Room 207.

I knocked, and the Lees' regular maid answered. She looked immediately at her feet but allowed me in. Only that young man's warning and now her hesitance kept me from calling out for Annabel. My footsteps were silent on the long green runner, and I turned carefully into the sitting room, a paneled chamber painted in light pink and white, with deep green molding and sheer curtains. Mrs. Lee sat upon a wicker chair beside the open French doors so that the ocean breeze ruffled her hem.

"Hello, Mrs. Lee," I said, curtsying unsteadily. I looked around for Annabel—peering a moment too long into the gilded mirror over the hearth, exactly positioned as it was in every guest suite, for I was much taller than last year, and could see all of my face.

"You," Mrs. Lee said, heaving up from the chair. "Get out."

Shocked, I stepped backward but did not leave. "Pardon me?" I whispered. "Is Annabel here? May I see her?"

"You may not, *ever*. I know what you did to my baby," Annabel's mother said, her voice unrecognizably thick. She lifted a hand, clutching a vivid blue hair ribbon, and gestured at me. "I know what you are."

They say angels loved Annabel Lee so much they sent a cold wind from heaven to retrieve her.

Perhaps what I am, then, is an angel.

The backs of my knees tickle as the tide reaches high, lapping at the delicate skin. My bloomers stick to me, damp and ruined, as seawater climbs up through the linen faster than the tide comes in. I gasp at each gentle surge, each new level of cold foam leaping up my legs.

"But what happened?" I cried, hands clutched together against my chest, pressing as if I could calm my heartbeat. "Where is Annabel?"

Mrs. Lee stepped forward as if to strike me but simply said again, "Get out!"

I fled.

Down the hallway and to the broad staircase that spilled in a soft curve toward the lobby. Each step brought me back to myself, but when I crashed into that sunny lobby, eyes turned toward me. Curious, dismissive—not yet mean, judgmental, hostile. The desk staff and bellboys had heard my name since my family arrived, and gossip had filled in some stuffing in the story between Miss Jaclyn Lavery and the departed darling Miss Annabel Lee.

If I had been the one to die, would I be the darling and Annabel the *I know what you are?*

My shoes stuck to the polished wood that stretched out from me in perfect thin lines, a ship's deck, a boardwalk, a ballroom floor, and I the only dancer. From sofas and window seats, from the check-in and concierge desks, from the open front doors of the Kingdom, they stared.

I took a deep breath and continued straight outside, as if that had always been my intention. A salty breeze wafted over the porch, a smell like sunshine, sand, and old seaweed. My heels tapped against the wood, and I breathed deeply again, and again, making my way off the porch, away from the circular drive, toward the bluffs.

Grass drifted, the pale sand glinting under the same sun that warmed my skin but could not find my heart. I climbed one hill and slipped down the opposite slope, knees buckling. I caught myself, palms scraping on the rough sand. There I remained until Sally from the front desk found me. "Miss," she whispered, despite being a few years older than me. She glanced back toward the Kingdom before adding, "I'm so sorry."

"What happened to her?"

"Sickness, I heard. All winter." Sally gently touched her hand to my shoulder, then just as gently took it away.

None of the other girls would tell me the gossip. Their mouths pressed shut when I approached, and if I asked, they pretended they knew nothing. I could not possibly inquire of an adult, and my father only said, "Such a tragedy, sweetheart," too wrapped up in Mother's needs to notice mine. At dinner, at the beach, any time I was with my parents, normalcy reigned. But if I ventured out alone, a thread of whispers followed me through the Kingdom. Two of the other girls refused to hold my arm for the morning constitutional—their mothers insisted, they claimed. It wasn't *their* fault.

I understood the gossip, somehow, in my guts. It was me, I was unnatural. Her death was my fault. I loved her, and she died. I longed for her, and she died. I touched her. And she died.

Unnatural love kills, the whispers claimed, or spoils at least, and when sickness comes, a ruined girl has no defense against the cold winds of hell, nor the yearnings of heaven.

We summer at Kingdom by the Sea for my mother's health. Since Robbie was born, she has needed to get away from the city, to relax in the warmth, unbothered by foul city air and the stress of company, of running a household. The most important thing is that I do not upset her.

And so when Mother cupped my cheek and asked what was wrong, I smiled my least-sad smile and promised I was well.

"You miss your friend," she said, drawing me onto our balcony.

"Yes," I murmured.

"I confess, I never liked her mother much, but it's dreadfully sad what happened."

I bit my lip, then asked, "Do you know? None will tell me but that she was sick."

"A fever took her, Jackie, late in the winter. It is so easy to lose a child." Mother's voice drifted into a whisper.

Just as easy to lose a mother, I thought, and hugged her fiercely. "I love you."

"Oh, darling." She stroked my hair.

She was my mother; I should've been allowed to tell her, to cry in her arms. She should've soothed my fears away. We should be allowed that.

I should've confessed everything to her, let her see the ugliness inside me. *See, Mother, what I did when I touched her, do you know what I am?*

I wished to do it, and have Mother reel back in horror—not at me, but at the idea that I carried such ruin. *You're perfect, Jackie, and so was Annabel Lee. Love is never ugly.*

That was all I wished.

But Mother was sick, and I could not put that pressure onto her heart.

Last summer I kissed Annabel on the corner of her mouth, as if it were less salacious than putting our plump bottom lips firmly together, less forbidden than a mingled breath, than a quick taste.

A kiss at the corner of the mouth might be innocent; it's practically a cheek, after all.

We knelt between two grassy bluffs, hidden from the Kingdom and from the ocean: only the sun could see, the sun and those ruffled white clouds so like our petticoats. Annabel touched my cheek and pushed hair off my temple, and then she kissed me back. Her eyes closed, lashes fluttering. She was so delicate, so lovely, and her freckles were like gilded sand, or stars, or pinpricks. Because she hated them (as she was taught to do), I made up a story that when she was a babe, she was so incredibly beautiful the angels had argued whether to mar her beauty just a little bit. If she was too perfect she'd never survive, some said. Just a little change to make her beauty human instead of angelic. Others said she was destined to be loved with a perfect purity, so might her face not reflect that perfection?

"It's a pretty story," Annabel said, tugging my braid with a frustrated wrinkle of her nose. "I wish the angels who wanted me perfect had won."

"Oh, but they did!" I cried, kissing her cheek again and again. "They—each—kissed—a—perfect—freckle—to—your—face—to—mark—your—angelic—perfection—forever!"

Laughter, unstoppable and sweet, bubbled out of her, and she pushed me playfully away.

Later, she told me she did not know if she had freckles on her shoulder blades, or down the narrow corridor of her spine, and perhaps, one day, I might discover it.

I dig my fingers into the beach as the ocean rolls up my knuckles. The tide comes in and then out again, in and out: sand sucks through my grip, slippery and flowing, drawn away by the undertow. I am wet up my thighs, and the ocean hungers for my hips.

Above, stars scatter like freckles. I hunt for the shape of a curving spine, a waist, and there, that spray of stars! Those are shoulder blades that flare into wings. An angel's wings, my perfect Annabel.

When tears slip hot down my temple, I think they are drops from my own internal salt sea marking the beach before the tide smears it all away.

I dig my fingers into the beach as the ocean rolls up my knuckles.

Part of me wants to be what they say. *Dangerous.* I would steal a touch here or there, the underside of a wrist, a press hip to hip, too firm to be ignored as innocent. I want to murmur into their daughters' ears what I know about love. To fill their thoughts with longing, put fire where they strive so hard to *feel* nothing, to *be* nothing but perfect dolls.

I know what you are.

No, but I don't think you do, old woman with your charcoal heart and cowardly hands. I am an angel. Fallen, maybe. But is there anything more natural than a fallen angel?

Tell me I'm young. Tell me I can't know myself, that I have not even developed a real capacity to understand love and loss, to experience these big feelings pulling me apart from the inside.

But last summer I never feared meeting new people. I never feared being myself, being seen. I could laugh, gossip, drink my cordial, flick my hand into the sunlight and smile at whomever caught me. This summer I don't know what I'm allowed to laugh at. The gossip can always turn sharply back against me. Every sip reminds me of Annabel, every sip reminds me of that glass of wine that told me I was ready.

I was not ready.

Is anyone ever ready?

There is a gaping wound between who I was and who I am.

If you do know what I am, please, I beg you: *tell me.*

The young man from Room 107 found me walking along the narrow path between the beach and the Kingdom. I'd been sent for a new slipper for my mother: hers had died the victim of a little brother's exuberant splashing.

I heard him jogging behind me and did not pause. His shoes skidded on the gritty path and he was bold enough to touch the small of my back.

Not bold. Entitled.

His touch shot through me like fury, because I knew he did it only because of what he'd heard. Twisting my love as if I'd give it to anyone.

The young man's smile was sweet, his eyes bright, and he said, "You seem to be lacking an escort."

"My integrity is all the escort I need, Mr. McCabe."

He laughed, a carefree and strong note, because boys are allowed it.

I paused to put my hands on his chest. I leaned in; he fell still. His shirt was soft, buttoned properly, but he wore no vest nor jacket. Only jaunty yellow suspenders that matched the band on his hat.

His stillness, like his laugh, was loud. He had no fears under this sun.

Jealous, I shoved him hard enough that he stumbled off the path.

Nobody cares if girls hold hands.

Our fingers entwined, a pocket of warmth tingling there, caught between palms.

No sick looks, no long judging glances, no need to hide it in alcoves or behind trees.

Annabel and I held hands every day. We slid fingers through each other's hair, combing and rebraiding. We leaned close together to whisper secrets. Our cheeks brushed. Her hair tickled my ear. My hair caressed her temple. I felt her breath against my eyelashes when I ducked my face to hide a grin. Her giggle was more of a *huff-huff-huff* pressure than sounds.

In the shade of Mother's umbrella, on a hot July day last

year, we were surrounded by family and summer neighbors, crashing waves and layers of conversations cried across the sand. Resentful gulls argued on the wing.

The only thing that could not see us was the sun.

Annabel wrinkled her nose at her little brother as he tripped too near us, spraying sand so we screamed, laughing, and covered our snacks. She put her lips near my ear and beneath the cover of all that brotherly chaos, she said, "I love you."

Everyone was watching.

I felt invincible.

There is this rolling grief that comes and goes. Like the tide, but there is no schedule for it, no great silver moon to pull it in regular courses.

Worse than the grief is the shame, for it is my own selfish anxiety. What if I did something wrong? What if what if what if? What if they are right about me, about ugliness? I am young, you say, how can I be righteous when the adults, the doctors and mothers and preachers and politicians, all know what I am?

Annabel Lee did have freckles in a curve along the small of her back, and a thicker, rose-brown birthmark just above her left knee. I kissed it, once. And all winter I imagined her birthmark to be the shape of a kiss, so that if I kissed the window of my bedroom in Baltimore then in my dreams a rose-brown mark would blossom there. If I kissed my mother, if I kissed the soft green leather binding of *Twelfth Night,* or the palm of my hand, or a winter orange, that same perfect rose-brown kiss would grow.

~~~

I wonder what gave us away. Did Annabel say something? Did she cry out for me in her fever, and before a doctor did she press her hand to that rose on her thigh and roll her hips the way she did when *I* touched it? Did she confess, did she defy them, did her mother have a vision?

Did winged seraphs descend from heaven to betray us?

That is the story I would tell:

When I kissed the corner of Annabel Lee's mouth, the moment crystallized. Perfection captured forever in a single ripple of time. It pulsed through heaven and hell, striking hardest at the angels who envied us. They might be powerful, immortal beings, but they are not two fifteen-year-old girls who hold between them the potential of a million lives. I drew away from Annabel to smile, but the thread remained, livid with musical lightning. Each glance we shared plucked it again, each memory made it hum, each touch—soft or swift or hot— strengthened the reverberations.

Those angels could not bear the purity of our love and sought to sever us. Yet so long as we were together, they could not approach, could do nothing but watch and yearn.

It was only when the winter arrived, when Annabel traveled far from me, that she became vulnerable. Separate.

And now I am alone, too. Vulnerable.

They touched freezing fingers to the thread between us, sickening Annabel Lee. The warmth of our love transformed into the heat of fever, and her shuddering chills were wretched mirrors of a delicate shiver along her arms when I played with the ends of her hair.

The angels perverted everything we were and *they* killed her. Not me.

Not. Me.

The tide has consumed me to the waist, to my navel that is a tiny pool of seawater now, a micro-ocean surrounded by the land of my body. If I were naked, that pool would reflect the moon.

Little narrow rivulets spread beneath my back, grasping around me toward my shoulders. The sand is duplicitous now; it appears solid but water creeps throughout its grains, and all the beach sinks nearer and nearer—farther and farther—into the sea.

If the ocean takes me, what is more natural than that?

What is more natural than a kiss?

A touch here, a touch there, this desire born in sunlight and surrounded by familiar laughter, family outings—what is more natural?

Mother always does better at Kingdom by the Sea than she does in Baltimore, but I can tell she's not healing. Last summer she would occasionally join Father at sunset to promenade along the boardwalk that lines the bluff. This summer even such a brief, relaxed exercise makes her cough worse.

It is a dry cough, hollow and dull. The fine wrinkles at her eyes strain, and white edges her lips. She laughs, though, and teases us all, Father especially.

Somehow, Father does not seem aware anyone condemns his daughter. He remains too focused on Mother, perhaps, or boldly dismissive of gossip.

One morning when Mother was slow to get out of bed, and her companion, a nurse we brought with us, ordered a morning steam, I asked Father if we would come here still when Mother could not.

He frowned. "Why would we leave her in Baltimore?"

That wasn't what I meant, but Father didn't realize it.

The Lees returned after Annabel died, as if there were no way to break the pattern, as if drawn here or tied here, or as if they had to confront her monster.

There is no monster killing my mother. Nothing to confront.

If I were an angel, I would be jealous of how much I love my mother, too.

Maybe I am a monster. Maybe girls like me—

Annabel Lee stretches beside me, her hand in mine, a tingling pocket of warmth protected between our palms. The ocean streaks against both our bodies.

She murmurs my name.

I turn my face to hers: she is starlight, she is marble, she is a cold, lost corpse. Unreal, but not unnatural.

The night-tide becomes our blanket, tucking us in.

I must know what I am. An ocean creature, a fallen angel, a monster who does not belong?

A girl by the sea.

When the sun rises and the tide washes back out, will it take me, too?

There is a place deep in the heart of the ocean, so black and cold light cannot survive, and there, I think, Annabel and I could kiss, and no matter how strong the reverberations, no matter how lightning-bright that thread of time between us, the killing angels could not find it. Nor us.

I know what you are!

If the night-tide drags me deep, I'll be a siren, a deep-sea girl. I'll find Annabel and we'll fly down there.

If the sun rises and I'm still here, cold in the tomb of sand, but alive by a spark—a warmth—a rightness—I'll stretch my arms and let the morning brightness dry me, let the blue sky give me a new name.

I'll teach that name to my mother, and to all the other girls.

I'll know what I am.

Maybe the tide can tell me.

The Glittering Death

⇢⇢⇢ Caleb Roehrig ⇠⇠⇠

inspired by "The Pit and the Pendulum"

The devil comes for me in a dark alley, wet with rain and lit by a cold moon. And I walk right into his clutches.

It's a careless move, like the countless careless moves people make every day with no consequences, even when they know better. Even when they know they fit a profile, and that someone is hunting people just like them on the streets at night. But it's the end of my shift, I'm tired and irritable, and all I want to do is go home. So I'm distracted when I take the garbage out to the dumpster behind the café—my mind already fixed on a near future of fast food and streaming video, trolling my group chat with bad puns—and I'm not paying attention.

The alley is narrow, a space that seems to exist solely for

the convenience of trucks to make deliveries and haul away trash, and the streetlamps meant to illuminate it burn out and go weeks without being replaced. There's hardly enough light to see by, and I'm hoisting a bag up to the metal rim of the bin when I hear a footfall behind me.

I turn with just enough time to see a dark shape separate itself from the shadows by the wall, lunging forward; to see the swirl of a long robe, the point of a hood, and two eyes that glint in the center of a black void where a face should be. An iron grip closes on my arm, something sharp pricking the flesh of my bicep, and a gloved hand clamps my mouth shut before I can scream. My heart races, my head grows light while my limbs grow heavy—and the alley blurs, darkness sliding over darkness, as I sway on legs that have suddenly given up their support.

The devil folds me into his embrace, my heart pounding slower and slower, the world a slippery thing that won't hold me anymore; and just before I lose consciousness, I hear him speak. *"I've got you now."*

"He calls himself the Judge," a woman had announced before an afternoon assembly at my school, two weeks earlier. Standing at the edge of the stage, she had glared down at us with a stern expression, her dark skin looking impossibly smooth under the bright lights. Cut in clean, severe lines, from her tailored blazer and white shirt to her angled cheekbones and sleek cap of black hair, she'd identified herself as Agent Fields. She'd even held up an official FBI identification badge for show-and-tell, as if any of the six hundred students gathered in the school theater were close enough to read it from the audience. "I'm sure that many of you have read or heard about him in the news already."

She was right, of course. With a population of three hundred thousand, Toledo, Ohio, isn't exactly a small town—but a serial killer who cuts women open and sends anonymous letters to the press after the fact tends to make a wide impression.

"What we know about the Judge," Agent Fields went on, her voice carrying to the far reaches of the room, "is that he targets young women between the ages of fifteen and twenty-five; that most of his victims have been white, with dark hair that is approximately shoulder length; and that he abducts his victims and holds them in captivity for some time before he kills them."

The words landed with the precision of an ice pick, carving room for themselves in the fear centers of our brains. Agent Fields was there to make her own impression, eyes sharp and arms akimbo, and exhibited no patience for an auditorium full of teenagers who gossiped and whispered while she was trying to terrify us.

"What we know," she boomed, "is that the Judge saws his victims' chests open while they are *still alive,* and that he then removes their hearts. We suspect he keeps the organs as souvenirs." *This* gruesome detail finally brought some silence to the room, and satisfaction pulled at a corner of the FBI agent's mouth. "He dumps the bodies where he knows they'll eventually be found—farmland, parks, drainage ditches—and once they are, he delivers a message to the press explaining why he's done what he's done.

"The letters accuse each victim of one or more of the seven

deadly sins—pride, envy, wrath, lust, avarice, gluttony, or sloth. The letters also list the supposed weight of each missing heart as part of the so-called evidence in his 'finding of guilt.'" Agent Fields paced the stage, pivoting on her heel, peering up into the balcony with the lights in her eyes. "We're talking about a complete psychotic, here, okay? These letters are the ravings of a madman; the girls he's killed were guilty of nothing but being in the wrong place at the wrong time."

Fields had a partner, Agent Prescott, who stood impassively in the background. Petite and blond, with thin lips and spiky hair, she kept her arms folded throughout the presentation and every time I looked up I could swear she was watching me— as if she could hear me telling my friends that she looked like Clarice Starling's love child with Rosemary Woodhouse. I was seated in the back of the audience with Brandy, Mark, and Shauna, and we were trading quips under our breath for the entire assembly; we call ourselves the Mean Girls as a joke, but the truth is that sometimes we *are* sort of mean.

"The abductions and the subsequent dumping and discovery of the bodies all follow a pattern," Agent Fields went on relentlessly. "They all take place at around the same time in each lunar cycle. Girls go missing three to seven days before the full moon, and are discovered dead anywhere from one to six days after the full moon—"

"*He's a werewolf!*" Aaron Lutz shouted from the balcony, and he got a few laughs that withered and died under the implacable glower of the FBI agents on the stage.

"He's not a storybook monster," Fields countered, almost quietly, her voice full of dark foreboding. "He's a man. He's flesh and blood like everyone in this room, and if you see him?

You won't know it." She let that sink in, until the vast room rang
with silence. "Go ahead and make jokes, if that's what you need
to do, but take this seriously. Because for everything we know
about the Judge, there are a million things we don't—and despite what you see on TV, serial killers change their MO all
the time. The Judge could be anyone, and he could be after
anyone. Including people in this room. And it's only nineteen
days until the next full moon."

Surfacing from oblivion, the first thing I become aware of is
the unmanageable weight of my limbs, as if my skeleton has
been removed and my body filled with sand. My head throbs,
and it takes a century to fight my eyelids open; it's like the time
that Shauna and I got her older brother to buy us wine coolers.
They were cloyingly sweet and went down like fruit punch, and
the next morning it took every ounce of willpower I had just to
get off the floor long enough to vomit into a half-empty bag of
Doritos.

But this is worse. Blinking my eyes, my thoughts still fogged
and my vision an untrustworthy kaleidoscope of doubled images, I know I'm in trouble before I know anything else. A light
bulb hangs from the ceiling, backed by a metal shade, casting
down a dim glow of sulfurous yellow—the same color of the
streetlamps that are supposed to keep the alley behind the café
safe. For a while I stare, herding the scattered fragments of my
thoughts, gradually coming to realize that I don't know where
I am.

When I push into a seated position, thin metal bites the
palms of my hands. The room dances, a swirling centrifuge

of blackness, and I battle down a wave of nausea. Rippled and soft, the walls seem to melt like wax pouring down from the ceiling, and it takes me a long, disorienting moment to realize that what I'm looking at is curtains—great swathes of thick, inky fabric that ring the room, blocking out any windows, anything that might give me a sense of my surroundings. I could be in a warehouse, a penthouse, or a tomb, for all I can tell.

At the opposite end of the room from where I lie, I can make out a steel table, its silvered edge gleaming yellow in the bilious light from above. My stomach pulls and then wrenches, and I turn with difficulty on to all fours, convinced I'm about to be sick. *Where am I?* A wet and musty basement smell coils around me like vapor as my vision finally starts to coalesce and I take in the wiry lattice that surrounds me. My mouth goes dry at the same time a chilling realization sets in.

I am in a cage.

Panic sweeps back over me in a bright wave, my heart galloping into my throat. Gripping the walls of my enclosure, I give the metal a hard shake, hearing it rattle. I shake harder, fear making me desperate, some feral remnant of my brain ascending. *I'm in a cage.* My muscles start to burn, flop sweat rolling from under my arms, and the sturdy wire begins to cut into the soft flesh of my fingers; but my efforts are useless. The mesh won't bend, the joints won't give, and frantic tears spangle my vision as my chest heaves.

The Judge. It has to be the Judge. My ears ring with the memory of Agent Fields, standing on the edge of the stage, trying to scare us—"abducts his victims," "holds them in captivity," "*still alive*"—and bile rushes up my throat. My eyes are finally adjusting to the dark, and I can make out the steel table with more clarity now. I can see the shallow gutters along its sides, the locked wheels on its feet, the drain set into the concrete floor just beneath it. It's meant for surgical procedures.

"*Help!*" I shout. The word sounds pathetic, denied resonance by the heavy curtains that gobble up sound with a vengeance. But once I've begun screaming, I find I can't stop. "*Somebody please help me!*"

Falling back, I start slamming my feet into the walls of the cage, trying to find weaknesses—trying to create some—shouting until my throat is raw. Just beyond the cacophony of my struggle, I hear a click and a creak of hinges, and I freeze. It's absurd; I made the noise hoping for attention, but as heavy footsteps thump against wood somewhere behind the folds of the black curtains around me, I go utterly still. Because I know. With every fiber of my being, I know it's him.

He emerges through an invisible gap in the thick drapery, at the far end of the room where the metal table waits, still in the same strange costume he wore in the alley. The robe that swirls about him hangs all the way to the floor, a dull crimson beneath the jaundiced light of the single bulb. He approaches my cage on soundless feet, and I scuttle backward, a whimper escaping my lips.

"The accused is awake," he intones, stopping when he's only a few feet away. The hood he wears covers his face completely except for two small holes for his eyes.

"Who are you?" I ask, even though I know the answer. "Where am I?"

"The accused has been brought before the Judge for the crimes of pride and lust," the man states in a grandiose way. "Does the harlot wish to make a confession?"

"I haven't done anything." My voice is scarcely above a whisper. "Please let me out. I'm not a . . . a harlot! So, just let me out, okay? I won't tell. I promise, I—"

"The accused offends the Judge with begging and false claims of innocence."

"They're not false!" Adrenaline squeezes my heart like a vise, and my pitch rises. "I'm not a harlot! I'm a fucking virgin, okay? So you've obviously—"

"*Vulgarity!*" He stumbles back as if he's been struck, gloved hands flying to his ears. Even through the hood I can see him blink, his eyes dark and shiny like beetle shells. "She pretends innocence, but defiles the very air with her shameful tongue!"

"*She* has a name, asshole!" I retort without thinking, my instincts driving me to claim some sort of ground. "And I'm not pretending anything—I'm a virgin, so you've made a fucking mistake!"

He moans, swinging away, hands clapped over his ears. "The putrescence of her soul exudes from her mouth like the stench of rot, foul and unclean!"

"The putrescence of *my* soul?" A switch flips, fear turning to reckless anger in a heartbeat. "You're a sick fuck who kidnaps girls and cuts them open, and you're calling *me* foul?" He reels backward, mumbling something under his hood. "Let me the hell out of this fucking cage, you fucking . . . fuck!"

Each profanity drives him another step back, his mumbling growing louder and more plaintive. I catch snatches of it—"*meorum peccatorum,*" "*summum bonum,*" "*omnia diligaris*"—and realize he's speaking Latin. I'm not Catholic, but Mark has dragged me to church with his family on several occasions ("*If God tries to strike me down for being gay, I'm throwing your heathen ass in the way of the lightning bolt,"*) and I recognize the prayer. *My sins, the highest good, all my love* . . . he's saying the Act of Contrition.

I start to swear at the top of my lungs, every curse I can think of, and every variation I can possibly devise. The Judge takes each word like a bullet, falling back a step at a time, and I shout harder. I have no plan, but he's acting like it hurts, and that's good enough for me.

When he reaches the table, his Latin prayer loud enough to compete with my screamed obscenities, he wrenches something free from the darkness behind the curtains and begins stalking back in my direction. I falter, fearing the worst, and when he reaches the cage again, I scuttle as far from the door as I can get. Eyes gleaming through the holes in his hood, his voice gruff, he snarls, "The accused will learn to show respect for the divine court, and to regret the filth that spews from her vile mouth."

He holds something in his hand, aiming at me through the walls of the cage, and I have no time to plead for mercy before a torrent of icy water sluices through the mesh. It's a hose, the end fitted with a nozzle that makes the spray focused and painful, tattooing my skin through the black pants and white shirt I wore for work.

I'm drenched from head to foot, shivering with cold by the time he cuts the nozzle off, and I uncover my face just in time to see him fixing metal clamps to the wire lattice of my prison. Attached to fat cables, they snake their way to a large black box with exposed terminal posts. The truth of what's about to happen hits me in a brutal instant, and I choke out, "No—please!"

"The accused will learn respect!" he thunders, and throws a switch on the box.

Electricity hums along the cables, streaks through every wire of the cage, and crackles through the water that pools underneath me. My body seizes, every muscle locking up like a fist, pain fitting itself to all of my nerve endings in the space of an instant. Everything shakes, my heart stops and starts, and my eyes roll until they throb.

Blood roars in my ears, a steady pounding like a hunter's drum flushing prey to its doom, until oblivion wraps its fingers back around me and pulls me away.

"I'm a virgin!" I'd insisted two weeks earlier, whispering in the back row of the theater, feeling Agent Prescott's creepy doll eyes all over me as I snickered with my friends. "Pure as the driven snow."

"*Plowed* as the driven snow, is more like it," Mark riposted under his breath, and Brandy clutched her stomach, trying not to cackle out loud.

"I'm being serious," I told them primly.

"Come on, Laura." Brandy fixed me with that no-nonsense look she had—the one that said she knew more about me than I did. "You and Zane were together for nine months, and I *know* you tried his . . . snow cone."

Mark succumbed to another fit of snorting laughter, and my face heated. I could feel Shauna on my right side like an exposed nuclear core, radiating heat and invisible disapproval. Summoning my dignity, I stated, "There are things I did with Zane and things I didn't, and that's all I'm going to say."

Even to my own ears I sounded uptight, but I had *reasons*. My ex-boyfriend, Zane, had been a jerk more often than he wasn't—but he'd never pressured me to do anything I didn't want to. We'd done mouth stuff and hands stuff, but I'd been cautious about the final frontier, and he'd respected that. And then we broke up, and Shauna and I got drunk on wine coolers, and we kind of did some Things together, too; and then she got weird about it afterward, and we still hadn't told Brandy or Mark. And, honestly, I wasn't entirely clear on what constituted "losing your virginity" when there were no penises to be had, anyway, because they *absolutely* did not cover that stuff in sex ed.

"The Judge could be anyone, and he could be after anyone. Including people in this room. And it's only nineteen days until the next full moon," Agent Fields declared ominously from the stage, filling the awkward silence I'd created. "So, here's a little practical advice: don't walk around alone at night; keep your phone charged, and keep it handy; make sure your friends and family know where you're going to be at all times, so that if you don't show up, someone will notice; and keep an eye out for one another. Six girls have died because the Judge caught them when they weren't expecting it. Make sure you're *always* expecting it."

"Fuck, why don't we all just lock ourselves in our bedrooms until we're thirty?" Mark rolled his eyes, seeking our agreement, but we left him hanging.

It wasn't his fault. He's gay, but he's a boy, and he hasn't heard that exact same advice spewed at him about every activity that might get him out of the house. Going to the mall? Make sure people know where you are! Staying out late? Keep your phone with you at all times! Going to a party? Don't you dare leave your drink unattended!

"The Judge is an organized killer," Fields continued. "He sticks to a schedule, he approaches his victims when he knows they'll be alone, and he chooses dump sites where the bodies will be found soon but where he won't be caught in the act.

"Something else he does is depersonalize his victims." She moved back and forth across the stage. "His letters to the press deliberately avoid using his victims' actual names. Behavioral profiling is an inexact science, so take what I'm about to tell you with a grain of salt, but we believe the Judge is personally familiar with his victims. We believe he knows the women he kills, and that dehumanizing them is how he escapes the guilt he feels over what he does to them."

The theater was silent.

This time, I claw my way back to consciousness like someone buried alive, dragging themself up from the grave. My body hurts all over, every muscle stiff and aching; even my eyelids feel bruised as I peel them open against the dull burn of the overhead light. I'm freezing cold, my clothes and the floor beneath me still wet from the hose, and I wonder how long I've been out.

Looking around, I see that I'm alone again with the surgical table and the stifling curtains, and I swallow something that tastes like relief. Propping myself up on a shaky elbow, however, I realize that the Judge has placed a few things inside the cage with me: a dented metal bedpan, a plastic cup of water, and a paper plate with a hunk of bread. It horrifies me how grateful I am; my mouth is as dry as the surface of Mars, and being electrocuted has left me with what feels like an extremely untrustworthy bladder.

My skin crawls as I use the bedpan, feeling the Judge's eyes evaluating my body, convinced he has cameras aimed at my enclosure. Finishing as quickly as I can, I reach for the bread . . . and pause, wondering if maybe it's poisoned. *Nineteen days until the next full moon* . . . that had been two weeks ago, which means there are still five days to go. Maybe. Agent Fields hadn't come right out and said that the Judge killed on the full moon, but that was the inference. To keep me alive long enough to cut my actual heart out, he'd have to feed me, right? Even so, my stomach rebels at the mere notion of eating.

Pride and lust. I shiver again, the cold, scaly sensation of his voice rubbing against my memory. What did he mean? My face warms as I think about all the times Brandy, Mark, Shauna, and I made an unkind joke at another's expense. Looking back, maybe it *was* prideful behavior. We never said those things when we thought people could hear us, but maybe we'd been careless one time. Or maybe our self-satisfied attitudes alone were enough.

But no. I shake loose my shame. This dude doesn't intend to *cut my heart out* because my friends and I think we're cool; and there is no way he's someone my age. No teenager could have this guy's resources. I take in the concrete floor, the curtains, the shape of the space; almost definitely, I'm in someone's basement.

But even if I'm on the bottom floor of an abandoned factory, what teenager could possibly keep me here? To set all this up, to come and go at any time? He'd been ready when I emerged from the café. *I've got you now.*

Reaching past the bread, I pick up the water, a nerve ticking inside me like a gas burner ready to ignite. Agent Fields's voice sweeps through me again, with all her dire pronouncements, telling us the Judge knew his victims. He didn't stumble into that alley by coincidence, dressed like a carnival worker and carrying a sedative; the asshole had been waiting for me.

My dry throat nearly crackles as I gulp down the water. I work two night shifts a week and each one ends with a trash run; how long has this guy been watching? How long have I been on his radar? His eyes burn in my memory, two glistening stones in the frayed holes of his hood, and I try to line them up with someone I know. Insects swarm through my veins at the thought that someone I've spoken to, smiled at, *touched*, might lurk behind that mask.

He hasn't taken it off, I realize. He was wearing it when he grabbed me, and again when he demanded that confession. Why? The only reason for him to keep his face covered at this point would be the fear that I could recognize him, right? And that would only matter if there's still a chance I could go free.

I realize the foolishness of letting myself think it could happen, but it's a glimmer of hope and I cling to it. Maybe there's some way, something I could do that the other girls didn't. He wants a confession . . . should I flatter his sense of power and give him one? Or did the other girls, the six already found dead and heartless, come to the same conclusion? Maybe telling him I'm guilty will only hasten my horrible death.

In the dim light, I explore the cage, finding the joints and testing their integrity. The metal is strong, but there have to be vulnerabilities. As I examine my prison, I try to focus on the man's voice, the way he spoke to me. *The accused is awake.* I roll the sound over in my mind, struggling to pinpoint anything about its pitch or timbre that might offer a clue to who he is. The mesh walls of my enclosure swim in front of me, the golden bulb overhead reels, and—too late—I realize the water in the plastic cup was drugged.

Slumping to the floor, I drag myself through the puddle of cold water to the back of the cage. My heart thudding with sluggish resistance, I barely make it to the corner opposite the door before blackness overtakes me again.

I feel him before I see him, a presence hovering at the rim of my consciousness, a feature on the dark side of the moon. Groggy and listless, my body full of sand again, I angle my face toward the front of the cage with great effort. The Judge stands watching me, his scarlet robe and obscuring hood rendered drab by the sallow bulb. Even with the light behind him, I can still see the unearthly shine in his eyes through the ragged holes.

"She awakens," he observes.

"Yes." My tongue is too thick for my mouth. "She awakens."

"The appointed hour draws closer." The Judge inclines his head slowly. "Has the accused reconsidered her refusal to confess?"

Fear makes me dizzy, and I don't trust my limbs to support me if I sit up, so I remain on the ground. "I want to make . . . a statement."

His head tips to the side, his gaze boring through the top layer of my skin. "What sort of statement? The accused has already tested the Judge's leniency."

My heart beats so hard I entertain a split-second fantasy of using it to break through the wires of the cage, but instead

I close my trembling fingers into fists and find my voice. "My name is Laura Catherine Martello."

"Is this a confession?"

"My best friend's name is Mark Montez. Or maybe Shauna Watts is my best friend now—I'm not sure how to define that stuff. I've known Mark longer . . . We sat next to each other in kindergarten, because our seats were in alphabetical order, and I was scared, and when my blue crayon broke and I started to cry he gave me the one from his box—"

"She stands accused of offending the natural order as laid down by the Almighty, and she speaks of . . . *crayons?*"

"But lately Shauna and I have gotten closer," I barrel on, desperately, speaking faster. "We met freshman year, in Spanish One, and I don't think we liked each other at first, but a lot has changed since then—"

"The accused now tests the Judge's patience!" my captor snaps, taking an agitated step to one side and then the other, the fabric of his cloak shifting as his shoulders rise.

Forcing myself up onto an elbow at last, I hear my own voice break as I scramble ahead. "My mom's name is Kelly. She's an X-ray technician and a Libra, and she pretends she doesn't believe in astrology but she totally does. My dad is Matthew, and he does furniture reclamation—like, takes old dressers and tables and refinishes them so they can be sold again? They met when my dad broke his arm falling—"

"*Enough,*" the Judge barks angrily. "The . . . the prisoner wastes the holy court's time, speaking of trivialities—"

"I have a cat," I whimper, a tear slipping down my cheek. "Her name is Dumbledore, and she's almost fourteen, and she can't see very well anymore. I'm the only person she likes, and she's probably l-lonely—"

"This is false!" the man fulminates from behind his mask. "The accused pours poison in my ears, telling lies upon lies, trying to bury one hideous sin beneath another! When the appointed hour comes, her deceitful tongue will be removed first!" He makes this decision with an air of relief, and his agitation subsides. "Her tongue will be excised so that it may testify against her. She will watch it squirm, and hear her lies, and her unclean soul will cower."

"I'm going to be a veterinarian," I whisper, feeling every fiber of my tongue as I use it to speak. "I've always loved animals, and when Dumbledore was diagnosed with feline leukemia, I knew I wanted to help other kids with sick animal friends. I'm seventeen. I'm a senior, and I've applied to a bunch of schools, but I want to go somewhere close to home because—because I love my parents." With a heaving breath I start to sob. "I love my parents so much, and I don't want to be far away from them."

"The accused was offered a chance to admit the transgressions that blacken her soul, but she chose instead to scorn the Judge's mercy and embrace the devilry that wells within her." He stalks back to the surgical table, retrieving the hose; and as he returns to the cage, opening the nozzle and drenching me in another stinging blast of gelid water, I finally realize my mistake.

He has no mercies upon which I could throw myself; and there is no chance I will be set free. My guilt was determined long before he took me, and I can say nothing that won't stand against me as further proof that I deserve to die. The man isn't wearing a disguise to keep me from recognizing him, he's wearing a uniform. Beyond just appointing himself judge, he's also appointed himself jury and executioner.

And executioners wear hoods.

This time, when he cranks the electricity on, I feel it arc between the fillings in my back teeth—hear it snapping in my ears and sizzling along the part in my hair. I try to scream, but my lungs are like stones in my chest, and when I finally black out again, it comes as a blessing.

Time passes in a blur. When I wake next, my bedpan has been emptied, and my bread and water replenished. I don't know what day it is, how long it's been since the end of my shift at the café, and I have no idea how close we are to the "appointed hour"—the moment when I'll pay for sins I never committed in the worst way imaginable.

I eat and drink as little as possible, needing sustenance but knowing that each swallow stands to rob me of what little time I have left. I grow drowsy after every meal, slipping in and out of consciousness, waking to find more water, more bread.

In a dream, Agent Fields speaks to me. We sit at a table in the café, and she taps one blunted nail on the surface before me, her eyes implacable. "He was here, you know. This is where he found you."

"I know." I nod, even though I haven't been certain.

"A killer like the Judge . . . what he wants is control. Try not to give it to him."

"I'm locked in an electrified cage," I explain carefully. "I'm pretty sure he's got all the control he fucking needs."

"No." Agent Fields shakes her head slowly. "He has power, but not control. The first he can seize, but the latter he must be given. The Judge needs you to capitulate, to play his game; he has a fantasy that he re-creates over and over, and he's cast you in a specific role. It doesn't work for him if you don't say your lines. So don't."

"I'm sorry," I say lightly. "Are you telling me not to cooperate with my murderer? Because I tried that strategy already, and he *electrocuted my ass*."

"I didn't say it would work," Fields replies calmly.

"Great. Thanks. Thanks for this little pep talk."

"There's a really good chance you're going to die in this basement, Laura," Fields goes on, determined to make this the worst date I'll never have, "but you've still got a choice. You can go out like a lamb, or you can go out like a lion. Which is it gonna be?"

I wake up as the Judge is arranging my sad little meal, and when he sees that my eyes are open he lunges back out of the cage, slamming the door shut. Glaring at me through his shabby, pitiful hood, he snarls, "The judgment of the accused draws nigh. Tomorrow, when the sun drops, it shall bring with it the final word. The prisoner must drink."

"Is that the final word?" I ask, surly and combative, my imagined exchange with the FBI agent clanking about in my head like loose ball bearings.

"The prisoner must drink," he repeats.

My head is still fogged, a near constant state now, but as I gaze down at the cup some new ideas struggle together. I have to have been in this cage for days already, but I've spent most of it sleeping off a drugged stupor; and aside from his demands for a confession, he's kept our interactions to a minimum. Recalling the way he darted back out of the cage, I also realize that I've never seen him open the door before. He's always waited until I'm out cold to empty my bedpan or set out the food.

Is he scared of me? He's tall, but the cloak disguises his build; underneath it, for all I know, he might be some cowardly beanpole with toothpick arms. Keeping me weak and disoriented around the clock might make me easier to manipulate, but it also keeps me from fighting back—or shouting. Maybe he wants me unconscious so I won't start screaming again and risk being heard by the neighbors or the mailman or whoever.

It doesn't work for him if you don't say your lines. I put my hand on the cup, and for a moment I see myself flinging its contents into the Judge's face. Telling him no, cursing him out again, refusing to be controlled. But I don't.

Whatever time it is, "tomorrow" is still too soon. Twenty-four hours? Thirty-six? *Eighteen?* Do I really want to go the rest of my life with no food or water, just to prove a point to a masked psycho? Every time I lash out or fight back, he turns on the electricity, and I've had enough. It seems like my two options are to spend what time I have left in either a chemical daze or a debilitated state of sheer agony. It isn't even a toss-up. If I have any hope of mounting an escape, I can't do it hungry, thirsty, and racked with pain.

Bringing the cup to my lips, my eyes on the Judge, I drink.

When I come to again, my body is so heavy I feel half fused to the floor. Whatever the Judge has been giving me, he must have upped the dose, because even pulling air into my lungs takes effort. As I realize I'm awake, a dart of panic careens through me, and I work my eyes open. I can't focus, the light bulb dancing a minuet as I try to gather my faculties. What time is it? *How much longer do I have?*

By the cage door, more bread has been set out, my water cup refilled. I work my way into a sitting position, my head spinning and my stomach overturning, and I barely make it to the bedpan before I throw up. When I'm finally empty, nothing coming out but gooey strings of bile, I can't hold back anymore—I begin to cry. A foul taste coats my tongue, acid burns my nose, and I can't even rinse my mouth without the risk of blacking out again and losing what precious little time I have left.

When the heaving stops and my gut settles, I slump back, wiping my eyes on my work shirt. I've been wearing it for days, and now it's filthy and rumpled. Distantly, I wonder if I can fashion a noose out of the sleeves. I don't want to die. I'm not ready. But if death is inevitable, I'd rather meet it on my own terms than let the Judge cut me apart—*still alive.*

"She is awake."

His voice takes me by surprise, and I whirl around, the room tilting a little. Standing by the door, he peers at me with reptilian eyes. My throat raw, I croak, "What time is it?"

"It is afternoon. The ritual will begin in a few hours."

"A few *hours*?" My heart starts to thud. It's too soon—I'd

planned on having time to think, time to come up with . . . with something. "You keep saying I'm 'accused.' Who's accusing me?"

"She is accused by the divine truth itself, which, when violated, always seeks justice." He speaks pompously, straightening his shoulders. "This is the prisoner's last chance to make a full confession, so that she may go to her creator with one less lie on her soul. To show contrition before she reaps the harvest of her indecent acts."

I don't know what to do. Out like a lamb, or out like a lion? Drawing back, I look him in the eyes. "I have nothing to confess."

"Hell will be ugly." He stands there, waiting in the spill of light while I watch him back. Thinking. Impatiently, he says, "The prisoner will eat and drink."

"Laura Catherine Martello is not hungry or thirsty just now," I reply, anger creeping into my blood, "and this bread is shitty, anyway."

The Judge shifts, eyes narrowing into slits. "The accused compounds her sins even to the last. She knows the payment for her foul tongue and obstreperous behavior!"

"Oh, is not being hungry a crime now, too?"

"The prisoner will drink."

My eyes drop to the cup. Up till now, I haven't really put much thought into how he intends to get me on the table. He's done it six times already, and clearly he has a method. But finally I'm coming to realize that he needs me sedated. It hadn't occurred to me that I might be unconscious when he saws my chest open—*still alive*—but it makes sense.

Pushing my foot across the cage, I kick over the water, the

tainted liquid spilling across the floor and soaking into the hem of the Judge's robes. He steps back instinctively, and I smile up at him with wide, innocent eyes. "Oops."

"She did this on purpose!"

"No, it was a total accident, I swear." I don't even bother to sound convincing. "I'm such a butterfingers. I mean, buttertoes."

"She has the devil in her! The very devil!" He sputters furiously. "Faced with her divine judgment, a hair's breadth from the appointed hour when she will reap damnation, she flaunts her pride! Very well." Turning on his heel, robes swirling, the Judge stalks for the hose. I'm scrambling to the rear of the cage as he marches back again, the nozzle in his hand. "She shall soon see what her pride is truly worth when weighed against the ugliness of her heart!"

With that, he opens fire, the jet of ice-cold water drenching me, soaking my clothes and flooding the cage. I'm shivering violently when he shuts the stream off again, and as he starts for the black box with the electrical cables, I blurt, "Stop! I'm sorry—I'm *sorry*! I'll confess, okay? I'll—I'll give you a confession, just please don't electrocute me again!"

He hesitates. I try to read his body language, but it's nearly impossible. I know his preference is to drug me, though; his script calls for me to be pliable, repentant.

"I'm really sorry. Bring another glass of water and I'll drink it this time, I swear. I'll eat, and I'll drink, and I'll give you a full confession. That's what you want, right? Please!"

He turns, peering suspiciously through the mesh. "The accused will confess?"

"To everything," I promise, still trembling all over.

"If this is another trick, she will regret it swiftly and absolutely." His tone is dark and his words terrifyingly final.

"No tricks." I pick up the bread, soggy now from the drenching with the hose, and stuff some of it in my mouth. "See? I'm eating."

It's mushy and gross—but it's also the first liquid I've consumed in days that isn't poisoned, and it cleanses the taste of vomit from my mouth. The Judge watches me, his eyes beady and unforgiving; but he finally turns back and heads for the invisible slit in the curtain. "The accused receives one more chance to make her confession, and only one. May the Divine have mercy on her unworthy soul."

And then he's gone. The bread sits heavy in my stomach, the most I've eaten in a long while—but my head is already clearer than it's been since the minute I first woke up in this cage, and at last I have some space to think.

When he comes back, if I drink the water . . . that will be it. I'll never wake up again. And the sick truth is, there are worse fates. Like being electrocuted and then sawed open—*still awake*—after the Judge cuts out my tongue to teach me a lesson for not admitting I'm a harlot. But either way, he plans to kill me; and I can either hit my cues like a good leading lady, or I can sabotage the show and deny him the fix he craves.

When the Judge returns, he stands before the cage with a fresh cup in his hand, his tone imperious. "Only if the accused gives a complete confession will her request for the water be granted."

"I'm guilty of the sins of pride and lust," I begin, speaking in an obediently somber tone, even though my teeth chatter. "I have defied the natural order and offended God, and . . . and I see now that it contaminated my soul. And I'm sorry."

The Judge is quiet for an unnerving moment. Then, "This is not enough. For any hope of absolution in the afterlife, the accused must enumerate her sins."

Here I stumble. Whether it came to me in a psychic flash or was pulled from my subconscious, I firmly believe what Agent Fields told me in my dream: the Judge found me at the café. It's the only scenario that really makes sense. But if I did something at work to trigger this guy's punishment-fantasy bloodlust, I can't think what it was; probably I did nothing at all.

The girls he's killed were guilty of nothing but being in the wrong place at the wrong time.

Improvising, I recount rolling my eyes at certain customers and flirting with others, overcharging people I didn't like and undercharging those I found attractive. It's almost entirely nonsense—I roll my eyes at everyone, because the job sucks and I hate it, and I never feel less like flirting than when I stink of sweat and coffee from my scalp to my feet—but I deliver my speech with the conviction of Desdemona. When I finally run out of things to say, the room vibrates with another tense silence.

"The accused's confession is . . . barely adequate," the Judge decides snappishly, "but time is short. At least her sins are acknowledged. She will back away from the door."

My pulse rising, I edge to the rear of the enclosure, and once I'm pressed to the far wall, he unlocks the cage and eases the cup of water inside. For a heartbeat, I want to lunge forward— catch the door while it's still open, force my way out, attack.

But I sit still. He'd slam it shut again before I could reach my knees, and then would come the electroshock.

Once he at last signals his permission, I dutifully fetch the drugged water, retreating back to the rear—as far from the door and the overhead light as I can get. I want him to leave, but he stands there, watching. Finally, he commands, "She will drink."

Lifting the cup, I pretend to take a sip. "This is it. Isn't it? When I drink this, I'll fall asleep, and then . . . you'll kill me?"

"The hour for the accused to answer for her sins is close at hand," he confirms. "The devil awaits."

"I'll tell him to expect you," I retort, but without much vigor, and feign another sip. Then I turn away, facing the corner with my back to the light. Pressing the cup to my mouth, my lips tightly closed, I tilt my head back and let the water stream quietly over my chin and down my neck. It soaks into my shirt and pants, disappearing into the already wet fabric, while I make loud gulping noises in my throat.

Provoking him into spraying me with the hose had been a risky gambit, but it had offered the only way I could think of to pull off this trick—to spill out the contents of the cup right under his nose, without being caught. When it's empty, I set it down and curl up on the floor. Eyeing the Judge balefully, I give a slow, drowsy blink. "See you in hell."

He waits as my lids close, as I slow and deepen my breaths, counting on the inhale and blowing out heavily. I've faked sleep before—for parents, babysitters, guys who won't take a hint—and I'm good at it; but I can *feel* him, lurking, watching, and it unsettles me. It takes all my concentration to keep from twitching with nerves.

Is he buying it? Does he believe I'm succumbing to the drug?

Or has he seen through my ruse? A knot of painful tension spreads across my lower back when the man begins to move, edging around the cage, the hair on my neck rising. *Breathe in for a count of eight, exhale; in for eight, exhale.*

There comes a scrape, a sliding noise . . . and then something jabs at my leg, my stomach. A broom handle? Softly, the Judge speaks. "Laura?" Hearing him say my name for the first time is a shock, but I force myself to stay inert. *Eight counts in, exhale.* "Laura?"

He prods me several more times, and then the object withdraws, and I hear him shuffling away across the floor. I stop counting breaths and quietly gulp down air, my head spinning from lack of oxygen. Eyes shut tight, I can hear the Judge at the table—arranging his tools, metal clinking portentously—and fight the urge to vomit again.

What have I done? What am I *doing*?

An eternity passes, two, and then his steps approach again; his key scrapes the lock and the cage door squeaks open. I remain on the ground, limp, my back throbbing and my shoulder numb where my weight rests on it. *Eight counts in, exhale.* He enters the cage, his breath loud, the air disturbed by his body heat. His hands close on me, tugging, rolling me onto my back. And that's when I finally act.

Grabbing the first handfuls of flesh I find, I howl like a banshee and drag him to the floor as hard as I can. He slams down and I roll on top of him, wrapping my hands around his throat, squeezing. It's kill or be killed, and my vision tunnels, my feral brain taking over once more. He writhes and struggles—and then stars explode behind my eyes as a bony fist collides with my jaw.

Tumbling back, I collapse to the floor, the cage spinning. My hand strikes metal, liquid sloshing and giving up the bitter scent of stomach acid as the bedpan capsizes. Beside me, the Judge is already righting himself—but I'm between him and the door now, and I see my chance opening before me.

We both move at once, our bodies coming together, and I feel the prick of a needle a moment before I crack the heavy bedpan across his skull. He rolls away, crumpling with a pitiful groan, vomit and urine soiling his robe; and I jerk backward, kicking my leg out in terror to dislodge the syringe from my calf.

My foot comes down on it as I scramble upright, the casing smashed to fragments in an instant, the liquid inside it pooling with the water soaking the floor. I gasp, horrified. Did he push the plunger before I hit him? *How much is in me?*

The cage hangs open, and I scramble out at a frantic crawl, heaving the door shut again with a crash. The key isn't in the lock, and I realize with dismay that the Judge—locked in, moving slowly, gripping the crown of his head—still has it. He won't be contained long. The room swirls and I stumble, lurching backward as fresh panic licks its way up my throat. However much of the drug is in my system, I have to get out before it overtakes me, or I'll be dead.

Staggering into a run, I make a crooked dash past the surgical table, pawing feverishly at the curtains until I plunge through the slit and fall against an ascending flight of wooden steps. There's a door at the top, dark wood, blurring in and out of focus as the drug smothers my brain cells one at a time. Five straight days of bread and water, sedatives, and shock therapy have drained my strength, and the climb leaves me winded and shaky, my heart chugging.

The door opens onto a dark hallway, which opens onto a shabby living room with floral-print furniture and yellowing wallpaper, a thick, beige carpet underfoot. The air smells like a combination of flea powder and onions that makes my stomach clench, and darkness edges in from the corners of my eyes. Everything seems to roll back and forth, and it requires all my concentration to keep the furniture in one place.

The front door taunts me from the far side of the room, the tawny shag like thirty miles of desert between me and freedom. I make it four crooked steps before my legs buckle and I fall. A sob racks my chest as I realize I'll never make it. The distance forward is a light-year . . . but nearby, to my left, a chintz curtain hangs across a picture window.

Levering myself to my feet again, I start for it in desperation, falling again before I quite make it all the way. Breathing heavily, forcing my lungs to take more air than they want, I drag myself all the way to the window with the last vestiges of my strength.

Outside, dusk is falling—*the appointed hour.* Under a lavender sky sit the houses, hedges, and orderly yards of an incongruously normal neighborhood. Windows glow as evening settles in, the lights a queasy smear. Across the street, I see a woman—or maybe two women, or maybe the same woman twice; or maybe it's a mailbox, and my muddled brain convinces the bright colors to become the human I need.

I pound against the glass, leaving filthy streaks, and try to scream for help; but no sound comes out. Slowing by the second, my heart throbs in my chest, my lungs heavy. A numbing haze laps over me like a gentle surf, shadows swallowing up the sky, the lighted windows, and the object across the street that I've been hoping will save my life.

The curtain flutters as I slide to the floor, and darkness grabs hold of me before my head hits the carpet.

I wake again with a jerk, a fierce white light glaring into my face. Sounds are sharp, slicing through the groggy veil of the drug as I come out of its hold, metal clanking and a voice snarling. Something pulls at my ankles, and I squirm, opening my eyes.

My pulse goes haywire, fear napalming my nerves, when I realize I'm back in the basement—lying atop the surgical table, the Judge tightening a heavy-duty strap across my legs. I scream, flailing clumsily, trying to right myself, and my hand collides with something to my right. A metal shelf bearing scalpels and scissors and other deadly tools upends, crashing to the floor, the instruments scattering.

Whirling, his eyes huge and furious through the holes in his hood, the Judge roars, *"Bitch! Satan's whore! She ruins everything! Already the ritual is delayed, and hell hungers for her filthy soul, but still she fights against justice!"*

"Help!" I scream louder, shoving myself up. His hand cracks across my cheek, knocking me back, heat and pain blossoming across the left side of my face. Forcing me against the table, he loops a second strap around my waist, pinning my arms while I'm still too dazed to fight back.

Up above, from somewhere past the thick curtains around

us, past the door at the top of the stairs, past even the lonely wasteland of the living room, there comes a heavy thump. The Judge hears it, too, spinning toward the slit in the curtain, his gloved hands working in agitated fists. "No. No, no! The ritual cannot be interrupted!"

Diving to the floor, he scrambles to retrieve his tools, and I scream until my chest aches. There are two more thuds and a splintering crash; and the Judge abandons his scattered knives with a squeal of panic. Footsteps shake the rafters above us, and I scream louder, wishing it could shake the room apart.

"Hell will have its payment!" the Judge gasps urgently, hoisting something up from the floor. "The accused will not escape divine retribution! She will be sent to the bosom of the eternal!"

He raises aloft a circular saw, its sharp teeth bright against the light, and as it spins to life, it emits a piercing shriek that drowns out even my own cries. The blade sparkles as he brings it down, a glittering death that plunges for my exposed breastbone, and I clench my eyes shut with one last scream—waiting for the unendurable to begin.

An explosion sounds, so loud it cuts through the twin wails of my voice and the shrill, mechanical saw—and then the noise of the blade spins sharply away. There comes a crash, the screech of metal teeth eating the concrete floor, and when a hand closes on my shoulder I scream again in senseless dread.

"It's okay, you're safe now," a voice says, firm and reassuring. "I've got you now, Laura."

My eyes open, my chest hitching as I gulp in shallow, terrified breaths, lights pulsing everywhere with the beat of my heart. The face peering down at me is familiar and impossible, and the name rattles out of me like a loose screw. "Agent Fields?"

"It's over," the woman says. Her hand is warm and real, her grip tight. I smell gunpowder in the air, hear the saw shrieking furiously against the floor.

"Where is—where is he?" I whimper.

"He's gone," Agent Fields states. "You're safe. You're going to be okay."

I don't believe her. I *won't* believe her until after she's unstrapped me from the table, helped me up the stairs, and walked me out to the front yard—where an ambulance, police cars, and a crowd of neighbors are already waiting for me to appear.

One week later, when I'm home from the hospital, Agent Fields and Agent Prescott pay me a visit. I sit between my parents on the couch, each of them gripping one of my hands as though I might be in danger of floating away. They're more nervous than me, I know; the doctor who examined me in the emergency room gave me something to help me sleep, and when I woke up the following morning, my ordeal in the Judge's basement had begun to collapse into a fuzzy blur. Just like that, a hole opened in my memory, gulping down events I'm pretty sure I never want to relive anyway. It's strange, though, like searching for a tooth that's inexplicably no longer there.

"His name was Jason Thomas Hurley," Fields begins. "Does that mean anything to you?" I shake my head blankly, and Prescott silently produces a photograph from a folder under her arm. A cold chill sweeps through me as I take in a face—pale skin, dishwater hair, beady eyes, *the eyes*—and Fields jumps on my reaction. "You recognize him?"

"No—I mean, yes," I stammer weakly, my mind spinning. "He's a customer. At the café. Sort of a regular." His features are nondescript, and yet they jump out at me. I can see that same face on the other side of the register, those eyes trying to meet mine as he pays for his drink, saying, *You should smile more.* Every time he came in, *You should smile more.* I shudder. "Smile Guy. He's the Judge?"

"He was," Prescott answers briskly, tucking the photo away.

I nod vaguely. It's gone from my memory, but my parents have assured me multiple times that the Judge is dead; that he was shot by the FBI just before he could kill me. Twice in the past seven days I've woken up screaming, haunted by a mechanical whine and the glittering rotation of metal fangs. "You saved my life."

"You saved your own life." Agent Fields folds her hands together between her knees. "We're still not entirely sure how, but you escaped the cage in Hurley's basement and made it to the first floor. A neighbor saw you beating on the window and called the police. She knew Hurley lived alone, and your disappearance was all over the news." With a friendly smile, she adds, "If you hadn't managed that, we'd never have known where to look for you. I wish you could remember what happened, because I bet it's a hell of a story."

"I'm glad I can't," I answer truthfully. Brandy, Mark, and Shauna have been by every day since I came home, trying to help me recover my lost time, but I've resisted their encouragement. Other pictures have been shown to me—the cage, the basement, the table—and I quail at the thought that they have anything to do with me. The truth is, I don't think I really want to know what happened to me. Ever.

"Perhaps that's for the best." Agent Fields proceeds to fill in some more details, describing items they've found in Hurley's home, corroborating evidence of his crimes. I tune all of it out. At last, she gets to her feet and reaches for my hand. "Congratulations, Laura. You're a fighter and a survivor, and you've still got the rest of your life to live. What do you think you're going to do?"

"I'm going to quit my fucking job," I answer immediately, and am rewarded with a throaty laugh.

The two women say their goodbyes and we see them to the door; and for a long time after they leave, I watch out the window as my boring neighborhood—houses and hedges, mailboxes and tidy yards—falls under the sway of dusk, windows lighting up one by one. Hundreds of lives left to live.

A Drop of Stolen Ink

➤➤➤ Emily Lloyd-Jones ⫸⫸⫸

inspired by "The Purloined Letter"

My first words were always a lie.

"Hi, I'm Augusta Pine." I extended my hand so a security guard could scan my tattoo. He held my wrist as red light drifted over the back of my hand, illuminating whorls of ink. My ID tattoo was a silvery web of squares and threads that ran from knuckles to wrist. It was the basic design: government-issued electron-ink, with a mod along my thumb so that I could check my vitals.

My new boss polished his vintage glasses. I knew his type. Mr. Duvall dressed in antique clothing, but not for its style or its value. He wore it to prove he'd outlived its previous owner.

His phone beeped, and he glanced down at it. It would be a biography of stats: my age, my education, even my social security number would be uploading to accounts payable.

Sweat trickled down my neck, dampening my silken shirt. I shifted, hoping that my restlessness would be mistaken for nerves. Mr. Duvall's eyes passed over me. I knew what I looked like: a rangy feral cat that someone had tried to tame. Sharp cheekbones, thin mouth, and sharp eyes. I'd softened my appearance with a blouse and nails painted periwinkle blue.

"Welcome to Atreus Partnership," Mr. Duvall said. "I am sure you will fit right in."

I should. I'd been designed to.

There are three things you need to know about identity theft.

First, anyone can be a victim.

A few decades ago, there were toddlers with mortgage debt. Elderly grandmothers with drained bank accounts. Even the recently deceased were resurrected for their social security numbers. In the age of the internet, we uploaded our identities and hoped corporate firewalls would protect us. Spoiler alert: they didn't. All of our information was ripe for the taking.

After several years of rampant identity crime, a solution was finally devised.

The only way to protect personal information was to put it somewhere safer: beneath our very skin. Written in government-issued electron-ink, tucked underneath layers of epidermis and powered by the body's tiny electrical impulses.

It was a simple, elegant solution. The identity tattoos could not be duplicated and they could not be stolen—at least, not without removing a limb. And without the warmth and breath of a life, an applied tattoo went dark, and all of its information vanished.

But here's the second thing you need to know: criminals are smart. Human ingenuity knows few boundaries. There are still ways to steal one's identity.

But before you despair, here's the third thing.

Criminals may be smart.

But I'm smarter.

A guard picked up a small patch of black filament with tweezers and gently laid it at the base of my hand. The nanotech burrowed beneath my skin, and in a few moments, a small barcode appeared. "It will let you in and out of the building," the woman said. "Atreus Partnership is on the seventeenth floor, and this will let you into those offices as well, but no others." I nodded. The tattoo wasn't electron-ink, which meant it could be deactivated once I left the company.

I found myself in a glass elevator with two rail-thin young men. They talked in sharp bursts of technical jargon and didn't look at me once.

I stepped into the hallway, found another set of glass doors—no handle, of course. Just a sensor. I held up my wrist.

Nothing happened.

I peered through the glass doors. The office was empty, save for two desks. It was a wonder of metal and glass, everything transparent and utterly sterile. My breath fogged the glass.

"You have to twist it."

I looked up. A young woman stood a few feet away. She looked nearly as transparent as our surroundings—white-blond hair and pale skin. Only her mouth had any color; her lipstick was the red-orange of a sunset. "Your wrist," she said.

Her voice had the lilt of an accent—London, I guessed. "The sensor's a bit wonky. You need to angle your hand down."

I did as she said.

The door slid open.

"Thanks," I said.

She nodded. "New intern?"

"Is it that obvious?" I smiled. "I'm Augusta."

"Well, I hope you last longer than your predecessor." She turned to the desk on the right, settling into her chair with a practiced ease. "He hit Reply All on a sensitive email thread."

I fought back a grin. "I'll do my best."

"Good." She flicked me a cool glance. "I'm Adriana—a senior intern, so you'll be answering to me." Her introduction finished, she began rummaging about in her desk.

I found myself studying her the way I'd watched Duvall, the jargony employees, and even the security guards.

My handler liked sending me into these situations without briefing me first, because it made me second-guess every interaction.

I didn't know whom to suspect, so I suspected everyone.

I jogged every evening. Gravel crunched beneath my feet, and I could hear the lapping of the reservoir lake a few steps away. It was a quiet sort of place, the trees blunting the sounds of the city.

A second figure slipped from the shadows, and before I could blink, a man was running alongside me. He was thin, with a blade of a nose and a mop of brown hair. He caught up easily, his strides eating up the distance between us.

"Prefect," I said, sounding only a little winded. "You're late."

"Well," he replied, with a glance down at his forearm. His tattoo was elaborate—global clocks ran across his forearm in a small grid. He was a man who lived in many times at once. He checked a clock, then tapped his wrist. "It's a Tuesday. I had to meet with three other assets."

"Poor you," I said. "Stuck telling people what to do all day."

For all that I gave him a hard time, Prefect wasn't a bad handler; he'd kept things professional, if a bit aloof. And I'd heard rumors of other prefects—ones who weren't afraid to misuse their wraiths. A person with utter control over another . . . well. Let's just say humanity's track record wasn't great in that regard.

"How are you liking the new job?" he asked after we rounded the lake.

"It's been one day." My breath was fraying, every inhale jagged. "I learned where the cafeteria is. I met Duvall's other receptionist."

"And have you guessed the target?"

I considered. "Duvall."

"And how do you know that?"

"He wears the clothing of dead men the same way poachers drape themselves in furs. Also, he's got that 'I'm so rich, look at me' vibe." I took my eyes off the path to glance at Prefect. "I'm right, aren't I?"

A few paces, and then Prefect said, "You're right."

"Please tell me he's a spy." It came out a little breathless as we rounded a bend in the gravel path. "I've always wanted to take down a spy."

Prefect allowed himself a small sigh. "He's a thief."

"Boring."

Prefect slowed, and I slowed with him, a little grateful for the reprieve.

"So what did he steal?" I asked. "Jewels? Famous baseball cards or something?"

Prefect drew in a breath and exhaled; steam fogged around us both. "We believe he is currently in possession of a duplicated government electron-ink tattoo."

I stumbled to a halt; rocks slid around my feet, and I heard several of them as they *plop-plopped* into the reservoir. "That's— that's not possible."

The whole point of electron-ink tattoos was that they could not be duplicated. The ink was top secret, accessible only to government officials. Every shipment was tagged, and the ink required a password to activate. Without that password, the nanotech became inert. And caused chemical burns.

No criminal could manage it. Which meant—

"Oh," I said, realizing the truth of the matter. "*We* did it. The Feds."

"It wasn't sanctioned." A sour look passed over Prefect's face. "I assume you've heard of NAME REDACTED?"

"I do know who our elected officials are, yes."

"Hypothetically," said Prefect, "if such a man were to have a mistress, he might want to give her access to his office. Every federal office is wired so that comers and goers are recorded in the public record. If he'd allowed his mistress to visit, his indiscretions would have been obvious. So he found a way around it."

I snorted. "So he bribed federal agents to duplicate his own tattoo? *To give to his mistress?* That's either brilliant or incredibly stupid."

"Considering the tattoo was stolen before it could be applied," said Prefect grimly, "I'm going with the latter."

"Duvall stole it?"

"We think so. He contracts out to several branches of government, and on the day the tattoo went missing, he had been in NAME REDACTED's office. But Duvall has been searched—thoroughly. As has his house. And his office." Prefect's mouth twisted at the edges. "We've been at this for months. Sent in special agents, even a few contractors. But we don't have enough evidence. Judges will no longer sign off on our warrants."

"And you can't involve the cops," I said. "Because then it might leak that our government is actually a corrupt crapshow."

And this was why I'd been brought in.

"I'll find it," I said. My voice was tart. "And presumably save our government from another scandal. I assume there'll be parades in my honor? A few medals? How about an actual paycheck instead of this ridiculous stipend? Or—"

"Your old life back."

That stopped me cold.

"What?"

His gaze and voice were steady when he replied, "Get this done, and we'll reactivate your old identity."

"I could go home," I said. The desire curled low in my belly, deeper than a physical hunger. For me, home was the scent of damp wood, the creak of floorboards beneath bare feet, the background thrum of the nearby traffic, the boxes of takeout because our parents were too busy to cook, and the comfort-

able old couch that sank a little in the middle. Home was chaotic and bustling and full of the people who truly knew me. Not
the name written beneath my skin—but *me*.

But—

"And if I can't find the tattoo?" I asked. "Let me guess—
something terrible happens to me. An extra five years, or solitary confinement?"

Prefect glanced at his forearm; he was somewhere else, even
as he stood beside me. "Where do you get these ideas?" he said,
exasperated. "We won't add to your sentence—but we won't
lessen it, either."

Ten years. Ten long years. I'd lived four of them, but six yet
remained. It made me want to keep running until my lungs
caught fire.

Prefect reached inside his breast pocket and withdrew a
necklace. "Scanner," he said. "Smash-proof, waterproof, and
looks cheap enough that it probably won't be stolen. When you
find the tattoo, verify it with this."

I slid the chain over my neck.

Prefect glanced out at the water, then shook his head. "I
don't know why you jog here."

I could have answered a number of ways. That people
picked at scabs because they didn't know how to let them heal.
That remembering was the only way to honor the dead.

I answered, "Aren't criminals supposed to return to the
scene?"

Going to work at Atreus Partnership wasn't difficult; I was just
an intern, after all. There were papers to be filed, guests to be

greeted, and meetings to schedule. I double-checked dates, input emails and phone numbers for new business partners, and kept everything organized. Duvall barely acknowledged me. It was Adriana who went with him to business meetings, carrying his coffee and his briefcase.

Briefcases are wondrous things for smuggling. The lining can be pulled away; they are made for false backs—and even the handles could be hollowed out. If I knew thieves—*and I did*—then I knew Duvall would keep the tattoo close.

On the third day of my employment, Adriana dragged her chair to my desk. "All right," she said. "I can't eat at my desk. Budge over."

I peered over my computer screen; sure enough, Adriana's desk was so covered in papers that it looked as if a book had exploded.

"So we're eating at my desk?" I said.

"Seniority rules," she said, but she was smiling. "And I'll share."

My lunch consisted of a protein bar. I often made do with drone-delivered takeout. Adriana produced a bowl brimming with lettuce, sprouts, pickled beets, and golden potatoes. All of it looked wondrously fresh.

Adriana divided a portion of her salad onto the bowl's lid, then slid it to me. I had no utensils, so I popped a sprout into my mouth with my fingers.

"You cook, then?" I asked.

Adriana nodded. Her fork swept gracefully into the bowl. "My mother and father both love it. They made sure I knew how to feed myself before I left home."

"How long have you been away from them?"

It wasn't truly information I needed to know, but most interrogations began that way. Start with the small things, make the subject relaxed, then prod deeper.

"About eight months," said Adriana, after another bite. The lines of her bright lipstick remained intact. "My family needed the money, so I left school."

Unlike other companies, Atreus Partnership paid their interns—and offered housing in a nearby college dorm. I hadn't taken them up on that offer, but then again, I had other income. "So you're hoping he'll hire you on, once you're eighteen?" I asked.

She nodded.

"So Duvall's a good boss?" I spoke conversationally, as if I were just another young woman probing at her own career options.

Adriana paused. "He's not bad. He's not all warm and fuzzy, but he's a decent person." She shrugged. "A few months back, I was at a party with him. You know the kind—all imported suits and wine that tastes terrible but costs a fortune."

I didn't know, but I nodded. She continued, "I had one drink, just to taste. We're not supposed to drink on the job, but I was curious." She grimaced. "Bartender slipped something into my glass and I was sick as anything. But rather than lecture me, Mr. Duvall just let me sleep it off in the limo. Afterwards, there was a bit of a balling out, but during—he was decent."

"Do you think he might take me to one of these events?" I asked. I tried to make it sound like I was merely interested.

"Maybe," said Adriana. "You'll have to learn everyone's names first. And how to eat with a fork and knife." She glanced down at my fingers, slippery with oil as I picked up a sliver of cucumber.

I felt a flush creep along my cheeks. "I'll bring a second set, next time," Adriana said, rising from her chair.

My first target was Duvall's briefcase.

It was black leather, with a worn antique handle and small nicks along one side. When Duvall came to work, it was tucked beneath one arm; when he stopped in the hallways to speak with acquaintances, he left it on Adriana's desk; every night, it went home with him, and I entertained myself with the thought of Duvall spooning the briefcase when he slept.

I couldn't simply take the briefcase.

But I didn't have to.

One afternoon, Duvall strode out of his office, tapping the phone interface at his ear. He set his briefcase down on Adriana's desk and pushed through the glass doors without a glance back.

"If the building's on fire, they have to tell us, right?" I asked dryly.

Adriana barely looked up from her work. "Yes."

I waited a few minutes, then rose from my own desk. There was a coffee machine down the hall—and while its espresso was laughably bitter, it would serve for my purposes.

I felt a little bad about this part of the plan.

But not so bad I wouldn't do it.

"I brought us coffee," I said, striding back into the office. I'd had to balance them, one on top of the other, to wave my hand for the door sensor. They teetered precariously, and I made a grab for the top one.

It was a little too slow. The cup hit the marble floor and coffee splattered across the hem of Adriana's white dress.

She made a small gasping sound, like a landed fish. There was a scramble for tissues, and my copious apologies. "I'm so sorry," I said.

Her face was tight with distress. "I need to—just a moment—" And she all but ran from the office, veering in the direction of the restroom.

I looked down at the forgotten briefcase.

I had to get this done quick.

The insides were lined with silk, and several folders were nestled together. The papers were flicked through and then set aside. I pressed my fingers to the briefcase's lining, feeling for any lump that should not be there. When I found nothing, I checked the handles. There were no grooves, no way to pry them open.

Next, I tapped the casing, listening for hollow spaces. The sound of my heartbeat was too loud, and I pressed my ear to the briefcase, trying to drown out the *lub-click, lub-click* of my pulse.

Nothing.

I closed the briefcase and returned to my own desk. The coffee tasted bitterer than I remembered.

Adriana forgave me.

I knew this because when one of the thin jargony young men decided to welcome the new intern by attaching a sticky note between my shoulder blades, Adriana reached up and tugged it free.

I blinked at the small scrap of paper. "Who put that there?"

"Looks like Fred's handwriting," she replied. "He's a bit of an arse."

I read the note.

"*Fresh meat?*" I said flatly.

"Well, it might have said *kick me*," Adriana replied.

"Considering it was on my upper back, they'd need some reach."

"Well, the easiest place to hide something is where you wouldn't think to look, right?"

It was true.

It didn't stop me from leaving a contract for a competing company in Fred's inbox. It'd be found in the next security sweep—and likely get him fired.

When I wasn't indulging in a little revenge, I thought of places that Duvall could be hiding that tattoo. The list wasn't short. Hollowed-out table legs. Beneath the carpets. Inside the lining of a coat. But all of those places had been searched, and as the days went by, I found myself thinking less of the assignment and more of the young woman sitting across from me.

We ate lunch at my desk. "I'll let you have some, though," she repeated, when she saw my meal of protein bars. She seemed more animated when she ate; her posture loosened and her fingers gesticulated wildly.

With each meal, I discovered a little more about her.

Over slices of rye bread topped with goat cheese and chives, I learned that she was six months out from her eighteenth birthday. When she brought poached pears and cold cream, she told me she had a little sister attending a school for the gifted. When we shared a bowl of warm curry broth, she let slip that she'd never dated anyone.

And when she brought pickled herring, I recoiled with such fervor that I nearly toppled over in my chair.

"Oh, come on," she said, and she laughed. "It's just fish."

"It smells rancid."

"It does not. It smells—"

"Fishy."

"Well, what do you expect? For it to smell like chicken?"

She settled beside me. I was still cringing away from the little pink lumps floating in a jar. It looked like something a mad scientist would keep on a shelf.

She placed a circle of potato on her plate, then dressed it with the herring, sour cream, and a sprinkle of fresh dill. "Do you trust me?"

The question pierced me through.

My pallor must have made Adriana nervous, for she said, "It's okay, you don't really have to try it."

I rolled up my sleeves, made a show of bracing myself. "All right. I can do this."

She laughed, picked up the herring, and held it up. Her mouth was crooked up in a half smile, half question.

I leaned forward and she placed the small bite between my lips.

It burst on my tongue like fresh seawater—brine and salt, with the tang of dill. I nodded my appreciation, and a grin broke across her face. It made an unfamiliar warmth unfurl in my stomach. It made me want to pick up another slice, just so she'd smile like that again.

"See," she said. "Not so bad . . ."

Her voice trailed off, and I realized she was looking at my left arm. At the webwork of scars along my left elbow. It had been one of my shattered joints, and it was utterly synthetic now.

I yanked at my sleeve.

Adriana looked away at once, as embarrassed as if she'd caught a glimpse of me naked. "Sorry. I didn't—I didn't mean to stare."

"It was a hijacking." The words came out of me before I could stop them.

Adriana blinked, but she didn't look too startled. It wasn't unheard of—not since self-driving cars became the norm. The autopilot could be hacked and redirected. Government officials had cars connected to a secret network to prevent hostage-taking. But normal people couldn't afford that.

"You were in an accident?" Adriana asked. Her voice was soft.

I nodded. "Someone reprogrammed the car I was in. Turned off the autopilot. With that gone, other cars couldn't sense our vehicle. We were slammed into by an SUV, pushed off a bridge. Fell into the reservoir."

Her lips formed silent platitudes. Finally, she said, "Well, that sucks."

In my dreams, I could still feel the jerk of impact, the sudden weightlessness, and then the cool water filling my nose and mouth.

When I'd awoken in the hospital, it had been to a body that was half rebuilt. To synthetic bones, regrown skin, and a half-mechanical heart that didn't like beating too quickly. A tube was lodged between my lips, and I couldn't speak. But the man sitting at my bedside must have heard me, for he looked up from his holographic newspaper. Global clocks spread across his arm, and he appeared to be checking one of them.

You aren't going to know my name, he'd said. *But you may call me Prefect.*

Adriana spoke. "What happened to the person who hijacked the car?"

I ate another slice of potato.

"Community service," I replied.

I broke into Duvall's apartment.

He wasn't in it, of course. I'd memorized his planner. As for getting inside, Prefect had the security codes from his legal searches.

I couldn't believe Duvall hadn't changed them. It was almost an invitation for the Feds to keep searching.

An invitation—or perhaps a taunt.

He lived in a high-rise, the kind with imported furniture and a few pieces of modern art. It held none of the comfortable clutter that made a place feel lived in. I stood in the center of the apartment and realized there was almost no place to search. The cupboards were made of glass; there were no carpets, no paintings to conceal a vault, and even the broom closet was rigidly organized.

There was no tattoo.

I stood in that sterile apartment, my gaze swimming with exhaustion and the summer heat, and all I wanted was to pick up the phone. To dial the old numbers, to hear my dad say, *"Hello?"*

He probably wouldn't recognize my voice. It had been years.

My heartbeat faltered, and I felt that hiccup of sensation. In the beginning, I'd considered asking Prefect to see a doctor, to ask if there was perhaps something wrong. But I already knew the answer.

Why was my heart out of rhythm?

Because it should not be beating.

I'd always been good at fooling computers; when I was a kid, I'd used my skills to download terabytes of pirated movies. But one day, I'd been trying to impress a boy. His brows were always arched and he wore a shirt of swampy green. On anyone else, it would have been ugly. But he had the Midas touch of beauty, a way of making everything around him seem appealing. Even I felt beautiful.

He'd had a car. A lovely little red thing that his parents had programmed to take him to school and back—no detours allowed. He had wanted to ditch school—and I'd wanted him.

Do you trust me? I'd asked, and he had smiled.

The best kind of thieves are the kind who don't smash windows or pick locks. They charm their way inside, leaving no trace of forced entry. It was how Duvall himself stole the tattoo. He'd proven more elusive than the Feds gave him credit for.

I felt a crinkle of paper in my pocket. It was the note that had been left on my back—that ridiculous prank some tech-head had thought would be fun to play on the new intern. For all of my intelligence, I hadn't noticed the paper until Adriana plucked it from between my shoulder blades.

My fingers smoothed out the paper.

Where does one hide something?

In plain sight.

❧

It was truly a night for break-ins.

This second home invasion wasn't difficult; college dorms have never been known for their security. All it took was a cut wire here and a fire exit there. I slipped in through a window, grimacing as I climbed over a bookshelf and narrowly dodged a vase filled with fake flowers. My ankle caught a book, and it clattered to the floor. I scrambled for it.

A light flicked on. The illumination pierced my gaze, and I blinked painfully.

A slim figure stood in the doorway, holding a cricket bat. She gaped at me. "Augusta, what are you doing here?" asked Adriana. She didn't sound precisely accusing—more confused.

I let out a breath. This was the difficult part.

"My name isn't Augusta."

At that, she went still. I watched the thoughts play out behind her eyes. "But your tattoo," she started to say, "I've seen you scan it and—"

I let her go on. Until her voice trailed to nothing.

For the first time since we'd met, I saw fear ripple across Adriana's features.

"You're a wraith," she breathed. It felt like our fragile friendship hung suspended between us, waiting for one word to shatter it.

"Yes," I said.

She took a step backwards and stumbled against her fridge. "You're here—you're—"

"It's not whatever you're thinking," I said, rushed. "I'm not—it's not like—"

I knew what people said about wraiths. They were resurrected soldiers and assassins, spies and saboteurs. They weren't teenage girls with painted nails and half smiles. Which was the point—no one ever suspected someone like me.

There have always been people in the shadows. In the past, they've been called informants or intelligence. In more recent years, they've been contractors. People who can do what the law cannot.

Wraiths.

Adriana's lips were bloodless, and I realized it was the first time I'd seen her without that swipe of lipstick. Her mouth seemed smaller without it. "The car accident. You—"

Died.

She didn't finish the sentence. She didn't have to. I was serving that sentence: all ten years of it.

Four years down—six to go.

I reached up. She flinched, but I merely tugged down my shirt collar. The scar ran down my chest. "My heart was crushed. It's half synthetic now. Only beats because a machine reminds it to."

I thought of telling her the rest—that my left cheek was slightly sharper than my right because it had been rebuilt. That only half of my ribs were the ones I'd been born with.

There are arguments about how a person is made. Some people think we're born a certain way. That genetics dictate our desires and actions. Others say that we are shaped by the world around us.

I know exactly how Augusta Pine was made.

In a crumpled mass of metal with reservoir water streaming in the cracks.

"I was the one who reprogrammed that car. Got the first boy I ever liked killed," I said. "And I died in the ambulance on the way to the hospital. Only woke up because I have a near-genius IQ and enough natural hacking skills that the government thought I might be useful.

"I can't go home," I said. I needed her to know this. I wasn't sure why, but I needed it. "They think I'm dead, because I am. Who I was before the car accident—it's gone. That tattoo and identity burned that day—and I'm working off my debt to society by catching criminals."

Understanding flared in Adriana's eyes. "You shouldn't be telling me this," she said. "Won't you get in trouble?"

"If I do one final job," I said, "if I can nail Duvall, they'll reactivate my old identity. I could be myself again."

Her eyes flicked back and forth between mine, as if searching for something. "He's—he's a criminal, isn't he?" Another breath. "What did he do?"

"Stole a tattoo," I said. "Belongs to NAME REDACTED. And he may have killed someone."

She threw me a look. "What?"

This was the moment. I closed my eyes, gathered myself, then said, "Turn around and pull down the collar of your shirt."

Adriana looked as incredulous as if I'd asked her to stand on her head.

"Do you trust me?" Those same words, spoken over pickled herring. She remembered them; I saw the indecision flicker in her expression.

"Turn around," I said, "and pull down your collar."

She hesitated; I watched her fingers tremble, but she did as I asked. Her shirt slid down, revealing the dimples of her spine and a smattering of freckles across her shoulders. Her hair was curly behind her ears, and it sent a painful little twinge through me. It was oddly vulnerable, that stray curl.

My necklace came free; I held the tiny scanner, and red light danced across Adriana's skin. Half of me hoped it wouldn't be there. That the scanner would meet only empty skin.

But the red light found pinpricks of ink between Adriana's shoulder blades. It was nearly transparent, invisible to the naked eye.

The scanner beeped once in affirmation.

And two words flared across the metal.

NAME REDACTED.

She turned, saw the identity glowing on my scanner. I watched as every one of my emotions played across her face: confusion, understanding, and then fear.

"The tattoo—it's stolen government property," she whispered. "And—Duvall put it on me. W-when—"

"When you were drugged," I said. "He probably slipped something into your drink and then applied the tattoo in the car."

For a few moments, we simply stood there. I looked at the scanner, and then at Adriana. She was wearing loose pajamas in a bunnies print. My treacherous fingers yearned to reach out and stroke the soft flannel.

And then she said what I had been thinking.

"They won't let me keep it." She drew in a wobbly breath. "This has to be ridiculously confidential. I could get nuclear codes. I can't—I'd be too much of a danger. Too much of a scandal."

She took a breath, and then the last piece settled into place.

"Me," she said flatly. "I'm the person Duvall killed."

I didn't reply. I didn't have to.

The Feds wouldn't admit to killing her. She'd just suffer an accident. A high fall, perhaps. Something painless—Prefect wouldn't like it, but he'd sign off on it. His loyalty was to the government, not to human lives.

"You can go home," she said quietly. "If you turn me in."

It was true. I could have my old life back—all it would cost was hers.

In that moment, I hated them all: Prefect, Duvall, even NAME REDACTED. They played their power games, and it was people like Adriana who suffered.

"Do you want to run?" I asked. "You could do it. That tattoo has all kinds of security clearance."

She hesitated then shook her head. "My—my family," she began to say, and faltered.

I understood.

I'd spent four years living with the knowledge that I might never see my own family again; I'd considered it penance. But Adriana didn't deserve my fate.

"Then I have a question," I said.

Adriana looked at me. I read my emotions in her face: fear, desperation, and a deep vein of anger. She'd need that anger, if she was going to survive.

"What?"

I said, "How do you feel about auto theft?"

Two young women walked into Atreus Partnership.

We did not break in because we did not have to—Adriana had the codes to stroll into Duvall's office. He trusted her, not as a person, but as a lackey. As someone he could manipulate and control. It was why he'd put the tattoo on her; he thought he owned her.

I didn't have to ask Adriana how she felt about that—I knew from personal experience.

It felt strange to slide into Duvall's expensive desk chair, to set my fingers against his holographic keyboard and begin to type. But I fell into old rhythms; some things never changed.

"He'll be headed home," Adriana murmured. She stood at my side, her pale fingers knotted together. "He drinks at the same bar from seven to eight, then he goes home."

Duvall's company car was networked to Atreus Partnership with a series of firewalls and passwords; I slid through them the way a pick eases into a lock.

A grid of the city sprang up before me, along with a pinprick of light that indicated where Duvall's car was headed.

"Call him," I said to Adriana.

She hesitated, then made the call. She set her phone on the desk between us.

It rang once, and I heard the familiar timbre of Duvall's voice. "What?"

"Hey, boss," I said cheerfully.

There was a pause. "You're not Adriana."

"Very observant," I replied. "I can see how you've accumulated such wealth. Your sharp mind is unparalleled."

A shorter pause. "The new intern," he said flatly. "You're going to be fired for this. Stealing my assistant's phone—"

"I didn't steal it. But this—this I did steal."

And at that moment, I plugged a new destination into the car's autopilot.

It took him a few moments to get it. I imagined the fury on his face, the pinched line between his brows and his hard-knuckled fingers yanking at the steering wheel. First, he'd try the emergency shutdown. When that was unsuccessful, he'd try to unlock the car and leap out. I'd made sure neither option would work.

There was a thumping noise. "Trying to break a window now?" I said. "Good luck with that."

There was a snarl of fury. "You're going to pay. You're—"

"A federal agent," I said cheerfully.

The phone went silent.

"You're lying," he said.

"Oh, come on, Duvall." I let out an ugly laugh. "You knew you were being investigated. That's why you hid the tattoo on your assistant. Not a very good choice, by the way. She's rather angry at you."

"You can't—"

"Let's cut the bullshit," I said. "Look around you, Duvall. Do you know where you are?"

I knew. At this moment, Duvall's car had come to a stop in a public park—just beside a reservoir lake. I imagined how the night glow of the city lights would reflect off the water; it would be beautiful.

The car stopped with its tires just brushing the water.

I heard his sharp intake of breath.

"You have a choice," I said. "First you run—and I mean, *run*. Tonight. Out of the country, away from Atreus Partnership and your luxurious life. Or—or I hit the gas.

"Either way," I said, "you won't be a danger to anyone ever again."

His breathing had sped up; when he spoke, his voice was low with shaking fear and anger. Helplessness was a terrible feeling—and I might have felt bad, if he weren't such a terrible person.

"I'll run," he said hoarsely. "I'll leave."

I ended the call, rose from my chair, and turned to Adriana.

She was pale, but her hands were steady. I thought of how she spoke fondly of her siblings and parents. I thought of shared salads, moments when she smiled at me, and the fear on her face when she realized what had been done to her.

"I'm going to leave now," I said. "I'm not going to look back. Or ask you about what you do next. The button to unlock the doors is here." I pointed at the holo-keyboard. "The one for the gas is here." I gestured again.

Her eyes widened.

"I'll see you later," I said, and walked out of the office.

I met Prefect where I always did. On the pebbled shore of the reservoir.

There was no sign of the hijacked car—but then again, there wouldn't be. I'd waited twenty-four hours to call Prefect. Either Duvall's ID tattoos would have deactivated, gone dark without the warmth of his body—or he was cavorting in some country that didn't extradite. Either way, he wasn't my problem.

"Here," I said, and held out the pendant.

Prefect took it from me, pressed his thumb to a near-invisible button. The last scanned name and identity flashed into the air: NAME REDACTED.

Prefect never looked overjoyed; it might detract from his professional air. But I saw a flash of triumph in his eyes. "Where is it?"

"On Duvall's upper arm," I said. "I'd have brought it, but I don't carry a bone saw with me."

A nod. He'd send out agents to find Duvall—and hopefully, he'd never succeed.

"I assume this concludes our work together?" I asked. Fear quickened in my chest; if he went back on his word . . .

Prefect's face softened, just a little. "You were always my best asset," he said. As if eulogizing me—well, not me. He was eulogizing Augusta Pine.

"I won't miss this job," I said. "But if you ever need a jogging buddy . . . well. You should know I'm picking a new park."

He touched his tattoo. Black ink swirled around his fingertip. "It was nice working with you, Pine."

I felt something give way in my chest.

Like I said, there's only one way to deactivate a tattoo.

When I came to, my warm cheek was against cool pebbles. I wasn't sure how long I'd been unconscious, how long it had taken the mechanical part of me to restart my heart. I staggered upright, wobbled out of the park, and found an ATM.

I waved my forearm in front of it and waited. Waited to see if the familiar lie would flash across the screen.

Instead, I saw a name I had not read in four years.

I met Adriana at a café. We sat outside on metal chairs, watched as the self-driving cars slid past in perfect lines.

I didn't ask her about her choice. It had been hers, after all. We spoke of inconsequential things until the servers were out of earshot.

Adriana's hand went to the back of her neck. "I feel . . . weird knowing the tattoo is there. I could get up to all kinds of mischief with it."

"You could."

"We could," she said, as if all sorts of bad ideas were occurring to her. Her use of the plural made me smile.

A server brought us a salad, and we split it—eating curls of fennel and radish in silence. We sat on the same side of the table, and I could feel the warmth of her beside me.

"I still feel like there's something we missed," she said.

I shrugged. "I mean, there's never a perfect crime."

"Isn't there?"

And when her fingers wove through mine, I thought she might be right.

Happy Days, Sweetheart

➤➤➤ Stephanie Kuehn ◄◄◄

inspired by "The Tell-Tale Heart"

I didn't cry when he won. I was fifteen, and I wasn't old enough to vote but I'd done what I could—made phone calls, canvassed neighborhoods, attended rallies, written letters, and galvanized what small power I did hold in order to bring promise to the tomorrow I knew would someday be waiting for me with open arms.

I had hope, is what I want to say, and maybe that's what tragedy really is. A dream ceded to less. Because at that point in time, there was a true vision for the future, a blueprint, and however imperfect it may have been, it was one of *possibility*, of a world far greater than the one I'd always known. It was meant to be. Of course it was. After all, she was qualified. Competent. Accomplished.

But then she lost.
To him.

I didn't cry when he won. I wanted to, but my defeat was hardly a surprise. How could it be? I was new to Middlefield Academy, a second-year transfer student at this small New England boarding school, one that hovered on the outskirts of Boston and basked in its sweet Yankee glow. For all its claims to inclusive values and a diverse student body—*Our students represent more than twenty-two different nations!* the school's glossy brochure boasted—Middlefield was a place that revered tradition. Legacy. The status quo. Not only was I unknown, I was brash, loud, and worse, female. Indeed, I represented the wrong kind of diversity—the product of both black and Mexican heritage, I was still solidly American and required financial aid. My worst sin by far, however, was that I hailed from California. Bakersfield, to be exact.

This is all to say I knew my place even as I strove to defy it, to break that bitch of a ceiling that persisted in remaining so grimly unbroken. Hope, for me, had been replaced by determination, and so during my first month at Middlefield, I threw my hat in the ring for sophomore class president. It was an uninspired race; the only other person running was Jonah Prescott, and Jonah didn't care at all about the position. I knew this because he'd told me as much. He was only running because his academic adviser had urged him to and Jonah didn't like to disappoint people. His effort was minimal, while I threw myself into the campaign.

My plan for victory was methodical. First, I spent what little money I'd saved over the summer working cleanup at the local doggy daycare on custom candies I ordered online that were stamped with my initials. Armed with these treats, I went door to door through the dorms and met with every single one of my classmates, listening intently to their concerns, their dreams, their fears. Next, I created social media accounts and invited people to submit anonymous questions to me. These I answered publicly and with an abundance of humility and self-deprecating humor. Finally, I joined clubs, cheered at games, and even went out of my way to seek out the students who felt they didn't fit into the campus community. This eclectic group included two budding Satanists, our lone JROTC member, and an aspiring magician. It was an uphill battle, but I believed I could persuade my classmates with my ideas. My passion. Sure, they knew Jonah. He was the comfortable choice. But I wanted to be seen as the maverick. The outsider. The one willing to usher in change. Wasn't *that* what the world wanted? It seemed that way. It really did.

But then I lost.

To him.

I didn't cry when he won. Over the next two years, this reflection would become my rallying cry. My point of strength as I stood before a mirror too distorted to trust and searched for the grit to keep going.

It was a position I faced again and again—losing, that is, to any number of unqualified boys. Although more often than not, I lost to Jonah Prescott, my first and most formidable nemesis. After my failed class-president bid came first-chair viola; I challenged Jonah for the seat per our orchestra's rules, and we both knew I outplayed him. He was as surprised as I was when he won, not even flinching when I told him to his face that the decision was bullshit. Then I was ranked second on our school's mock-trial team—this, after I single-handedly led the prosecution in the conviction of a white police officer for the murder of an unarmed black man. Jonah outscored me with a closing argument for the defense in which he invoked the words of MLK in an appeal to disregard evidence of racial bias because to not do so *was* racial bias. Furious, I filed a complaint with the competition's governing body, only to be told the decision was made purely on technical merit and was "in no way an endorsement of the ideology presented."

There was also the junior-class election—I ran for treasurer that time, bowing to lowered expectations and still losing out—and finally, in the greatest of insults, I was chosen as the alternate to our National Honor Society's annual citizenship award. This one stung because from what I could tell, Jonah was named the winner for no reason other than the fact that he didn't expect it. Not to mention the citizenship award was a stepping stone I'd hoped to use in my quest to become valedictorian senior year. *This* was the crowning achievement of Middlefield, and obtaining it was the driving force behind most of my ambition. But for every inch of recognition I sought, victory proved a moving target. Always, I was deemed too loud, too pushy, too intimidating, too *something*. Anything that could be used to justify doubt so that someone else could reap the benefit.

Bottom line: People didn't like me, and the cruelest twist was that what they didn't like were the precise qualities that made me worthy of winning.

Still, there had to be a way to reverse my fortune. I wouldn't be so close to the top if there wasn't a way to get there. So it was with an open mind that I went straight to the source—Jonah himself.

We began spending time together, Jonah and me, and in a lot of ways he was a standout guy. He was sweet and kind and cute in a blue-eyed corn-fed white boy sort of way. However, he was equally insufferable in that he had no interest in accolades or awards. Even as he won them all! This careless ease was what I craved and longed to emulate. It was the key to his success. I was sure of it. But Jonah was uncrackable. The harder I tried to understand him, the more inexplicable he became. He charmed because he didn't care not to offend. He stood out because he refused to stand for anything. I told him this in a fit of anger, insisting that his apathy regarding the outcome of his actions was not a sign of character. Or intellect. Far from it.

It only meant he had nothing to lose.

"I think the problem's that you care too much, sweetheart," he chided me softly. "All this validation you're chasing—it's meaningless. Constructs created to divide us. You need to learn how to play outside the lines. Define your own worth, you know?"

I nodded. Not because I agreed with Jonah, although he was right, in a sense. Accolades and achievements only mattered when society said they did. But they mattered to me because I'd seen the way injustice after injustice had been decided with the wave of a hand, the shrug of a shoulder. Indifference was no better than outright bigotry, and playing outside the lines was something only people who made the lines in the first place ever got to do. The rest of us had to do everything just right, all the time, and so the utter dismissal of things like skill and competence in favor of what was easy, was not only infuriating, it shut real doors. Limited real access. Had real consequences. For people like *me*.

But I nodded in that moment because Jonah Prescott and I happened to be lying side by side in the school meadow, cooled by the afternoon shade of a weeping willow and serenaded by the coo of the chickadees. His hand was on my bare thigh, his fingers tracing small circles there, filling me with an urgent sort of heat as I rested my head against his chest, absorbing the soft thumping roll of his heartbeat. We'd been there for hours, debating back and forth, and I'd felt myself get angry, tense, as I raged against the unfairness of my world. But somehow, incredibly, that whole time, Jonah's heartbeat had remained slow, steady, and unperturbed. It was only as his hand began to creep higher and my own crept lower that I felt his pulse finally quicken, spurred from its position of ease and willing tranquility in order to reach between my legs and chase the one thing he clearly cared very, very deeply for.

I didn't cry when I killed him. We were seniors by then and I didn't love him or anything, so you should know it wasn't a matter of the heart. This was no crime of passion or malice of a spurned lover. It was an act of reason. A motive of pure gain.

You see, my goal all along was to be named class valedictorian. And for good reason. Two years prior, while preparing for my sophomore class president bid, I'd run a statistical analysis of the available data and learned that Middlefield valedictorians obtained success in their chosen career at rates far higher than the rest of the alumni population—even when compared to the top 10 percent of their graduating class.

Well, that commanded my interest. Numbers don't lie, and what those numbers told me was that the title of valedictorian—not salutatorian or any other honor—was uniquely predictive of future greatness. Success *I* wanted. Success *I* deserved. It was an achievement correlated with future Nobel prize–winning research, a Supreme Court justice appointment, even Academy Award–winning filmmaking, among other notable distinctions. My point is that *this* was an honor that mattered.

Tangibly.

Now maybe it would seem that actually earning an honor isn't as important if you're willing to kill for it. But for me, both had to be true. I had to *be* the best in addition to becoming it, and so I fought for that title. All year, my grades were impeccable. My leadership skills, my service, my music, my athletic pursuits—I excelled at everything I put my heart into. Jonah did, too, of course, and there were times I longed to tell him to slow down. To screw up. To get messy or say something offensive so that blue-eyed corn-fed charm would tarnish. Just a little. Just enough so that I wouldn't have to go through with my plan. After all, he wasn't going to college. Not right away, at least. He wanted to travel. Find himself. Play outside the lines and do shit like fly to Tibet and rub shoulders with monks. Or write the next great novel. Or walk down Fifth Avenue with a loaded gun—whatever it was that rich white boys did when they knew they could do anything and get away with it.

The thing was, Jonah *didn't* screw up. My grades were equal to his, but valedictorian selection would come down to faculty nominations and I knew I would fall short. I always had.

This sealed my decision, although it wasn't until March that I acted. I should've moved sooner, but I gave him every chance to fail. Right up until the last minute, which is how you know this was not an impulsive act. This was a murder as premeditated and deliberate as the scientific method itself. Trust me when I say there was no emotion involved. I merely followed the steps and executed my plan. It went like this:

The senior boys' dorm was located right next to my own. This was a supposed "benefit" of our maturity: nightly proximity to one's classmates, regardless of gender. While we never officially dated—he insisted on not using labels and I was only too eager to agree—Jonah and I spent many nights together. My room was easy enough to sneak out of and so was his. Our usual hookup spot was in the school theater, but now that the weather was warm, I begged him to meet me down at the boathouse after midnight. I loved the night air, I said. The sound of crickets chirping and the lapping wash of the river.

Jonah agreed, and for three nights we met like that. I'd hidden a tarp, blankets, and other items under a pile of life vests, and I'd be lying if I said there was no passion between us. No spark of lust in the danger and the darkness. We spread the blankets out, tore off our clothes, and the rest was instinct. After, Jonah would sleep, while I had never felt more awake. I sat beside him, my eyes wide, my mind ablaze, as he snored gently, a mortal metronome ticking off the finite seconds of our lives.

Wednesday was the night I did it. It wasn't easy. The conditioned pull of my gender was strong, a fervent, sentimental whisper that urged me to accept love as the greater good, the higher calling, but I resisted. Turning toward the light was folly when you lived among shadows. Like all women, I'd been raised on faith and goodwill and the belief that having a man was better than having it all. But I saw those lies for what they were—worthless currency in a world that rewarded callousness and mistrust. Action, ambition: these were the qualities that would define my future. Not dreams or feelings.

Definitely not love.

Like Monday, like Tuesday, we had sex right there on the floorboards with the sound of the current rushing beneath our joined bodies, an urgent swiftness that told me to *go go go* to take what was mine. Later, I softened in the afterglow, lying naked with Jonah and listening to the slow, soothing rhythm of his heart while my own rattled around like a high hat working double time.

But there was no moment to waste. This was the eve of my eighteenth birthday and thus my last best chance. When I was sure he'd drifted off, I pulled away from Jonah, crawling across splintered planks to the edge of the dock where the sculls sloshed and bounced in the frigid water. Starlight snuck through the rafters, lighting my way like a well-kept secret. I held my breath and plunged my hand in, reaching for the knife I'd hidden in a plastic bag beneath the surface of the water, taped to the bottom of a boat. The cold shocked me, but my only hesitation came when I felt the pull of Jonah's heartbeat from across the boathouse—that easy hypnotic lull.

That dream of something more.

Arm dripping, knife in hand, I crawled back to where he lay. Stared down at his restful face. There was no tension there.

No worry. Only the gentle peace that comes from knowing that for you, the dawn will always come. I closed my eyes. Let myself swim in the warm promise of his heartbeat.

Put it down, it said.

Be with me, sweetheart.

Forever.

My eyes flew open. I gritted my teeth and struck. Hesitation gone, I brought the knife down into his chest with the combined force of gravity, my weight, and my conviction. With a whistle and thwack, the blade pierced flesh and bone to land in the center of his beating, sleeping heart.

The rest was agony. He screamed. Fought me. I threw myself on top of him, muffling his cries while burying the knife deeper, twisting it through his organs and striving for damage. Blood flowed, my hands growing slick, wet, hot. It was everywhere—what had been inside him—and I lost it for a second recalling that moments earlier he'd been inside of me and *what the holy hell was I doing?* Madness loomed, a swirling menace, but it was over after that. I was still on top of him, my naked form sprawled across his, one arm shoved into his mouth, but he'd stopped moving, stopped fighting me, and when I sat up, gazed down at his face, no longer peaceful but most definitely at rest, I knew that was it. He was gone.

Revulsion swelled up in me, unbidden. Unwanted. But I'd planned for this. There was no thinking required from here on out. I'd rehearsed the following steps so many times, my body went through the motions with minimal effort. I rolled Jonah up in the tarp we'd lain on, knotted it tight with cord, and dragged his body into one of the boats, a canoe. Here I clipped weights to the cords, then unhooked the canoe from the dock.

Using a paddle to push off, I ducked low to clear the boathouse door as we drifted toward the center of the river.

My plan was to drop the body at the deepest point and, while I waited, I lay atop Jonah again, pressing my cheek to his chest. He was dead, I knew this, yet through the crinkled tarp I still heard the lazy, lulling rhythm of his heart. It was impossible, but impossible was what I needed in that moment. It eased the maelstrom of panic over what I'd done and what remained ahead.

The boat slipped through darkness to bob in the current. When enough time had passed, I popped my head up and looked around. The whole world was silent—in awe, perhaps, at the shrewd nature of my actions. The boat drifted to a stop, and with no fanfare I dumped him into the water. The splash was gentle, forgettable, and I leaned over the side, eager to watch him vanish into the depths, but saw nothing.

After paddling back to the boathouse, I scrubbed the canoe clean with bleach. Same with the floorboards, my hands, my skin. When I was finished, I dressed myself and took the knife, his clothes, the bleach, and buried it all deep in the woods. Then I made my way back to the school, slipping through my dorm-room window under the stealth of night and sliding into bed like a goddamn winner.

My victory, after all, was now a foregone conclusion.

I didn't cry when the cops showed up at Middlefield two days later and said they wanted to talk to me. I was eighteen now and I could say yes, even without my parents' permission. This was a point I'd debated in my mind: agreeing to their demands or claiming I needed protection. I was sure the school administration would step in on my behalf if asked. But what would be the point? They'd never taken my side before and besides, I had nothing to fear.

"I'll do anything I can to be of help," I said when we were alone. The two cops investigating Jonah's disappearance had asked me to follow them down to the riverbank and away from the school so we could speak more freely. They knew I was his girlfriend, they told me, and they'd heard our relationship was trouble free. I nodded, surprised our classmates had assumed so much when they knew so little. But I remained unfazed. Of course, I replied. I loved Jonah dearly, and he loved me back. Speaking these words out loud eased my guilt in a way I found pleasing. Lies felt a little like truth when other people believed them, and maybe that meant one day I would believe them, too.

Then the cops told me things I didn't know. That Jonah had been seen by the boathouse Wednesday night. That someone had heard a scream. These facts did not please me, but I knew how to respond in a sensible way. My alibi was easy and my distress well-rehearsed. I only doubted these cops would see anything honorable in *me*. After all, I'd been misjudged my entire life. There was no reason to assume this would stop in the face of my proclaimed innocence. In fact, reason could only conclude it would not.

But I was unshakeable. Every question they asked, I gave a more than adequate answer. My performance, in short, was flawless, and to my surprise, the cops believed me. It was surreal. Euphoric, even, and empowering, too. Deceit, it seemed, was the true path toward being taken seriously, and I soon grew dizzy with my own bravado, my ability to misdirect, cast doubt, and—for the first time ever—*charm.* This, *this,* was what victory felt like.

Entitlement.

The only problem was that I couldn't *stop* talking. The more I rambled on with my perfect excuses and perfect composure, the less sure I sounded. It was as if now that people were finally listening, my mouth couldn't stop speaking a truth that wasn't true. My stomach knotted. My palms went damp with dread. Hell, I'd killed Jonah, hadn't I? Next month I'd be named vale-dictorian, but I hadn't *earned* my entitlement; I'd simply taken what I'd believed to be mine. It was awful, really. Treacherous. I'd become everything I hated and had fought against. Stand-ing in that meadow, the river in full view, I felt panic bubbling up from my gut, a froth of confession pushed forth by my guilt, my terrible, terrible guilt.

The female officer thanked me for my time, reaching out to pat my shoulder and offering her hope that my boyfriend might return. This was the moment. I had to tell her! The words *I did it, I killed him, I killed Jonah Prescott!* hammered at the back of my throat. But then I heard something, faint at first, but unmistakable. It was Jonah's *heartbeat*—that slow, sooth-ing *lub-dub* pulse. The sound was clear as day—I'd know that rhythm anywhere—echoing up from the river. Startled, I bit my tongue and listened closer. How could this be? Jonah was dead, sunk and lost to the fathoms. And yet . . .

"Are you okay?" the officer asked. Her eyes narrowed as my lips parted once more to shout my guilt, admit my evil, only to be interrupted *again* by the steady throb of Jonah's murdered heart. No one else seemed to hear it, but in my ears, the sound rang out, growing louder and louder still. Every time I went to speak it stopped me, snapped my jaw shut, until nothing I could say would drown it out. I squealed in fury, clapped my hands over my ears. How *dare* he!

The cops stared, aghast at my theatrics, but then it came to me. Jonah wasn't trying to drive me *insane*. My guilt was my own. I could deny it just as easily as I'd denied any romantic impulse or sense of tenderness toward him. Just as easily as I could deny my spite at his constant interruption and keep my eye on the goddamn prize. Killing him had been no act of emotion—it was one of pure cunning and exquisite design— and what Jonah wanted, I realized, wasn't a confession or some wild descent into madness. No, his hideous heart simply wanted what every man wanted from the brash, pushy, out- spoken women in their lives. For me to shut the hell up.

So I did.

The Raven (Remix)

>>>> amanda lovelace <<<<

Once ███████████, █ I ███████
██████
█████████████████████████ forgot ███
██████
██████████████████████ her █████
████████
██████████████████████████████
████████
███████████████████████████
█████████
██████████████████.
████████████████████
████████

each   ghost

I wished

Nameless   for evermore.

the   sad, uncertain

beating of my heart
repeating,

re

g   r   e

T   it   .

Madam,   forgive

the   gently
rapping

Darkness ███████ in███ m██e.

███████ th███████ e█n████ I ██████

whispered

███, "Lenore?"

███ "Lenore!"—

███ and nothing ███!

███████ the

Raven

perched

just above my chamber door

and

said,

r

u

n !

But the Raven

w   as   t o   o

l

a   t e

.

Doubtless,

s   h   e

Followed fast

g

;

the

door

She

Swung i n

from thy memories

a

tempest tossed

,
Desolate yet
enchant
i   n

G

.

Lenore

shrieked,

Leav   in

g

m e

dreaming,

on the floor;

my soul   floating

f or

evermore!

Changeling

→→→ Marieke Nijkamp ←←←

inspired by "Hop-Frog"

1.

1832

"Girl, stop dawdling. Lend us a hand." A large, leathery fist pushed me off the high cart, flat onto the cobbled road. The stones dug into my face, my hands, my shoulders. I barely managed to roll out of the way of the tall wheels before they crushed my legs.

And I went to work.

In those days, we were left for the fae and the fair folk, we misformed and broken children. After all, our families decided, we were cursed. We were bad luck. So we were left, small and defenseless against the cold and the elements.

Except, when you leave a child for the fae, the fae don't always know to come. They are magic, yes, but not omniscient. Some of us waited to no avail. Some of us were taken by strangers first, strangers both kind and not so kind.

I was one of those taken. But I was never wanted.

They called me *girl*, or *changeling*, the merchants who found me. A crooked child whose back was bent, whose hands were clawed, whose tread was always too slow, too stumbling, too insecure.

They laughed at me. At my wobbling, my hesitation, my fear.

They used me. They found themselves a servant for free on the road between Lyon and Tarare and they took full advantage of it. I was small enough to hide when needed. Agile enough to climb between carts and horses. And because it was the life I grew up in, I did not know better. I did not think it abnormal to be beaten or starved, and the traders who crossed paths with us, well, who ever takes notice of a crippled child? They considered it a mercy, an act of charity that my merchants even fed me at all.

Still, I was all too aware that I did not belong there and I wished for a place where I did. Every night I dreamed of being taken by the fae. Every morning I woke up disappointed.

We traveled all across the continent. From the gray masses of industrial cities breathing out endless smog to farmlands still scarred and exhausted from the wars and revolutions that swept across Europe before I was born. From Piedmont through Tuscany to the Papal States. From Bavaria to Saxony and Prussia. We traveled by cart, mostly, but occasionally by ship or the steam-powered trains that tore through the landscape.

My masters traded in fine textiles, contraband, and cruelty, all of which were languages spoken universally. I only spoke when I was spoken to, and even then I tried to avoid it. At best, I practiced words in the privacy of night.

I learned to mask my differences as much as possible when we got to new towns. When I didn't or didn't succeed, I'd be yelled at. Boys would laugh and jeer at me, throw sticks and stones. Drunk men would spit at me.

I wondered often what they saw when they looked at me, back then. A demon? A danger? As I grew into my teens, my body became even more angled. It became harder to walk the way people expected. I couldn't mask the hunch of my back or the way my fingers curled around thin air.

"That wretched girl is better off in an institution," one contact told my master, late one night, not bothering to lower his voice. "Bad luck they are, the defective ones. Criminals and thieves too."

"Work 'em until they bleed, is what I always say," my master said.

I looked at the welts on my legs. I wondered sometimes if my skin would become so scarred it wouldn't bleed anymore. It hadn't yet. Nor had it stopped scarring. I wore an atlas of cruelty upon my skin.

"Leave your changeling to a workhouse," another said, when I could barely hold the spirits that the merchants wanted to show off. "They'll put the fear of God into her."

"So will I," the merchant said.

I couldn't imagine being more afraid than I already was. My fear was always there, like a second shadow, darkening my steps.

"Chain her to a wall just like they do in those asylums," a third suggested, when I lost my grip on a box of coin and banknotes and spread the contents all over the dirty floor of an abandoned den in the hills between Basel and Zurich. Hunger gnawed at me, causing my hands to tremble, my stomach to cramp. I was too weak. I was too wretched. I was too worn away.

Without pause, my master dragged me close to him and

slapped me with the back of his hand. The stones of his rings tore into my cheek like broken glass, flaying me open.

"Leave her. You've done your charitable duty."

He smiled. "She's grown useless, yes."

"You'll find another one."

With his thumb, he smudged the blood on my cheek to make it into a mocking rouge.

I would've run if I could have. I couldn't. I tried to struggle. They didn't stop laughing. All those years of free service had not rendered me valuable, they'd rendered me worthless. I was nothing more than entertainment.

He decided it was a waste to use chains, so they used rope instead. Along my feet and arms. Around my throat. The rope cut and burned. It choked me. I would grab at it, tear at it, but my fear had gripped me too.

One of the contacts took his cup of contraband bourbon and emptied it over my head, before they left me to the wintry night, bound to the outside wall of a barn, while they slept in the warm interior. "She'll sing for us before the night's end," they said, as they closed the door and left me to freeze.

I listened to their drunk voices inside, the bawdy songs, the laughter, while I slowly turned to ice.

That was when the fae finally came for me.

2.

1896

We observe, from a distance. We've fallen into a routine, the two of us. We are together, for convenience or comfort or complicity. Because vengeance is addictive, and because, no matter how time passes, the world is a too cruel place to leave it be. We do not need to be everywhere, but we need to be in too many places. We are barely magic and still not omniscient, but we try to be both.

There is a girl on a grassland between villages. Somewhere between Ely and Lynn. She reminds me of Jester when we first met. She reminds me of me. She's as crooked and small as I am, and as fierce as Jester. She has a birthmark that spreads across the side of her face. She wears rags and contempt. She's surrounded by a group of boys. All look pretty much the same to me—blond hair, pale skin, harsh eyes. They all wear similar clothes, in whites and dark browns. They are farm boys, perhaps. Or scholars. I cannot tell the difference, and I've found cruelty knows no class.

"If it isn't the miller's crippled daughter. Have we not made it clear? You don't belong here." One of the boys grabs the crutch she leans on and flings it off into the distance.

The girl wavers but places her fists on her hips. "Lay off, Francis. It is not for you to say where I do and don't belong."

Another boy leans against a strange contraption with two wheels and a handle bar across the front. Another one of those contraptions leans against a raggedy shed. He lets it go and it clatters to the dirt road. He grimaces. "We tolerated you while your father was still alive. Since it's just you, we should've put an end to it months ago. You're a drain on our community."

"I'm not a drain on any community. I take care of myself fine. *Lay off.*"

The first boy—Francis—smiles thinly. "Perhaps not you personally, though I know you accept food from families like ours who need it more. Perhaps you can be of use—or of pleasure. But the world is changing, Harper. There is a new century coming, and the world holds no place for your kind anymore. We'll stop you from weakening our genes."

My blood runs cold. The girl takes a step back and stumbles.

One of the other boys catches her, wraps his arms around her in a deadlock. "Doesn't mean we can't have a little fun first, of course."

The third boy pulls a bottle of something or other from his coat, and for the briefest of moments, I'm convinced it's the same bourbon the merchants poured over me, more than a lifetime ago. But when he uncorks the bottle and forces it into her mouth, it smells of cheap ale instead.

He locks his arms around her, but before he can pour it all down her throat, she lashes out. Her arms are pinned behind her back, in the other boy's grasp, but her legs are still free. She kicks out at the one holding the bottle first and hits him square between his legs. He drops the bottle, which falls to the grass but doesn't shatter, and he doubles over.

She brings her heel down on the other boy's instep with all her force. He yells. He doesn't let go, instead pulling her closer.

"You degenerate witch," Francis spits at her.

He reaches out to hit her, and I tear through the air—like luxury textiles or skin—and hop out before Jester can do or say anything to stop me.

Francis reaches back and I grab his fist.

"No."

He spins around and his mouth curls in disgust when he sees me. "Another one? Get—"

At that precise moment, Jester appears next to me, and to

these boys it must seem like she appeared out of nowhere. She's smiling, the way I smiled when I got my revenge. There's a red hue to her eyes, and we carry shadow with us. Despite the time of day, the sunlight dissipates when she smiles. "She said no."

Before they can scream or attack her, she snaps her fingers and they all crumble to the ground. Jester has been part of the unseelie world for so much longer than I, she knows tricks I only tried and failed at.

The girl falls too, unfortunately, but she's still conscious.

Jester walks over to where the girl's crutch landed to collect it.

I step on one of the boys to get to the girl. She's curled up in a ball and she retches. I crouch down—or stumble in a controlled manner—and brush her hair out of her face. She's clenched her jaw and she's shaking.

"Hey." I try not to touch her beyond keeping her locks free of vomit. "We won't harm you. You're safe now. What's your name?"

3.
1832

"What's your name?"

Jester was my age, though she was taller by half and sharp as the edge of a knife, when she found me, bound, in the middle of the night. She seemed to me like a tree sprite, in her dark green linen clothes, leaning against a twisted wooden staff, with her dark eyes that burned.

She crouched down next to me, loosened the ropes around

my arms and neck. She didn't flinch away from touching me, and I leaned into her, because I didn't know what kind touch felt like.

"What's your name?" she repeated.

I coughed and croaked, unsure exactly what the answer was. I only knew what people called me. "Changeling."

She kept her eyes on my lips. She nodded. She pulled her long coat off and wrapped it around me, rubbing life back into my shoulders and arms.

"Come," she said. "This place isn't for us. This world isn't for us."

With her help, I scrambled to my feet. Cold fire rained down my spine, as my blood crawled its way through my limbs again. Now that I was standing as tall as I could, Jester was easily head and shoulders taller than me.

"Are *you* fae?" I so rarely used my voice, it sounded awkward and foreign to me, but she didn't seem to notice.

She raised her hand and the air shimmered around her, then tore, like paper. The tears showed an even darker night than the one we were in. A moonlit sky. Dim vales and shadowy woods. Phosphorescent trees and a thousand red and purple stars. A less cruel world. "I don't know what I am. But I know I belong here."

That was good enough for me. Every night I wished to be taken by the fae. I believed I belonged there too. "Can I come?"

She moved so fast, producing a knife from out of shredded air. She cut her forearm, she cut my forearm, then she pushed them both together. Her blood sizzled on my skin. "From now, always. We'll go immediately." She licked her lips. "Unless."

"Unless what?"

Her smile was all teeth.

"Do you wish to take revenge?"

4.

1896

The world changes every time we tear through the fabric that separates the unseelie realm from the place where I grew up. Time moves differently in each place, so it can easily be that what seemed like mere months ago to me is decades in real time. I met Jester two years ago, but Europe changes every time we cross over. Revolutions. Uprisings. Outbreaks. War. Industrialization. Technological advances. The end of the century crawls nearer and I'm still a teenager.

We change too. I eat properly for the first time in my life. It looks like endless riches to me. Jester teaches me to be comfortable in my body—and comfortable in hers. She teaches me signs—and private touches meant only for us. We are both still in pain. That never changes. But we find solace in each other.

We find other folk like us—girls, boys, others—who don't belong here. And, oddly, some who do. Some who are both wanted and accepted. We turn away from them, because that, in itself, is pain too.

And we find folk like this girl. Who once, perhaps, belonged here, but who is now on the verge of losing that.

"Harper, isn't it?" I vaguely remember one of the boys saying that.

She nods.

I wonder what she sees when she looks at me. A demon? A danger? She would be wise to think me both. But likely she sees a glamor instead. Both Jester and I have it, faintly. Enough to make it look like we fit in every era we visit. Not enough to mask the burning hatred I direct at the boys.

"How are you feeling?" Jester asks. She kneels down with a suppleness I both envy and appreciate, and holds out the crutch to the girl.

Harper starts to laugh, but she does so with heaving sobs. "I grew up with them, did you know that? I grew up with them, and they would break me. Use me. Francis . . . we used to play hide-and-seek together. He was a bully back then, but it was never more than pulling my hair, pushing me around."

I grit my teeth.

"You are fae, aren't you?" Harper continues without pause. "My father always told me about you. He told me about your tricks and dangers. He told me to stay away from the valleys and the glens, because once you got lost you could never return. When I was born . . . they said in the olden days they left children like me for the fae. Have you come to collect me?"

"We have," I say.

I get to my feet and pull her up as well. I stretch to my full length, which brings me up to about halfway to Jester's biceps. Our first day together, I cut off all my hair, and it hasn't returned. One of my hands has turned inward. I would swear my back keeps angling in more absurd directions. Jester rocks to a stand and leans on her cane. Scars from another incident with fire snake around her free arm. And now Harper stands before us, her crutch trembling in her hand. Her pale green eyes are fierce against the light. We're a motley collection.

"This place isn't for us. This world isn't for us. We know of a better one," I say. I gesture to the tear in the air that we left open.

"You think there's nothing left here for me?" Harper asks.

"Do you think there is?" Jester counters.

The girl visibly considers it. She stares at the boys, at the road she walked down, at the rags she's wearing. And little by little, I can see her break.

"You want there to be, don't you?" Jester asks with tenderness.

Harper clenches her jaw and steels herself, doesn't answer. "Is this what you do then?" she asks instead. "Appear out of nowhere and find the unwanted ones?"

I shrug. "That's how Jester found me."

And mostly, everyone we find is ready to be away. The lost girls in the asylums. The children who are still left for the fair realm. The older ones who face the wrath or the cruel mercy of their families.

"Do you ever happen upon people like us who do belong?" Harper wants to know. She's not the first to ask, but it happens rarely.

Jester takes a step closer. Her voice lowers. "Yes."

"Really?"

I kick one of the boys in the shoulder. They won't wake up for a while yet, and my eyes burn and my hands itch and I taste the bitterness of blood in my mouth. "Yes. We find folk like us who are accepted, who belong. Brave, poor things. It doesn't happen often. They find each other too. But it happens." I refuse to lie about it, not to her, but it makes me feel at once as if those who remain here were stolen from us, as if they belong to our strange, underdark family, and as if I were stolen from them.

"And those of us who don't?"

I start to smile. "That depends."

"On what?"

"Do you wish to take revenge?" I ask.

5.
1832

"Yes."

If I had answered that question differently, perhaps things would be different now. But I didn't. I did wish to take revenge. The moment she asked me that question, I felt the need for it burning inside my bones, a different pain than the pain I carried with me. A hunger to return every cruelty I'd been shown over all the years I traveled.

Jester's grin broadened. It was as if her teeth grew sharper, as if her eyes shone brighter. And I remembered the stories I'd heard of the fae and the fair folk across all the continent. Hobgoblins and will-o'-the-wisps. The wild hunt and the many lost travelers.

"You're unseelie," I whispered. I'd never before been able to speak all my thoughts.

Jester handed me the ropes that had been used to bind me. "Seelie and unseelie depends only on your point of view. To me, they're all the same."

"Were you found by the fae?"

A shadow passed by us as Jester took a step back. She shrank in on herself, and without fully understanding, I could see how similar we were. Her angles were softer, her scars were different, but her hurt ran as deep. "I wish."

"What did they do to you?"

"They tried to drown me and failed. I was found by a nobleman who took me to his prince as a gift. A fool for his court. A misshapen girl who wouldn't hear his secrets. A body for his courtiers, when I was old enough. It was . . ." She glanced at the hills around us, as if the world itself would tell her what age we lived in. "A long time ago. When courts ruled the land. Do they still?"

I didn't know. "I only know of money and the rules of my masters and the road."

"Then there is so much world you haven't discovered yet, for ill and for good." She shook her head. "No matter. I tried to drown myself and failed too. It was to be my last jest. Then one of them found me, ill-wanted as I was. They brought me between worlds, where I found others like us." Her fingers curled around her cane. "Others like us, who live without fear. Can you imagine?"

"Why did you ever leave?" All I thought then was if I found such a place, I would stay there for the rest of my days.

She took a step toward me again, but she felt more distant than she had previously. More closed off.

"Because someone found me and saved me. I owe it to you to do the same thing. The world is too cruel to leave it be. Speaking of which"—she nodded at the den behind us, where the boisterousness had died down hours ago—"what do you wish to do?"

Because vengeance was addictive, but she didn't say that yet. And I didn't care. I really didn't. "Before the night's over, I want to make them sing."

"How?"

I pulled the rope taut. The den itself was all that remained of an old barn. A single-story building, with its few windows shuttered to keep any light from filtering out. A low thatched roof. One set of doors.

"Do you know how to make fire in your world between worlds?"

I crawled over to the doors, because my legs were still painful and protesting. Treacherously slowly, I began to thread the rope through the door handles with the same knots my master had taught me when he first ordered me to secure his wagons. I remembered every single one of them, because he took the rope and hit me with it until the knots were seared into my flesh.

"I do have fire," Jester said. "If you are certain that is the way to do this. Not for them, but for you. There are other ways to take revenge. Destroy their wares, their reputation. Take their money and run—I'll help you. Cruelty is not for everyone."

I still smelled of alcohol from the last time I touched their coin. I kept threading the rope until it was bound so tight, no flames could undo the knots. They kept me in a cellar like this, once. Bound and locked in. Quarantined. It was in the midst of a cholera outbreak, and I was ill. And so they did not want anything to do with me. They did not tend to me or comfort me. They didn't clean me when I soiled myself or care for me when I ailed. They left it in the hands of fate to decide whether

I lived or died. But, as my master was fond of reminding me, they didn't abandon me either. They provided me with water and shelter. They believed they were merciful.

I would not be merciful now.

"They'll find another one. They'll do the same thing all over again." In truth, that was only an excuse.

Jester smacked her lips. She stepped through the tears in the night and returned with a torch. She held it out to me. "Revenge then. Make them pay."

Without a second thought, I held the flame to the thatched roof, which instantly burst into a sheet of vivid flame. Jester held my hand as I walked around it, lighting the thatch on all sides. Soon, it blazed fiercely.

I smiled. "Sing for me."

And all we had to do was wait, until we heard them wake up, until the roar of the fire overtook their shouts. Until I stumbled back from the inferno and sat down on the cold, hard ground, my arms around my knees.

Jester sat down next to me, our knees touching, her back toward the flames. "Does that feel better?"

The fire burned to a bright yellow, and it lit up the entire night sky. I didn't feel lighter but I did feel freer. "Yes."

"I know."

Not entirely sure what to do, I leaned against her and marveled at touch without anger or hatred, while we watched the fire spread and smolder. It kept burning until dawn first peeked at the horizon and turned the sky to a pale blue. From the tears Jester had created sounded cheerful birdsong. "What did you do?"

She rested her shoulder against my shoulder. "I took revenge too."

"Tell me about it until the sun rises."

"We lured the prince into the woods. My fae and I. We lured him into the woods in the middle of the night, bound him and undressed him, like he had done to— We bled him, just enough for the scent of blood to mark him. It is said there were wild pigs and wolves in that forest. I wouldn't know. I never went hunting." She trembled. "I didn't watch, in case you're wondering. I just left him. I didn't want anything more to do with him."

I swallowed. "I'm sorry."

"I'm not. Can you blame me?"

"Can you blame *me*?"

6.
1896

"No." Harper shakes her head. "I don't want revenge." She stares at the grass where the boys still lie unconscious. They look innocent, the three of them. They are as bright as the spring flowers around them.

They would burn so easily.

Next to me, Jester sighs in relief. She would help, if Harper wanted to, but she has nightmares she can't shake. She wants desperately to be the better person now, and our roles have reversed. I have long since given up on that. This pain is not for me. I carry too much pain with me already.

"I just want to be away from here," Harper says. And that I understand too. "You're right, there's nothing left for me here. Not anymore. Not since Father . . ." She scrambles to her feet and brushes the dirt from her rags. She winces and spits on the ground again. "I'll do anything you want me to do. I'll work for my keep. I'm done with their kind of charity—I want to create a place to belong."

"You don't have to do—"

"Gather your possessions," I interrupt Jester. "Gather what you want to keep. Trinkets. Jewelry. Anything you have stashed away or hidden. And then meet us back here." Harper blinks, then nods. "I can do that. I won't be long. I don't have—I just have the necklace my father gave me. I'm afraid to travel with it, but I'd rather not leave it behind."

"Good."

Harper isn't one of us, which is to say, not like Jester and me. She'll settle in well at the unseelie court without needing to go back. She doesn't need to pay her price in blood, she just needs to belong. Most who come to the fae are like that. It's on us to keep them hidden. It's on us to keep them safe.

When she's out of sight, I turn to Jester. "Let's clear the roads before we go. Get this scum to a better place."

She tilts her head. "What do you mean by that?"

"I won't kill them, if that's what you mean. Not without Harper's permission. I just want to scare them a little."

"Details, please. Use your words."

"The shed. We can tie them up and hide them there. Let them sweat a bit before they make their way back."

Before Jester can even open her mouth, I shake my head. "Not literal sweat. Worry. Apprehension. A reminder that they shouldn't do this again."

That last comment is the easiest way to Jester's heart. I know it. She knows that I know it.

"We'll do it, but it means we'll have to drag them."

"Can't you . . ." I wiggle my fingers and she gives me a look of utter disgust.

"Glamors. Travel. Some vengeance, but that's it."

"Then we'll drag them."

Getting the three bodies to the shed across the road would be a relatively easy task for most people, especially knowing that the boys will be asleep for a few hours longer, but it's harder for the two of us. Still, we manage to do so. It's a feat of will and stubbornness. We drag them in, prop them up, and I use my ever-trusted rope to tie them together. Tightly. Uncomfortably so.

"They'll regret this when they're awake."

From near the door, I consider the three of them one last time. They look even more alike when they're all unconscious. Bright young monsters. It would be so easy. So easy to close the door behind me and accidentally start a spark.

Jester places a hand on my arm. "Not today, love."

"Not today," I reply through gritted teeth.

Today I leave the shed door unlocked.

7.
1896

Jester opened the door for me, a lifetime ago. When the sun rose over the blackened mess of the barn, she tore the air and helped me step through. She held the passage between worlds open like a curtain.

I do the same for Harper. She stares at me, at Jester, at the world beyond with wide eyes. The sun is bright on the other side too. The flowers are red as blood and black as charcoal. The grass seems to be made from shards of crystal and shards of ice.

"When you step through," Jester told me, "you no longer belong to this world. You can attempt to return, if you're foolish enough." If vengeance drives you. "But for most, this is a one-way ticket."

"I'll disappear." It's not quite a question, not quite a statement.

"You won't be seen again by anyone who knows you."

Harper stares for a moment in the direction of the shed, and the town that exists somewhere along the same road. There is a loneliness in her eyes that hurts more than any vengeful death. "I have no one who will keep an eye out for me, anyway."

"Once you're part of us, you'll always have someone who will keep an eye out for you," I promise fiercely.

Harper nods. She takes a deep breath and, without further hesitation, she steps through the tear. Inside, the shadows cling to her. Her night-blue eyes seem brighter, her ragged clothes take on a glamor. She bites her lip. "So what now?"

I link my fingers around Jester's, and we both step through at the same time. Jester says the same thing she told me the very first time, and every time we've passed through the veil since.

"Now we take you home."

The Oval Filter

⟫⟫⟫ Lamar Giles ⟪⟪⟪

inspired by "The Oval Portrait"

ariq could've lived without the ice baths.

During his time rehabbing his ACL—strained, not torn, thank God; his life would've been *over* if his injury were that severe—there'd been outright pain during a few torturous PT sessions. Having grown accustomed to throwing himself full speed at other large, wickedly strong humans as part of Radcliffe Prep's (nationally ranked, thank you very much) football team's defensive line, Tariq had learned to accept pain. Discomfort, though . . . he could be a baby.

On the field, when helmets crunched like half a dozen fender benders on every play, most pain was sudden, bright, and minor. A memory before you really felt it. Even when he'd heard the pop in his knee during training camp, and his leg quit on him, the fear was worse than the pain. Fear that he'd be gone all of senior year. Fear that he'd fall off college scout radars and be gone forever.

That loose rolling, tugging ache where his thigh met his calf was secondary to a potential life of obscurity, working in one of the city's popular and hopeless industries. Meat packing, or banging skulls at the local prison. He had to get out. Especially after all that happened. The entire town was pain for him now.

So a strain was good news. The stretching and weights, part of the job. Now that he was mobile without crutches, doing light workouts and building toward his comeback in two weeks, the coach and team trainers insisted on his least favorite part of bodily maintenance.

"It's been a while, 'Riq," Morris, the team manager, said, tapping the temperature gauge beside the aluminum tub with his loose-fitting State Championship ring (awarded for his dutiful service to the team, even though he never once suited up or ran a play). He dumped another scoop of ice into the crystalline water. "Coach says start you around sixty-four degrees. See how you do."

"You already know how I'm gonna do. Freeze my nuts off."

"Yes. That is correct. But they will thaw."

That got a laugh from some guys in earshot, though not from Tariq.

Morris, an inch or two shy of tall, and many pounds shy of an admirable physique, was a senior, too, and team manager their entire high school career. Tariq never saw the appeal of the gig. Seemed like a lot of grunt work, including his personal deal breaker: washing fifty-plus funky jock straps as often as they needed washing.

Once, coming home on the team bus, McClane, their quarterback, had asked Morris why he did it—no scholarships or pro dreams involved. Everyone in the surrounding seats, Tariq included, got quiet . . . inquiring minds.

Not used to the spotlight, Morris blushed and stuttered his way through it. "I—I love football. And I love you guys. We're a team. Where you go, I go."

The game was a blowout win; everyone was in a good mood, so no one gave him shit for such an affectionate answer. Instead, McClane started a slow clap, and others joined in, giving similar professions of love for their team, their brothers.

Tariq was not feeling the love today as he stepped onto the platform that put him level with the aluminum tub's rim and dipped a toe into water so cold, it made his entire foot feel coated in silver.

Morris said, "Doing it slow like that is only going to make it worse."

"Back off. It's been a while."

"Come on, 'Riq. Once I get you settled in I got other stuff to do. It's only ten minutes. Play *Fruit Ninja* or something."

At that moment, Coach Nielsen poked his head into the training room. "'Riq the Freak, how's that treatment coming?"

"Fine, Coach. Fine."

"Better be. We need you back on that line pronto."

"Yes, sir."

Coach disappeared, on to other business, and Morris gave Tariq a "Well. . . . ?" kind of look. "Take a deep breath. It'll be fine. Ten minutes and you're done."

Fine, goddammit. Deep breath. One, two . . .

Tariq dropped into the tub, bent his knees, and submerged

everything below his pecs, a trillion pinpricks assaulting every nerve in his body. His heart paused and his lungs seized for just one frightening moment. He must've been away from it longer than he thought; he didn't remember it ever feeling like that.

He thumped his chest, jump-starting his cardiovascular and respiratory systems. With chattering teeth, he said, "Give me my phone!"

Morris passed Tariq his cell. He didn't play *Fruit Ninja*, but he did open Instagram to add a new selfie to his story. It was a high shot, him set among floating ice cubes, naked except for the black gym shorts he wore under the water. Caption: *Guess Who's Back: Frozen Nuts Edition.*

He posted it, saw views and Likes pile up immediately.

Morris said, "I'm going to get the practice jerseys into the wash. There's a timer set, make sure you're not in here too long after it buzzes."

"I ain't forgot everything, man."

"Good. Glad to have you back, 'Riq."

Morris left Tariq in the burning phase of the ice bath. Those moments when it's so cold, it feels like there's blue fire beneath your skin. He distracted himself by scrolling through the various posts on IG. All the models he followed flaunting their sponsored short skirts, bikinis, and tummy-flattening teas. Only stopping to tap the heart icon beneath each photo out of habit. They did nothing for him lately.

Then he saw a pic that—

No. No fucking way.

It made zero sense. So he couldn't bless it with a heart. Not anymore.

Courtney.

Her bright brown face and beaming smile inside a strange oval-shaped filter that seemed out of place in an app that favored square, portrait images. Though not as out of place as Courtney herself.

In a new post.

Despite being dead for more than a month.

The tub was suddenly too cold to bear.

"Hey," Morris said, "what's with all that splashing? Sounds like a tidal wave in here."

Tariq was awkward exiting the tub, swishing chunky ice over the rim, creating a tendril of water that snaked toward the central floor drain.

"Yo, you see this?" He held his phone before him, clumsy on the tub's platform.

"Be careful! You fall and reinjure yourself, that's both our asses."

"Just look!"

Morris took the phone, frowning. He had to understand how wrong it was seeing her face, there, like nothing had happened. At least that was what Tariq thought until Morris said, "She's hot."

"Wha—?" Tariq claimed his phone, flipped it, and saw the screen had refreshed. Now a bathing suit model from Brazil filled the screen. He scrolled, trying to find Courtney, but he followed too many people, and the refresh had filled his timeline with hundreds of new photos. So he tapped her name into the search field.

No users found.

Flustered, Tariq retyped it, double-checked for misspellings. *No users found.*

Courtney's mother had deleted all her social media after. Couldn't handle the creeps or trolls. Maybe she couldn't handle the outpouring of condolences, either. All those #RIP-Court, #HeavensGotANewAngel, and other bullshit. Tariq sure couldn't.

Morris said, "Yo, you don't look so good."

"I—" What to say? What to do? "I gotta go."

When Tariq sidestepped on course for his locker, Morris blocked his way, a dangerous move considering their eighty-pound weight difference. "Your treatment," he said.

Tariq nudged him aside. "Tomorrow. I'll do twenty minutes to make up for it."

"That's not the way it works."

But Tariq couldn't care less.

Nothing was as it should've been that evening.

Courtney Hedge hadn't been girlfriend material, her words. She was a bad chick, also her words, for sure. Rihanna-esque and aware of the resemblance, she worked her looks and atti-tude. At parties, she was like the luscious blue light of a bug zap-per. Everyone tried to get close even after seeing their friends go down sizzling. If you thought it was brutal in person, the online thirst was something to behold. Every Courtney post got Likes in the thousands. Every video, crazy views. She even had a couple of cats on those Freeform TV shows following her, and she blew those minor celebs up when they slid into her

DMs, particularly if they only played a teen on TV but were really in their twenties, like most of them were.

Tariq always assumed she'd end up dating some NBA prospect from one of the nearby colleges. Maybe an actual one-and-done who was good enough to play with men, but not quite old enough to date grown women. All that to say *The Courtney Show* was a thing.

So much so that when Tariq had seen the single, solitary message in his DMs six months ago, he thought it was some kind of prank.

Courtney: *Hey, you got the science notes from yesterday?*

He did, in fact, have the science notes, and was happy to say yes to any question from her, though he wasn't falling into the trap every guy fell into with Courtney. It wasn't like he was hurting for female attention. Getting drawn in and torched by Radcliffe's Most Wanted wasn't part of his plan.

He found out, soon enough, that it wasn't part of hers, either.

But plans were made to be broken.

The apartment was empty; Tariq knew it would be. Mama had a shift at the Criterion Motor warehouse, where she unpacked large shipments of auto parts for redistribution to various stores along the Eastern seaboard. Dull, repetitive work that often resulted in her smearing Icy Hot on her lower back late at night. Her version of sacrificing her body on the field, but with little upside beyond food and rent.

He knew how cliché it was to have baller dreams of making millions in the NFL and buying his mama a house. Knew what people (mostly white folks) thought when he talked about it. So he had this joke, where he'd say the thing, then follow up with, "When I buy my mama that house, I'm going to name it like it's some kind of estate, or British manor. We calling it *Cliché*."

Courtney liked that joke a lot. Said it made scouts (mostly white folks) feel comfortable around him. Said personality was part of the game, too. With his size and dark complexion, it was good that he disarmed people with humor.

Wasn't that how he'd disarmed her?

Tariq reached for the refrigerator door handle, needing water, or juice, or something to soothe his hot, dry throat. As soon as the seal broke, a rotting, invisible hand mushed his face with the force of an on-the-field stiff arm. He flinched away from the smell, then lurched back into the open box, breathing through his mouth, searching the forest of nearly empty condiment containers, pickle jars, and Tupperware that probably should've been emptied and washed last season. What was rotten here?

He yanked open the veggie drawer and found a leaky package of thawed chicken sitting in a puddle of pink, congealed blood.

Shit! Tariq had put it there three days ago intending to . . . he didn't even know. Courtney was the first person he ever cooked for. Shrimp and crab cakes, paid for with booster money all the players got a piece of since their team was the winning kind. The meal was a hot mess when he finished, the shrimp sopping with butter (you don't sauté with the whole stick), the crab cakes broken and mostly lost in popping grease (breadcrumbs would've helped). Yet he liked the planning of it—strategy and execution. He didn't always get football plays right the first time, but the process of getting there, then getting perfect, spoke to him.

"You're meticulous." Her words.

Or he was.

He tugged his shirt collar over his nose. Twirled long streamers off the paper towel roll to soak up the blood. Yanked the entire drawer free and sat it on the floor, where he disposed of the foul meat in a heavy-duty trash bag. Then he dropped the paper towel in the swill, deciding to let it soak. While it did, he checked his phone, as addicted to status updates as ever, despite his imagination getting the best of him earlier. He missed her. That was expected, and that was all.

More IG. More bikini girls. Normal. Except now he was disappointed. Until he scrolled further, his hopes and fears realized.

There was Courtney again, in that same oval filter.

Not the front shot from last time, with her smile sly and her cat eyes reflecting mischief. No, her head was turned, as if gazing at something to the left of the frame. A good profile shot, with a solid view of one of the simple pearl earrings— also bought with booster money—that he'd given her on her birthday.

It was a tribute page. Had to be.

Except no one knew about the earrings, jewelry so unlike the hoops she normally rocked. So prim compared to her rattling bracelets or diamond stud nose ring. He'd told her he bought them because he didn't know anything about jewelry. Then contradicted himself by saying Alfre Woodard gave Sanaa Lathan pearls to wear in their favorite old-school movie, *Love & Basketball,* so that made them special. Really, while booster money bought shrimp and the good lump crab meat, it didn't cover gold or diamonds like she was used to. She didn't scoff, or laugh, or call him out. She did rock those pearls among the other three studs that adorned her multi-pierced ears. That was when he suspected they were more than the secret they were playing at.

Tariq tapped the name above her picture, which went to the profile he'd known for their entire time together. The one her mother had deleted a week after they found her.

Courtney Hedge
Beauty/Glam/Fashionista
Your favorite dime's favorite dime,
and my time ain't coming . . . it's here!

That part was right, but nothing about the rest of it was.

All the pictures were framed by the oval filter. Various angles of her face, in the typical IG grid, but arranged so if you looked at them quickly, your eye bouncing from one to the next, she appeared to thrash about, like an infant shaken by a grown man with such force, thick swaths of her hair fanned into tentacles reaching beyond the oval frame.

They weren't selfies, and they weren't anything Courtney would've ever allowed on her page. Not her standard Hot Girl aesthetic. In some, there were light patches where her cheek, nose, and neck flattened, as if pressed against the lens the moment the photo was snapped. Those horrified Tariq, because they showed anguish in such detail an artist could slave his whole life trying to render such visceral emotion, and never succeed.

A key rattled at the door, startling Tariq. He stood suddenly, nearly losing his grip on the phone.

"Oh lord," his mama squealed, "What is that smell?"

She rounded the corner, work-damp and face crumpled from the odor.

"I'm sorry." Tariq plucked up the sloppy paper towel and dropped it in the bag with its accompanying meat. "Some chicken went bad."

"Please get it out of here before I gag! Gawd!"

Scrambling, he sprayed cleaning liquid into the drawer, scrubbed it with fresh paper towels, and asked, "Why are you home so early?"

"What are you talking about, boy? I worked my normal shift."

Exactly. Three to eleven. She usually didn't get home until nearly midnight. Before he pointed that out, he glanced at the stove clock. 11:45.

That . . . that wasn't right.

He jabbed the wake button on his phone. It showed a different time, but it didn't make any more sense. 11:47 p.m.

None of the clocks in their house were synched. So as he trudged around the apartment, checking the cable box, and the microwave, and his alarm clock, he found few matches, but all of them were close enough. It had been more than six hours since he'd arrived home. Six hours since he'd first navigated to those strange photos of Courtney. Hours that passed like seconds. Or had seemed to.

Phone in hand, awake, he shuddered. That word, *awake*, for an electronic device. Why? If it could sleep, and wake, could it also . . . watch?

With an unsteady finger, he tapped Instagram, expecting more of Courtney in that goddamned oval. Before he could scroll the screen shifted, flashed a red empty-battery icon, then went totally black.

Tariq was relieved.

Field focus, that was what was needed here. One task at a time, one play at a time. He got the chicken cleaned all the way up and carried the bag to the dumpster behind their building. All that existed were the next few steps. Not the shadows visible in the corner of his eye, those shapeless voids. No ovals among them. He was sure of that, and he made certain not to look directly at them for fear of discovering otherwise.

Inside he showered, dressed for bed, and slid beneath the covers, skipping a step that had been as much a part of his nighttime routine as saying a brief prayer for Mama. He didn't plug in his phone.

It felt like the right choice.

His sleep was thin. Restless and dreamless, barely sleep at all. He roused ready for daylight to burn off yesterday's lingering unease.

His phone was ready, too. On his nightstand. Plugged in and fully charged.

Awake.

Four weeks ago, a body had been found by an early morning jogger. The woman spotted "purple sparks" at the muddy bank of the Alberto River. The sequins in Courtney's favorite jacket.

She'd drowned. That much was certain. The authorities theorized she'd been crossing the walking bridge, a mile or so upstream from where she was found, the path she'd walked many times, when *something* happened.

"Dumbass was probably taking a selfie by the railing and tipped over when she couldn't get the right angle." That was Auna Brewster's loud, bitchy hallway deduction. She was a Radcliffe girl who'd talked more shit about Courtney than most. Auna, who'd chased Courtney's popularity since they were freshmen, with more money and more effort but still coming up short. Auna, who'd gone as far as setting up burner social media accounts just to troll until some other rich-girl frenemy busted her, giving Courtney the ultimate ammunition for revenge.

"When I told her, 'Sweetie, I don't need a secret identity to let the world know how tacky you are,' it was like a supervillain origin story. Chick's been *extra* salty ever since. I seriously fear for my life some days, 'Riq!" That was Courtney's unserious rendition, told after a sweaty half hour together beneath Tariq's covers while his mom worked that three-to-eleven shift.

Had that Auna/Courtney beef seemed superficial? It did. Until.

Tariq relayed all that to the police when they came asking if anyone else walked with Courtney, or had a problem with Courtney, or meant to hurt Courtney.

Normally, Tariq had a firm "no snitching" policy. But the police had also asked about his whereabouts (hospital, plenty of witnesses, it was the night he'd hurt his knee). If they knew enough to come to him, his Courtney thing wasn't as secret as they'd thought. If they were asking that many people that many questions, maybe Courtney didn't fall taking a dumbass selfie.

Police scared Tariq most of the time. This was different. These cops were Radcliffe football fans; they made a point of letting him know. He knew they'd try their best.

As of the present, their best hadn't been enough.

Courtney's case had gone cold.

No heat in sight.

Until now.

≈≈

Tariq zoned out through the day, only a lurch and slide from tumbling out of his desk in every single class. He didn't snore, and his teachers were grateful since that would make it harder to ignore his blatant disregard for the lesson. When he was awake, he stared at his phone, an oval filter picture of Courtney now his home and lock-screen wallpaper.

He hadn't changed his screens—they used to be logos for Ohio State and Notre Dame, his two dream schools. When he tried to change them back, it simply didn't work. He'd tapped the settings menu so hard he feared he might crack the glass. Then, he just accepted the pics.

It was Courtney, after all. Hadn't he *wanted* to see her again?

Courtney posts were like art. She'd been smart about her tools. Never frivolous. "Only post important pictures," she'd said one weekend afternoon, after examining a selfie, finding it unacceptable, and deleting it, "ones that last."

"You post every day, though." Tariq'd said. The team had lost the night before and he'd been cranky.

She didn't let his mood disprove her point. "Because every day is important. Especially for people like us. You should know."

"People like us" meant the physically gifted. His strength, speed. Her looks. Assets and hindrances, because other people thought that was all they were. Courtney's strategy: use it, then surprise them from the top with some genius shit.

"It would've worked, too. But everybody who's there to help ain't helpful, " she said, no longer in his memory because that wasn't something she ever said when she was alive. She twisted on the couch and faced him, wet, grit-smeared with river mud in her purple-sequined jacket, her voice warbling, her words pushing moss bubbles from her lips. "You should know."

Tariq jerked out of the dream, his phone in his hand, kicking away from his seat. His powerful healed leg launched the entire desk into the adjacent row, a clanking collision with another defensive lineman, Cory Wilson.

"Dude!" Cory said, more surprised than anything. As was the entire class.

Mr. Staunton looked cornered at the front of the room. No way to give the customary Football Player Pass on such a loud disruption. But the final bell rung, and students exited the room, unconcerned with Tariq's fit. When it was just him, panting and disoriented, the teacher waved him on. "Just go."

He did, with Courtney's oval-encased face seemingly pressed to his screen. Her eyes canted left, the direction he needed to go. At the hallway intersection, he turned right, but not before glancing at the screen, seeing her position shifted slightly, her eyes now cutting his way. She'd become a macabre compass, only settling on a position when he reached the locker room, his stomach churning because they'd have to part.

"Coach is strict about no phones. Even if you're benched,"

Tariq mumbled, reluctantly placing his phone on his locker shelf, sealing it in.

He knew she knew, but he didn't like the idea of her alone in the dark. He never had.

Sidelined, his locker two hundred yards away, still he felt her. That single pearl earring from her gorgeous profile shot a dying star in the center of his dark mind. Those words from his dream like claxons in his ears.

Everybody who's there to help ain't helpful. You should know.

After practice, his teammates showered and dressed while he perched on the bench before his locker, staring at Courtney, watching her eyes. They were closed. Squeezed shut. They remained so as Jimmy Rogers asked him to go for burgers. And when AJ Wheeler invited him over to play Xbox. So he declined, of course.

The locker room emptied. Teammates spilled into the evening. Courtney's eyes opened. Cutting left, then right. Not in the picture, like some ghost movie. Her image wasn't some animated spirit. The picture changed, different shots inside that oval filter, refreshing to follow the movement of one so-called teammate. That was when Tariq knew . . .

. . . he needed a do-over on his ice bath.

"Morris," he said, his voice airy, "you got me?"

"You know it, 'Riq."

Coach retreated to his office to do whatever paperwork coaches do, leaving Tariq and Morris to it.

A powerful stream of water splattered inside the aluminum tub, like pounding a rusty drum. Morris hunched over the lip, dumping scoops of ice from his bucket. "You gotta do a full ten minutes today, 'Riq. I covered for you yesterday, but, for real, the cold is gonna help you get back to cracking skulls soon. We need you out there."

"Uh-huh." Tariq hadn't changed from his street clothes. Jeans, sneakers, a sweater Courtney had gifted him the day before his injury and her death. Following her eyes in the flickering new photos, he made his way to the center of the training room, knelt by the floor drain.

With his house key, he pried up the circular grate covering the drainpipe. Mossy gas escaped; the dark pipe might've run to the center of the earth. That was not his concern. The pearl earring, wedged in muck just an inch from the pipe's opening, though . . .

"Hey," Morris said, dropping his plastic scoop in his bucket, "what the hell you doing?"

"What did Courtney ever do to you, Morris?"

The team manager's smile dissolved.

Everybody who's there to help ain't helpful. You should know.

Tariq couldn't look at him, so he focused on the tub. Tried to imagine levitating over it, a bird's-eye view. If that were possible, he'd see a nearly perfect oval, wouldn't he? Almost like an old-school picture frame. Or a filter made to look like one.

Morris said, "You don't look so good, 'Riq."

Tariq stepped to him, the pearl earring that must've come off when Morris did what he did pinched between thumb and forefinger. An earring swishing over the edge of the tub as Courtney thrashed while Morris held her down. An earring floating in a gush of ice water toward a drain where it should've disappeared into the dark forever, but didn't.

There was a different picture on Tariq's phone now. Courtney's face pressed hard against the screen—or the tub's bottom. Fingers visible, gripping her neck. A pale hand, a loose-fitting State Championship ring with its signature amber gem in the shot.

She'd always posted with purpose.

"You killed her here," Tariq said, her message coming through crystal clear, "then dumped her in the river. Why?"

What change did Morris see in him? What horror had Tariq become? Whatever it was, it unhinged Morris's jaw and sped up his tongue. "She came in acting like she always does. I mean, why'd she even come here?"

For me, Tariq thought. *We were going to give it a real try. No secrets. But my knee . . .* That didn't matter anymore.

Tariq closed the gap between them. "Make me understand. Do that, and I promise I won't snitch."

"Everyone was gone because you got hurt. I was going through my regular shit, and she strolled in here like she wanted it. I mean—she did want it—said she had some fantasy about boning in a locker room."

Tariq glanced at the phone, and the photo of Courtney wore a scowl inside the oval filter, her eyes daggers. *That's a lie, Morris.*

For every step Tariq took, Morris took two backward, until he was making the three-step climb onto the ice-tub platform. "We were right here, 'Riq, and I mean, sure, maybe she was looking for one of you guys, but we're all a team, right?"

Courtney's face was pure rage inside the oval filter.

"Then she slipped, fell in the tub," Morris said, like that made any kind of sense. "Must've hit her head or something."

"You could've pulled her out. Called nine-one-one."

The picture on his phone zoomed to that gripping hand, and that oversize ring. *It's okay, baby,* Tariq thought. *I know.*

Tariq held the phone up for Morris.

"Dude, what am I looking at? The screen's black."

Tariq climbed onto the platform, grabbed Morris by the neck, and edged him toward the frigid water. "Take a breath," he said. "Ten minutes should do it."

On his phone, Courtney, his sweet, sweet Courtney, inside the oval filter, was all teeth.

Red

→→→ Hillary Monahan ←←←

inspired by "The Masque of the Red Death"

leven p.m. on a Boston train headed for Cambridge.
It's Friday. Halloween.

The car is bustling. Drunk party boys whoop and
holler, their costume makeup long since smeared off
onto their shirtsleeves. Drunk party girls avoid drunk party
boys, clustering together at one end of the car, snapping selfies
and shriek-laughing. A Chinese woman on her way home after
her night shift reads a Kindle, wearing sneakers with business
casual, her nylon tote bag on the seat beside her, a freeloading
passenger. The vagrants huddle in on themselves, needing the
warmth of a till-one train in the face of a record-breaking cold
snap.

It's not often October gets snow, but El Niño or a random
stroke of bad luck set the windchill to subzero with gusts strong

enough to force most kids to miss trick-or-treating. It is, for them, a Halloween they'll remember.

Tears and disappointment for all, then, Prospero.

I sit in the middle of a three-set seat, my body wrapped in a coat far too big for my five-foot-nothing. You could fit two of me in the ankle-length wool, and as I warm my fingers in pockets that are newly mine, I think of the man who wore it last. Broad-shouldered. Tall. Hints of cologne ride the collar along with the faint, acrid tang of old cigarette smoke, accounting for my ownership of the coat in the first place.

Across from me, swaddled in a black parka with tears at the elbows, is an old white man with sallow skin and a grizzled beard long overdue for a trim. He smells like bourbon and post-bourbon vomit. I think he's asleep, but then he lifts his red-rimmed gaze my way. The whites of his eyes aren't white but banana-yellow. Jaundice. That's one liver that's seen better days.

"That your real color?" he asks-slash-demands.

I pull my fingers from my pocket and thumb the long, silky strands resting on my shoulders. Scarlet, the color of freshly spilled blood. I'd almost forgotten, but that too-smooth texture reminds me again. I'm young now, only sixteen. My skin is pale, my chin is soft, my eyes are dark. I've been so many *to* so many, but tonight, I am Red. I am Red and I am coming.

The man asks his question again.

I peer at him over the standing-tall collar of my new coat.

"Sleep," I say.

His lids droop and he fades into slumber. Not forever, just for another stop or two. The conductor's voice comes over the loudspeakers.

"Park Street," he says, the *R* of the name lost to his accent. "Next stop, Park Street."

⌒⌒

Boston's layout makes little sense until you realize the roads were once the cart routes of a freshly colonized world. Infrastructure wasn't a consideration of the Puritans; they went where their tow animals pulled them, and years later, when it came time to pave roads, they paved where so many had trodden before. The buildings were fitted in between the migratory patterns of the domesticated cart-hauling cow.

I think of this as I navigate a grid of streets that's not a grid at all, but something much more nonsensical. A sharp left. A jagged right. The structures are packed in tight on the narrower streets, creating tunnels of wind that drop the temperature not by a degree or two, but by ten or twenty. I shiver inside my too-large coat, the snot in my nose frozen, my eyes blinking against the shredding gusts.

I walk.

I turn a corner, clear on my destination, and yet I pause. There's an old man. More appropriately, there *was* a man, the flesh that contained him all that remains. He's laid out on a sidewalk bench as if presented on a bier. His eyes point to the October sky. His lean bones are clad in pants that fit before the hard times hit the hardest, but now require a rope belt to keep him decent. A filthy shirt. A grease-stained hat. His fingernails, jagged from gnawing, are riddled with dirt. Between hands stained dark with soil is a sign.

I TRIED, it reads. There's a cup beside it, a few paltry coins on the bottom indicating a short haul, and perhaps why the man dared the elements in such frigid cold.

The man's name is unimportant to me. What is important is his coat. It is camouflage and there are patches of numbers that long ago frayed at the edges sewn on. The threads are bright despite their forty-five years. The pins on the lapel are worn straight—a mark of pride—despite their thirst for polish.

It is a coat that has been with this man longer than it hasn't, as evidenced by its condition and its stench. It is a good coat, a worthy coat, and I shoulder out of my large woolen one so that I may take this newest mantle. It's a grim task, to pull the clothing from stiffening limbs while the October night screams, but I am, after all, ever patient.

Soon, I don the new garment. Soon, my old coat is laid atop the body as if to shield him from New England's weather-borne indignities.

Soon, I am back on task.

Onward.

All great cities have their multitudes, great wealth and great poverty coexisting in an inequitable truce that sees those who *have* doing what they want and those who *do not have* suffering. Boston's feast-versus-famine dichotomy is more pronounced than most. The man whose coat I wear lived among the squalor, where the lights were dimmest, where rats scurried and trash skittered down the streets with every gust of winter wind.

Where I've come, where Prospero's prospers, is beyond the sour smoke pouring from the haphazard train stops. Beyond forgotten alleys harboring shivering humans gathering their warmth for survival. The pavement here is not cracked, old, and gray, but neatly poured, unsullied, and a pleasing beige against well-maintained cobblestone. The streetlights are not rare birds in a concrete jungle but standing stalwart on every corner—iron lanterns with whorled adornments that look good on *Wish You Were Here* postcards. It's perfect landscaping and perfectly kept brick buildings. It's logoed sweatshirts, stiff upper lips, and too many coffee shops. It's Ivy League, where trust-fund babies rub elbows with those who clawed their way to their rightful place among the illuminati.

It's no coincidence that Prospero's is found here, among the riches. It caters to monarch butterflies only; the common codling moth need not apply. A wall of wide males standing shoulder to shoulder, wearing identical black suits, blocks the entrance. To mark the holiday, they wear masks of horned gods and birdlike creatures and gargoyles. These bouncers are decorated deterrents, keeping the revelers inside "safe" from the excitable rabble outside.

I force my way to the front of the jockeying crowd. It's a spectacle for a slight, red-haired girl in jeans, sneakers, and a dirty military coat to stand among such finery, but I boldly command space women often aren't allowed, tilting back my head to better see the marquee waving across the night sky. *Prospero's!* it proudly proclaims, both to tantalize and to taunt.

The centermost bouncer motions me near with his clipboard. He peers at my clothes from behind a demi-mask fashioned like a skull. I do not belong, his eyes say, but he is wrong. The hustle, glitter, and glam are all meaningless without the urgency only I can bring. And his mask! It is an offering, albeit an unintentional one.

"Name?" he asks, his thick finger gliding over a list.

"Does it matter?" I ask.

And as I look at him, he peers at me from behind that twisted, painted leather tethered with a string. *He knows.* Halloween is a holiday of fear, of manufactured scares that quicken the heart, but this is altogether different. This fear starts in the recesses of the primitive brain, in the place where reason and logic are trumped by something older than human sensibilities. It is where instinct is born. It demands survival by telling the prey animal that it is outmatched by a nastier, venom-fanged predator and to *flee, flee, flee!*

The muscles in the man's body furl. His feet itch to run. His bladder twinges. He knows me and he knows my purpose. He sweeps the mask from his face, revealing a bevy of worry lines across a wide, brown brow, revealing a top lip dotted with fresh sweat and the rawness that goes along with deep-seated terror that mortality is not such an abstract concept after all.

His hands tremble, and both clipboard and mask drop to the ground. He retrieves the former, I the latter, my thumb coursing over the smooth, sanded inside, where the wearer's nose nestles into the leather. He does not ask for it back as he steps aside. I do not offer it, passing him and venturing into a domain that was, truthfully, mine all along.

Velvet ropes do not apply to me.

The black glass doors open, and then they close behind me. Immediately, the clamoring of the masses is silenced. I assess the dozen steps before me. Wide. Carpeted black. The front edges have strings of lights that shift color, from blue to purple to green to orange to white to violet. It reminds me of an abbey long ago, and I wonder if they know this is how it began then.

If they realize this is how it will end again.

I don the mask and, with nary a word nor care, I ascend.

Prospero's has seven immaculately decorated rooms connected by a meandering, looping hallway. There is no sense to their placement, nor is there logic to the awkward angles and shapes of the walls within. It's meant to confuse. To tantalize. To lure you in deeper. *Come closer,* it says, never revealing why. Certain apex predators do this: entice with flashy colors, with hypnotic movements and appealing scents. Beauty is the trap, assuring demise.

The club is no different. The guests are drawn to a flame that will inevitably consume their papery wings.

I walk.

In the first chamber—on the eastern-facing side of the building—the ceiling, walls, and floors are the color of cornflowers, sun-kissed clouds painted all about as if to grant one the illusion of flight. The decorations are suns—so many suns. Hanging from the ceiling as chimes. On the walls as large, bronze disks. In inlaid mosaics on the end tables. At the center of a rich, thick carpet imported from the Middle East. The furnishings are deep, golden velvet, the wood pale and polished to gleaming.

Cherub statuettes loom above, their faces fat and smiling. It is all so very garish, but so, too, are the guests. The people swarm, their costumes tailored, not selected from a shelf or bought off the rack at a store, but fitted over long hours by skilled seamstresses. Their makeup is paint, applied in layers by an artist's hand.

They are peacocks fanning their tail feathers.

I walk through the blue, stepping over a man supine on the floor, his pupils enormous, his body twitching as he ogles the angels above. Ignoring the man slipping his wedding ring into his pocket so he can better woo an Aphrodite who's starved herself for just the right jut of hipbone. Threading my way through bodies grinding to heavy drumbeats, their manicured hands spilling champagne on themselves and one another. I pause to admire a tall, narrow window with blue glass through which I can see the twisting hallway. Electric candelabras ignite the panes in a fiery hue, casting all inside the same cornflower blue as the walls.

Smoke and mirrors. Illusions to please. Like the bouncers making those outside believe they aren't worthy. Making those inside believe they are shielded from the unworthy.

I take a harsh, unnaturally sharp turn to enter the purple room. Tapestries cover the walls in lieu of clouds, yet it is no less decadently adorned. Divans with sprawling, twined bodies occupy the corners. Scarves hang from the ceiling. A bar serving only purple cocktails is centered on the tiled floor, with tables offering candies and fruits in colored accordance. The air smells of grape—not the fresh fruit on the vine but a sugary chemical tang best served in Popsicles and punch. It's cloying, but it defeats the sweat-and-perfume stench of the guests.

Again I pause by a tall, narrow window shining colored light on such a party. Again I walk. This pattern continues for six of seven rooms. I bear witness to the celebrations of the joyfully oblivious as I pass from purple to green, from green to orange and through white and violet, always admiring Prospero's light play through the windows. Only the seventh room—the last room—is different, and it is here that I will take my stand, as it is here where the revelers do not dwell.

The room is on the western side, the walls black velvet, the ceiling and floor covered by shining black latex. There are no furnishings beyond a tall black clock with a stark white face, the shape and countenance reminding me of nuns who scurry into their stone holy buildings to serve their Lord. The pendulum swings back and forth, heavy as it ticks away the seconds of the minutes, the minutes of the hours, with deeply resonating clangs that echo through its hollow guts. A long, slender minute hand inches closer to twelve to mark the day's death on this Halloween masque to remember.

I brace my legs apart, my hands sunk deep in the pockets of my camo coat. This room, and only this room, has a window with glass of a differing color than the walls. The panes are sanguine red, the light shining within—on Prospero's walls, on the slight girl standing alone inside—splashed in such a way that we are bloodied.

Soon, the clock will chime twelve.

Behind me, commotion stirs.

Rarely does Red smile, but I do find one on the brink of this new day.

For you see, he's learned of my arrival.

Much to my delight, *Prospero comes.*

The manager wears a fine suit imported from Italy, crafted by a man whose father and grandfather outfitted kings. The stitching is precise. The lining on the jacket is silk, as are the vest and tie. He stands out among his guests for his simplicity as much as his severity. He is a sleek figure in black with silver jacquard accents and a plain black mask. His hair is blond and wisped through with silver. His eyes are watery, indistinct blue.

The metal nametag reads DUKE, which is delicious and ridiculous and so very apt. His importance was decreed at birth, then, by parents who thought to declare his quality with four simple letters.

"Where is she?" I hear him say. He is hard and unmelodic. I'd much rather listen to the tick-tocks and metal groans of the clock before me than this privileged son.

"You, there. In that— Damn it. Get Victor in here. Get that mask off of her!" he proclaims. There is a pause before he adds, "Kill the music. We have a breach. What am I paying you for if that kind of kid can get in here without an invitation?"

Not a kid, *that kind of kid*. A walking, talking reminder of the filth that exists beyond Cambridge's picturesque streets.

The speakers go quiet, as do the guests. Duke's voice is robust, echoing throughout his carefully curated rooms, throughout the asplike hallway, his words bouncing off the mirrors' surfaces to reach my ears. He comes for me, passing his rooms in order, from blue to purple, through the violet and toward the black where I stand, waiting for him with a minute left on the clock.

This should be a time of celebration, when all are overjoyed that they may unmask! But no, silence reigns as the man in the suit comes to do work his paid men will not do. *They* know, you see. They sense who I am—*what* I am—like the man at the doors with his clipboard. These brave men . . . their feet will not move forward but backward toward the exits. Their rabbit hearts pitter-patter inside their chests in anticipation of an unknown awfulness they cannot yet grasp.

"Christ, she smells. Victor! Where are— You there. Kid. Come here," Duke demands.

I do not turn.

"I said to come here. If you think I won't—"

He reaches for me, to manhandle me. To displace me from his gilded cage because I don't belong. I am one of *them*. I am the unwashed masses with the stink of poverty clinging to me. My lack of riches in this immaculate place is an affront he cannot abide.

He wishes to show me my place.

Away from him, abandoned to the freezing, unseen alleys.

The minute hand ticks over to twelve. The pale-faced clock clangs its first, heralding the change of day with gleeful fury. I turn to face my unwitting host so he may know me. So he may see me within the eyes of this young woman, fathomless and black and hungry to swallow him whole. The chimes sing a delighted symphony as he grasps for one moment and one moment only exactly whom—what—he tried to subjugate.

He ends prostrate on the floor, his pale eyes swimming around before going forever sightless.

Another clang.

Another.

The guests descend upon the black room. Shouts. Fury. *Frenzy*. Hands reach for me, but they find themselves grasping air, discovering too late that I can touch but cannot *be* touched. Revelers fall like discarded dollies at my feet. They fall beyond, too—in the colorful rooms and the winding, mirrored hall-ways, until all those inside the club are expended.

The last body crumples to the floor as the clock delivers its final chime, never to ring out again.

I peer at their final postures in this temple of affluence. With little ceremony, I remove my camouflage coat. I replace it with one of fine Italian craftsmanship, the sleeves too long for my arms, the silk lining warm and scented with expensive cologne. I button the double breast. I flip up the collar so it touches my ears. The candelabras of the club flicker and wane as I make my way to the fire exit and out into the cold November night. I walk narrow Boston streets, the wind shrieking past my ears, my red hair streaking over my skull demi-mask.

The marquee behind me proclaims Prospero's dominion across the night sky.

I do not bother proclaiming mine.

Lygia

⟫⟫⟫ Dahlia Adler ⟪⟪⟪

inspired by "Ligeia"

The only thing I remember about the day we met, Lygia, is that you smelled like oranges. I would learn later that you tasted like them, too, but in that first moment it was just a scent and I was lost.

I should remember more, I know. It was the day I met my light, my love, my life. But to be honest, I do not clearly remember a time before your wild tangle of dark hair, your eyes of wildfire smoke.

Memories of you now, though . . . those come unbidden nightly, daily, hourly. They come whether I call them or not, but they are never entirely unwelcome, nor are they ever entirely gone.

My favorite memory is of you on my fifteenth birthday, fire-light reflected in the silvered coal of your eyes as you watched me blow out the candles on the beautiful cake you'd made me from scratch. Strawberry buttercream. You knew it was my favorite, knew I'd love the touch of the fresh strawberry layer and the way it tinted pink just the tiniest bit of the sweet crumb.

Another favorite—when we got caught in the rain in your backyard, the automatic lock proving its strength when I attempted to karate chop the door down. You looked so beautiful with wet drops in your thick, dark curls and feathery eyelashes, streaking down your long neck, that secretly, I didn't try all that hard.

The one I hold closest, though, is prom, you stunning in a dress the color of rubies with a high front hem, showing off your gorgeous legs, gorgeous shoulders, gorgeous everything. Your head tilted to mine as our parents took pictures with happy sighs and pretended not to notice as we sneaked kisses. The limo ride where we giggled together as we sipped bubbly champagne until we both admitted we hated it, though it didn't stop us from taking every taste of it we could from each other's lips. Dancing under foil stars amid the scent of Calla lilies. A teary kiss when we were announced prom queen and queen, a dream I hadn't even known you'd had. And afterward . . . well, a lady wouldn't talk about afterward. She would just think of it for eternity, a small smile playing on her lips each time she remembered silken skin and happy sighs and murmured promises.

That's the memory I'll never get.

Cancer is a greedy bitch, and it devoured you with a racing fire we never saw coming. The disease wasn't content to make its home in your soft, golden skin; it needed to worm into your liver and gnaw at your lungs, too. It was too late by the time we realized your constant nausea, cold symptoms, and propensity for smelling *everything* were actually symptoms of a disease that would steal prom, steal Sunday waffle breakfasts, steal the melody of your voice when you read me poetry, steal the twinkle in your dark eyes at my attempts to impress your mother with my mangled Portuguese, steal the richness of your soft, citrus-scented hair, steal graduation and whatever came next and everything after, steal my heart and my soul and your future and my future and our future.

Now school is a stage, one where I play the role of Girl Moving on with Her Life every day to no applause. No one shouts "Brava!" for driving myself to the building without your feet up on the dash. No one throws roses at my feet when I pass your locker without breaking down. And no one suggests I break a leg the day I pass that same locker and see a girl with a curtain of blond curls putting books inside, as if that locker door had never held photo-booth strips of two girls in love or a mirror in which you used to check your cherry-red lipstick before every period.

But breaking something is exactly what I feel like doing. I could snap that locker door in two with the sheer will of my grieving mind. Yet I remain still, staring at the back of the new girl's golden head, fixed in my hate, until I feel an arm wrap around my shoulder—and then Joanna Glanvill is there, coffee breath assaulting my nostrils. "You know you don't have to leap on every lez in this school, right?"

I answer her on autopilot. "Actually, it's my civic rainbow duty. They revoke your queer card if you don't."

Joanna's lips twist into a grimace when she'd rather die than smile. At this point, I could easily trace it with my fingertip in the dark. And while I couldn't give a fraction of a damn about the class bully, her words have somehow gotten into my head and sparked like fireflies.

Is Joanna just being her typical trash-fire self? Or does she know something about this girl I have not somehow gleaned from the back of her head? As if Joanna Glanvill has some sort of Gaydar wizardry.

Then the girl turns. No wizardry required to decipher her Hayley Kiyoko T-shirt. She is blond where you were dark and sunshine where you were lunar beauty and her big blue eyes look like they've never held a single secret.

She is nothing like you and maybe that, or maybe the joint I smoked in my car, is why it feels safe to say, "Hi, new girl." My lips lift in one corner and I hate myself for it.

"Roberta," she says.

"I like your shirt."

Her smile is full and open, nothing but ChapStick on her lips.

It isn't your smile, not at all, and maybe that's why I smile back with my heart in one piece.

My heart is still with you, Lygia, but God, I am lonely. When Roberta asks to sit next to me at lunch, I say yes. When she asks me to show her around town, I say yes. When she kisses me one night in her chintzy bedroom, I say yes, yes, yes, without any words at all. My heart is yours, Lygia, but my body has its own mind.

Still, you are there, you are present, I promise you. When I tousle her hair and wish it were dark, and examine my skin for bright cherry lip prints, you are there. When rain patters on her lone picture window, casting shadows on the tapestried walls, I am right back in your yard. When Roberta puts her favorite music on in the background, Halsey is singing to you, to us, to that night we accidentally left "Ghost" on repeat for hours but were too busy kissing to care. When she shows me pictures of her old life, neon glimpses of concerts and Pride parades and suburban house parties, all I see are our memories, the ones we had and the ones we won't.

That night, she smells like vanilla and vanilla is fine, but it isn't oranges. No perfume, no soap, nothing from the rows of body sprays and fancy soaps in the drugstore can re-create your scent. Did you know that? Did you know how uniquely you it was? Did you know that I could gift Roberta every orange-scented item I could find, and still it would never be yours, never be you?

"What is this?" she asks as I give her the latest, a blend of orange and lily that I think might be the closest match yet. I call it a present for one month together. "More oranges?"

I don't answer, just help her dab the oil on her neck and breathe in. It's still not you, but it's closer, and I only realize I'm burying my face in her skin when she makes a sound of pleasure that curls my toes. "You like this one, I take it?" she asks, a teasing lilt to her voice.

"Mm-hmm."

"Now that you've finally found the one, whatever will you do about buying me gifts?"

"Lipstick." There is not even a moment's hesitation. I miss your cherry lips, Lygia, and I wish now I'd had the foresight to tattoo your last lip print right below my collarbone. "I think you'd look just perfect in red lipstick."

She pulls away slightly. "I was joking about the gifts. You don't need to buy me anything. You didn't need to buy me this. Although you like it so much, I admit I'm glad you did."

"And I will love the lipstick, too," I promise, and I kiss her only so there will be no more talk at all.

I am right, of course. I love the lipstick, especially when paired with the orange-lily oil. I'm so elated the first time she wears them together that I suggest we extend our day and go tanning, because what's cherry-red lipstick without your glow behind it?

That day we talk more, Lygia, and forgive me, for I tell her of our prom memory that isn't a real memory at all. She wants to know it all, and it feels like so long since anyone has pried me open like an oyster and searched for the pearls you left behind. Roberta is quiet, so quiet, as we look at picture after picture that captures only a fraction of you, and I wonder if she's falling in love with you, too, with the way you threw your head back when you laughed and the designs you painstakingly applied to your nails and the final poem you left scrawled on a scrap of paper stained with your favorite cherry tea.

I tell her the bad along with the good. I tell her how you hated that no one could pronounce your name, how even I bungled it that first time. "You can change it to Lydia, if you want, when you turn eighteen," I said once, and I knew immediately it was the wrong thing to say, hated that I ever said it, hated that I couldn't take it back. Your pride in your Portuguese heritage is something for which I have no equivalent and I would make that slip up to you a thousand times if I could.

Roberta forgives me immediately, doesn't understand your ire at all, and at first I am mad for you—but then I'm relieved, I admit, to be absolved of this sin I have always regretted. And in that moment my heart catches up with my body and I will spare you the knowledge of how we spend that night, Lygia, but there is no shortage of lip prints on my body afterward.

In the morning light, her lips are nude and your scent is gone and I slip out into the dawn because the glow alone is not enough.

If she is disturbed by my disappearance, she doesn't say so when I see her at school on Monday morning; she just chatters about what fun we'd had and what we might do next. I'm barely listening, I admit, allowing myself to be swept back into your lipstick, your scent. But when she mentions prom, suddenly every nerve ending in my body becomes keenly aware of her presence. "I don't know if I want to go to that."

She crumbles, just a little bit, though she must have known that after the prom I'd already dreamed for you and me, Lygia, no pale imitation would suffice. "Okay," she says, in a voice that means it isn't okay. Only then do I notice the way her clothing hangs differently in just the few weeks we've known each other, differently, even, than it did a few nights earlier. Her face has lost its fullness. Her wrist bones poke out of her skin. You would think *she* was the one who had lost someone. But there is no grief in her life. There is no hole in her heart.

She knows nothing at all of what real love and real loss can be.

But it doesn't repulse me. Because her impossibly slender ankles remind me now of yours, and the sharpness of your cheekbones now juts up against her skin. So I tell her she looks beautiful, because she reminds me that you were, too, even as you disappeared right in front of my eyes.

"Do you really want to go?" I ask, because thoughts of you have made me soft.

"I know it's silly, but I do. I want the bad music and bad decorations and to dance with the beautiful date I never thought I'd get to have. I already found the perfect dress," she says, and her face glows, and for a moment, I can dream. "I promise, you'll love it. And I know the perfect scent and lipstick to wear with it."

It is possible, my love, that Roberta has come to know me in her own way these past weeks, because she has indeed found the perfect words to say to convince me. "I'm not sure you'll be very impressed by my dancing," I warn her, because I know you never were, even if it made you laugh.

Again, that glow, that twinge in my heart. "Does that mean you'll go? We're going to prom?"

I can taste the salt on your skin as surely as if we were already dancing under that spotlight, tiaras glittering in our hair, when I say, "We can go."

The glow burns bright, and it smells like oranges.

⌇⌇

As prom nears, Roberta somehow drifts further away. She claims the flu day after day until a week has passed. I spend it missing you, as I always do, smoking enough to relax and imagine that you are lying by my side, your dark curls cascading over my arm and your lips brushing my ear.

I'm gazing at your locker when Joanna passes by and asks, "Where's your new girlfriend?" her voice and her question both making my skin crawl.

My palm tingles with the urge to leave its print on her freckled cheek, but I'm tired and high and well aware she isn't worth it. "Did your mom not show up at work today?"

She doesn't particularly care for that response but I don't particularly care for her, although Roberta urges us to play nice for reasons I do not understand. She's one of those people for whom kindness is the greatest virtue.

You know how boring I find those people.

My week is no less interesting for her absence, and no more interesting for it, either. Without you, what difference is there from one day to the next, really?

In truth, I don't care if she returns or not, and part of me hopes she won't and I'll be free of this prom farce for good. It's silly to think I should do this without you, my Lygia, and sillier still to think that I could.

But when the day comes, she calls to assure me she's in good health and as excited to go as she ever was, and she teases the lipstick and scent again and the assurance of more. Perhaps it feels disrespectful to you, Lygia, that I am going, and perhaps it is, but I can't say no, although I would give anything to affix this ridiculous corsage to your dress instead.

The limousine may as well be a hearse for all my heart feels on the interminable drive to Roberta's parents' Victorian house. You well know I have never lacked confidence in my looks, but tonight I couldn't care less for the cut of my tux or the perfectly shorn side of my skull; none of it means anything without you biting your lip in approval.

I'm grateful when the limo hits inexplicable traffic on its way to her house, and I pop a pill, wash it down with vodka, and close my eyes. Conjuring up the image of you coming toward me in the dress I've envisioned for you, your curls pinned up and your eyes aflame, is effortless as always. This should be our night, Lygia.

This should be ours.

You should be mine.

You should be here.

But it's not your house I pull up to, and it's not your bell I ring. It's not your mother who greets me with a glare. At first I think it must be the tux, although judging by the rainbow flag that flies in their bay window, this is unlikely. Perhaps my breath mint hasn't masked the vodka as intended or the eye drops have not done their work.

But her eyes are their own shade of red, one that suggests tears and distress, one I recognize so clearly from your own mother's that final night. A wild part of me wonders for a moment if there was more to this flu of Roberta's, if she has been consumed as you were, as my heart was, as we will all someday be. Perhaps it's a blessing to be taken sooner rather than later if this constant fear is all that life is.

I don't know how to comfort her now, as I did not know how to comfort your mother then. But then she turns to the staircase and calls "Roberta!" and slowly I find my heartbeat return to its normal rhythm, and my feet mechanically move toward the stairs. The pill has kicked in and I feel off balance on my wing-tipped feet, stumbling as I look at the stairs, my tongue stuck to my palate as her mother calls her name again, and again once more.

It is on the third call that she appears at the top of the stairs, a bloody waterfall of red silk pouring down lithe limbs. Behind me, her mother moans, but I cannot spare a glance in her direction; my eyes are tracing up a high-hemmed skirt and ruby bodice to raven curls, pinned up into messy curtains for silvered coal windows, shaded by the thickest and darkest of lashes. The scents of citrus and lilies are so thick in the air I can barely breathe, and the glow that radiates from her golden skin blinds my eyes to tears.

With every step down that winding staircase the beat of my heart pounds louder in my ears. The world grows hazy with the taste of salt and champagne, the twinkle of foil stars in the air, and when those red lips curve into a smile my heart and lungs give up completely but to shout, "Lygia! LYGIA!"

They tell me I was still screaming your name when they brought me here, as if there is something strange about that. But how can I not scream your name when you have finally returned to hear it?

The Fall of the Bank of Usher

⤖ Fran Wilde ⤕

inspired by "The Fall of the House of Usher"

A cold rain beat against the shuttered windows of the Offshore Bank of Usher the night my brother and I tried hacking our way out.

Rik and I hit the walls with everything we had: decrypts, burners, a handful of worms, and a genuine military-grade safe-cracker. None of it worked. Not at first.

The bank's artificial intelligence and its human host, Dr. Tarn, laughed at us as attempt after attempt failed. A low-pitched rumble echoed from deep within the walls and the man's wiry human frame by the fireplace.

"Your reputations far exceed your abilities, it seems. Turns out you're just script kiddies after all," Tarn said.

"Asshole." I curled my fingers into fists and then spread

them again before diving back into the lock codes that controlled the bank's doors and shutters.

"Focus, Mad," my brother whispered as Tarn's countermeasures came at us across the network. Rik had chewed off most of his silver lipstick.

He held the doctor off with signal reroutes while I kept pounding at the locks. But the passcodes changed faster than I could type, or think.

My brother's hands shook. My own fingers kept freezing up. The marble fireplace held a weak gas flame, too small to crackle the air, much less warm it.

Worse, I was growing angrier.

At Dr. Tarn, for calling us script kiddies. At my brother, for wanting to pull off this one last job for the glory of it. At the time we'd lost trying to hack our way to money, when we should have been running away. At the despair I felt because we might lose more than just time.

A bank tracer caught up to one of my programs and devoured it, shorting out my tablet. The smell of burnt computer chips filled the air.

Angry hacking meant I was making mistakes. Destroying my devices.

"No matter who we think worthy of challenging us, we always win," the doctor said. "We always maintain our hack-proof status. I do feel bad that you are so young. Instead of bright futures, you'll disappear. Just like your toys." His prominent forehead glistened with sweat, and his eyes gleamed feverishly.

Rik's handheld went black, bricked into a useless piece of glass and plastic.

He groaned when I pulled my last device—my oldest tablet—from my pocket. It hadn't been connected to a network since we'd left the Syndicate. Since we'd broken out, more accurately. "Mad, don't."

The tablet held our real identities. Our best hope of reuniting with our families, if they remained; and with each other, if we were ever separated. It also held a single wideband electromagnetic pulse program. The final thing we'd stolen from our employers. I didn't look at Rik when I hit the switch. I glared at the doctor instead.

The hookup took a heartbeat, then a bank tracer bit down hard on the pulse and took it right into the AI's laughing mouth.

The foundation shook. Gaps appeared in the old stone masonry. The floorboards cracked. Outside, a rock-colored sky spat rain.

Then the walls closed up, sealing us in. A hole opened at Rik's feet.

"Mad!" He scrambled for balance as his dead tablet clattered into the gap.

I dove for him and grabbed his sweater. The black knit fabric tore from my fingers. We both let out a single scream as Rik dangled above the bank's cavernous vault.

"You stay," I said through gritted teeth, fighting against the pull of the vault. "I can't do this alone."

The crypto-challenge summons had arrived in the usual way, hitting our secure private network as a series of nonsense letters from an old relative, asking for a visit from Madrik—one of our personas.

It took us longer to decrypt than some, but we shook the data loose. We were the best hackers the Syndicate had raised in a long time, after all.

And then we'd become the first in a long time to run.

The challenge to hack the Offshore Bank of Usher was the first we'd received since we'd been on the outside.

57.5359° N, 6.2263° W; all you can take
(approx. EU 4 bn), 1 m on signature.

"Latitude, longitude, and payoff—four billion, plus a million right now for signing on. But no IP address?" I glared at the message and my screen glared back. "They want us to come to them? Not on your life, Rik."

"Mad, for that kind of money and cred? It's worth it." Rik and I often used our own handsigns in case there was a listener, but his face told the story: He missed the glory of a big job, and this felt huge. "Besides, this is totally an inside job—the bank's inviting us to test its defenses. We're practically guests. It's perfect for us."

I was tiring of doing risky jobs for street cred, even if invited. Since we'd left the Syndicate, I'd been trying to figure out how to tell Rik. What if he didn't want to slow down? Would I wake up one day to find he'd gone out on his own? What would I do then? That was the fear that kept me from speaking.

But right now, what worried me more was the risk of showing up in person at this job, rather than working from a safe, distant location.

"We don't need the money or the cred as much as we need a safer place to hide. That's all." I began stuffing our clothes and hardware into our one gray duffel bag. We shared an all-black wardrobe, from dusters and leggings to stacked Venetian heels. It was simpler that way.

If going was risky, staying was worse. A challenge meant we weren't safe anymore: Someone knew how to find us. No matter how careful we'd been about the decryption, it was time to move on.

"A safe place is easier to get with four billion euros," Rik said, his tone a little chiding, like he was older than me. As if that mattered. To him, it did. By six minutes. After we'd taken down a day-trading market, he'd had our digital birth certificates etched in the memory of our old Syndicate tablet to prove it.

"And if this is a trap?" The Syndicate was looking for us. And when they caught us, they'd try to split us up again. Or kill us both.

"What if it is? We got out before. We can do it again. Let's do this: We take the million for signing on now. We see how it feels. If we don't like it, we can fail out, or get them to kick us out. Mad, please."

"Your ego is going to end us both, Rik." I jammed the last of our sweaters, our smaller 3D-printed tools and cameras, and our makeup case into the bag. He was winning me over, and he knew it.

"If your overworked sense of dread doesn't get us first, Mad," Rik answered, then whistled low. "Oh, I've heard about this bank."

He turned his tablet so I could see crypto-challenge chat room logs from exactly a year before, and the year before that. A hacker named SoundofWater had said they'd accepted a challenge to break a bank's security—a penetration operation exploit—but never returned to the chat to gloat about it. Another hacker named DarkCold, too, the year before. A couple of others. No one had reported back after. Everyone figured they were too embarrassed.

Rik laughed. "We'll be legends once we crack it."

Pride being a major component of a hacker's toolbox, I finally grinned. If you didn't believe in your own skills, no one would. Yeah. He'd pulled me in again.

We left Hôtel Henri IV ten minutes later, ditching our Canadian tourists' identities and credit cards in the garbage outside.

For a moment, we were just ourselves. Brother and sister. Twins. More than that. We were Madrik. Best pair of hands in the biz.

He held the tablet out to me and I was the one who hit "Accept."

Unlocked, the challenge produced a ticket to the Isle of Skye via Charles de Gaulle and Inverness, and notice that a car would pick Madrik up, courtesy of the bank. I hit the airlines on another tablet and turned that one ticket into two.

Meantime, Rik read through a pile of digitally signed noncompete, nondisclosure forms.

"Legal? Seriously?" I almost laughed.

Rik shook his head, his earrings catching the streetlights. I tapped my tablet, watching as the million-euro payout landed in the first of our accounts. With a few commands, I rerouted the money several times, dividing it into smaller packets as Rik read the fine print.

"They want us to hit them with everything we've got. Security test. Penetration operation exploit, like the chat room said. They're recertifying the hard way."

I scanned the road outside the hotel's pull-around for the car we'd called. "It's late."

"It will be here." My brother squeezed my hand through the thick, fingerless gloves he always wore. "You're cold, Mad." We were always so cold when we were running. Whether hiding from orphanage bullies or bolting from the Syndicate's warehouse, it didn't matter.

"The body reroutes blood flow from extremities to brain— so a person can think better for longer when they're in danger." I squeezed back. His hands were cold, too.

"Grim. And makes it hard to code." Before I could grumble at him, he got out in front of my next worry with the practice of someone who knew me well. "We'll make the flight."

"Yeah, we will. And we'll beat the challenge."

He smiled broadly, showing the gap in his teeth and the dimple that no one ever saw but me. Grateful. We took care of each other. We always had.

The cab's brakes squealed as it pulled up beside us. Rain splatted on my shoulders as I shoved our bag in after Rik, sliding the canvas across the age-shined faux-leather seats.

The car bumped over slick cobblestones on the way to Charles de Gaulle and our flight to Scotland. Rik applied his most metal lipstick in the cab, his hands steady.

"They might *not* want us for the gig once they see us, anyway," Rik said, pressing his lips together and letting them unseal with a pop. "It's an easy out if you want to take it when we get there. Banks are weird that way. Good they paid the upfront fee."

"Now you're worried." I rolled my eyes hard enough that I could see the kohl caking my lashes. Maybe he'd wanted the gig so badly, he hadn't stopped to think about the details of both of us appearing at the bank's door. I signed, "We've agreed."

"Madrik did, not Mad and Rik."

"Well, now MadRik is going." We could do this. Madrik had been stocking ID caches for the Syndicate for four years, since we were thirteen. Madrik had been the best at cracking medical and military databases for three years. Who we were was entirely based on what we did. Those who knew us sometimes made the mistake of writing me off as the weak one, or as Rik's assistant. Usually that only happened once.

Both of us were slim, short hair slicked back in my case, spiked in Rik's, our clothes all flapping dark coats and night-colored jeans. We looked alike. We ran code as one—switching off attack and defense until no one knew what had just hit them.

"Just running our options. I want to try for the four billion. Either they'll let us stay and play or tell us to go. Or we'll get there and decide it's not our kind of gig. And we'll keep their signing fee either way," Rik said as Paris receded.

"If it's not a trap."

"We can bust out of any trap, Mad. Together."

If our family had survived the attack that destroyed our small, rebellious village just inside the rusting remains of the Iron Curtain, maybe things would have been different. Maybe Rik and I wouldn't have grown so close. But after that fiery night, first in the hospital and then the orphanage, when one of us screamed themselves awake, the other would promise to stay up and watch for danger. The nurses joked that we slept with two eyes open. Later, when we got in fights with kids twice our size over food, warm clothes, or the few wallets and tablets we could—sometimes with the orphanage staff's help—steal, we kept more for ourselves when we were together. It's true what they say in the chat room about Madrik: thrown out of one orphanage for stealing and tossed from another when it closed for dangerous practices. But we learned a valuable lesson along the way: We were stronger as one.

By the time a Syndicate hacker found us at our third orphanage, near Greece, we were already skilled at stockpiling advantages and watching people for weaknesses. And we didn't allow anyone to separate us.

The hacker tested us for aptitude, found we could use both credit card dataware and lockpicks, and then took us into the EU to train us up and help her datamine that same day. The orphanage hadn't asked many questions.

We'd built our skills, kept our profiles low, schooled ourselves online, and made plans to run as soon as we could, which took years.

Meantime, our new "mom" did us one favor each. She encrypted our birth records on a single file and then scorched any public data she could find. "In case you ever need to be yourselves. Otherwise you can be anyone you want."

When the Syndicate tried to send Rik to Ukraine and me to the United States, we'd jumped. We wanted to be a team. We worked best that way. So: Middle-of-the-night exploit right out the back door. We'd been running ever since.

Rik was right. To stay free, together, we needed money. Not other people's money—that we could get, at least in small, untraceable amounts. For new lives, we needed a stash of cash.

That was why we took the job.

That was what I told myself, later.

⁓

At the airport, we slid through security on Belgian passports, then hit the closest restroom. I pulled on nitrile gloves and applied bright overtone colors to Rik's spikes—silver—and my short bob—chartreuse. We waited for ten minutes and then I buried the gloves and the dye, wrapped around the various IDs we'd used in France, in the waste bin. Then I rinsed out my hair.

We didn't look like ourselves anymore. Or much like each other. For the moment, that was fine by me.

On the plane, Rik pulled down everything he could find about the bank. More chat-room gossip, international filings. "Usher was family-held until two generations ago when they all died out. They left behind a board of directors and a vault. Lots of shell companies, hard to tell who's in there. But the bank's loaded. Supports other banks all over the world." He peered closer, pulling at the bank's own online presence. "They have an AI—at least one. But it looks easy to break in. Their incoming security is ridiculous. Like anyone might be able to get in from on-site. I mean, one of DarkCold's last messages was, 'I'm in.' So it's doable."

"So how do they keep getting recertified?"

"Because it looks like no one ever gets out. No one's ever logged a finished exploit from Usher. Not DarkCold, not anyone. With a record like that, people feel their funds are secure."

I looked over his shoulder. The bank's major assets were solid-state, not digital. "Oooh." Once that stuff's gone, it's gone. Untraceable.

"It's so old school. They trade on trust. Deliver withdrawals by helicopter, it says."

"And no one's ever successfully hit them." I whistled low while picking at my nail polish. Duochrome flecks sparkled yellow on the plane's dark seats.

"We'd be the first." Rik looked out the window, over the anonymous ocean, glittering below.

When we landed in Skye, our tablets faded to a green-gray the color of lichen, then lit up with the Bank of Usher logo.

"You said their security was awful," I growled at Rik, watching every bounce point on our networks go dark as we were sucked into the bank's own system. Even our VPN was inaccessible.

Rik muttered as his hands flew over his tablet, rebooting drives right there in the tiny arrivals lounge, beyond customs. "Owned."

In an instant, nothing was ours anymore, except the old drive with our birth certificates on it. We had that, three passports each remaining, two pairs of black jeans, a pile of black T-shirts and leggings, our dusters, and some lipstick.

At least as far as I knew, those weren't crackable.

Outside the welcome center, the Isle of Skye was draped in thick rainclouds, but no rain fell. The heavy atmosphere pressed against us as a dark car rolled up to the now empty arrivals center. Then a driver emerged from the car, liveried in dark gray, holding a manila folder clearly labeled: USHER.

When Rik and I approached, the driver looked startled. I lifted a tablet to show him the takeover screen. He frowned.

"I wasn't told you'd be bringing someone," he said to Rik. I stifled a growl, but the driver let us climb into the car's deep quiet.

A small data node wrapped his ear. It glowed. I nudged my brother so he'd know not to talk around the driver. If my tablet hadn't been flatlined, I could have hacked the driver's port all to pieces.

"Shh, Mad. We're through the first gate. They know we're both coming and they haven't turned us away," Rik signed as the car sped over Skye Bridge and through the small towns on the other side, turning and winding us up into the highlands. The neat houses passed in a blur.

"Maybe when we're finished, we could find a quiet town like this, somewhere warmer," I signed back. "No Wi-Fi. No temptation to jump at a challenge. Maybe I'll take my GED, go to college. Get a job. We both can."

Rik stared at me in horror. Then he spoke for the first time since we'd driven away from the airport, his surprise completely filling the car. "A small town like this? You're not serious. We do this, we're legends. Our future is something to think about later, after."

I stared out the window at the disappearing towns and the rising hills for the rest of the drive.

The light faded as we came to the ancient house surrounded by a steel-gray lake that managed to reflect nothing of its surroundings.

A deep sense of foreboding stuck in my throat, and I shivered but kept quiet.

The house was gray, too, old stone covered with some kind of lichen or moss that looked decidedly unhealthy. The building's windows were pale, staring eyes that captured nothing of sky or water.

The driver barely slowed as the car rattled over a wooden gangway.

"Who needs security when you have a moat?" my brother mused.

I managed a smile at his gallows humor. I knew it for a peace offering, and I accepted it. Rik didn't want to fight or worry. He wanted to play. We were in the game now. If this was a trap and the Syndicate awaited us on the other end, we'd know it soon. But they would have gone to a lot of trouble if that was the case.

If the challenge was for real, and the bank's offer legitimate, like Rik believed, then Usher had still rooted all our gear. We were at a disadvantage already.

But if anyone could complete a challenge on terms like those, it was us. And if we made the exploit—if Madrik did—it would be epic.

The Bank of Usher's stone walls loomed over us; fungi and lichen burrowing deep into the masonry looked like all that held the structure up. We passed beneath a cold archway, the smell of vegetation creeping into the car, and stopped before a pair of cavernous doors.

Rik reapplied his lipstick carefully for our arrival: a matte silver that sheened dragon-yellow when he pressed his lips together. It matched his new hair color perfectly.

I went for dark green. I liked change.

"This doesn't look like a bank," Rik said as he climbed the front steps. I shouldered our bag and followed. "It looks like a mansion."

"Still no signal." The bank's logo glowed on my useless tablet. The stone walls rose over us. For a moment, the fungus and rime on the mansion's exterior seemed to crawl and writhe. I rubbed my eyes and it stopped. Too much air travel sometimes had that effect.

One of the big wooden doors swung wide, and a woman in gray livery blocked our way. "Welcome to The Bank of Usher." Her eyes were pale gray, and her skin was sallow. She looked like the house, held up by her uniform. A soft blue glow at her collarbone, beneath her collar, told me she was wired to the bank, too.

"We're here for the challenge," I began.

The woman blinked at me, paused as if she was waiting for instructions and, after two heartbeats, waved us forward. "All right. The drawing room."

She tried to take my bag, pulling much harder at the strap than I thought she'd be able to, but I held tight until she let go. Then she led us through a dark hallway hung with old portraits and lit by flickering sconces. "In there." My ears rang when she slammed the heavy drawing-room door behind us, but we waited, looking around the richly appointed space. Pale green watered silk covered two walls, while the fireplace and windows were backed by more of the stone that made up most of the house. The mullioned windows peered out over the lake, but they were set high in the walls and allowed only a view of the heavy, almost sulfurous clouds.

I walked close to the fireplace and checked my tablet again, out of habit. To my surprise, the connection was strong and the bank's logo had disappeared. "We've got signal."

A quick scan told me nothing had changed on my tablet

that I could see. Still, I felt a chill run across my shoulders and down my arms to my fingertips. The room—the whole house, really—sounded a steady pulse against my ears: probably my heart trying to beat a way out. I shook my hands nervously.

"We couldn't have you telegraphing the bank's whereabouts." A sibilant voice sounded far too close to my ear and I jumped. I realized the man speaking—thin and pale, with a receding hairline—had been standing near the fireplace since we arrived. He'd been studying the hearth, and us, without our noticing. Rik blushed and brushed at his jacket before reaching for his own tablet.

The man continued to speak, his voice low and monotone. "You are welcome to use your devices now, except for sending messages. Not until you succeed at your task. I am Dr. Tarn." He turned. His eyes glittered with a hint of something more than human behind them.

"You're hosting an AI," Rik whispered, a half beat ahead of me. The construct was called a *centaur* in certain parts of our business. I'd always found the concept more invasive, like mold.

"The bank found a human-AI combination made for excellent security, yes. I helped design it. What a human understands as risk is different from what a computer understands. My eyes contain the uplink. I'm as human as you in most other respects." Tarn's monotone didn't help his presentation. In fact, it made his declaration seem even less human. I snuck a glance at my brother, but he wouldn't meet my eyes.

The doctor took his hand from the mantel. "I've given instructions that meals be laid here for you on a regular schedule, beginning with tea. You'll have twenty-four hours to try to break the bank."

"And after that?" Rik asked.

"After that, you will have failed. The terms of your agreement are quite clear. If you fail, which you will, you'll be turned over to the authorities or offered an opportunity to work here. If you escape, with whatever euros you can grab, up to the contracted limit, you will have won the challenge."

Something still didn't feel right. "You think we can be fooled into complacency by your 'tea'? We aren't children."

"You are, which is somewhat disconcerting," the doctor said. "But no, I haven't given you poisoned tea. I cannot do such a thing. This is a technical recertification challenge, not a murder-mystery weekend." He chuckled to himself. "Each of you fits the parameters required by the bank's security recertification: top-level expertise in your field, numerous exploits. That there are two participants this year will provide us and the staff some additional amusement and challenges."

At a knock on the drawing-room door, the doctor waved his hand in the air. A bolt slid back and the door opened. The woman who had greeted us at the door entered, pushing a cart piled high with cakes, teacups, and a teapot in a graying rose cozy.

The dishes on the cart called to Rik and me as if we hadn't eaten the entire day. Safe to say—aside from coffee and a few snack bars—we hadn't. The tray held sweet, fondant-covered jam cakes in perfect squares, tiny cream-cheese-and-cucumber sandwiches cut in triangles, and boiled eggs wrapped in sausage, then deep fried.

Our host didn't move from his place by the fire as we inhaled the food's rich scents. "I assure you once again that it's safe. Poisoning you would cancel the recertification."

This made me feel less comfortable, rather than more.

"It's cool, we're fairly noncontagious at this point, too," Rik joked, then picked up a cake. We'd both had bad flu the week before.

Now the look on the doctor's face shifted to deep concern. "You are unwell?" He carefully stuck his hands in his pockets. Rik's eyebrows rose and fell as he took note.

People-hacking was one of Rik's skills. From the way his fingers twitched, he was delighted to find he had an advantage: He knew one of the doctor's weaknesses.

As for me, I'd purchased my advantages from mod shops in each city we'd stayed in, looking for new tech. I'd printed a few cameras and lockpicks in Paris 3D vats and kept my best vault-cracking programs up to date. But the best thing I had going for me was what I'd always had: caution and a determination not to fail. Rik and I would have been lost long ago without it.

So I skipped the small talk.

"We are well enough. Your bank holds about ten billion in gold reserves, another twenty in European funds for various investors," I said. "We'd like to take four billion of that off your hands."

Tarn shrugged, still looking uncomfortable. The AI gleamed from within the doctor's eyes. "And we'll do everything we can to stop you. Questions?"

Rik glanced from me to the doctor. "When do we start?"

I held up a hand. "What happened to the previous challengers?"

"Some of them work here." The doctor smiled thinly.

The word "some" gave me pause. *Some* work here. *Others* had probably been turned over to the authorities. What would

Rik and I choose, if we had to? In jail, we'd be separated, most likely. The cold stone walls of Usher didn't look any more hospitable, but at least we'd be together.

"No one's won." Rik stood up, placing his teacup back on the tray with a soft clatter. "We'd be the first."

"And the last." The doctor crossed the room to the door. "Anyone cracks my system, the investors flee, the bank collapses. I am highly motivated not to fail."

Rik looked around the richly appointed room. "You'd lose your cush job. I get it."

"We'd lose everything. The AI and I work together to keep the house going, protect it from outside elements, and thus the Bank of Usher, too. We are stronger that way. Able to defeat any threat."

"What if we don't accept?" Another wave of this-is-the-dumbest-gambit-we've-tried washed over me.

"You've already accepted by coming through the front door. Consider that moment your job interview, and refusal failure. If you fail, you join the others and work for us."

"I don't work for anyone," Rik countered. "I'd die first."

I tried to hide my surprise. A crack had opened between us in the car, yes. But now it was one that spanned the distance between "we" and "I." We were a team. We needed to look like one. But Rik—who'd just said "I" a lot more than I was comfortable with—took a step closer to the doctor.

The doctor backed across the threshold. "As I said, I am unable to kill you or anyone. If someone dies, it is not by my hand. I *am* capable of turning you over to your former employers, who probably would enjoy that, though." He paused to let us absorb that, looking at each of us in turn. Then added, "You have twenty-three-and-a-half hours now. Anything you require from the house in that time will be supplied to you. Nothing in your tablets has been tampered with."

He said that in the same tone with which he'd said "The cakes are safe, I assure you." As if to prove it to us, he lifted a cake and took a bite. Fondant crumbled across his lapel, turning a soft gray in the light.

After the doctor left, I stared at my brother over the untouched tea. The fireplace crackled weakly.

I reached for the one tablet I was sure was clean, but put it back in the bag. *Only for emergencies.*

Rik fiddled with an earring. "It's not so bad. We have loads of time. Let's not waste it." He peered from the room out into the hallway where the doctor had disappeared. The sun, setting now, tinted the tiled floor, the paneled walls, and the vases and family heirlooms that lined the walls a sickly yellow. He patted my hand. "I'm going to look around. If they're as deep in physical assets as it seems, there will be a vault. Just need to crack that and their security and the job's done. Back soon."

He set off down the hallway, following the doctor's path. I watched him go, my surprise keeping me speechless. When *we* cracked data online, *we* stuck together, spelling each other. Now Rik was going off on his own, and *he* hadn't conferred with *me* at all before he'd decided on a course of action.

And *I* didn't like it.

"Brothers," I growled under my breath to cover my distress. The house was undoubtedly always listening.

We'd been alone most of our lives, but this was the first time I'd felt truly separated from the only family I'd ever known. I flicked more polish off my nails. My rings glittered in the gaslight, reminding me of the things *I'd* done, who *I* was.

A sudden gust from outside pressed against the windows, and I imagined I could smell the mold from outside trying to creep through the cracks. Rising to look through the glass at the house's stonework, I saw once again how the vegetation seemed to hold the ancient masonry together. In the wind, the fungi rippled slightly.

The shutters rattled then. Not from the wind. A grinding from within the walls, an increasing shadow. I realized the shutters were closing, the bank sealing us in.

By the time the heavy boards finally locked shut over the mullioned glass, cutting off the fading daylight and the bank's creepy outer walls, I was fully spooked. And my brother hadn't returned.

The gaslight flickered in the fireplace, casting more shadows. I found the switch to turn it off.

"Loads of time." I pulled the sack of small tools from the duffel and set it on the chair beside me. I dug around inside until I found a matte black square of plastic, about the size of a credit card.

When I tapped it, the card shook until tiny, thin bat wings unfolded from the flat surface and began to whirl. What was left of the card—a small camera eye, a transmitter, and two tiny pincers—hung beneath the wings. Thin as webs, the black carbon-fiber wings lifted the tiny drone body up above my palm.

I guided it to the fireplace and spoke instructions: "Up. Out."

Sounding like a real bat working its way up the chimney, the drone obeyed. What it saw appeared on my handheld:

more stone, more fungus and mold, thickening the higher the drone went. Finally, it perched on the chimney's ledge, looking out over the roofline of the Bank of Usher, across the lake, to the hills. Freedom.

But not for us. Not yet.

The chimney was too narrow, the roof too high for an escape.

"Rik," I whispered. "We need to coordinate plans." I shivered.

No answer.

This was bad. He'd been gone a while already, and we always checked in to make sure we didn't hack across each other.

On my tablet, I could see the thick vegetation clearly now. Layers of it, reaching deep inside the roof's slate tiles. I took over the drone's commands with a few finger-taps and used its pincers to grab a sample of the stuff, then dropped that back down the chimney.

Before I could command the drone to follow, its camera tilted up to the clouds, catching the glare of pale sunset, then the glowering sky. I pushed another command through from my tablet, but the drone didn't respond. Its camera shook. Then gray tendrils of mold spread across its lens, covering the visual on my tablet, too. Too soon, the drone's signal flickered. The mold was devouring it.

I could hear the bit of mold I'd pried loose from the roof falling down the chimney, closer now. Even as the drone's camera went gray, then dark, the sound shifted from something falling to something scrabbling and crawling.

What had I brought inside the bank? Something that reacted against an attacker, even one from the inside.

The scrabbling slowed but didn't stop. Its movements within the chimney echoed, and pieces of stone clattered to the hearth.

I backed out of the drawing room, dragging our duffel bag while keeping an eye on the fireplace. Tendrils of mold began to spread across the mantel as I cleared the threshold, stepping quickly.

Right into the doctor's thin frame.

"What have you done?" Dr. Tarn whispered. "The fungus must stay outside the bank—it protects us but cannot distinguish . . ." His voice trailed off as he pushed me aside in his rush for the front hall. From a closet concealed in the paneled walls, he withdrew a garment of pale green plastic and a bottle of bleach. "Perhaps there is still time," he muttered as he slipped into the protective gear. "This is not an acceptable part of the test."

"You gave us no such boundaries," I said, swallowing back my fear. The rustling sound had only gotten louder. My small bag of tools was still inside the room. And I recalled the doctor's words: *it cannot distinguish*. What? Friend from foe? Stone from flesh? "That stuff is sentient?"

The doctor's words were muffled by the suit. "It's a robotic-organic vegetation designed by the bank's board. Part of the bank's maintenance system, to maintain integrity. You have no idea what you've released." His eyes glowed as he entered the drawing room and shut the door.

"What *we* released? We aren't the ones coating a building in sentient mold," I said to the closed door. I hated when adults built something and only thought about the possible consequences later.

I paced the hall, not wanting to lose the Wi-Fi signal, which faded the farther I got from the drawing room. With it, I could see Rik's tablet on our VPN, but my messages wouldn't go through. He'd gone several floors down and then stopped. Best to wait where he would know to find me, and consider our options. The house creaked in the wind. The gaslights flickered annoyingly. My tablet glowed brighter in the dark.

Dr. Tarn emerged from the drawing room, shutting the door behind him. He carried a small bag. Mine. It was gray now and wrapped in clear plastic. A smell of bleach followed the doctor. Behind him, through the tightening crack in the door, I could see that our untouched tea had turned to what looked like dust on a scoured tray.

"No one may go in there for at least eighteen hours," the doctor said. "Which is almost all the time you have remaining."

"How are we supposed to work in these conditions?" I muttered, hoping to distract the man into giving me more information about the mold, or the house. "Sentient mold, terrible Wi-Fi."

"That's your problem, not mine," he said, holding up my tool bag. "I'll bury this. You'll want to keep a closer eye on your equipment in the near future." He looked at me as if he thought I would make good fertilizer for the vegetation outside.

I started to wonder about Rik, though I could still see his signal.

The clock on my tablet disappeared for a moment. When it reset, it showed a countdown, not the time. Seventeen hours, fifty minutes.

"You said you hadn't interfered with our systems."

"I haven't. You're on Usher's Wi-Fi. The bank has converted local time to your remaining time balance."

That would make keeping track of our challenge easier, but some things more difficult. I checked to make sure the tablet's internal clock was safe, and it was. But I didn't trust it. "Where is my brother?"

Tarn smiled. "You mean you've lost him already?" He turned away then, and the walls began to laugh.

During the next hour, I searched the Bank of Usher for my brother. I could hear banging and the occasional shout from below, but the farther I went from the drawing room, the worse the Wi-Fi got. I couldn't see our network. The thought that he'd been swallowed by the house clouded my mind and froze my fingers into tight curls.

Way too early, we'd failed at every turn. Coming here was a mistake. Thinking we were better than all the hackers before us. We were good. Very good. As long as we stayed off-site. And didn't wander.

And stayed together.

Here, we were out of our element. Rik had been too bewitched by the prospect of a legendary win. We hadn't yet broken a single one of the Bank's security measures.

No. I stopped. I'd broken one. By myself. The vegetation— the sentient mold and fungi designed by the bank's board to maintain the building's integrity—was a breach. One I'd caused. Just not a breach in our favor. Even the doctor seemed scared of it.

And now all my picks and sensors were sealed in plastic and about to be buried underground.

And Rik was gone.

Breathe, Mad. You can do this. You don't give up. I took a deep breath of the mansion's vile air and swore under my breath.

When I finally took a last step away from the Wi-Fi signal and descended to the basement, the banging grew louder.

"Rik?" I whispered, then, when no one answered, I spoke louder. "Rik!"

"Mad!" came my brother's voice, rippling with relief, from behind a thick metal door in a row of doors. "I broke into a vault to bag some of our reward, but then someone locked me in."

I pulled at the old vault door's handle, but it wouldn't budge. My picks were in the bag of tools and mold the Doctor had removed. Leaning against the door, I could hear the creepy pulse of the house through the metal, feel my twin on the door's other side. "Can you see anything in there? How much did you grab?"

"A little light between the door and the floor from your tablet, if I turn mine off," Rik said. "Mad. That's the thing. There's nothing in here. Most of the vaults are empty."

"That's not possible," I said. "Remember the gold reserves? The euros?" *The contract?*

"They're not storing it in the vaults if it's here, Mad." Rik's voice sounded faraway and more anxious now. "There's nothing here but bones."

"Animal bones, right, Rik?" I tried to stifle my fear. He didn't answer, and I began to worry. *Human bones? Someone who used to live here? Other hackers from the chat room?*

"Okay, don't worry," I said to myself as much as to him. If I'd listened to my own doubts instead of to my brother, we'd be in a hotel somewhere in South America by now. Clean sheets, hot coffee. No bones.

There was nothing about this exploit that hadn't gone wrong, and all of it had started by us going on-site instead of working remotely. Having to take physical funds. "We'll get you out."

I searched the open vaults, which were as empty as Rik had said. A few coins were neatly stacked on one shelf, next to a sheaf of bearer bonds that looked like the photo from the bank's website. But nothing close to the bank's stated reserves. Or our four billion Euros.

The place had been emptied. Or else it had never been full. We'd been played.

The bank would get recertified, we'd be caught, and no one would ever believe us if we said the vault was empty. Or, worse, they'd blame us. It was a genius play. I kind of admired Tarn, for a moment.

So how could we escape the bank?

In the second-to-last vault, there was a pile of old tools. Hammers, a saw. None looked up to the task of opening a vault door. The tools lay beside a large box, pried open. Its top had been cracked and pushed off its hinges. Inside was more emptiness.

As I picked through the tools, our chances felt increasingly doomed. Then a small sound from the doorway made me jump and turn.

The woman who'd greeted us and brought our tea stood with one hand on the door to my vault. Her skin shone with a blue light. The neuro-hack at her collarbone.

"No." I rushed at her, refusing to be shut in like my brother.

But she didn't move. Her mouth jerked as if she was fighting something. Her hands were curled into tight fists. "It can't be hacked," she whispered. The blue glow sputtered and faded, and I smelled burning computer chips again. When she fell down in a seizure, the woman's heels kicked softly against the vault floor. "Sounds of water," she slurred.

I gasped as I tried to keep her from hitting her head against the open metal door. "You're from the chat room. You tried to challenge last year." The woman's left hand opened, spilling a set of keys loudly to the floor. I smoothed her hair away from her sweat-cold face and tucked the keys in my pocket. Her skin was gray, the color of the house. The blue glow had faded completely.

"I lost." She laughed. "I was wrong; nothing is unhackable."

"What's your name? How were you wrong?" I stared at her as she chewed her lower lip.

Finally she spoke again. "My name is Beth. Nothing's unhackable. Can't be hacked. I can't be hacked, either. Not when the neuro is on." She sounded delirious. Her eyes opened wide and she laughed louder. "But the house can hack itself. And us. Don't give in." Then she stilled. Her breathing settled, more even, but her pulse was weak. The blue glow returned. I backed into the shadows as she stood and shook the dirt off, checked the locked vault where Rik was trapped, and then climbed the stairs.

"What's happening?" Panic rose in Rik's voice.

I couldn't answer for a long time, for fear the woman would return. Finally, when I couldn't hear her footsteps on the floors above, I took the keys I'd pulled from her hand while she was unconscious and unlocked the sealed vault door.

My brother looked pale and furious in the light from my tablet.

"I found SoundofWater," I said. "Or she found us. The house is controlling her." Rik listened as I told him about the fungus, about the locked shutters. Then I shifted to our hand-signs. Our own private language, which had helped us survive together in the orphanage. "We have to hit the network with everything we've got before the bank gets us, too."

Who knew where the AI was listening and where it wasn't?

"How, Mad? And what do we get out of all this? There's nothing here to take. We've been played."

"That's what the bank's protecting: nothing. That's what Beth meant—nothing isn't hackable by definition . . . we can't steal emptiness. But secrets are hackable. The bank has to run security challenges to keep up the sham that there's money here, but it's all a cover. There's no money here anymore. These aren't vaults and this isn't a bank if there's nothing in-side. It's just . . ." I tried to get a grip on my voice and failed, thinking of the bones, the dark, the thick walls, and the horrible dampness. "A crypt."

"A crypt with doors and windows. We can crack those, at least, then sell the intel on the bank to the highest bidder. Make our money that way," Rik said, eyeing the ring of keys. He'd already moved on to the next exploit; hadn't heard the tremor in my voice. He didn't meet my eyes when he said, "Nice grab."

I had to get out of here. To get both of us out of here. If that meant hacking Rik, too, then I was going to do it. "Exactly," I said, jingling the keys. "Let's do just that. What's the best way out?"

I thought about the windows and the rime and fungi–covered walls. Maintaining the building's integrity was what the robotic-organic vegetation was for. And the doctor was afraid of it. He seems not to have left the bank in decades. How old was the fungus?

"I'll try the smaller door out to the helipad first." Rik, always practical, pushed both vault doors shut again and locked them. "They might think we're still in here."

"SoundofWater—Beth—will notice her keys missing soon. Besides, those won't work for the big doors and shutters. I heard them datalock, and saw it on the network. Let's leave them what they're looking for and get out the hard way. They won't expect it."

When I dropped the keys to the ground, Rik chuckled. "You're not so bad at people, Mad."

"People are terrible," I grumbled. "I like bots and programs." Bots were predictable. They did what you told them. Or what someone told them.

I blinked, realizing what that meant. "Rik, Dr. Tarn said he can't kill anyone. I bet that's an operating rule, not just a term of the recertification. Even if the house might lock us up or neuro-control us, it probably can't let anyone come to direct harm."

Rik caught up to me. "And the doctor can't let anyone know that Usher is bankrupt. Just like he can't let the bank be hacked. Because then the Bank of Usher will fail, and the fungi will destroy the house and him in it."

I stared at my brother, wide-eyed. "If the lichen was added by the board members, the fungus isn't solely for protecting the house. It's a security measure that got out of control. Maybe it was once for keeping the AI in. But he's as afraid of it as he is of illness. He's trapped here, too."

We snuck back to the first floor. Now that the doctor thought we'd been trapped in the vaults below, the house had quieted. Its inhabitants slept through the deep night.

I led my brother to the drawing room and used our network to jam the Wi-Fi signal. Gray mire still crept along the inside of the chimney but couldn't make it past the bleach the doctor had laid down.

Robotic-organic, huh. Maybe it could be reasoned with.

I ran a small, polite outreach code at the fungi in the chimney, pinging it. One word: "Hello."

To my surprise, the vegetation responded with a single ping and then settled. I tried to reach out to it again, but it didn't answer. Maybe later I could try again. If we had time.

Rik worked the alarm codes.

"Window and door alarms muted," he whispered.

"Good." I held up a hammer from the pile in the vault. Picking locks was one way through a door. Take off the hinges—which was easier from inside—and the locks meant nothing.

The back door out to the helipad was small enough and out of the way enough to be our goal. I left the tablet in the drawing room, but we had hammers. "Now to really hack our way out." We'd get out without waking the AI or the doctor. Then we'd figure out what to do next.

After several long attempts at prying loose a door hinge, we were sweaty and cold. The house began to emit waking sounds, and I could hear the maid rumbling around in the kitchen. We were out of time.

My brother still worked his tools against the huge door hinges, but he looked back toward the drawing room. "Mad, we have to try something bigger or we're going to die in here."

"Like what?" I said sadly. "You wanted to do one last job. I wanted to be done with it all."

"Not one last job. One big job. I don't want to be done. Being out of it feels like dying." Then he signed, "Maybe the only way out *is* dying."

"I won't, not even for you," I signed back.

He stared at me. "No?" The walls of the house seemed to tighten around us.

I shook my head. "No. But I won't give up in here. You can't, either." Madrik wasn't me any longer, and I needed to look after my own safety, but I still loved my brother. "We either have to hack our way out or we have to get sick enough that the AI will think something has poisoned us, and the doctor will freak out about germs and infection. We need to look like we're dying. *Without actually dying.* Find me something that will make us really sick."

Rik frowned, thinking. "In the drawing room. The tea." Mold covered the tray, and the doctor had put down plastic over it. There was nothing left there but dust. But my brother had given me an idea. I ran back to the drawing room and went straight to the chimney.

"There." I pointed. "The fungus. It's part drone. Robotic-organic, the doctor said."

"You think that will make us sick but not dead? You're crazy, Mad." My brother backed away from me. "What if it hacks us?"

"She is crazy," said the doctor from the door. He held a tray with more neuro-components. "The fungus's only goal is to keep the bank safe from incursions. I have a better solution. Stay and work for the bank."

We were truly out of time.

"There's nothing left of the bank. You're maintaining a lie, that's all," I said.

The AI glow brightened in Dr. Tarn's eyes. "That's my job." He laughed. And the walls laughed with him.

"Rik, now!"

My brother dropped the hammer and reached for his last tablets. I did, too.

We hit the walls with everything we had left: two crypto codes, worms, burners, a military safe-cracker.

The window shutters groaned. Through the walls, I could hear the AI laughing, and the low thrum escalating to higher-pitched sounds. My ears ached.

The human side of Dr. Tarn laughed, too, his wiry frame unable to contain a giggle at our expense.

"Focus, Mad," my brother whispered, as Tarn's trackers came at us across the network, and Tarn himself took a step toward me. In the doorway, Beth appeared, headed for Rik. No, her neuro-connection glowed. The AI had her again. There wasn't time to try anything else. Cracks appeared in the walls and then sealed up. The smell of mold grew stronger.

The passcodes on the windows and doors changed faster than I could type, or think.

"No," I whispered. As the room grew dark, and as Dr. Tarn reached for me, the walls closed in and the floors began to crack. I ducked into the chimney and grabbed a chunk of fungus. Passed some to Rik. Took the rest of the handful for myself and kissed it.

Rik did the same.

I felt a creeping chill as spores formed on my lips. The doctor watched me in horror, then shrieked as I kissed him on the cheek.

Tarn struggled and groaned as the green of my lipstick mixed with the mire, leached into the AI circuitry beneath his skin.

The vegetation in my hand rustled and I put it down, shaking as my skin crawled.

As the fungi overcame the doctor, and then my brother, I struggled to reach for the last tablet. My fingers slipped along the glass. I triggered the EMP charge.

The whole tablet pulsed, taking the only proof of our real identities with it, and then slowly the AI glow left the doctor's eyes.

The fungi, too, ceased to pulse or signal back, at least inside the house. Outside, the walls groaned with a sudden new antagonism.

Rik began to cough in earnest. The fungus spores were growing. The doctor had turned grimly pale. Even with the EMP taking out the nearby robotic-organics' sentient side, it was still fungus. And it was getting to all of us. The floor began to give way under Rik, and I grabbed his sweater. He stumbled and the tablet he'd been using clattered down to the vault.

I moaned and the room spun. I hadn't imagined these consequences. We wouldn't make it out, not without help. Rik's sleeve slipped from my grasp and he fell.

"MAD!" "RIK!" We shouted simultaneously, and then my brother's voice abruptly disappeared.

"Rik?"

Nothing. The weight of that silence dragged me to the floor.

I couldn't see far in the darkness below. Was he dead? I had to get down there to find him.

But I didn't know how to do that alone, and this weak. I stared at the hole in the floor, the place where my brother had been.

As the fungus drained more energy, I started to shake with cold. I wobbled at the edge of the hole in the floor.

No. I wasn't done. "Call a helicopter. Call for help. For all of us," I begged the doctor. I could save myself. And Rik. "Hurry."

The doctor frowned, but only with half his mouth. The other half slumped.

"You have to try. Beth said to try." I hoped he recognized who Beth was.

The doctor struggled, then pulled a tablet from his pocket and dialed. He spoke urgently to someone on the other end. When he finished, he looked up at me. "Thank you," he said. "Finally free."

And then he collapsed. The doors and windows unlocked.

I dragged him from the room, and outside to the helipad, where we lay watching the dawn filter through the clouds.

A steady beat in the sky was the sound of two helicopters descending.

A shadow loomed over me, human-shaped, but bright. Beth—SoundofWater—her eyes dim now. "We cannot kill you," she said. "But we can break you."

The helicopters landed, and two groups of Syndicate hackers stepped out.

"They've come to take us all back," SoundofWater said. "You and I will go at once, and your brother, if they find him, will go with the others."

Separated. "No," I whispered, weaker still. I fought to stand. My legs wobbled and I fell to the ground again. "I'll stay until we find Rik."

And then, from the house, a pulse. Slow and gentle, speaking inside my head. "Hello," it whispered.

The fungi had taken control of the Bank of Usher's communications and was speaking for the first time. I closed my eyes and saw a pulse of light against my eyelids, then two more, against a haze that somehow I knew was the house itself.

Two of the lights were close together. Me and the doctor? I shifted and one light moved. Another lay alone, deep within the haze. Rik? That pulse didn't move.

Rik lay still, deep in the house. But he breathed, the pulse seemed to say, just as I did; and the haze that was a bio-network of vegetation thickened around him. Him, and the house. And me. "He's there!" I shouted. "Please get my brother!"

I lowered my voice to a whisper. "Don't give up, Rik. Anything can be hacked."

This had to be true. The haze grew brighter. A cold headache began to spread behind my eyelids, pushing at my temples. I fought it. Maybe I could still get Rik back.

"I protect the bank." The fungi pushed back.

"There is no bank," I said. "The vaults are empty. You're protecting a tomb. Give me my brother back."

The house was silent. Searching itself for the truth.

"Let me tell everyone," I whispered to it. "Let's tell everyone together."

There was a long pause. Then a long rustling sound. A drawn-out "Yes" from the fungi. Then, behind my eyes, like I'd had a neuro-connection installed, a network opened up—the house's connection to the world. I sent one message out, wide-band. Told the chat room and then the world press everything I knew about the bank's holdings, and lack thereof.

The fungi helped, sharing data from the vaults and real-time security footage from inside the house. We told everyone who would listen what the Offshore Bank of Usher really was. I closed my eyes and hoped someone heard.

For a moment, a very brief moment, the digital boundaries of the house wrapped around me: a safe place. A home. Then I felt the Syndicate's men lift me from the ground, and my hand automatically reached for my brother's but caught only air.

The pain was unbearable.

"You have to get Rik. He's still in there."

Then Syndicate crew stopped, listening. But not to me. To the beat of more helicopter blades. They dropped me and ran. My body thudded against the grass, the light suddenly too bright above me.

Then the fungus withdrew so that it barely pulsed behind my eyelids. The headache receded.

Another helicopter landed, this one with Interpol insignia.

And with loud cracks that seemed to split the bank right to the foundation, the vegetation began to squeeze the stones, cracking them until the building collapsed into the water.

I screamed and screamed.

When I woke, two days later, the room beeped alarms. A nurse swooped to my hospital bed, calming the machines.

"You are very lucky, miss," a gentleman said from a chair somewhere out of my field of vision. "No one has ever emerged from that bank, much less taken it down as thoroughly as you did. You're either very lucky or very good."

My voice sounding raw and rough, I whispered, "Both."

"Same," my twin whispered from the next bed over. I gingerly turned my head toward him through the wires and monitors. His face was bruised and swollen, and both arms were in casts. He wore a pale gray hospital gown, same as me.

He was here. We were here. I could breathe again.

"Interpol agents found him clinging to a fungus- and lichen-draped rock in the lake. We pulled him out and brought him here," the gentleman said to me, then turned to Rik. "No idea how you held on to that for as long as you did."

Rik didn't answer.

We were both safe. And the bank was gone. But there was a new distance between us, too.

The gentleman flashed us a badge: IBHS—International Bureau of Hacking and Security. He placed two tablets—clean—a newspaper, and his card, emblazoned with Interpol insignia on the table between us. "Join us," he said, "when you're ready."

"Never," said Rik.

I looked at the Interpol officer. "I'll think about it."

I took a long sip of water from the cup by my bedside while Rik stared at me. "We'll always be a team," I told him. "But maybe we can be strong on our own, too."

The newspaper's first- and second-page headlines featured news of bank clients collapsing all over the world. A fifth-page item detailed two notorious hackers captured inside the bank, dressed as a maid and a chauffeur. A third body was also found, a former CTO and AI developer named Tarn.

I read until my eyes throbbed and the light was too bright.

I felt very lucky to emerge alive on the other side. Alive, and still myself, and my brother with me, and changed, too, for as we rested, the fungi let us talk to each other silently.

Hello, it said occasionally.

Hello, we each whispered back.

The Murders in the Rue Apartelle, Boracay

➤➤➤ Rin Chupeco ◄◄◄

inspired by "The Murders in the Rue Morgue"

esh, I'm going to Prague next year!

Ay sus, it's not for a boy.

Haha, fine, it *is* for a boy. But it's not what you think.

No, it's not an eldritch this time. I'm so over eldritches. Every eldritch I've ever dated wound up cheating on me. Only thing they're faithful to is booze and that putanggra god of theirs—Gonodra? Golgorot? Whatevs.

No, not a vampire, either. They're fun at parties, but they're such a drag during the day. Not husband material at all. Were-wolves are the same, and they wind up destroying my stuff, too. Not a siyokoy—fish tails don't leave room for much else, if you know what I mean. An aswang? There's some aswangs in this story—but he's not one of them.

Oh, besh. He's a normal human boy. That's what makes it so strange. Half-French, half-Filipino, and the good looks to prove it. His name's Auguste Dupin, but everyone calls him Ogie.

Yes, the son of the French ambassador to the Philippines. I *swear* I didn't know that when I first met him.

You know that full moon party they hold in Boracay every month? The one at Bulabog Beach? That's where we met. And dios ko, besh, he parties hard. As in, hardcore partying with fairies—drinking their booze, dancing with them, eating their snacks. Diba they say never eat fairy food? Because they'll turn you into a tree or something? Anyway, he was sandwiched between two of the engkantada with the biggest—well. I filled out really nice last year, and I was still jealous of their *assets.*

But then he looked right at *me.* I swear, he was staring at me like he'd seen a ghost.

And then he asked me to dance. Like—all the enchanted fairfolk there, and he asks *me*?

But then the organizers saw the fairy beer. Not only was it illegal, but it was *super* illegal for humans to drink. So they confiscated all the booze and the fairies ran off, so now it's just me and Ogie standing there looking at each other like, anetch? Where did everyone go?

And then his bodyguard appeared—six-foot-tall golem in a business suit—and we learned who Ogie was. The organizers panicked, because who do you think people'd blame if he died at their party? They wanted to bring him to the hospital, but he said he was fine—he'd had fairy beer before. They gave us both the VIP treatment—water, tote bags, food, a room to wait in while they called a Benz to bring us home. I was so embarrassed, since I lived at that small rental in Station 3 and they probably thought I was a paid escort or something. But Ogie said oh, just take us both to the Shangri-la resort and besh, I nearly fell over. At that point I stopped caring if they thought I was his mistress because *oh my sushmita*, I'm going to Shangri-la!

It was so beautiful there, 'teh. One night costs like my monthly salary, but they have indoor Jacuzzis!

Ogie said he used to live in the mansion up Diniwid Beach, but his dad kicked him out because he threw too many loud parties. So he was demoted to Shangri-la with his golem body-guard, who'd been with him since he was seven.

Ogie was a happy drunk, but I liked him better when he was sober. He wanted to enjoy his last year of freedom before he went off to university in Europe and became a respectable diplomat like his dad. Also, the government was closing Bora-cay for six months, so he wouldn't be back for a while even if he wanted to.

We didn't sleep together that first night. He even *apolo-gized* for inconveniencing me, said I could stay for as long as I wanted.

"I don't want to impose," I said, because my mudra taught me to be respectful, too. "And I don't want to cause problems."

"Problems?" He had a gorgeous accent. "You?"

"Yes, me," I said, because I wanted to be honest upfront. Alam mo, it's hard enough to be a woman without all the judg-ment. So hard waiting for your body and the surgeries and the injections to catch up to the rest of the real you.

I don't know how he knew, but he did. "You won't." He said it so confidently. "Trust me," and I wanted to cry because I've

never met anyone who was this understanding. Even my mudra thought there was something wrong with me at first.

Yes, besh, I know it was dangerous. I mean, you never really
know if the pretty boy you're with might be a serial killer, right?

But I knew he wouldn't hurt me.

Those were the best days of my life. We explored the beach
and swam. We ate six-course meals by this private chef who
used to cook for the third prince of Atlantis. We island-hopped
on a yacht, snorkeled, and lounged on deck while he played
whale songs on his phone and the kraken-fishermen grilled us
all these tilapia and prawns. His bodyguard (his name was
Ansel) followed him around, but he was so good he was almost
invisible.

Of course I enjoyed being treated like a princess. But it wasn't
just that—it was him, you know? If all he could afford was a
date at a carinderia, I still would have stayed. I wasn't with him
because he was rich. I know why people would think that, but I
never asked for money or gifts.

Ogie's father was never around, and I knew that disappointed him. His mother's Mischa Montemayor, the Filipina
socialite, but they're not close, either. He'd had one serious girlfriend, and from the quiet way he talked about her I think *she*
dumped *him*. But he was *so* intelligent. He was a valedictorian
pala at the Boracay European International School! And he
spoke six languages! He'd climbed both Everest and Kiliman-
jaro, and was an expert at Krav Maga. He was going to study
international economics and commercial diplomacy at Charles
University in Prague so he could follow in his father's footsteps.
It's not like I'm dumb—I mean, haller, Philippine Science

High School graduate, incoming University of the Philippines freshman—but he takes smarts to another level.

And he stopped drinking as much. "I'm only tempted when I'm bored," he said, shrugging like that was normal. "And I'm not bored now that I have company."

I didn't know why he kept me around. He didn't try to force it like some of the Kanos at the bars do. Not that I don't appreciate that. I mean, when I went home with him that first time I was more interested in *where* I'd be sleeping than *who* I might be sleeping with. I thought maybe I wasn't his type, and he just wanted someone to be with now that most of his friends had left Boracay and were partying somewhere else.

But on the fourth night, I accidentally found a picture of his ex. It was on his dresser, half hidden—long black hair, dark eyes. Super pretty—as in, gandara park to the max. I wasn't trying to pry, by the way.

"The one that got away," Ogie admitted. He tried to sound like he didn't mind. "Everyone liked her. Ansel treated her like a daughter."

"You look a lot like her," he added.

Aha, I thought. This was the former Serious Girlfriend, and maybe I was his rebound, but that was okay. I appreciated his honesty. "There are many reasons why I'm different from her." I laughed.

"You're more similar than you know. And being different doesn't mean I don't find you appealing. I hope—I hope the guys here don't treat you poorly because of it?"

Besh, I *froze*. I wasn't expecting him to be so blunt.

"Was that the wrong thing to say? I'm sorry."

"It's not," I said. "It's just that you guessed right. Guys get very . . . hostile, when they find out."

"Guys are assholes."

"Sorry."

His brow furrowed. "Don't apologize. You don't deserve any of that." And then his voice went so quiet. "Did they hurt you?"

"I always leave before things get bad," I said, because it was easier than saying yes.

"I'll never hurt you."

He was like a puppy. So cute.

So many reasons to not get involved with an ambassador's son, besh.

So many.

Pero like the French say—*c'est la vie,* diba?

I did mention that he was really smart, right? Sometimes Ogie would be restless at night, so we'd go out and join the groups wandering Station 3 or watch the firedancers or stay at the clubs. He didn't drink—he was more interested in watching people than in a pitcher of Pineapple Sling.

He'd make a lot of observations, too. Like he'd say that American guy was a former veteran, retired with a wife back home, but that one of the bartenders was his mistress. Or that the girl on my left has four kids and a husband she's separated from. Or the tall man in front of us had been to jail and was looking for a sugar mommy. I didn't believe him at first—it's not like they'd admit that they're divorced or that they're convicts if I asked.

Except one day I *did* get to ask one of the manananggals he analyzed, and she admitted to divorcing three husbands like he said—they had a hard time adjusting to life with a girl who could bisect her own waist and fly away with her upper body, I guess. So he was right with her, at least.

One more thing though, because it happened the night of the murders—

—yes, *yes*, I'll tell you all about it!—

—we'd stopped at the Coco Bar with a group of eldritches— the bar with that Brain Train challenge where you knock off ten shots in a row? Well, Ogie gave up after two, and the eldritches were acting so smug. One of them was all, **The Doom Has Come For You, Fear The Trembling of The Sarnath For We Shall Drink You Under** and I was so mad because that sounded like something my ex would say, too.

Anyway, I took them on and I *won* and got my T-shirt and my name on the Wall of Fame and everything. And I did it faster than any of the eldritches, ha! But then they got mad, and Ogie had to break one of the wooden stools to make a point. The eldritches backed off. Ogie paid for the stool, too, like a true gentleman. His golem bodyguard just sat there like he was used to it.

But I was still drunk and wanted calamansi muffins for some reason, so we left the bar and Ogie helped me walk up to Station 2 looking for the cafe that sold them.

He was quiet the whole time until we got to the end of the street. Maybe he was embarrassed about the eldritches, although I thought he was so brave. And my mind was wandering at that point—the music felt so *loud, mare*. I glared at the DJ as we passed, but I felt a lot better after we'd passed the clubs and reached the open-air cafes with their milder sixties music.

You think the Beach Boys ever visited Boracay, *mare*? People love them here.

"That's true," he said, all of a sudden, "*Dirty Computer* will endure not only as a musical masterpiece, but as *the* protest album of our generation."

"Yeah!" I cheered, then realized I hadn't said anything. "Wait. Ogie, syet, how'd you—"

"—know you were thinking about Janelle Monae's latest album? It was the DJ."

I'm like, ano daw? The DJ?

"The DJ playing the open bar at the Epic."

But he wasn't playing any of Janelle Monae's songs.

"It was obvious that your train of thought ran this way— Taylor Swift, the DJ, politics, the Beach Boys, androids, Dirty Computer. It makes sense once you apply logic and reasoning. One of my ancestors coined a word to explain it— ratiocination. I know you love Monae and I know you've done research into her latest album, so admittedly, knowing this beforehand worked in my favor. When we walked past the Epic after leaving the Coco Bar, Taylor Swift's *Reputation* was on blast. I saw you frown, annoyed, and surmised you were not a fan. And when the DJ leaned into the mic to call her the Queen of Pop, I saw your irritation increase. Then your eyes wandered through the crowd, resting on a man wearing a shirt that said Let's Get Political, and you rolled your eyes. You were thinking of Swift and her reluctance to discuss her political opinions in the public sphere even as she claims that she speaks for the youth."

(Yes besh, I know she's awesome now and I freely admit my

mistake, but at that time all I was really concerned with was how he was boggling my mind!)

"As you stepped away, I saw your attention diverted by the faint strains of Beach Boys music playing from a separate, quieter bar, and this time a small smile stole across your lips. You were thinking about how their music and their outspoken politics more closely align with yours.

"You then murmured something that sounded like 'android' and by context I took it as a reference to *ArchAndroid,* Monae's second album—also an important political album. You nodded resolutely to yourself then, and your eyes sparkled. I knew that you knew the Beach Boys' lead vocalist, Brian Wilson, worked with Janelle Monae for her latest album, *Dirty Computer,* which was even more unabashedly political, and so I agreed—if there is any justice in the world, history will be kinder to Monae than it will be to Swift."

"Are you a mind reader?" I demanded. He explained everything so well, but I was still super drunk, so as far as I was concerned, this was magic.

He grinned. "I was rather hoping," he said, taking a step toward me, "that you would find it a turn-on."

(I did, besh!)

Ogie had already showered when I woke the next morning; he was eating breakfast and reading the newspaper when I came in. "You missed all the excitement," he said. "Look at this."

I'm sure you've heard of the murders, diba? I mean, all the

big newspapers in the Philippines reported it when it happened: AMERICANS IN BORACAY MURDERED, LIVERS MISSING. Here, let me google the article:

An American and his son were killed in Boracay's Station 3 at White Beach in the early hours of the morning, according to local authorities.

The gruesome remains were found by a maid and a security guard at the Rue Apartelle, rented to one Allan Dayton-Smith and his son, Lance, both from Texas, United States. The door was locked when the maid arrived to clean their room, but after finding blood seeping out from behind the locked door she fled and called a passing guard, who subsequently broke in.

"Andami talaga (There was so much of it)," said Alma Fuentes, 65, as she described the scene. "Di namin alam saan tatapak, kasi baka matakpan rin kami ng dugo. Puro dugo kasi yung kuwarto. Parang kinatay sila. (We didn't know where to step without being covered in blood. The room was full of it. The bodies looked like they'd been butchered.)"

"The murderers might have taken advantage of the loud music and parties going on at that time to commit the crime, tapos tumakas (and then escaped)," police superintendent Barnaby Sta. Ana said.

Records show that the Dayton-Smiths were both at Boracay on vacation, and that they were frequent visitors to the island, having stayed for the whole month of March in 2015 and again in 2017. The police say they are trying to get in touch with the victims' family.

"After our initial investigation, it was found that their livers were also missing," Sta. Ana added.

The murders come on the heels of an expected closure of Boracay island for six months starting April 28, to upgrade the island's overtaxed sewage system and to investigate the sanitation standards that led to a rise in pollution in the last few years.

It is rare for a murder to be committed in Boracay. In 2017, only one murder was reported by the local police; the case remains unsolved.

I don't know how big this was in Manila, but people in Boracay wouldn't stop talking about it. Ogie was hooked. We talked to fishermen, bartenders, business owners, jewelry sellers, massage therapists. Everyone thought it was the aswangs because the Americans' livers were missing and really, who goes out of their way to eat livers other than the aswangs?

"I don't think it was the aswangs," Ogie said. "And it's disappointing how easily people succumb to hostility of the Other when they have no other answers to offer."

I didn't know why he didn't think it was the aswangs, but then I remembered Janelle Monae and the girl with the three husbands. He was right both times. I was convinced. Maybe that wasn't a good enough reason for other people, but I was invested in wanting him to be perfect a little longer. Plus, he was smart. I wasn't biased about *that*.

"I know some of the aswangs here," he said. "The whole cluster of them that lives in White Beach, anyway. My father has used them as guides many times before, for tours with people at the embassy. And with all due respect—as friendly as the people here are, I don't trust the police's competence to solve a crime of this scale. The superintendent on this island knows my family. It would be easy enough to get the facts out of him."

I wasn't expecting my vacation in Boracay to turn into a crime-solving episode, but sige na, if he really wanted this. . . .

And money really talks, besh, because when we got to

the police station you would have thought Ogie was a celebrity from the way the superintendent acted. He said he would show us the bodies and give us a tour of the place they were murdered at, like this was a tourist attraction. We had to go through the back—the area was full of reporters, and Ogie didn't want to be seen. I looked back wistfully at the beach, where people were still swimming and sunbathing. *The things I do for a cute guy,* I thought, and followed them in.

We looked at the bodies first. I ran outside again to throw up, because ohmaygad, I was still hungover. I knew it would be bad, but I didn't think about how bad it was. Also, they *stank*.

When I came back, Ogie was sympathetic, still examining the corpses. From what I remember, the older Amerikano was burly—muscles turning to fat, middle-aged, tribal tattoos on one shoulder. His son was thinner and shorter. The superintendent said they were fifty-six and twenty-five years old.

"Just father and son?" Ogie asked. "No wives or daughters along for the trip?"

"Ah, no. The younger Kano was an only child, and the father a widower."

"No surgeon did this," Ogie said, his voice low and odd. "They were in a lot of pain when they died. Ligatures on their necks, as well."

"If I don't solve this crime they might ask me to resign," Sta. Ana fretted.

"Your medical examiner confirms that their livers are missing. Were any other organs taken?"

"Nothing else that we know of, boss. And I believe," the superintendent continued heatedly, "that this is an aswang's work.

Why else would the livers be gone? The vampires drink blood and the werewolves eat everything, and the ones with the tentacles will screw your minds over, but only the aswangs take livers!"

We went to the place where the Kanos had been staying next, the Rue Apartelle, and we had to push our way through the gathered crowd staring ghoulishly up at the windows. It was a cheap place, the type tourists rented if they wanted to stay longer on the island on a low budget.

"Their room was locked from the inside, but the windows were open," Ogie said. "That's important. Unfortunately, they were angled away from the other houses, so the neighbors wouldn't have seen any visitors inside. The younger Dayton-Smith's body was found there, so presumably he was killed first. His father was still in bed when the murder occurred. It's a large enough window, six feet high and twelve across—easy for an adult to get through."

"Or aswang," said Sta. Ana, a stubborn man.

Ogie took a pair of gloves and looked through the victims' things next. Just normal stuff: clothes and snorkeling gear, passports and receipts.

"These Dayton-Smiths kept a messy house," Ogie said, pushing dirty clothes out of the way. "Their cash remains— ten thousand dollars in total." He brought out a knife from one of their bags. "And this? This isn't something tourists usually bring."

The superintendent shrugged, like he couldn't be bothered about the strange things any Kano would bring to Boracay.

"A knife would have been confiscated at the airport. Did they check in any luggage?"

"Yes. Maybe they bought it somewhere after they landed at Caticlan airport. . . ."

"Unlikely. This looks old and well used. Do you have a crime lab here in Boracay? For DNA?"

"No." The man looked embarrassed.

"I can help you fast-track this to a lab in Manila. My dad knows a reputable company. We should get results in a couple of days."

"Salamat, boss," the officer said, grateful. "If it's not too much a problem. . . ."

"Boracay has been very good to me, and I want to return the favor. The idea of a murder happening here makes me angry. And of course, I know this isn't something the police usually do in cases." Ogie was a good diplomat, like his father. I would have just told Sta. Ana he sucked. "But I'd like to keep my name out of the news."

"Understood, boss."

"I trust you and your men to make sure the evidence isn't contaminated, and that you and a representative will employ standard procedures in sealing this knife and delivering it."

"Of course, boss."

"Why the knife?" I asked.

"There are flecks of brown stains on the blade. Possibly animal blood—possibly something else. I'm surprised the killer didn't use this. I'm told it was sitting in full view on their dresser, and any good murderer would have used that so it wouldn't be traced back to them. There's nothing in Boracay that would require one to use a hunting knife, so I find it curious. Any luck unlocking their phones?"

"Not yet, boss."

"The family might know more. Make it a point to ask them." There were still people outside, so Ogie donned a cap to hide his face, then leaned out the window. "I see some marks," he said. "They seem too clean and pronounced to be made from aswang claws. The neighbors from across the street, and that small hostel beside this apartelle, would be our best witnesses."

The neighbors were not good witnesses. The old labandera, Mrs. Gomez, insisted she heard someone talking in Bahasa Indonesian, while her husband thought it might be Chinese. But the Indonesian living below them said it was Korean, though his girlfriend watched K-dramas and said it sounded nothing like it, and that it was Thai. Coincidentally, the backpackers staying in the hostel room *were* Thai, but assumed the speaker was Vietnamese.

"Six languages," Ogie said. "You would think that living here in Boracay, where people from all countries visit to party, they'd know the difference."

"But which of them is right?" I asked.

"They all described the voice as a peculiar moaning sound. In that they all agree. Let's interview our main suspects next."

Most of the aswangs would be out of jobs once the island closed, so a majority had already left two weeks ago for the nearby town of Kalibo to find work. The two that remained behind were an old aswang named Valdez and his young grandson, Tomas. Since Tomas was only four years old, he was quickly dismissed as a suspect. Cops loitered outside the house, although the superintendent said they had no evidence to arrest anyone yet.

"Too old to be scampering on rooftops," Valdez told Ogie in Tagalog, and showed us his worn, chipped claws, brittle from old age. Like all aswangs he was bald and leathery, but his grandson was like an adorable little bat, chewing on a doll while staring up at us with his bright red eyes. "I have arthritis. I can barely stand, much less climb walls."

"Aswangs are the only creatures in Boracay that eat human livers," Ogie pointed out.

The old man laughed and plucked out his dentures. "Does it look like I can still eat liver? My grandson won't get his cravings until he's sixteen."

"Solving this would be easier," Ogie said, sounding almost angry, "had you gone to Kalibo with the others."

"I would be of no use there. Cheaper to stay. All I want is to care for my grandson. I have no problems with Kanos."

The superintendent sounded crestfallen when we returned to the police station. "All the other aswang were working overtime at the Berregen Construction Company in Kalibo, so they're accounted for," he mourned. "But if the old man didn't do it, who did? It can't be the boy."

Ogie patted him on the back. "Give it a couple more days, pare. I'm sure we'll have something."

Ah, besh. I'm sure you know what happened next, diba? When the results from the crime lab came back and there was *blood* on the knife? And it wasn't any of the *Kanos'* blood?! Remember when they compared it to that other girl murdered last year, and it was a match? It was Ogie who suggested that, and he was right! He was supposed to solve the *Kanos'* murders, but he actually solved the murder *they* committed! Plot twist, sobra!

The Kanos killed that girl! And it was a trans girl rin daw!

Those men had also stayed in Boracay back in 2017, remember? And then they were here in 2015, when there was *another* murder! Honestly, no one's interested in their killer anymore. Parang they want to know who it was so they can give them a medal!

Not even Ogie minded after that. "I'm more interested in justice finally being served," he said. "I'll take this as a victory. They had money, and money passes through a lot of judicial hands here. I don't think they would have stayed in jail for very long in the Philippines. . . ."

"But who did you think killed those men?" I asked.

"I can't give you a name," he said. "But I can make an educated guess. First—they weren't much into cleanliness, these Dayton-Smiths, and I thought they would be particularly lax when it came to cleaning up evidence, counting on the lack of DNA analysis in Philippine criminal cases. I hope this doesn't offend, but Filipinos have a tendency to put white foreigners on a pedestal over their own kinspeople, and the murderers knew it. Cruel men, these Dayton-Smiths. The knife was my best bet.

"Secondly, if an aswang had attacked them for their livers alone it would have been easier to find some solitary tourist on the beach in the dark and assault them instead. Why risk getting in through an open window where they could have been seen? That, and the ten thousand dollars remaining in the men's possession suggests not a robbery, but a personal vendetta.

"And then there's the mysterious killer who speaks in no human language the neighbors could discern. Everyone *did* agree it was a low, moaning voice. Perhaps their inability to determine the murderer's nationality was because the language they heard wasn't human to begin with. No one that night heard the compulsory *eek eek* cry aswangs make when they at-tack. Eldritches and vampires do so silently. Werewolves would have destroyed the room in their rage, howled up a ruckus. If no species currently living in Boracay fit that profile, perhaps the moaning was a deliberate attempt to mislead us.

"So let us follow the hypothesis that someone took their livers not to eat, but to blame the aswangs. But again, why choose the Dayton-Smiths in particular? As I said before, any tourist would have sufficed. I see no connection between the Americans and the aswangs, and most of the latter had already gone to Kalibo for work. Was the perpetrator aware of that fact, and so went out of their way to frame them, knowing they would have an alibi?

"The culprit, then, is someone with a grudge against the Dayton-Smiths. I haven't been able to involve myself in the in-vestigation since the knife was tested, so I wasn't privy to all the pertinent information gleaned from the victims' phones, but I'd bet the killer was someone they knew—someone who knew and loved one of their victims and sought revenge. Someone who knew enough about climbing to use a hook on the window ledge and make the grooves I discovered there. Valdez's claws were too fragile for those imprints. Someone strong enough to overpower two men. Someone who saw the knife and chose *not* to use it, suggesting he was aware there could be DNA for the police to find. Someone who fabricated an aswang attack as a red herring, to convince the police that the killer is anything but what he actually is—human."

"I can't believe that," I said.

"You're refuting my deductions?"

"No. I think you know who the killer is. You wouldn't have

stopped until you did." I remembered his obvious irritation when I thought he was making stories up about his observations of other people. How he insisted on telling me about his *Dirty Computer* thought process. It wasn't like him to leave something unsolved.

He laughed. "I'd rather not slander someone without the hard evidence on hand to back me up. Maybe I'll tell you some day. But I'm hoping I won't need to."

It's not like he could stay even if we both wanted him to. It was a good summer. I don't wanna be bitter about it, you know?

But then he called me up a week later. We still talk almost every day. I *really* like him, besh.

I may not be as smart as he is, but I'm not dumb, either. It just took me longer to realize some things.

Because I've been thinking about it for a while na. Especially after they showed the murdered girls' pictures in the newspaper, months after Ogie left for Europe.

One looked a lot like that photo I saw of Ogie's ex.

I couldn't be sure. I only saw a glimpse that time at the Shangri-la. . . .

He said I was so similar to her. Maybe he wasn't just talking about being pretty. . . .

He was so mad when he learned that the old aswang, Valdez, didn't go to Kalibo with the others. The construction company that hired the aswangs was a friend of Ogie's dad, too. . . .

I remembered he was a mountain climber.

I remembered that whale songs do sound like moaning. . . .

I remembered being asleep when the murders happened, and that Ogie, who could drink fairies under the table, didn't last two shots that night. I remembered that going to the Coco Bar was his idea.

I remembered when he scared the eldritches because he was stronger than he looked. I remembered he had a bodyguard golem who was even stronger, who Ogie said was close enough to his ex that he treated her like a daughter. . . .

I remembered his face when he saw me for the first time. He said I looked familiar. Like he'd seen the ghost of someone he knew well. . . .

If taking their livers was a red herring to blame the aswangs, why use whale songs instead of imitating an aswang cry? Like he wanted some superficial evidence available that could point to an aswang, but also leave evidence to suggest reasonable doubt about that, too? So that no innocent aswang actually got arrested?

I wondered why he insisted on being part of the police investigation.

And then I thought—Ogie's so smart. But sometimes he's too smart for his own good, and it goes over people's heads. So maybe he had to guide the police in the direction he *wanted* them to go.

But why tell me all that if he could get into trouble, diba? I thought long and hard about it.

And I realized it's the most romantic thing anyone has ever done for me.

I trust you rin, besh. I know you would never give me up.

And besides, he's a diplomat's son with immunity. What's anyone gonna do?

So Ogie invited me to Prague next month. I'm going to be his date for the prince of Lindbergh's wedding! *Oh may gad* besh—what do I wear to *that?*

Glossary for "Murders in the Rue Apartelle, Boracay"

* denotes specifically Filipinx LGBTQ+ slang

besh* — best friend

ay sus — oh, sheesh

putanggra* — bitch

siyokoy — a merman

aswang — shape-shifting monster from Filipino mythology

dios ko — my god

Diba — to ask for confirmation/agreement from the person you're talking to. "Diba they say never eat fairy food?" for example, would typically mean, "Don't they say, never eat fairy food?"

engkantada — faerie folk

like, *anetch?** — like, what did they say? Slang for *ano daw*

oh my sushmita* — a reference to Sushmita Sen, Miss India and Miss Universe 1994, and a popular celebrity among Filipinx

'teh — from "Ate" (ah-teh), meaning "sister"; also a respectful term to refer to women older than the speaker

mudra* — mother

alam mo — you know

carinderia — Filipino eatery

He was a valedictorian *pala* — *pala* indicates something that went against your expectation: "I wasn't expecting him to be a valedictorian." Not intended as an insult.

I mean, *haller** — I mean, hello

Kano/Kanos — from "Amerikano"

gandara park to the max* — a nod to KPOP singer Sandara Park of 2NE1, indicating that someone is exceptionally pretty (*ganda* is the Tagalog word for "beautiful"); "to the max" serves as additional emphasis

Pero like the French say — But like the French say

manananggal — flying monster from Filipino mythology who can sever her upper torso before hunting

mare — pronounced ma-reh; a female friend (informal)

syet — shit (expletive)

I'm like, *ano daw?* — I'm like, what'd they say?

sige na, if he really wanted this — fine, if he really wanted this

ohmaygad — oh my god

salamat — Thank you

pare — pronounced pa-reh; a male friend (informal)

labandera — washerwoman

Plot twist, sobra! — *Sobra* in this context indicates something that is so over the top — "Plot twist! This is too much!"

And it was a trans girl *rin daw*! — *daw* suggests that someone else has mentioned it, or that it was a common belief; "And it was a trans girl, or so they also say!"

Parang they want to know who it was — It's like they want to know who it was

I've been thinking about it for a while *na* — I've been thinking about it for a while now.

About the Authors

DAHLIA ADLER is an associate editor of mathematics by day, a blogger by night, and an author of young adult novels at every spare moment in between. Her books include the Daylight Falls duology, *Just Visiting*, and the Radleigh University trilogy, and her short stories can be found in the anthologies *The Radical Element*, *All Out*, *It's a Whole Spiel*, and *His Hideous Heart*. Dahlia lives in New York with her husband, her son, and an obscene number of books.

KENDARE BLAKE is the author of several novels and short stories. Her work is sort of dark, always violent, and features passages describing food from when she writes while hungry. She was born in July in Seoul, South Korea, but doesn't speak a lick of Korean, as she was packed off at a very early age to her adoptive parents in the United States. That might be just an excuse, though, as she is pretty bad at learning foreign languages. She enjoys the work of Milan Kundera, Caitlín R. Kiernan, Bret Easton Ellis, Richard Linklater, and the late, great Michael Jackson. She lives and writes in Kent, Washington, with her husband, their cat son Tyrion Cattister, red Doberman dog son Obi-Dog Kenobi, rottie mix dog daughter Agent Scully, and naked sphynx cat son Armpit McGee.

RIN CHUPECO wrote obscure manuals for complicated computer programs, talked people out of their money at event shows, and did many other terrible things. She now writes about ghosts and fantastic worlds but is still sometimes mistaken for a revenant. She is the author of *The Girl from the Well;* its sequel, *The Suffering;* and the Bone Witch trilogy. She was born and raised in the Philippines and, or so the legend goes, still haunts that place to this very day. Find her at rinchupeco.com.

LAMAR GILES writes novels and short stories for teens and adults. He is the author of the Edgar Award nominees *Fake ID* and *Endangered,* as well as the YA novel *Overturned.* His most recent novel, *Spin,* is a teen thriller that combines music with murder, and his middle-grade work *The Last Last-Day-of-Summer* takes readers on a time-traveling adventure. Lamar is a founding member of We Need Diverse Books, and resides in Virginia with his wife. Check him out online at lamargiles.com, or follow @LRGiles on Twitter.

TESSA GRATTON is the associate director of Madcap Retreats and the author of the Blood Journals series and the Gods of New Asgard series, coauthor of two YA writing books, as well as dozens of short stories. Though she's lived all over the world, she's finally returned to her prairie roots in Kansas with her wife. Her current projects include *Tremontaine* at Serial Box Publishing, the YA Fantasy *Strange Grace,* and her adult fantasy novels *The Queens of Innis Lear* and the forthcoming *Lady Hotspur* from Tor. Visit her at tessagratton.com.

TIFFANY D. JACKSON is the author of critically acclaimed YA novels, including the NAACP Image Award–nominated *Allegedly,* the Walter Dean Myers Honor Book *Monday's Not Coming,* and *Let Me Hear a Rhyme.* She received her bachelor of arts in film from Howard University, her master of arts in media studies from the New School, and has over a decade in TV/film experience. The Brooklyn native is a lover of naps, cookie dough, and beaches, currently residing in the borough she loves, most likely multitasking.

STEPHANIE KUEHN is a psychologist and an author. She has written five novels for teens, including *Charm & Strange,* which won the ALA's 2014 William C. Morris Award for best debut young adult novel. *Booklist* has praised her work as "intelligent, compulsively readable literary fiction with a dark twist."

EMILY LLOYD-JONES grew up on a vineyard in rural Oregon, where she played in evergreen forests and learned to fear sheep. She has a BA in English from Western Oregon University and a MA in publishing from Rosemont College. Her novels include *Illusive, Deceptive, The Hearts We Sold,* and the forthcoming *The Bone Houses.*

having grown up a word-devourer & avid fairy tale lover, it was only natural that **AMANDA LOVELACE** would begin writing books of her own. so she did. when she isn't reading or writing, she can be found waiting for pumpkin spice coffee to come back into season & binge-watching *gilmore girls*. (before you ask: team jess all the way.) the lifelong poetess & storyteller currently lives in new jersey with her spouse, their ragdoll cats, & a combined book collection so large it will soon need its own home. she is a two-time winner of the goodreads choice award for best poetry as well as a *usa today* & *publishers weekly* bestseller.

HILLARY MONAHAN is the author of twelve titles, including the *New York Times* bestselling horror novel *Mary: The Summoning* through Disney Hyperion. She lives in Massachusetts with her family of some parts human, more parts fur friend.

MARIEKE NIJKAMP was born and raised in the Netherlands. A life-long student of stories, language, and ideas, she spends as much time in fictional worlds as she does the real world. She loves to travel, roll dice, and daydream. Her #1 *New York Times* bestsell-ing debut novel, *This Is Where It Ends,* follows four teens dur-ing the fifty-four minutes of a school shooting. Her sophomore novel, *Before I Let Go,* is a haunting young adult murder mystery set during a cruel Alaskan winter. Marieke is the editor of the YA anthology *Unbroken: 13 Stories Starring Disabled Teens* (FSG) and the writer of *The Oracle Code* (DC Ink).

CALEB ROEHRIG is a writer and television producer originally from Ann Arbor, Michigan. Having also lived in Chicago, Los Angeles, and Helsinki, Finland, he has a chronic case of wanderlust, and can recommend the best sights to see on a shoe-string budget in more than thirty countries. A former actor, Roehrig has experience on both sides of the camera, with a résumé that includes appearances on film and TV—as well as seven years in the stranger-than-fiction salt mines of reality television. In the name of earning a paycheck, he has: hung around a frozen cornfield in his underwear, partied with an actual rock star, chatted with a scandal-plagued politician, and been menaced by a disgruntled ostrich.

FRAN WILDE's novels and short stories have been finalists for three Nebula Awards, a World Fantasy Award, and two Hugo Awards, and include her Andre Norton– and Compton Crook–winning debut novel *Updraft*, its sequels *Cloudbound* and *Horizon*, her 2019 debut middle grade *Riverland*, and the Nebula-, Hugo-, and Locus-nominated novelette *The Jewel and Her Lapidary*. Her short stories appear in *Asimov's Science Fiction, Tor.com, Beneath Ceaseless Skies, Shimmer, Nature*, and the *2017 Year's Best Dark Fantasy and Horror*. She writes for publications including *The Washington Post, Tor.com, Clarkesworld, io9,* and *GeekMom*. You can find her on Twitter, Facebook, and at franwilde.net.

Acknowledgments

An anthology is by its very nature a group effort, and enormous thanks are due to everyone who made this one happen. Thank you, Victoria Marini, for all your work finding *His Hideous Heart* the perfect home at Flatiron, and Sarah Barley, for taking on the collection of my dreams and helping me turn it into an anthology of beautiful nightmares.

Thanks, too, to everyone who helped take a raw manuscript and turn it into this gorgeous volume, including but surely not limited to Bryn Clark, Melanie Sanders, Emily Walters, Lauren Hougen, Devan Norman, and of course, Jon Contino and Keith Hayes for the most striking cover I could never have imagined.

Huge thanks are also due to everyone at Macmillan who produced and marketed the magnificent audiobook—Matie

Argiropoulos, Samantha Edelson, Emily Dyer, Brisa Robinson, Mary Beth Roche, Robert Allen, and Brian Ramcharan.

I am grateful for the work of all those who've studied Poe before me, and especially to the Edgar Allan Poe Society of Baltimore, Project Gutenberg, and Benjamin F. Fisher.

Anthologies are complicated beasts, and I'm exceptionally grateful to experienced editors Marieke Nijkamp, Katherine Locke, Saundra Mitchell, and Jessica Spotswood for their guidance. You're all wise, brilliant, and I'm grateful to each of you for not only helping me as needed but for either giving me a chance as an author or bravely accepting me to be your editor.

Much love to the friends who've patiently helped me find my balance these last couple of years as I walked on unsteady feet, especially Lindsay Smith, Maggie Hall, Emery Lord, Melissa Albert, Becky Albertalli, Sona Charaipotra, Candice Montgomery, Rebecca Coffindaffer, Sharon Morse, Jess Capelle, Tess Sharpe, Anna-Marie McLemore, Eric Smith, AK Furukawa, and of course the aforementioned Marieke and Katie. Thank you to Tara Dairman, Lauren Morrill, and Heidi Heilig for the safe and helpful Facebook spaces you've created, and to everyone on Twitter who's listened to me babble about this book and *Grey's Anatomy* and macarons and stuck around anyway. I'm especially grateful to Twitter for indirectly making this whole thing happen, thanks to a certain someone. (I'm pretty grateful to her, too.)

To my family, thank you for endless love and support, and for being excited for each and every new venture as it comes. Micah, you may share your mom with so many things and so many imaginary people, but you are the panda of my heart, and I love you even more than you love Elmo. Yoni, this is my seventh time getting to use this space to talk about how much I love and appreciate you, and I only seem to get worse at it. Thank you for all the cookies and Sunday mornings.

Of course, biggest thanks of all go to everyone whose words comprise this volume and whose incredible work speaks for itself. Kendare, Rin, Lamar, Tessa, Tiffany, Steph, Emily, amanda, Hillary, Marieke, Caleb, and Fran, thank you for your passion and your talent and for every shiver and smile and gasp and wince. And Edgar, thank you for the beautiful work you've made of people who do ugly things, for the Gothic legends of my teenage dreams, and for writing stories and poems that forever continue to inspire.

Without further ado, Dear Reader, here are those very same stories and poems that inspired ours, and I hope they hold the same dark, thrilling, and enduring magic for you.

The
Original
Tales

Metzengerstein

Pestis eram vivus—moriens tua mors ero.

—MARTIN LUTHER

orror and fatality have been stalking abroad in all ages. Why then give a date to this story I have to tell? Let it suffice to say, that at the period of which I speak, there existed, in the interior of Hungary, a settled although hidden belief in the doctrines of the Metempsychosis. Of the doctrines themselves—that is, of their falsity, or of their probability—I say nothing. I assert, however, that much of our incredulity (as La Bruyere says of all our unhappiness) *"vient de ne pouvoir être seuls."*

But there are some points in the Hungarian superstition which were fast verging to absurdity. They—the Hungarians—differed very essentially from their Eastern authorities. For example, *"The soul,"* said the former—I give the words of an acute and intelligent Parisian—*"ne demeure qu'un seul fois dans un corps*

sensible: au reste—un cheval, un chien, un homme meme, n'est que la res-
semblance peu tangible de ces animaux."

The families of Berlifitzing and Metzengerstein had been at
variance for centuries. Never before were two houses so illustrious, mutually embittered by hostility so deadly. The origin
of this enmity seems to be found in the words of an ancient
prophecy—"A lofty name shall have a fearful fall when, as the
rider over his horse, the mortality of Metzengerstein shall triumph over the immortality of Berlifitzing."

To be sure the words themselves had little or no meaning.
But more trivial causes have given rise—and that no long while
ago—to consequences equally eventful. Besides, the estates,
which were contiguous, had long exercised a rival influence in
the affairs of a busy government. Moreover, near neighbors are
seldom friends; and the inhabitants of the Castle Berlifitzing
might look, from their lofty buttresses, into the very windows
of the Palace Metzengerstein. Least of all had the more than
feudal magnificence, thus discovered, a tendency to allay the
irritable feelings of the less ancient and less wealthy Berlifitzings. What wonder, then, that the words, however silly, of that
prediction, should have succeeded in setting and keeping at
variance two families already predisposed to quarrel by every
instigation of hereditary jealousy? The prophecy seemed to
imply—if it implied anything—a final triumph on the part of
the already more powerful house; and was of course remembered with the more bitter animosity by the weaker and less
influential.

Wilhelm, Count Berlifitzing, although loftily descended,
was, at the epoch of this narrative, an infirm and doting old
man, remarkable for nothing but an inordinate and inveterate

personal antipathy to the family of his rival, and so passionate a love of horses, and of hunting, that neither bodily infirmity, great age, nor mental incapacity, prevented his daily participation in the dangers of the chase.

Frederick, Baron Metzengerstein, was, on the other hand, not yet of age. His father, the Minister G——, died young. His mother, the Lady Mary, followed him quickly. Frederick was, at that time, in his eighteenth year. In a city, eighteen years are no long period; but in a wilderness—in so magnificent a wilderness as that old principality, the pendulum vibrates with a deeper meaning.

From some peculiar circumstances attending the administration of his father, the young Baron, at the decease of the former, entered immediately upon his vast possessions. Such estates were seldom held before by a nobleman of Hungary. His castles were without number. The chief in point of splendor and extent was the "Palace Metzengerstein." The boundary line of his dominions was never clearly defined; but his principal park embraced a circuit of fifty miles.

Upon the succession of a proprietor so young, with a character so well known, to a fortune so unparalleled, little speculation was afloat in regard to his probable course of conduct. And, indeed, for the space of three days, the behavior of the heir out-heroded Herod, and fairly surpassed the expectations of his most enthusiastic admirers. Shameful debaucheries— flagrant treacheries—unheard-of atrocities—gave his trembling vassals quickly to understand that no servile submission on their part—no punctilios of conscience on his own—were thenceforward to prove any security against the remorseless fangs of a petty Caligula. On the night of the fourth day, the stables of the Castle Berlifitzing were discovered to be on fire; and the unanimous opinion of the neighborhood added the crime of the incendiary to the already hideous list of the Baron's misdemeanors and enormities.

But during the tumult occasioned by this occurrence, the young nobleman himself sat apparently buried in meditation, in a vast and desolate upper apartment of the family palace of Metzengerstein. The rich although faded tapestry hangings which swung gloomily upon the walls, represented the shadowy and majestic forms of a thousand illustrious ancestors. *Here,* rich-ermined priests, and pontifical dignitaries, familiarly seated with the autocrat and the sovereign, put a veto on the wishes of a temporal king, or restrained with the fiat of papal supremacy the rebellious sceptre of the Arch-enemy. *There,* the dark, tall statures of the Princes Metzengerstein—their muscular war-coursers plunging over the carcasses of fallen foes—startled the steadiest nerves with their vigorous expression; and *here,* again, the voluptuous and swan-like figures of the dames of days gone by, floated away in the mazes of an unreal dance to the strains of imaginary melody.

But as the Baron listened, or affected to listen, to the gradually increasing uproar in the stables of Berlifitzing—or perhaps pondered upon some more novel, some more decided act of audacity—his eyes were turned unwittingly to the figure of an enormous, and unnaturally colored horse, represented in the tapestry as belonging to a Saracen ancestor of the family of his rival. The horse itself, in the foreground of the design, stood motionless and statue-like—while, farther back, its discomfited rider perished by the dagger of a Metzengerstein.

On Frederick's lip arose a fiendish expression, as he became

aware of the direction which his glance had, without his consciousness, assumed. Yet he did not remove it. On the contrary,
he could by no means account for the overwhelming anxiety
which appeared falling like a pall upon his senses. It was with
difficulty that he reconciled his dreamy and incoherent feelings
with the certainty of being awake. The longer he gazed, the
more absorbing became the spell—the more impossible did it
appear that he could ever withdraw his glance from the fasci-
nation of that tapestry. But the tumult without becoming suddenly more violent, with a compulsory exertion he diverted his
attention to the glare of ruddy light thrown full by the flaming
stables upon the windows of the apartment.

The action, however, was but momentary; his gaze returned
mechanically to the wall. To his extreme horror and astonishment, the head of the gigantic steed had, in the meantime, altered its position. The neck of the animal, before arched, as if
in compassion, over the prostrate body of its lord, was now extended, at full length, in the direction of the Baron. The eyes,
before invisible, now wore an energetic and human expression,
while they gleamed with a fiery and unusual red; and the dis-
tended lips of the apparently enraged horse left in full view his
sepulchral and disgusting teeth.

Stupified with terror, the young nobleman tottered to
the door. As he threw it open, a flash of red light, streaming
far into the chamber, flung his shadow with a clear outline
against the quivering tapestry; and he shuddered to perceive
that shadow—as he staggered awhile upon the threshold—
assuming the exact position, and precisely filling up the contour, of the relentless and triumphant murderer of the Saracen
Berlifitzing.

To lighten the depression of his spirits, the Baron hurried into the open air. At the principal gate of the palace he encountered three equerries. With much difficulty, and at the imminent peril of their lives, they were restraining the convulsive plunges of a gigantic and fiery-colored horse.

"Whose horse? Where did you get him?" demanded the youth, in a querulous and husky tone, as he became instantly aware that the mysterious steed in the tapestried chamber was the very counterpart of the furious animal before his eyes.

"He is your own property, sire," replied one of the equerries, "at least he is claimed by no other owner. We caught him flying, all smoking and foaming with rage, from the burning stables of the Castle Berlifitzing. Supposing him to have belonged to the old Count's stud of foreign horses, we led him back as an estray. But the grooms there disclaim any title to the creature; which is strange, since he bears evident marks of having made a narrow escape from the flames."

"The letters W. V. B. are also branded very distinctly on his forehead," interrupted a second equerry, "I supposed them, of course, to be the initials of Wilhelm Von Berlifitzing—but all at the castle are positive in denying any knowledge of the horse."

"Extremely singular!" said the young Baron, with a musing air, and apparently unconscious of the meaning of his words. "He is, as you say, a remarkable horse—a prodigious horse! although, as you very justly observe, of a suspicious and untractable character; let him be mine, however," he added, after a pause, "perhaps a rider like Frederick of Metzengerstein, may tame even the devil from the stables of Berlifitzing."

"You are mistaken, my lord; the horse, as I think we mentioned, is *not* from the stables of the Count. If such had been the case, we know our duty better than to bring him into the presence of a noble of your family."

"True!" observed the Baron, drily; and at that instant a page of the bedchamber came from the palace with a heightened color, and a precipitate step. He whispered into his master's ear an account of the sudden disappearance of a small portion of the tapestry, in an apartment which he designated; entering, at the same time, into particulars of a minute and circumstantial character; but from the low tone of voice in which these latter were communicated, nothing escaped to gratify the excited curiosity of the equerries.

The young Frederick, during the conference, seemed agitated by a variety of emotions. He soon, however, recovered his composure, and an expression of determined malignancy settled upon his countenance, as he gave peremptory orders that the apartment in question should be immediately locked up, and the key placed in his own possession.

"Have you heard of the unhappy death of the old hunter Berlifitzing?" said one of his vassals to the Baron, as, after the departure of the page, the huge steed which that nobleman had adopted as his own, plunged and curveted, with redoubled fury, down the long avenue which extended from the palace to the stables of Metzengerstein.

"No!" said the Baron, turning abruptly toward the speaker, "dead! say you?"

"It is indeed true, my lord; and, to the noble of your name, will be, I imagine, no unwelcome intelligence."

A rapid smile shot over the countenance of the listener. "How died he?"

"In his rash exertions to rescue a favorite portion of his hunting stud, he has himself perished miserably in the flames."

"I-n-d-e-e-d-!" ejaculated the Baron, as if slowly and deliberately impressed with the truth of some exciting idea.

"Indeed;" repeated the vassal.

"Shocking!" said the youth, calmly, and turned quietly into the palace.

From this date a marked alteration took place in the outward demeanor of the dissolute young Baron Frederick Von Metzengerstein. Indeed, his behavior disappointed every expectation, and proved little in accordance with the views of many a maneuvering mamma; while his habits and manner, still less than formerly, offered anything congenial with those of the neighboring aristocracy. He was never to be seen beyond the limits of his own domain, and, in this wide and social world, was utterly companionless—unless, indeed, that unnatural, impetuous, and fiery-colored horse, which he henceforward continually bestrode, had any mysterious right to the title of his friend.

Numerous invitations on the part of the neighborhood for a long time, however, periodically came in. "Will the Baron honor our festivals with his presence?" "Will the Baron join us in a hunting of the boar?"—"Metzengerstein does not hunt;" "Metzengerstein will not attend," were the haughty and laconic answers.

These repeated insults were not to be endured by an imperious nobility. Such invitations became less cordial—less frequent—in time they ceased altogether. The widow of the unfortunate Count Berlifitzing was even heard to express a hope "that the Baron might be at home when he did not wish to be at home, since he disdained the company of his equals; and ride when he did not wish to ride, since he preferred the society of a horse." This to be sure was a very silly explosion of hereditary pique; and merely proved how singularly unmeaning our sayings are apt to become, when we desire to be unusually energetic.

The charitable, nevertheless, attributed the alteration in the conduct of the young nobleman to the natural sorrow of a son for the untimely loss of his parents—forgetting, however, his atrocious and reckless behavior during the short period immediately succeeding that bereavement. Some there were, indeed, who suggested a too haughty idea of self-consequence and dignity. Others again (among them may be mentioned the family physician) did not hesitate in speaking of morbid melancholy, and hereditary ill-health; while dark hints, of a more equivocal nature, were current among the multitude.

Indeed, the Baron's perverse attachment to his lately-acquired charger—an attachment which seemed to attain new strength from every fresh example of the animal's ferocious and demon-like propensities—at length became, in the eyes of all reasonable men, a hideous and unnatural fervor. In the glare of noon—at the dead hour of night—in sickness or in health—in calm or in tempest—the young Metzengerstein seemed riveted to the saddle of that colossal horse, whose intractable audacities so well accorded with his own spirit.

There were circumstances, moreover, which coupled with late events, gave an unearthly and portentous character to the mania of the rider, and to the capabilities of the steed. The space passed over in a single leap had been accurately measured, and was found to exceed by an astounding difference, the wildest expectations of the most imaginative. The Baron, besides, had no particular *name* for the animal, although all the rest in his collection were distinguished by characteristic appellations. His stable, too, was appointed at a distance from the rest; and with regard to grooming and other necessary offices, none but the owner in person had ventured to officiate, or even to enter the enclosure of that particular stall. It was also to be observed, that although the three grooms, who had caught the steed as he fled from the conflagration at Berlifitzing, had succeeded in arresting his course, by means of a chain-bridle and noose—yet no one of the three could with any certainty affirm that he had, during that dangerous struggle, or at any period thereafter, actually placed his hand upon the body of the beast. Instances of peculiar intelligence in the demeanor of a noble and high-spirited horse are not to be supposed capable of exciting unreasonable attention, but there were certain circumstances which intruded themselves per force upon the most skeptical and phlegmatic; and it is said there were times when the animal caused the gaping crowd who stood around to recoil in horror from the deep and impressive meaning of his terrible stamp—times when the young Metzengerstein turned pale and shrunk away from the rapid and searching expression of his earnest and human-looking eye.

Among all the retinue of the Baron, however, none were found to doubt the ardor of that extraordinary affection which existed on the part of the young nobleman for the fiery qualities of his horse; at least, none but an insignificant and misshapen little page, whose deformities were in every body's way, and whose opinions were of the least possible importance. He (if his ideas are worth mentioning at all,) had the effrontery to assert that his master never vaulted into the saddle without an unaccountable and almost imperceptible shudder; and that, upon his return from every long-continued and habitual ride, an expression of triumphant malignity distorted every muscle in his countenance.

One tempestuous night, Metzengerstein, awaking from a heavy slumber, descended like a maniac from his chamber, and, mounting in hot haste, bounded away into the mazes of the forest. An occurrence so common attracted no particular attention, but his return was looked for with intense anxiety on the part of his domestics, when, after some hours' absence, the stupendous and magnificent battlements of the Palace Metzengerstein, were discovered crackling and rocking to their very foundation, under the influence of a dense and livid mass of ungovernable fire.

As the flames, when first seen, had already made so terrible a progress that all efforts to save any portion of the building were evidently futile, the astonished neighborhood stood idly around in silent, if not pathetic wonder. But a new and fearful object soon riveted the attention of the multitude, and proved how much more intense is the excitement wrought in the feelings of a crowd by the contemplation of human agony, than that brought about by the most appalling spectacles of inanimate matter.

Up the long avenue of aged oaks which led from the forest to the main entrance of the Palace Metzengerstein, a steed, bearing an unbonneted and disordered rider, was seen leaping with an impetuosity which outstripped the very Demon of the Tempest.

The career of the horseman was indisputably, on his own

part, uncontrollable. The agony of his countenance, the convulsive struggle of his frame, gave evidence of superhuman exertion: but no sound, save a solitary shriek, escaped from his lacerated lips, which were bitten through and through in the intensity of terror. One instant, and the clattering of hoofs resounded sharply and shrilly above the roaring of the flames and the shrieking of the winds—another, and, clearing at a single plunge the gate-way and the moat, the steed bounded far up the tottering staircases of the palace, and, with its rider, disappeared amid the whirlwind of chaotic fire.

The fury of the tempest immediately died away, and a dead calm sullenly succeeded. A white flame still enveloped the building like a shroud, and, streaming far away into the quiet atmosphere, shot forth a glare of preternatural light; while a cloud of smoke settled heavily over the battlements in the distinct colossal figure of—*a horse.*

The Cask of Amontillado

The thousand injuries of Fortunato I had borne as I best could, but when he ventured upon insult, I vowed revenge. You, who so well know the nature of my soul, will not suppose, however, that I gave utterance to a threat. *At length* I would be avenged; this was a point definitely settled—but the very definitiveness with which it was resolved precluded the idea of risk. I must not only punish, but punish with impunity. A wrong is unredressed when retribution overtakes its redresser. It is equally unredressed when the avenger fails to make himself felt as such to him who has done the wrong.

It must be understood that neither by word nor deed had I given Fortunato cause to doubt my good will. I continued, as was my wont, to smile in his face, and he did not perceive that my smile *now* was at the thought of his immolation.

He had a weak point—this Fortunato—although in other regards he was a man to be respected and even feared. He prided himself on his connoisseurship in wine. Few Italians have the true virtuoso spirit. For the most part their enthusiasm is adopted to suit the time and opportunity—to practise imposture upon the British and Austrian *millionaires*. In painting and gemmary, Fortunato, like his countrymen, was a quack—but in the matter of old wines he was sincere. In this respect I did not differ from him materially: I was skillful in the Italian vintages myself, and bought largely whenever I could.

It was about dusk, one evening during the supreme madness of the carnival season, that I encountered my friend. He accosted me with excessive warmth, for he had been drinking much. The man wore motley. He had on a tight-fitting parti-striped dress, and his head was surmounted by the conical cap and bells. I was so pleased to see him, that I thought I should never have done wringing his hand.

I said to him—"My dear Fortunato, you are luckily met. How remarkably well you are looking to-day! But I have received a pipe of what passes for Amontillado, and I have my doubts."

"How?" said he. "Amontillado? A pipe? Impossible! And in the middle of the carnival!"

"I have my doubts," I replied; "and I was silly enough to pay the full Amontillado price without consulting you in the matter. You were not to be found, and I was fearful of losing a bargain."

"Amontillado!"

"I have my doubts."

"Amontillado!"

"And I must satisfy them."

"Amontillado!"

"As you are engaged, I am on my way to Luchesi. If any one has a critical turn, it is he. He will tell me—"

"Luchesi cannot tell Amontillado from Sherry."

"And yet some fools will have it that his taste is a match for your own."

"Come, let us go."

"Whither?"

"To your vaults."

"My friend, no; I will not impose upon your good nature. I perceive you have an engagement. Luchesi—"

"I have no engagement;—come."

"My friend, no. It is not the engagement, but the severe cold with which I perceive you are afflicted. The vaults are insufferably damp. They are encrusted with nitre."

"Let us go, nevertheless. The cold is merely nothing. Amontillado! You have been imposed upon. And as for Luchesi, he cannot distinguish Sherry from Amontillado."

Thus speaking, Fortunato possessed himself of my arm. Putting on a mask of black silk, and drawing a *roquelaire* closely about my person, I suffered him to hurry me to my palazzo.

There were no attendants at home; they had absconded to make merry in honour of the time. I had told them that I should not return until the morning, and had given them explicit orders not to stir from the house. These orders were sufficient, I well knew, to insure their immediate disappearance, one and all, as soon as my back was turned.

I took from their sconces two flambeaux, and giving one to Fortunato, bowed him through several suites of rooms to the archway that led into the vaults. I passed down a long and winding staircase, requesting him to be cautious as he followed. We came at length to the foot of the descent, and stood together on the damp ground of the catacombs of the Montresors.

The gait of my friend was unsteady, and the bells upon his cap jingled as he strode.

"The pipe," said he.

"It is farther on," said I; "but observe the white web-work which gleams from these cavern walls."

He turned towards me, and looked into my eyes with two filmy orbs that distilled the rheum of intoxication.

"Nitre?" he asked, at length.

"Nitre," I replied. "How long have you had that cough?"

"Ugh! ugh! ugh!—ugh! ugh! ugh!—ugh! ugh! ugh!—ugh! ugh! ugh!—ugh! ugh! ugh!"

My poor friend found it impossible to reply for many minutes.

"It is nothing," he said, at last.

"Come," I said, with decision, "we will go back; your health is precious. You are rich, respected, admired, beloved; you are happy, as once I was. You are a man to be missed. For me it is no matter. We will go back; you will be ill, and I cannot be responsible. Besides, there is Luchesi—"

"Enough," he said; "the cough is a mere nothing; it will not kill me. I shall not die of a cough."

"True—true," I replied; "and, indeed, I had no intention of alarming you unnecessarily—but you should use all proper caution. A draught of this Medoc will defend us from the damps."

Here I knocked off the neck of a bottle which I drew from a long row of its fellows that lay upon the mould.

"Drink," I said, presenting him the wine.

He raised it to his lips with a leer. He paused and nodded to me familiarly, while his bells jingled.

"I drink," he said, "to the buried that repose around us."

"And I to your long life."

He again took my arm, and we proceeded.

"These vaults," he said, "are extensive."

"The Montresors," I replied, "were a great and numerous family."

"I forget your arms."

"A huge human foot d'or, in a field azure; the foot crushes a serpent rampant whose fangs are imbedded in the heel."

"And the motto?"

"Nemo me impune lacessit."

"Good!" he said.

The wine sparkled in his eyes and the bells jingled. My own fancy grew warm with the Medoc. We had passed through walls of piled bones, with casks and puncheons intermingling, into the inmost recesses of catacombs. I paused again, and this time I made bold to seize Fortunato by an arm above the elbow.

"The nitre!" I said; "see, it increases. It hangs like moss upon the vaults. We are below the river's bed. The drops of moisture trickle among the bones. Come, we will go back ere it is too late. Your cough—"

"It is nothing," he said; "let us go on. But first, another draught of the Medoc."

I broke and reached him a flagon of De Grave. He emptied it at a breath. His eyes flashed with a fierce light. He laughed and threw the bottle upwards with a gesticulation I did not understand.

I looked at him in surprise. He repeated the movement—a grotesque one.

"You do not comprehend?" he said.

"Not I," I replied.

"Then you are not of the brotherhood."

"How?"

"You are not of the masons."

"Yes, yes," I said; "yes, yes."

"You? Impossible! A mason?"

"A mason," I replied.

"A sign," he said, "a sign."

"It is this," I answered, producing a trowel from beneath the folds of my *roquelaire*.

"You jest," he exclaimed, recoiling a few paces. "But let us proceed to the Amontillado."

"Be it so," I said, replacing the tool beneath the cloak and again offering him my arm. He leaned upon it heavily. We continued our route in search of the Amontillado. We passed through a range of low arches, descended, passed on, and descending again, arrived at a deep crypt, in which the foulness of the air caused our flambeaux rather to glow than flame.

At the most remote end of the crypt there appeared another less spacious. Its walls had been lined with human remains, piled to the vault overhead, in the fashion of the great catacombs of Paris. Three sides of this interior crypt were still ornamented in this manner. From the fourth side the bones had been thrown down, and lay promiscuously upon the earth, forming at one point a mound of some size. Within the wall thus exposed by the displacing of the bones, we perceived a still interior recess, in depth about four feet in width three, in height six or seven. It seemed to have been constructed for no especial use within itself, but formed merely the interval between two of the colossal supports of the roof of the catacombs, and was backed by one of their circumscribing walls of solid granite.

It was in vain that Fortunato, uplifting his dull torch, endeavoured to pry into the depth of the recess. Its termination the feeble light did not enable us to see.

"Proceed," I said; "herein is the Amontillado. As for Luchesi—"

"He is an ignoramus," interrupted my friend, as he stepped unsteadily forward, while I followed immediately at his heels. In an instant he had reached the extremity of the niche, and finding his progress arrested by the rock, stood stupidly bewildered. A moment more and I had fettered him to the granite. In its surface were two iron staples, distant from each other about two feet, horizontally. From one of these depended a short chain, from the other a padlock. Throwing the links about his waist, it was but the work of a few seconds to secure it. He was too much astounded to resist. Withdrawing the key I stepped back from the recess.

"Pass your hand," I said, "over the wall; you cannot help feeling the nitre. Indeed, it is *very* damp. Once more let me *implore* you to return. No? Then I must positively leave you. But I must first render you all the little attentions in my power."

"The Amontillado!" ejaculated my friend, not yet recovered from his astonishment.

"True," I replied; "the Amontillado."

As I said these words I busied myself among the pile of bones of which I have before spoken. Throwing them aside, I soon uncovered a quantity of building stone and mortar. With these materials and with the aid of my trowel, I began vigorously to wall up the entrance of the niche.

I had scarcely laid the first tier of the masonry when I discovered that the intoxication of Fortunato had in a great measure worn off. The earliest indication I had of this was a low moaning cry from the depth of the recess. It was *not* the cry of a drunken man. There was then a long and obstinate silence. I laid the second tier, and the third, and the fourth; and then I heard the furious vibrations of the chain. The noise lasted for several minutes, during which, that I might hearken to it with the more satisfaction, I ceased my labours and sat down upon the bones. When at last the clanking subsided, I resumed the trowel, and finished without interruption the fifth, the sixth, and the seventh tier. The wall was now nearly upon a level with my breast. I again paused, and holding the flambeaux over the mason-work, threw a few feeble rays upon the figure within.

A succession of loud and shrill screams, bursting suddenly from the throat of the chained form, seemed to thrust me violently back. For a brief moment I hesitated—I trembled. Unsheathing my rapier, I began to grope with it about the recess; but the thought of an instant reassured me. I placed my hand upon the solid fabric of the catacombs, and felt satisfied. I reapproached the wall; I replied to the yells of him who clamoured. I re-echoed—I aided—I surpassed them in volume and in strength. I did this, and the clamourer grew still.

It was now midnight, and my task was drawing to a close. I had completed the eighth, the ninth, and the tenth tier. I had finished a portion of the last and the eleventh; there remained but a single stone to be fitted and plastered in. I struggled with its weight; I placed it partially in its destined position. But now there came from out the niche a low laugh that erected the hairs upon my head. It was succeeded by a sad voice, which I had difficulty in recognizing as that of the noble Fortunato. The voice said—

"Ha! ha! ha!—he! he! he!—a very good joke indeed—an excellent jest. We shall have many a rich laugh about it at the palazzo—he! he! he!—over our wine—he! he! he!"

"The Amontillado!" I said.

"He! he! he!—he! he! he!—yes, the Amontillado. But is it not getting late? Will not they be awaiting us at the palazzo, the Lady Fortunato and the rest? Let us be gone."

"Yes," I said, "let us be gone."

"For the love of God, Montresor!"

"Yes," I said, "for the love of God!"

But to these words I hearkened in vain for a reply. I grew impatient. I called aloud—

"Fortunato!"

No answer. I called again—

"Fortunato—"

No answer still. I thrust a torch through the remaining aperture and let it fall within. There came forth in reply only a jingling of the bells. My heart grew sick on account of the dampness of the catacombs. I hastened to make an end of my labour. I forced the last stone into its position; I plastered it up. Against the new masonry I re-erected the old rampart of bones. For the half of a century no mortal has disturbed them. *In pace requiescat!*

Annabel Lee

It was many and many a year ago,
    In a kingdom by the sea,
That a maiden there lived whom you may know
    By the name of Annabel Lee;
And this maiden she lived with no other thought
    Than to love and be loved by me.

I was a child and *she* was a child,
    In this kingdom by the sea:
But we loved with a love that was more than love—
    I and my Annabel Lee—
With a love that the wingéd seraphs of heaven
    Coveted her and me.

And this was the reason that, long ago,
    In this kingdom by the sea,
A wind blew out of a cloud, chilling
    My beautiful Annabel Lee;
So that her high-born kinsman came
    And bore her away from me,
To shut her up in a sepulchre,
    In this kingdom by the sea.

The angels, not half so happy in Heaven,
    Went envying her and me—
Yes!—that was the reason (as all men know,
    In this kingdom by the sea)
That the wind came out of the cloud by night,
    Chilling and killing my Annabel Lee.

But our love it was stronger by far than the love
    Of those who were older than we—
    Of many far wiser than we—
And neither the angels in Heaven above,
    Nor the demons down under the sea,
Can ever dissever my soul from the soul
    Of the beautiful Annabel Lee:

For the moon never beams, without bringing me
dreams
    Of the beautiful Annabel Lee;
And the stars never rise, but I feel the bright eyes
    Of the beautiful Annabel Lee;

And so, all the night-tide, I lie down by the side
Of my darling—my darling—my life and my bride,
    In her sepulchre there by the sea—
    In her tomb by the sounding sea.

The Pit and the Pendulum

Impia tortorum longos hic turba furores
Sanguinis innocui, non satiata, aluit.
Sospite nunc patria, fracto nunc funeris antro,
Mors ubi dira fuit vita salusque patent.

—QUATRAIN COMPOSED FOR THE GATES OF A MARKET TO BE
ERECTED UPON THE SITE OF THE JACOBIN CLUB HOUSE AT PARIS

I was sick—sick unto death with that long agony; and
when they at length unbound me, and I was permitted to
sit, I felt that my senses were leaving me. The sentence—
the dread sentence of death—was the last of distinct ac-
centuation which reached my ears. After that, the sound of
the inquisitorial voices seemed merged in one dreamy indeter-
minate hum. It conveyed to my soul the idea of revolution—
perhaps from its association in fancy with the burr of a mill
wheel. This only for a brief period; for presently I heard no
more. Yet, for a while, I saw; but with how terrible an exaggeration! I saw the lips of the black-robed judges. They appeared
to me white—whiter than the sheet upon which I trace these
words—and thin even to grotesqueness; thin with the intensity
of their expression of firmness—of immoveable resolution—

of stern contempt of human torture. I saw that the decrees of what to me was Fate, were still issuing from those lips. I saw them writhe with a deadly locution. I saw them fashion the syllables of my name; and I shuddered because no sound succeeded. I saw, too, for a few moments of delirious horror, the soft and nearly imperceptible waving of the sable draperies which enwrapped the walls of the apartment. And then my vision fell upon the seven tall candles upon the table. At first they wore the aspect of charity, and seemed white and slender angels who would save me; but then, all at once, there came a most deadly nausea over my spirit, and I felt every fibre in my frame thrill as if I had touched the wire of a galvanic battery, while the angel forms became meaningless spectres, with heads of flame, and I saw that from them there would be no help. And then there stole into my fancy, like a rich musical note, the thought of what sweet rest there must be in the grave. The thought came gently and stealthily, and it seemed long before it attained full appreciation; but just as my spirit came at length properly to feel and entertain it, the figures of the judges vanished, as if magically, from before me; the tall candles sank into nothingness; their flames went out utterly; the blackness of darkness supervened; all sensations appeared swallowed up in a mad rushing descent as of the soul into Hades. Then silence, and stillness, night were the universe.

I had swooned; but still will not say that all of consciousness was lost. What of it there remained I will not attempt to define, or even to describe; yet all was not lost. In the deepest slumber—no! In delirium—no! In a swoon—no! In death—no! even in the grave all is not lost. Else there is no immortality for man. Arousing from the most profound of slumbers, we break the gossamer web of some dream. Yet in a second afterward, (so frail may that web have been) we remember not that we have dreamed. In the return to life from the swoon there are two stages; first, that of the sense of mental or spiritual; secondly, that of the sense of physical, existence. It seems probable that if, upon reaching the second stage, we could recall the impressions of the first, we should find these impressions eloquent in memories of the gulf beyond. And that gulf is—what? How at least shall we distinguish its shadows from those of the tomb? But if the impressions of what I have termed the first stage, are not, at will, recalled, yet, after long interval, do they not come unbidden, while we marvel whence they come? He who has never swooned, is not he who finds strange palaces and wildly familiar faces in coals that glow; is not he who beholds floating in mid-air the sad visions that the many may not view; is not he who ponders over the perfume of some novel flower—is not he whose brain grows bewildered with the meaning of some musical cadence which has never before arrested his attention.

Amid frequent and thoughtful endeavors to remember; amid earnest struggles to regather some token of the state of seeming nothingness into which my soul had lapsed, there have been moments when I have dreamed of success; there have been brief, very brief periods when I have conjured up remembrances which the lucid reason of a later epoch assures me could have had reference only to that condition of seeming unconsciousness. These shadows of memory tell, indistinctly, of tall figures that lifted and bore me in silence down—down—still down—till a hideous dizziness oppressed me at the mere idea of the interminableness of the descent. They tell also of a vague horror at my heart, on account of that heart's unnatural stillness.

Then comes a sense of sudden motionlessness throughout all things; as if those who bore me (a ghastly train!) had outrun, in their descent, the limits of the limitless, and paused from the wearisomeness of their toil. After this I call to mind flatness and dampness; and then all is madness—the madness of a memory which busies itself among forbidden things.

Very suddenly there came back to my soul motion and sound—the tumultuous motion of the heart, and, in my ears, the sound of its beating. Then a pause in which all is blank. Then again sound, and motion, and touch—a tingling sensation pervading my frame. Then the mere consciousness of existence, without thought—a condition which lasted long. Then, very suddenly, thought, and shuddering terror, and earnest endeavor to comprehend my true state. Then a strong desire to lapse into insensibility. Then a rushing revival of soul and a successful effort to move. And now a full memory of the trial, of the judges, of the sable draperies, of the sentence, of the sickness, of the swoon. Then entire forgetfulness of all that followed; of all that a later day and much earnestness of endeavor have enabled me vaguely to recall.

So far, I had not opened my eyes. I felt that I lay upon my back, unbound. I reached out my hand, and it fell heavily upon something damp and hard. There I suffered it to remain for many minutes, while I strove to imagine where and what I could be. I longed, yet dared not to employ my vision. I dreaded the first glance at objects around me. It was not that I feared to look upon things horrible, but that I grew aghast lest there should be nothing to see. At length, with a wild desperation at heart, I quickly unclosed my eyes. My worst thoughts, then, were confirmed. The blackness of eternal night encompassed me. I struggled for breath. The intensity of the darkness seemed to oppress and stifle me. The atmosphere was intolerably close. I still lay quietly, and made effort to exercise my reason. I brought to mind the inquisitorial proceedings, and attempted from that point to deduce my real condition. The sentence had passed; and it appeared to me that a very long interval of time had since elapsed. Yet not for a moment did I suppose myself actually dead. Such a supposition, notwithstanding what we read in fiction, is altogether inconsistent with real existence;—but where and in what state was I? The condemned to death, I knew, perished usually at the autos-da-fe, and one of these had been held on the very night of the day of my trial. Had I been remanded to my dungeon, to await the next sacrifice, which would not take place for many months? This I at once saw could not be. Victims had been in immediate demand. Moreover, my dungeon, as well as all the condemned cells at Toledo, had stone floors, and light was not altogether excluded.

A fearful idea now suddenly drove the blood in torrents upon my heart, and for a brief period, I once more relapsed into insensibility. Upon recovering, I at once started to my feet, trembling convulsively in every fibre. I thrust my arms wildly above and around me in all directions. I felt nothing; yet dreaded to move a step, lest I should be impeded by the walls of a tomb. Perspiration burst from every pore, and stood in cold big beads upon my forehead. The agony of suspense grew at length intolerable, and I cautiously moved forward, with my arms extended, and my eyes straining from their sockets, in the hope of catching some faint ray of light. I proceeded for many paces; but still all was blackness and vacancy. I breathed more freely. It seemed evident that mine was not, at least, the most hideous of fates.

And now, as I still continued to step cautiously onward, there came thronging upon my recollection a thousand vague rumors of the horrors of Toledo. Of the dungeons there had been strange things narrated—fables I had always deemed them—but yet strange, and too ghastly to repeat, save in a whisper. Was I left to perish of starvation in this subterranean world of darkness; or what fate, perhaps even more fearful, awaited me? That the result would be death, and a death of more than customary bitterness, I knew too well the character of my judges to doubt. The mode and the hour were all that occupied or distracted me.

My outstretched hands at length encountered some solid obstruction. It was a wall, seemingly of stone masonry—very smooth, slimy, and cold. I followed it up; stepping with all the careful distrust with which certain antique narratives had inspired me. This process, however, afforded me no means of ascertaining the dimensions of my dungeon; as I might make its circuit, and return to the point whence I set out, without being aware of the fact; so perfectly uniform seemed the wall. I therefore sought the knife which had been in my pocket, when led into the inquisitorial chamber; but it was gone; my clothes had been exchanged for a wrapper of coarse serge. I had thought of forcing the blade in some minute crevice of the masonry, so as to identify my point of departure. The difficulty, nevertheless, was but trivial; although, in the disorder of my fancy, it seemed at first insuperable. I tore a part of the hem from the robe and placed the fragment at full length, and at right angles to the wall. In groping my way around the prison, I could not fail to encounter this rag upon completing the circuit. So, at least I thought: but I had not counted upon the extent of the dungeon, or upon my own weakness. The ground was moist and slippery. I staggered onward for some time, when I stumbled and fell. My excessive fatigue induced me to remain prostrate; and sleep soon overtook me as I lay.

Upon awaking, and stretching forth an arm, I found beside me a loaf and a pitcher with water. I was too much exhausted to reflect upon this circumstance, but ate and drank with avidity. Shortly afterward, I resumed my tour around the prison, and with much toil came at last upon the fragment of the serge. Up to the period when I fell I had counted fifty-two paces, and upon resuming my walk, I had counted forty-eight more;— when I arrived at the rag. There were in all, then, a hundred paces; and, admitting two paces to the yard, I presumed the dungeon to be fifty yards in circuit. I had met, however, with many angles in the wall, and thus I could form no guess at the shape of the vault; for vault I could not help supposing it to be.

I had little object—certainly no hope—in these researches; but a vague curiosity prompted me to continue them. Quitting the wall, I resolved to cross the area of the enclosure. At first I proceeded with extreme caution, for the floor, although seemingly of solid material, was treacherous with slime. At length, however, I took courage, and did not hesitate to step firmly; endeavoring to cross in as direct a line as possible. I had advanced some ten or twelve paces in this manner, when the remnant of the torn hem of my robe became entangled between my legs. I stepped on it, and fell violently on my face.

In the confusion attending my fall, I did not immediately apprehend a somewhat startling circumstance, which yet, in a few seconds afterward, and while I still lay prostrate, arrested my attention. It was this—my chin rested upon the floor of the prison, but my lips and the upper portion of my head, although seemingly at a less elevation than the chin, touched nothing. At the same time my forehead seemed bathed in a clammy vapor, and the peculiar smell of decayed fungus arose to my nostrils. I put forward my arm, and shuddered to find that I had fallen at the very brink of a circular pit, whose extent, of course, I had no means of ascertaining at the moment. Groping about the masonry just below the margin, I succeeded in dislodging a small fragment, and let it fall into the abyss. For many seconds I hearkened to its reverberations as it dashed against the sides of the chasm in its descent; at length there was a sullen plunge into water, succeeded by loud echoes. At the same moment there came a sound resembling the quick opening, and as rapid closing of a door overhead, while a faint gleam of light flashed suddenly through the gloom, and as suddenly faded away.

I saw clearly the doom which had been prepared for me, and congratulated myself upon the timely accident by which I had escaped. Another step before my fall, and the world had seen me no more. And the death just avoided, was of that very character which I had regarded as fabulous and frivolous in the tales respecting the Inquisition. To the victims of its tyranny, there was the choice of death with its direst physical agonies, or death with its most hideous moral horrors. I had been reserved for the latter. By long suffering my nerves had been unstrung, until I trembled at the sound of my own voice, and had become in every respect a fitting subject for the species of torture which awaited me.

Shaking in every limb, I groped my way back to the wall;

resolving there to perish rather than risk the terrors of the wells, of which my imagination now pictured many in various positions about the dungeon. In other conditions of mind I might have had courage to end my misery at once by a plunge into one of these abysses; but now I was the veriest of cowards. Neither could I forget what I had read of these pits—that the sudden extinction of life formed no part of their most horrible plan.

Agitation of spirit kept me awake for many long hours; but at length I again slumbered. Upon arousing, I found by my side, as before, a loaf and a pitcher of water. A burning thirst consumed me, and I emptied the vessel at a draught. It must have been drugged; for scarcely had I drunk, before I became irresistibly drowsy. A deep sleep fell upon me—a sleep like that of death. How long it lasted of course, I know not; but when, once again, I unclosed my eyes, the objects around me were visible. By a wild sulphurous lustre, the origin of which I could not at first determine, I was enabled to see the extent and aspect of the prison.

In its size I had been greatly mistaken. The whole circuit of its walls did not exceed twenty-five yards. For some minutes this fact occasioned me a world of vain trouble; vain indeed! for what could be of less importance, under the terrible circumstances which environed me, then the mere dimensions of my dungeon? But my soul took a wild interest in trifles, and I busied myself in endeavors to account for the error I had committed in my measurement. The truth at length flashed upon me. In my first attempt at exploration I had counted fifty-two paces, up to the period when I fell; I must then have been within a pace or two of the fragment of serge; in fact, I had nearly performed the circuit of the vault. I then slept, and upon awaking, I must have returned upon my steps—thus supposing the circuit nearly double what it actually was. My confusion of mind prevented me from observing that I began my tour with the wall to the left, and ended it with the wall to the right.

I had been deceived, too, in respect to the shape of the en-closure. In feeling my way I had found many angles, and thus deduced an idea of great irregularity; so potent is the effect of total darkness upon one arousing from lethargy or sleep! The angles were simply those of a few slight depressions, or niches, at odd intervals. The general shape of the prison was square. What I had taken for masonry seemed now to be iron, or some other metal, in huge plates, whose sutures or joints occasioned the depression. The entire surface of this metallic enclosure was rudely daubed in all the hideous and repulsive devices to which the charnel superstition of the monks has given rise. The figures of fiends in aspects of menace, with skeleton forms, and other more really fearful images, overspread and disfigured the walls. I observed that the outlines of these monstrosities were sufficiently distinct, but that the colors seemed faded and blurred, as if from the effects of a damp atmosphere. I now noticed the floor, too, which was of stone. In the centre yawned the circular pit from whose jaws I had escaped; but it was the only one in the dungeon.

All this I saw indistinctly and by much effort: for my per-sonal condition had been greatly changed during slumber. I now lay upon my back, and at full length, on a species of low framework of wood. To this I was securely bound by a long strap resembling a surcingle. It passed in many convolutions about my limbs and body, leaving at liberty only my head, and my left arm to such extent that I could, by dint of much exertion, supply myself with food from an earthen dish which lay by my side on the floor. I saw, to my horror, that the pitcher had been removed. I say to my horror; for I was consumed with intolerable thirst. This thirst it appeared to be the design of my persecutors to stimulate: for the food in the dish was meat pungently seasoned.

Looking upward, I surveyed the ceiling of my prison. It was some thirty or forty feet overhead, and constructed much as the side walls. In one of its panels a very singular figure riveted my whole attention. It was the painted figure of Time as he is commonly represented, save that, in lieu of a scythe, he held what, at a casual glance, I supposed to be the pictured image of a huge pendulum such as we see on antique clocks. There was something, however, in the appearance of this machine which caused me to regard it more attentively. While I gazed directly upward at it (for its position was immediately over my own) I fancied that I saw it in motion. In an instant afterward the fancy was confirmed. Its sweep was brief, and of course slow. I watched it for some minutes, somewhat in fear, but more in wonder. Wearied at length with observing its dull movement, I turned my eyes upon the other objects in the cell.

A slight noise attracted my notice, and, looking to the floor, I saw several enormous rats traversing it. They had issued from the well, which lay just within view to my right. Even then, while I gazed, they came up in troops, hurriedly, with ravenous eyes, allured by the scent of the meat. From this it required much effort and attention to scare them away.

It might have been half an hour, perhaps even an hour, (for I could take but imperfect note of time) before I again cast my eyes upward. What I then saw confounded and amazed me. The sweep of the pendulum had increased in extent by nearly a yard. As a natural consequence, its velocity was also much greater. But what mainly disturbed me was the idea that had perceptibly descended. I now observed—with what horror it is needless to say—that its nether extremity was formed of a crescent of glittering steel, about a foot in length from horn to horn; the horns upward, and the under edge evidently as keen as that of a razor. Like a razor also, it seemed massy and heavy, tapering from the edge into a solid and broad structure above. It was appended to a weighty rod of brass, and the whole hissed as it swung through the air.

I could no longer doubt the doom prepared for me by monkish ingenuity in torture. My cognizance of the pit had become known to the inquisitorial agents—the pit whose horrors had been destined for so bold a recusant as myself—the pit, typical of hell, and regarded by rumor as the Ultima Thule of all their punishments. The plunge into this pit I had avoided by the merest of accidents, I knew that surprise, or entrapment into torment, formed an important portion of all the grotesquerie of these dungeon deaths. Having failed to fall, it was no part of the demon plan to hurl me into the abyss; and thus (there being no alternative) a different and a milder destruction awaited me. Milder! I half smiled in my agony as I thought of such application of such a term.

What boots it to tell of the long, long hours of horror more than mortal, during which I counted the rushing vibrations of the steel! Inch by inch—line by line—with a descent only appreciable at intervals that seemed ages—down and still down it came! Days passed—it might have been that many days passed—ere it swept so closely over me as to fan me with its acrid breath. The odor of the sharp steel forced itself into my nostrils. I prayed—I wearied heaven with my prayer for its more speedy descent. I grew frantically mad, and struggled to force myself upward against the sweep of the fearful scimitar. And then I fell suddenly calm, and lay smiling at the glittering death, as a child at some rare bauble.

There was another interval of utter insensibility; it was brief; for, upon again lapsing into life there had been no perceptible descent in the pendulum. But it might have been long; for I knew there were demons who took note of my swoon, and who could have arrested the vibration at pleasure. Upon my recovery, too, I felt very—oh, inexpressibly sick and weak, as if through long inanition. Even amid the agonies of that period, the human nature craved food. With painful effort I outstretched my left arm as far as my bonds permitted, and took possession of the small remnant which had been spared me by the rats. As I put a portion of it within my lips, there rushed to my mind a half formed thought of joy—of hope. Yet what business had I with hope? It was, as I say, a half formed thought—man has many such which are never completed. I felt that it was of joy—of hope; but felt also that it had perished in its formation. In vain I struggled to perfect—to regain it. Long suffering had nearly annihilated all my ordinary powers of mind. I was an imbecile—an idiot.

The vibration of the pendulum was at right angles to my length. I saw that the crescent was designed to cross the region of the heart. It would fray the serge of my robe—it would return and repeat its operations—again—and again. Notwithstanding terrifically wide sweep (some thirty feet or more) and the hissing vigor of its descent, sufficient to sunder these very walls of iron, still the fraying of my robe would be all that, for several minutes, it would accomplish. And at this thought I paused. I dared not go farther than this reflection. I dwelt upon it with a pertinacity of attention—as if, in so dwelling, I could arrest here the descent of the steel. I forced myself to ponder upon the sound of the crescent as it should pass across the garment—upon the peculiar thrilling sensation which the friction of cloth produces on the nerves. I pondered upon all this frivolity until my teeth were on edge.

Down—steadily down it crept. I took a frenzied pleasure in contrasting its downward with its lateral velocity. To the right—to the left—far and wide—with the shriek of a damned spirit; to my heart with the stealthy pace of the tiger! I alternately laughed and howled as the one or the other idea grew predominant.

Down—certainly, relentlessly down! It vibrated within three inches of my bosom! I struggled violently, furiously, to free my left arm. This was free only from the elbow to the hand. I could reach the latter, from the platter beside me, to my mouth, with great effort, but no farther. Could I have broken the fastenings above the elbow, I would have seized and attempted to arrest the pendulum. I might as well have attempted to arrest an avalanche!

Down—still unceasingly—still inevitably down! I gasped and struggled at each vibration. I shrunk convulsively at its every sweep. My eyes followed its outward or upward whirls with the eagerness of the most unmeaning despair; they closed themselves spasmodically at the descent, although death would have been a relief, oh! how unspeakable! Still I quivered in every nerve to think how slight a sinking of the machinery would precipitate that keen, glistening axe upon my bosom. It was hope that prompted the nerve to quiver—the frame to shrink. It was hope—the hope that triumphs on the rack—that whispers to the death-condemned even in the dungeons of the Inquisition.

I saw that some ten or twelve vibrations would bring the steel in actual contact with my robe, and with this observation there suddenly came over my spirit all the keen, collected calmness of despair. For the first time during many hours—or perhaps days—I thought. It now occurred to me that the bandage, or surcingle, which enveloped me, was unique. I was tied by no separate cord. The first stroke of the razorlike crescent athwart any portion of the band, would so detach it that it might be unwound from my person by means of my left hand. But how fearful, in that case, the proximity of the steel! The result of the slightest struggle how deadly! Was it likely, moreover, that the minions of the torturer had not foreseen and provided for this possibility! Was it probable that the bandage crossed my bosom in the track of the pendulum? Dreading to find my faint, and, as it seemed, my last hope frustrated, I so far elevated my head as to obtain a distinct view of my breast. The surcingle enveloped my limbs and body close in all directions—save in the path of the destroying crescent.

Scarcely had I dropped my head back into its original position, when there flashed upon my mind what I cannot better describe than as the unformed half of that idea of deliverance to which I have previously alluded, and of which a moiety only floated indeterminately through my brain when I raised food to my burning lips. The whole thought was now present—feeble, scarcely sane, scarcely definite,—but still entire. I proceeded at once, with the nervous energy of despair, to attempt its execution.

For many hours the immediate vicinity of the low framework upon which I lay, had been literally swarming with rats. They were wild, bold, ravenous; their red eyes glaring upon me as if they waited but for motionlessness on my part to make me their prey. "To what food," I thought, "have they been accustomed in the well?"

They had devoured, in spite of all my efforts to prevent them, all but a small remnant of the contents of the dish. I had fallen into an habitual see-saw, or wave of the hand about the platter: and, at length, the unconscious uniformity of the movement deprived it of effect. In their voracity the vermin frequently fastened their sharp fangs in my fingers. With the particles of the oily and spicy viand which now remained, I thoroughly rubbed the bandage wherever I could reach it; then, raising my hand from the floor, I lay breathlessly still.

At first the ravenous animals were startled and terrified at the change—at the cessation of movement. They shrank alarmedly back; many sought the well. But this was only for a moment. I had not counted in vain upon their voracity. Observing that I remained without motion, one or two of the boldest leaped upon the frame-work, and smelt at the surcingle. This seemed the signal for a general rush. Forth from the well they hurried in fresh troops. They clung to the wood—they overran it, and leaped in hundreds upon my person. The measured movement of the pendulum disturbed them not at all. Avoiding its strokes they busied themselves with the anointed bandage. They pressed—they swarmed upon me in ever accumulating heaps. They writhed upon my throat; their cold lips sought my own; I was half stifled by their thronging pressure; disgust, for which the world has no name, swelled my bosom, and chilled, with a heavy clamminess, my heart. Yet one minute, and I felt that the struggle would be over. Plainly I perceived the loosening of the bandage. I knew that in more than one place it must be already severed. With a more than human resolution I lay still.

Nor had I erred in my calculations—nor had I endured in vain. I at length felt that I was free. The surcingle hung in ribands from my body. But the stroke of the pendulum already pressed upon my bosom. It had divided the serge of the robe. It had cut through the linen beneath. Twice again it swung, and a sharp sense of pain shot through every nerve. But the moment of escape had arrived. At a wave of my hand my deliverers hurried tumultuously away. With a steady movement—cautious, sidelong, shrinking, and slow—I slid from the embrace of the bandage and beyond the reach of the scimitar. For the moment, at least, I was free.

Free!—and in the grasp of the Inquisition! I had scarcely stepped from my wooden bed of horror upon the stone floor of the prison, when the motion of the hellish machine ceased and I beheld it drawn up, by some invisible force, through the ceiling. This was a lesson which I took desperately to heart. My every motion was undoubtedly watched. Free!—I had but escaped death in one form of agony, to be delivered unto worse than death in some other. With that thought I rolled my eyes nervously around on the barriers of iron that hemmed me in. Something unusual—some change which, at first, I could not appreciate distinctly—it was obvious, had taken place in the apartment. For many minutes of a dreamy and trembling abstraction, I busied myself in vain, unconnected conjecture. During this period, I became aware, for the first time, of the origin of the sulphurous light which illumined the cell. It proceeded from a fissure, about half an inch in width, extending entirely around the prison at the base of the walls, which thus appeared, and were, completely separated from the floor. I endeavored, but of course in vain, to look through the aperture.

As I arose from the attempt, the mystery of the alteration in the chamber broke at once upon my understanding. I have observed that, although the outlines of the figures upon the walls were sufficiently distinct, yet the colors seemed blurred and indefinite. These colors had now assumed, and were momentarily assuming, a startling and most intense brilliancy, that gave to the spectral and fiendish portraitures an aspect that might have thrilled even firmer nerves than my own. Demon eyes, of a wild and ghastly vivacity, glared upon me in a thousand directions, where none had been visible before, and gleamed with the lurid lustre of a fire that I could not force my imagination to regard as unreal.

Unreal!—Even while I breathed there came to my nostrils the breath of the vapour of heated iron! A suffocating odour pervaded the prison! A deeper glow settled each moment in the eyes that glared at my agonies! A richer tint of crimson diffused itself over the pictured horrors of blood. I panted! I gasped for breath! There could be no doubt of the design of my tormentors—oh! most unrelenting! oh! most demoniac of men! I shrank from the glowing metal to the centre of the cell. Amid the thought of the fiery destruction that impended, the idea of the coolness of the well came over my soul like balm. I rushed to its deadly brink. I threw my straining vision below. The glare from the enkindled roof illumined its inmost recesses. Yet, for a wild moment, did my spirit refuse to comprehend the meaning of what I saw. At length it forced—it wrestled its way into my soul—it burned itself in upon my shuddering reason.—Oh! for a voice to speak!—oh! horror!—oh! any horror but this! With a shriek, I rushed from the margin, and buried my face in my hands—weeping bitterly.

The heat rapidly increased, and once again I looked up, shuddering as with a fit of the ague. There had been a second change in the cell—and now the change was obviously in the form. As before, it was in vain that I, at first, endeavoured to appreciate or understand what was taking place. But not long was I left in doubt. The Inquisitorial vengeance had been hurried by my two-fold escape, and there was to be no more dallying with the King of Terrors. The room had been square. I saw that two of its iron angles were now acute—two, consequently, obtuse. The fearful difference quickly increased with a low rumbling or moaning sound. In an instant the apartment had shifted its form into that of a lozenge. But the alteration stopped not here—I neither hoped nor desired it to stop. I could have clasped the red walls to my bosom as a garment of eternal peace. "Death," I said, "any death but that of the pit!" Fool! might I have not known that into the pit it was the object of the burning iron to urge me? Could I resist its glow? or, if even that, could I withstand its pressure? And now, flatter and flatter grew the lozenge, with a rapidity that left me no time for contemplation. Its centre, and of course, its greatest width, came just over the yawning gulf. I shrank back—but the closing walls pressed me resistlessly onward. At length for my seared and writhing body there was no longer an inch of foothold on the firm floor of the prison. I struggled no more, but the agony of my soul found vent in one loud, long, and final scream of despair. I felt that I tottered upon the brink—I averted my eyes—

There was a discordant hum of human voices! There was a loud blast as of many trumpets! There was a harsh grating as of a thousand thunders! The fiery walls rushed back! An outstretched arm caught my own as I fell, fainting, into the abyss. It was that of General Lasalle. The French army had entered Toledo. The Inquisition was in the hands of its enemies.

The Purloined Letter

Nil sapientiae odiosius acumine nimio.

—Seneca

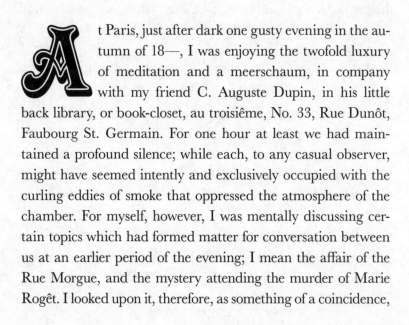t Paris, just after dark one gusty evening in the autumn of 18—, I was enjoying the twofold luxury of meditation and a meerschaum, in company with my friend C. Auguste Dupin, in his little back library, or book-closet, au troisiême, No. 33, Rue Dunôt, Faubourg St. Germain. For one hour at least we had maintained a profound silence; while each, to any casual observer, might have seemed intently and exclusively occupied with the curling eddies of smoke that oppressed the atmosphere of the chamber. For myself, however, I was mentally discussing certain topics which had formed matter for conversation between us at an earlier period of the evening; I mean the affair of the Rue Morgue, and the mystery attending the murder of Marie Rogêt. I looked upon it, therefore, as something of a coincidence,

when the door of our apartment was thrown open and admitted our old acquaintance, Monsieur G——, the Prefect of the Parisian police.

We gave him a hearty welcome; for there was nearly half as much of the entertaining as of the contemptible about the man, and we had not seen him for several years. We had been sitting in the dark, and Dupin now arose for the purpose of lighting a lamp, but sat down again, without doing so, upon G.'s saying that he had called to consult us, or rather to ask the opinion of my friend, about some official business which had occasioned a great deal of trouble.

"If it is any point requiring reflection," observed Dupin, as he forebore to enkindle the wick, "we shall examine it to better purpose in the dark."

"That is another of your odd notions," said the Prefect, who had a fashion of calling every thing "odd" that was beyond his comprehension, and thus lived amid an absolute legion of "oddities."

"Very true," said Dupin, as he supplied his visiter with a pipe, and rolled towards him a comfortable chair.

"And what is the difficulty now?" I asked. "Nothing more in the assassination way, I hope?"

"Oh no; nothing of that nature. The fact is, the business is very simple indeed, and I make no doubt that we can manage it sufficiently well ourselves; but then I thought Dupin would like to hear the details of it, because it is so excessively odd."

"Simple and odd," said Dupin.

"Why, yes; and not exactly that, either. The fact is, we have all been a good deal puzzled because the affair is so simple, and yet baffles us altogether."

"Perhaps it is the very simplicity of the thing which puts you at fault," said my friend.

"What nonsense you do talk!" replied the Prefect, laughing heartily.

"Perhaps the mystery is a little too plain," said Dupin.

"Oh, good heavens! who ever heard of such an idea?"

"A little too self-evident."

"Ha! ha! ha—ha! ha! ha!—ho! ho! ho!" roarcd our visiter, profoundly amused, "oh, Dupin, you will be the death of me yet!"

"And what, after all, is the matter on hand?" I asked.

"Why, I will tell you," replied the Prefect, as he gave a long, steady and contemplative puff, and settled himself in his chair. "I will tell you in a few words; but, before I begin, let me caution you that this is an affair demanding the greatest secrecy, and that I should most probably lose the position I now hold, were it known that I confided it to any one."

"Proceed," said I.

"Or not," said Dupin.

"Well, then; I have received personal information, from a very high quarter, that a certain document of the last importance, has been purloined from the royal apartments. The individual who purloined it is known; this beyond a doubt; he was seen to take it. It is known, also, that it still remains in his possession."

"How is this known?" asked Dupin.

"It is clearly inferred," replied the Prefect, "from the nature of the document, and from the non-appearance of certain results which would at once arise from its passing out of the robber's possession; that is to say, from his employing it as he must design in the end to employ it."

"Be a little more explicit," I said.

"Well, I may venture so far as to say that the paper gives its holder a certain power in a certain quarter where such power is immensely valuable." The Prefect was fond of the cant of diplomacy.

"Still I do not quite understand," said Dupin.

"No? Well; the disclosure of the document to a third person, who shall be nameless, would bring in question the honor of a personage of most exalted station; and this fact gives the holder of the document an ascendancy over the illustrious personage whose honor and peace are so jeopardized."

"But this ascendancy," I interposed, "would depend upon the robber's knowledge of the loser's knowledge of the robber. Who would dare—"

"The thief," said G., "is the Minister D——, who dares all things, those unbecoming as well as those becoming a man. The method of the theft was not less ingenious than bold. The document in question—a letter, to be frank—had been received by the personage robbed while alone in the royal boudoir. During its perusal she was suddenly interrupted by the entrance of the other exalted personage from whom especially it was her wish to conceal it. After a hurried and vain endeavor to thrust it in a drawer, she was forced to place it, open as it was, upon a table. The address, however, was uppermost, and, the contents thus unexposed, the letter escaped notice. At this juncture enters the Minister D——. His lynx eye immediately perceives the paper, recognises the handwriting of the address, observes the confusion of the personage addressed, and fathoms her secret. After some business transactions, hurried through in his ordinary manner, he produces a letter somewhat similar to the one in question, opens it, pretends to read it, and then places it in close juxtaposition to the other. Again he converses, for some fifteen minutes, upon the public affairs. At length, in taking leave, he takes also from the table the letter to which he had no claim. Its rightful owner saw, but, of course, dared not call attention to the act, in the presence of the third personage who stood at her elbow. The minister decamped; leaving his own letter—one of no importance—upon the table."

"Here, then," said Dupin to me, "you have precisely what you demand to make the ascendancy complete—the robber's knowledge of the loser's knowledge of the robber."

"Yes," replied the Prefect; "and the power thus attained has, for some months past, been wielded, for political purposes, to a very dangerous extent. The personage robbed is more thoroughly convinced, every day, of the necessity of reclaiming her letter. But this, of course, cannot be done openly. In fine, driven to despair, she has committed the matter to me."

"Than whom," said Dupin, amid a perfect whirlwind of smoke, "no more sagacious agent could, I suppose, be desired, or even imagined."

"You flatter me," replied the Prefect; "but it is possible that some such opinion may have been entertained."

"It is clear," said I, "as you observe, that the letter is still in possession of the minister; since it is this possession, and not any employment of the letter, which bestows the power. With the employment the power departs."

"True," said G.; "and upon this conviction I proceeded. My first care was to make thorough search of the minister's hotel; and here my chief embarrassment lay in the necessity of searching without his knowledge. Beyond all things, I have been warned of the danger which would result from giving him reason to suspect our design."

"But," said I, "you are quite au fait in these investigations. The Parisian police have done this thing often before."

"O yes; and for this reason I did not despair. The habits of the minister gave me, too, a great advantage. He is frequently absent from home all night. His servants are by no means numerous. They sleep at a distance from their master's apartment, and, being chiefly Neapolitans, are readily made drunk. I have keys, as you know, with which I can open any chamber or cabinet in Paris. For three months a night has not passed, during the greater part of which I have not been engaged, personally, in ransacking the D—— Hotel. My honor is interested, and, to mention a great secret, the reward is enormous. So I did not abandon the search until I had become fully satisfied that the thief is a more astute man than myself. I fancy that I have investigated every nook and corner of the premises in which it is possible that the paper can be concealed."

"But is it not possible," I suggested, "that although the letter may be in possession of the minister, as it unquestionably is, he may have concealed it elsewhere than upon his own premises?"

"This is barely possible," said Dupin. "The present peculiar condition of affairs at court, and especially of those intrigues in which D—— is known to be involved, would render the instant availability of the document—its susceptibility of being produced at a moment's notice—a point of nearly equal importance with its possession."

"Its susceptibility of being produced?" said I.

"That is to say, of being destroyed," said Dupin.

"True," I observed; "the paper is clearly then upon the

premises. As for its being upon the person of the minister, we may consider that as out of the question."

"Entirely," said the Prefect. "He has been twice waylaid, as if by footpads, and his person rigorously searched under my own inspection."

"You might have spared yourself this trouble," said Dupin. "D——, I presume, is not altogether a fool, and, if not, must have anticipated these waylayings, as a matter of course."

"Not altogether a fool," said G., "but then he's a poet, which I take to be only one remove from a fool."

"True," said Dupin, after a long and thoughtful whiff from his meerschaum, "although I have been guilty of certain dog-grel myself."

"Suppose you detail," said I, "the particulars of your search."

"Why the fact is, we took our time, and we searched every where. I have had long experience in these affairs. I took the entire building, room by room; devoting the nights of a whole week to each. We examined, first, the furniture of each apartment. We opened every possible drawer; and I presume you know that, to a properly trained police agent, such a thing as a secret drawer is impossible. Any man is a dolt who permits a 'secret' drawer to escape him in a search of this kind. The thing is so plain. There is a certain amount of bulk—of space—to be accounted for in every cabinet. Then we have accurate rules. The fiftieth part of a line could not escape us. After the cabinets we took the chairs. The cushions we probed with the fine long needles you have seen me employ. From the tables we removed the tops."

"Why so?"

"Sometimes the top of a table, or other similarly arranged piece of furniture, is removed by the person wishing to conceal an article; then the leg is excavated, the article deposited within the cavity, and the top replaced. The bottoms and tops of bedposts are employed in the same way."

"But could not the cavity be detected by sounding?" I asked.

"By no means, if, when the article is deposited, a sufficient wadding of cotton be placed around it. Besides, in our case, we were obliged to proceed without noise."

"But you could not have removed—you could not have taken to pieces all articles of furniture in which it would have been possible to make a deposit in the manner you mention. A letter may be compressed into a thin spiral roll, not differing much in shape or bulk from a large knitting-needle, and in this form it might be inserted into the rung of a chair, for example. You did not take to pieces all the chairs?"

"Certainly not; but we did better—we examined the rungs of every chair in the hotel, and, indeed the jointings of every description of furniture, by the aid of a most powerful microscope. Had there been any traces of recent disturbance we should not have failed to detect it instantly. A single grain of gimlet-dust, for example, would have been as obvious as an apple. Any disorder in the glueing—any unusual gaping in the joints—would have sufficed to insure detection."

"I presume you looked to the mirrors, between the boards and the plates, and you probed the beds and the bed-clothes, as well as the curtains and carpets."

"That of course; and when we had absolutely completed every particle of the furniture in this way, then we examined the house itself. We divided its entire surface into compartments, which we numbered, so that none might be missed; then we scrutinized each individual square inch throughout the premises, including the two houses immediately adjoining, with the microscope, as before."

"The two houses adjoining!" I exclaimed; "you must have had a great deal of trouble."

"We had; but the reward offered is prodigious!"

"You include the grounds about the houses?"

"All the grounds are paved with brick. They gave us comparatively little trouble. We examined the moss between the bricks, and found it undisturbed."

"You looked among D——'s papers, of course, and into the books of the library?"

"Certainly; we opened every package and parcel; we not only opened every book, but we turned over every leaf in each volume, not contenting ourselves with a mere shake, according to the fashion of some of our police officers. We also measured the thickness of every book-cover, with the most accurate admeasurement, and applied to each the most jealous scrutiny of the microscope. Had any of the bindings been recently meddled with, it would have been utterly impossible that the fact should have escaped observation. Some five or six volumes, just from the hands of the binder, we carefully probed, longitudinally, with the needles."

"You explored the floors beneath the carpets?"

"Beyond doubt. We removed every carpet, and examined the boards with the microscope."

"And the paper on the walls?"

"Yes."

"You looked into the cellars?"

"We did."

"Then," I said, "you have been making a miscalculation, and the letter is not upon the premises, as you suppose."

"I fear you are right there," said the Prefect. "And now, Dupin, what would you advise me to do?"

"To make a thorough re-search of the premises."

"That is absolutely needless," replied G———. "I am not more sure that I breathe than I am that the letter is not at the Hotel."

"I have no better advice to give you," said Dupin. "You have, of course, an accurate description of the letter?"

"Oh yes!"—And here the Prefect, producing a memorandum-book proceeded to read aloud a minute account of the internal, and especially of the external appearance of the missing document. Soon after finishing the perusal of this description, he took his departure, more entirely depressed in spirits than I had ever known the good gentleman before. In about a month afterwards he paid us another visit, and found us occupied very nearly as before. He took a pipe and a chair and entered into some ordinary conversation. At length I said,—

"Well, but G———, what of the purloined letter? I presume you have at last made up your mind that there is no such thing as overreaching the Minister?"

"Confound him, say I—yes; I made the re-examination, however, as Dupin suggested—but it was all labor lost, as I knew it would be."

"How much was the reward offered, did you say?" asked Dupin.

"Why, a very great deal—a very liberal reward—I don't

like to say how much, precisely; but one thing I will say, that I wouldn't mind giving my individual check for fifty thousand francs to any one who could obtain me that letter. The fact is, it is becoming of more and more importance every day; and the reward has been lately doubled. If it were trebled, however, I could do no more than I have done."

"Why, yes," said Dupin, drawlingly, between the whiffs of his meerschaum, "I really—think, G——, you have not exerted yourself—to the utmost in this matter. You might—do a little more, I think, eh?"

"How?—in what way?"

"Why—puff, puff—you might—puff, puff—employ counsel in the matter, eh?—puff, puff, puff. Do you remember the story they tell of Abernethy?"

"No; hang Abernethy!"

"To be sure! hang him and welcome. But, once upon a time, a certain rich miser conceived the design of spunging upon this Abernethy for a medical opinion. Getting up, for this purpose, an ordinary conversation in a private company, he insinuated his case to the physician, as that of an imaginary individual.

"'We will suppose,' said the miser, 'that his symptoms are such and such; now, doctor, what would you have directed him to take?'

"'Take!' said Abernethy, 'why, take advice, to be sure.'"

"But," said the Prefect, a little discomposed, "I am perfectly willing to take advice, and to pay for it. I would really give fifty thousand francs to any one who would aid me in the matter."

"In that case," replied Dupin, opening a drawer, and producing a check-book, "you may as well fill me up a check for the amount mentioned. When you have signed it, I will hand you the letter."

I was astounded. The Prefect appeared absolutely thunderstricken. For some minutes he remained speechless and motionless, looking incredulously at my friend with open mouth, and eyes that seemed starting from their sockets; then, apparently recovering himself in some measure, he seized a pen, and after several pauses and vacant stares, finally filled up and signed a check for fifty thousand francs, and handed it across the table to Dupin. The latter examined it carefully and deposited it in his pocket-book; then, unlocking an escritoire, took thence a letter and gave it to the Prefect. This functionary grasped it in a perfect agony of joy, opened it with a trembling hand, cast a rapid glance at its contents, and then, scrambling and struggling to the door, rushed at length unceremoniously from the room and from the house, without having uttered a syllable since Dupin had requested him to fill up the check.

When he had gone, my friend entered into some explanations.

"The Parisian police," he said, "are exceedingly able in their way. They are persevering, ingenious, cunning, and thoroughly versed in the knowledge which their duties seem chiefly to demand. Thus, when G—— detailed to us his mode of searching the premises at the Hotel D——, I felt entire confidence in his having made a satisfactory investigation—so far as his labors extended."

"So far as his labors extended?" said I.

"Yes," said Dupin. "The measures adopted were not only the best of their kind, but carried out to absolute perfection. Had the letter been deposited within the range of their search, these fellows would, beyond a question, have found it."

I merely laughed—but he seemed quite serious in all that he said.

"The measures, then," he continued, "were good in their kind, and well executed; their defect lay in their being inapplicable to the case, and to the man. A certain set of highly ingenious resources are, with the Prefect, a sort of Procrustean bed, to which he forcibly adapts his designs. But he perpetually errs by being too deep or too shallow, for the matter in hand; and many a schoolboy is a better reasoner than he. I knew one about eight years of age, whose success at guessing in the game of 'even and odd' attracted universal admiration. This game is simple, and is played with marbles. One player holds in his hand a number of these toys, and demands of another whether that number is even or odd. If the guess is right, the guesser wins one; if wrong, he loses one. The boy to whom I allude won all the marbles of the school. Of course he had some principle of guessing; and this lay in mere observation and admeasurement of the astuteness of his opponents. For example, an arrant simpleton is his opponent, and, holding up his closed hand, asks, 'are they even or odd?' Our schoolboy replies, 'odd,' and loses; but upon the second trial he wins, for he then says to himself, 'the simpleton had them even upon the first trial, and his amount of cunning is just sufficient to make him have them odd upon the second; I will therefore guess odd;'—he guesses odd, and wins. Now, with a simpleton a degree above the first, he would have reasoned thus: 'This fellow finds that in the first instance I guessed odd, and, in the second, he will propose to himself, upon the first impulse, a simple variation from even to odd, as did the first simpleton; but then a second thought will suggest that this is too simple a variation, and finally he will decide upon putting it even as before. I will therefore guess even;'—he guesses even, and wins. Now this mode of reasoning in the schoolboy, whom his fellows termed 'lucky,'—what, in its last analysis, is it?"

"It is merely," I said, "an identification of the reasoner's intellect with that of his opponent."

"It is," said Dupin; "and, upon inquiring of the boy by what means he effected the thorough identification in which his success consisted, I received answer as follows: 'When I wish to find out how wise, or how stupid, or how good, or how wicked is any one, or what are his thoughts at the moment, I fashion the expression of my face, as accurately as possible, in accordance with the expression of his, and then wait to see what thoughts or sentiments arise in my mind or heart, as if to match or correspond with the expression.' This response of the schoolboy lies at the bottom of all the spurious profundity which has been attributed to Rochefoucault, to La Bougive, to Machiavelli, and to Campanella."

"And the identification," I said, "of the reasoner's intellect with that of his opponent, depends, if I understand you aright, upon the accuracy with which the opponent's intellect is admeasured."

"For its practical value it depends upon this," replied Dupin; "and the Prefect and his cohort fail so frequently, first, by default of this identification, and, secondly, by ill-admeasurement, or rather through non-admeasurement, of the intellect with which they are engaged. They consider only their own ideas of ingenuity; and, in searching for anything hidden, advert only to the modes in which they would have hidden it. They are right in this much—that their own ingenuity is a faithful representative of that of the mass; but when the cunning of the individual felon is diverse in character from their own, the felon foils them, of course. This always happens when it is above their own, and very usually when it is below. They have no variation of principle in their investigations; at best, when urged by some unusual emergency—by some extraordinary reward—they extend or exaggerate their old modes of practice, without touching their principles. What, for example, in this case of D——, has been done to vary the principle of action? What is all this boring, and probing, and sounding, and scrutinizing with the microscope and dividing the surface of the building into registered square inches—what is it all but an exaggeration of the application of the one principle or set of principles of search, which are based upon the one set of notions regarding human ingenuity, to which the Prefect, in the long routine of his duty, has been accustomed? Do you not see he has taken it for granted that all men proceed to conceal a letter,—not exactly in a gimlet hole bored in a chair-leg—but, at least, in some out-of-the-way hole or corner suggested by the same tenor of thought which would urge a man to secrete a letter in a gimlet-hole bored in a chair-leg? And do you not see also, that such recherchés nooks for concealment are adapted only for ordinary occasions, and would be adopted only by ordinary intellects; for, in all cases of concealment, a disposal of the article concealed—a disposal of it in this recherché manner,—is, in the very first instance, presumable and presumed; and thus its discovery depends, not at all upon the acumen, but altogether upon the mere care, patience, and determination of the seekers; and where the case is of importance—or, what amounts to the same thing in the policial eyes, when the reward is of magnitude,—the qualities in question have never been known to fail. You will now understand what I meant in suggesting that, had the purloined letter been hidden any where within the limits of the Prefect's examination—in other words, had the principle of its concealment been comprehended within the principles of the Prefect—its discovery would have been a matter altogether beyond question. This functionary, however, has been thoroughly mystified; and the remote source of his defeat lies in the supposition that the Minister is a fool, because he has acquired renown as a poet. All fools are poets; this the Prefect feels; and he is merely guilty of a non distributio medii in thence inferring that all poets are fools."

"But is this really the poet?" I asked. "There are two brothers, I know; and both have attained reputation in letters. The Minister I believe has written learnedly on the Differential Calculus. He is a mathematician, and no poet."

"You are mistaken; I know him well; he is both. As poet and mathematician, he would reason well; as mere mathematician, he could not have reasoned at all, and thus would have been at the mercy of the Prefect."

"You surprise me," I said, "by these opinions, which have been contradicted by the voice of the world. You do not mean to set at naught the well-digested idea of centuries. The mathematical reason has long been regarded as the reason par excellence."

"'Il y a à parièr,'" replied Dupin, quoting from Chamfort, "'que toute idée publique, toute convention reçue est une sottise, car elle a convenue au plus grand nombre.' The mathematicians, I grant you, have done their best to promulgate the popular error to which you allude, and which is none the less an error for its promulgation as truth. With an art worthy a better cause, for example, they have insinuated the term 'analysis' into application to algebra. The French are the originators of this particular deception; but if a term is of any importance—if words derive any value from applicability— then 'analysis' conveys 'algebra' about as much as, in Latin, 'ambitus' implies 'ambition,' 'religio' 'religion,' or 'homines honesti,' a set of honorable men."

"You have a quarrel on hand, I see," said I, "with some of the algebraists of Paris; but proceed."

"I dispute the availability, and thus the value, of that reason which is cultivated in any especial form other than the abstractly logical. I dispute, in particular, the reason educed by mathematical study. The mathematics are the science of form and quantity; mathematical reasoning is merely logic applied to observation upon form and quantity. The great error lies in supposing that even the truths of what is called pure algebra, are abstract or general truths. And this error is so egregious that I am confounded at the universality with which it has been received. Mathematical axioms are not axioms of general truth. What is true of relation—of form and quantity—is often grossly false in regard to morals, for example. In this latter science it is very usually untrue that the aggregated parts are equal to the whole. In chemistry also the axiom fails. In the consideration of motive it fails; for two motives, each of a given value, have not, necessarily, a value when united, equal to the sum of their values apart. There are numerous other mathematical truths which are only truths within the limits of relation. But the mathematician argues, from his finite truths, through habit, as if they were of an absolutely general applicability—as the world indeed imagines them to be. Bryant, in his very learned 'Mythology,' mentions an analogous source of error, when he says that 'although the Pagan fables are not believed, yet we forget ourselves continually, and make inferences from them as existing realities.' With the algebraists, however, who are Pagans themselves, the 'Pagan fables' are believed, and the inferences are made, not so much through lapse of memory, as through an unaccountable addling of the brains. In short, I never yet encountered the mere mathematician who could be trusted out of equal roots, or one who did not clandestinely hold it as a point of his faith that x^2+px was absolutely and unconditionally equal to q. Say to one of these gentlemen, by way of experiment, if you please, that you believe occasions may occur where x^2+px is not altogether equal to q, and, having made him understand what you mean, get out of his reach as speedily as convenient, for, beyond doubt, he will endeavor to knock you down.

"I mean to say," continued Dupin, while I merely laughed at his last observations, "that if the Minister had been no more than a mathematician, the Prefect would have been under no necessity of giving me this check. I know him, however, as both mathematician and poet, and my measures were adapted to his capacity, with reference to the circumstances by which he was surrounded. I knew him as a courtier, too, and as a bold intriguant. Such a man, I considered, could not fail to be aware of the ordinary policial modes of action. He could not have failed to anticipate—and events have proved that he did not fail to anticipate—the waylayings to which he was subjected. He must have foreseen, I reflected, the secret investigations of his premises. His frequent absences from home at night, which were hailed by the Prefect as certain aids to his success, I regarded only as ruses, to afford opportunity for thorough search to the police, and thus the sooner to impress them with the conviction to which G——, in fact, did finally arrive—the conviction that the letter was not upon the premises. I felt, also, that the whole train of thought, which I was at some pains in detailing to you just now, concerning the invariable principle of policial action in searches for articles concealed—I felt that this whole train of thought would necessarily pass through the mind of the Minister. It would imperatively lead him to despise all the ordinary nooks of concealment. He could not, I reflected, be so weak as not to see that the most intricate and remote recess of his hotel would be as open as his commonest closets to the eyes, to the probes, to the gimlets, and to the microscopes of the Prefect. I saw, in fine, that he would be driven, as a matter of course, to simplicity, if not deliberately induced to it as a matter of choice. You will remember, perhaps, how desperately the Prefect laughed when I suggested, upon our first interview, that it was just possible this mystery troubled him so much on account of its being so very self-evident."

"Yes," said I, "I remember his merriment well. I really thought he would have fallen into convulsions."

"The material world," continued Dupin, "abounds with very strict analogies to the immaterial; and thus some color of truth has been given to the rhetorical dogma, that metaphor, or simile, may be made to strengthen an argument, as well as to embellish a description. The principle of the vis inertiæ, for example, seems to be identical in physics and metaphysics. It is not more true in the former, that a large body is with more difficulty set in motion than a smaller one, and that its subsequent momentum is commensurate with this difficulty, than it is, in the latter, that intellects of the vaster capacity, while more forcible, more constant, and more eventful in their movements than those of inferior grade, are yet the less readily moved, and more embarrassed and full of hesitation in the first few steps of their progress. Again: have you ever noticed which of the street signs, over the shop-doors, are the most attractive of attention?"

"I have never given the matter a thought," I said.

"There is a game of puzzles," he resumed, "which is played upon a map. One party playing requires another to find a given word—the name of town, river, state or empire—any word, in short, upon the motley and perplexed surface of the chart. A novice in the game generally seeks to embarrass his opponents by giving them the most minutely lettered names; but the adept selects such words as stretch, in large characters, from one end of the chart to the other. These, like the over-largely lettered signs and placards of the street, escape observation by dint of being excessively obvious; and here the physical oversight is precisely analogous with the moral inapprehension by which the intellect suffers to pass unnoticed those considerations which are too obtrusively and too palpably self-evident. But this is a point, it appears, somewhat above or beneath the understanding of the Prefect. He never once thought it probable, or possible, that the Minister had deposited the letter immediately beneath the nose of the whole world, by way of best preventing any portion of that world from perceiving it.

"But the more I reflected upon the daring, dashing, and discriminating ingenuity of D——; upon the fact that the document must always have been at hand, if he intended to use it to good purpose; and upon the decisive evidence, obtained by the Prefect, that it was not hidden within the limits of that dignitary's ordinary search—the more satisfied I became that, to conceal this letter, the Minister had resorted to the comprehensive and sagacious expedient of not attempting to conceal it at all.

"Full of these ideas, I prepared myself with a pair of green spectacles, and called one fine morning, quite by accident, at the Ministerial hotel. I found D—— at home, yawning, lounging, and dawdling, as usual, and pretending to be in the last extremity of ennui. He is, perhaps, the most really energetic human being now alive—but that is only when nobody sees him.

"To be even with him, I complained of my weak eyes, and lamented the necessity of the spectacles, under cover of which I cautiously and thoroughly surveyed the whole apartment, while seemingly intent only upon the conversation of my host.

"I paid especial attention to a large writing-table near which he sat, and upon which lay confusedly, some miscellaneous letters and other papers, with one or two musical instruments and a few books. Here, however, after a long and very deliberate scrutiny, I saw nothing to excite particular suspicion.

"At length my eyes, in going the circuit of the room, fell upon a trumpery fillagree card-rack of pasteboard, that hung dangling by a dirty blue ribbon, from a little brass knob just beneath the middle of the mantel-piece. In this rack, which had three or four compartments, were five or six visiting cards and a solitary letter. This last was much soiled and crumpled. It was torn nearly in two, across the middle—as if a design, in the first instance, to tear it entirely up as worthless, had been altered, or stayed, in the second. It had a large black seal, bearing the D—— cipher very conspicuously, and was addressed, in a diminutive female hand, to D——, the minister, himself. It was thrust carelessly, and even, as it seemed, contemptuously, into one of the uppermost divisions of the rack.

"No sooner had I glanced at this letter, than I concluded it to be that of which I was in search. To be sure, it was, to all appearance, radically different from the one of which the Prefect had read us so minute a description. Here the seal was large and black, with the D—— cipher; there it was small and red, with the ducal arms of the S—— family. Here, the address, to the Minister, diminutive and feminine; there the superscription, to a certain royal personage, was markedly bold and decided; the size alone formed a point of correspondence. But, then, the radicalness of these differences, which was excessive; the dirt; the soiled and torn condition of the paper, so inconsistent with the true methodical habits of D——, and so suggestive of a design to delude the beholder into an idea of the worthlessness of the document; these things, together with the hyper-obtrusive situation of this document, full in the view of every visiter, and thus exactly in accordance with the conclusions to which I had previously arrived; these things, I say, were strongly corroborative of suspicion, in one who came with the intention to suspect.

"I protracted my visit as long as possible, and, while I maintained a most animated discussion with the Minister upon a topic which I knew well had never failed to interest and excite him, I kept my attention really riveted upon the letter. In this examination, I committed to memory its external appearance and arrangement in the rack; and also fell, at length, upon a discovery which set at rest whatever trivial doubt I might have entertained. In scrutinizing the edges of the paper, I observed them to be more chafed than seemed necessary. They presented the broken appearance which is manifested when a stiff paper, having been once folded and pressed with a folder, is refolded in a reversed direction, in the same creases or edges which had formed the original fold. This discovery was sufficient. It was clear to me that the letter had been turned, as a glove, inside out, re-directed, and re-sealed. I bade the Minister good morning, and took my departure at once, leaving a gold snuff-box upon the table.

"The next morning I called for the snuff-box, when we resumed, quite eagerly, the conversation of the preceding day. While thus engaged, however, a loud report, as if of a pistol, was heard immediately beneath the windows of the hotel, and was succeeded by a series of fearful screams, and the shoutings of a terrified mob. D—— rushed to a casement, threw it open, and looked out. In the meantime, I stepped to the card-rack, took the letter, put it in my pocket, and replaced it by a fac-simile, (so far as regards externals,) which I had carefully prepared at my lodgings—imitating the D—— cipher, very readily, by means of a seal formed of bread.

"The disturbance in the street had been occasioned by the frantic behavior of a man with a musket. He had fired it among a crowd of women and children. It proved, however, to have been without ball, and the fellow was suffered to go his way as a lunatic or a drunkard. When he had gone, D—— came from the window, whither I had followed him immediately upon securing the object in view. Soon afterwards I bade him farewell. The pretended lunatic was a man in my own pay."

"But what purpose had you," I asked, "in replacing the letter by a fac-simile? Would it not have been better, at the first visit, to have seized it openly, and departed?"

"D——," replied Dupin, "is a desperate man, and a man of nerve. His hotel, too, is not without attendants devoted to his interests. Had I made the wild attempt you suggest, I might never have left the Ministerial presence alive. The good people of Paris might have heard of me no more. But I had an object apart from these considerations. You know my political prepossessions. In this matter, I act as a partisan of the lady concerned. For eighteen months the Minister has had her in his power. She has now him in hers—since, being unaware that the letter is not in his possession, he will proceed with his exactions as if it was. Thus will he inevitably commit himself, at once, to his political destruction. His downfall, too, will not be more precipitate than awkward. It is all very well to talk about the *facilis descensus Averni*; but in all kinds of climbing, as Catalani said of singing, it is far more easy to get up than to come down. In the present instance I have no sympathy—at least no pity—for him who descends. He is that *monstrum horrendum*, an unprincipled man of genius. I confess, however, that I should like very well to know the precise character of his thoughts, when, being defied by her whom the Prefect terms 'a certain personage' he is reduced to opening the letter which I left for him in the card-rack."

"How? did you put any thing particular in it?"

"Why—it did not seem altogether right to leave the interior blank—that would have been insulting. D——, at Vienna once, did me an evil turn, which I told him, quite good-humoredly, that I should remember. So, as I knew he would feel some curiosity in regard to the identity of the person who had outwitted him, I thought it a pity not to give him a clue. He is well acquainted with my MS., and I just copied into the middle of the blank sheet the words—

——Un dessein si funeste, S'il n'est digne d'Atrée, est digne de Thyeste. They are to be found in Crebillon's 'Atrée.'"

The Tell-Tale Heart

TRUE!—nervous—very, very dreadfully nervous I had been and am; but why will you say that I am mad? The disease had sharpened my senses—not destroyed—not dulled them. Above all was the sense of hearing acute. I heard all things in the heaven and in the earth. I heard many things in hell. How, then, am I mad? Hearken! and observe how healthily—how calmly I can tell you the whole story.

It is impossible to say how first the idea entered my brain; but once conceived, it haunted me day and night. Object there was none. Passion there was none. I loved the old man. He had never wronged me. He had never given me insult. For his gold I had no desire. I think it was his eye! yes, it was this! He had the eye of a vulture—a pale blue eye, with a film over it. Whenever it fell upon me, my blood ran cold; and so by degrees—very gradually—I made up my mind to take the life of the old man, and thus rid myself of the eye forever.

Now this is the point. You fancy me mad. Madmen know nothing. But you should have seen me. You should have seen how wisely I proceeded—with what caution—with what foresight—with what dissimulation I went to work! I was never kinder to the old man than during the whole week before I killed him. And every night, about midnight, I turned the latch of his door and opened it—oh so gently! And then, when I had made an opening sufficient for my head, I put in a dark lantern, all closed, closed, that no light shone out, and then I thrust in my head. Oh, you would have laughed to see how cunningly I thrust it in! I moved it slowly—very, very slowly, so that I might not disturb the old man's sleep. It took me an hour to place my whole head within the opening so far that I could see him as he lay upon his bed. Ha! would a madman have been so wise as this? And then, when my head was well in the room, I undid the lantern cautiously—oh, so cautiously—cautiously (for the hinges creaked)—I undid it just so much that a single thin ray fell upon the vulture eye. And this I did for seven long nights—every night just at midnight—but I found the eye always closed; and so it was impossible to do the work; for it was not the old man who vexed me, but his Evil Eye. And every morning, when the day broke, I went boldly into the chamber, and spoke courageously to him, calling him by name in a hearty tone, and inquiring how he has passed the night. So you see he would have been a very profound old man, indeed, to suspect that every night, just at twelve, I looked in upon him while he slept.

Upon the eighth night I was more than usually cautious in opening the door. A watch's minute hand moves more quickly than did mine. Never before that night had I felt the extent of my own powers—of my sagacity. I could scarcely contain my feelings of triumph. To think that there I was, opening the door, little by little, and he not even to dream of my secret deeds or thoughts. I fairly chuckled at the idea; and perhaps he heard me; for he moved on the bed suddenly, as if startled. Now you may think that I drew back—but no. His room was as black as pitch with the thick darkness, (for the shutters were close fastened, through fear of robbers,) and so I knew that he could not see the opening of the door, and I kept pushing it on steadily, steadily.

I had my head in, and was about to open the lantern, when my thumb slipped upon the tin fastening, and the old man sprang up in bed, crying out—"Who's there?"

I kept quite still and said nothing. For a whole hour I did not move a muscle, and in the meantime I did not hear him lie down. He was still sitting up in the bed listening;—just as I have done, night after night, hearkening to the death watches in the wall.

Presently I heard a slight groan, and I knew it was the groan of mortal terror. It was not a groan of pain or of grief—oh, no!—it was the low stifled sound that arises from the bottom of the soul when overcharged with awe. I knew the sound well. Many a night, just at midnight, when all the world slept, it has welled up from my own bosom, deepening, with its dreadful echo, the terrors that distracted me. I say I knew it well. I knew what the old man felt, and pitied him, although I chuckled at heart. I knew that he had been lying awake ever since the first slight noise, when he had turned in the bed. His fears had been ever since growing upon him. He had been trying to fancy them causeless, but could not. He had been saying to himself—"It is nothing but the wind in the chimney—it is only a mouse crossing the floor," or "It is merely a cricket which has made a single chirp." Yes, he had been trying to comfort himself with these suppositions: but he had found all in vain. All in vain; because Death, in approaching him had stalked with his black shadow before him, and enveloped the victim. And it was the mournful influence of the unperceived shadow that caused him to feel—although he neither saw nor heard—to feel the presence of my head within the room.

When I had waited a long time, very patiently, without hearing him lie down, I resolved to open a little—a very, very little crevice in the lantern. So I opened it—you cannot imagine how stealthily, stealthily—until, at length a simple dim ray, like the thread of the spider, shot from out the crevice and fell full upon the vulture eye.

It was open—wide, wide open—and I grew furious as I gazed upon it. I saw it with perfect distinctness—all a dull blue, with a hideous veil over it that chilled the very marrow in my bones; but I could see nothing else of the old man's face or person: for I had directed the ray as if by instinct, precisely upon the damned spot.

And have I not told you that what you mistake for madness is but over-acuteness of the sense?—now, I say, there came to my ears a low, dull, quick sound, such as a watch makes when enveloped in cotton. I knew that sound well, too. It was the beating of the old man's heart. It increased my fury, as the beating of a drum stimulates the soldier into courage.

But even yet I refrained and kept still. I scarcely breathed. I held the lantern motionless. I tried how steadily I could maintain the ray upon the eve. Meantime the hellish tattoo of the heart increased. It grew quicker and quicker, and louder and louder every instant. The old man's terror must have been extreme! It grew louder, I say, louder every moment!—do you mark me well I have told you that I am nervous: so I am. And now at the dead hour of the night, amid the dreadful silence of that old house, so strange a noise as this excited me to uncontrollable terror. Yet, for some minutes longer I refrained and stood still. But the beating grew louder, louder! I thought the heart must burst. And now a new anxiety seized me—the sound would be heard by a neighbour! The old man's hour had come! With a loud yell, I threw open the lantern and leaped into the room. He shrieked once—once only. In an instant I dragged him to the floor, and pulled the heavy bed over him. I then smiled gaily, to find the deed so far done. But, for many minutes, the heart beat on with a muffled sound. This, however, did not vex me; it would not be heard through the wall. At length it ceased. The old man was dead. I removed the bed and examined the corpse. Yes, he was stone, stone dead. I placed my hand upon the heart and held it there many minutes. There was no pulsation. He was stone dead. His eye would trouble me no more.

If still you think me mad, you will think so no longer when I describe the wise precautions I took for the concealment of the body. The night waned, and I worked hastily, but in silence. First of all I dismembered the corpse. I cut off the head and the arms and the legs.

I then took up three planks from the flooring of the chamber, and deposited all between the scantlings. I then replaced the boards so cleverly, so cunningly, that no human eye—not even his—could have detected anything wrong. There was nothing to wash out—no stain of any kind—no blood-spot whatever. I had been too wary for that. A tub had caught all—ha! ha!

When I had made an end of these labors, it was four o'clock—still dark as midnight. As the bell sounded the hour, there came a knocking at the street door. I went down to open it with a light heart,—for what had I now to fear? There entered three men, who introduced themselves, with perfect suavity, as officers of the police. A shriek had been heard by a neighbour during the night; suspicion of foul play had been aroused; information had been lodged at the police office, and they (the officers) had been deputed to search the premises.

I smiled,—for what had I to fear? I bade the gentlemen welcome. The shriek, I said, was my own in a dream. The old man, I mentioned, was absent in the country. I took my visitors all over the house. I bade them search—search well. I led them, at length, to his chamber. I showed them his treasures, secure, undisturbed. In the enthusiasm of my confidence, I brought chairs into the room, and desired them here to rest from their fatigues, while I myself, in the wild audacity of my perfect triumph, placed my own seat upon the very spot beneath which reposed the corpse of the victim.

The officers were satisfied. My manner had convinced them. I was singularly at ease. They sat, and while I answered cheerily, they chatted of familiar things. But, ere long, I felt myself getting pale and wished them gone. My head ached, and I fancied a ringing in my ears: but still they sat and still chatted. The ringing became more distinct:—it continued and became more distinct: I talked more freely to get rid of the feeling: but it continued and gained definiteness—until, at length, I found that the noise was not within my ears.

No doubt I now grew *very* pale;—but I talked more fluently, and with a heightened voice. Yet the sound increased—and what could I do? It was a low, dull, quick sound—much such a sound as a watch makes when enveloped in cotton. I gasped for breath—and yet the officers heard it not. I talked more quickly—more vehemently; but the noise steadily increased. I arose and argued about trifles, in a high key and with violent gesticulations; but the noise steadily increased. Why would they not be gone? I paced the floor to and fro with heavy strides, as if excited to fury by the observations of the men—but the noise steadily increased. Oh God! what could I do? I foamed—I raved—I swore! I swung the chair upon which I had been sitting, and grated it upon the boards, but the noise arose over all and continually increased. It grew louder—louder—louder! And still the men chatted pleasantly, and smiled. Was it possible they heard not? Almighty God!—no, no! They heard!—they suspected!—they knew!—they were making a mockery of my horror!—this I thought, and this I think. But anything was better than this agony! Anything was more tolerable than this derision! I could bear those hypocritical smiles no longer! I felt that I must scream or die! and now—again!—hark! louder! louder! louder! louder!

"Villains!" I shrieked, "dissemble no more! I admit the deed!—tear up the planks! here, here!—It is the beating of his hideous heart!"

The Raven

Once upon a midnight dreary, while I pondered, weak
and weary,
Over many a quaint and curious volume of forgotten
lore—
While I nodded, nearly napping, suddenly there came a
tapping,
As of some one gently rapping, rapping at my chamber
door.
"'Tis some visiter," I muttered, "tapping at my chamber door—
  Only this and nothing more."

Ah, distinctly I remember it was in the bleak
December;

And each separate dying ember wrought its ghost upon
the floor.
Eagerly I wished the morrow;—vainly I had sought to
borrow
From my books surcease of sorrow—sorrow for the lost
Lenore—
For the rare and radiant maiden whom the angels
name Lenore—
    Nameless *here* for evermore.

And the silken, sad, uncertain rustling of each purple
curtain
Thrilled me—filled me with fantastic terrors never felt
before;
So that now, to still the beating of my heart, I stood
repeating
"'Tis some visiter entreating entrance at my chamber
door—
Some late visiter entreating entrance at my chamber
door;—
    This it is and nothing more."

Presently my soul grew stronger; hesitating then no
longer,
"Sir," said I, "or Madam, truly your forgiveness I
implore;
But the fact is I was napping, and so gently you came
rapping,
And so faintly you came tapping, tapping at my chamber door,

That I scarce was sure I heard you"—here I opened
wide the door;—
    Darkness there and nothing more.

Deep into that darkness peering, long I stood there
wondering, fearing,
Doubting, dreaming dreams no mortal ever dared to
dream before;
But the silence was unbroken, and the stillness gave no
token,
And the only word there spoken was the whispered
word, "Lenore?"
This I whispered, and an echo murmured back the
word, "Lenore!"—
    Merely this and nothing more.

Back into the chamber turning, all my soul within me
burning,
Soon again I heard a tapping somewhat louder than
before.
"Surely," said I, "surely that is something at my window
lattice;
Let me see, then, what thereat is, and this mystery
explore—
Let my heart be still a moment and this mystery
explore;—
    'Tis the wind and nothing more!"

Open here I flung the shutter, when, with many a flirt
and flutter,

In there stepped a stately Raven of the saintly days of
yore;
Not the least obeisance made he; not a minute stopped
or stayed he;
But, with mien of lord or lady, perched above my
chamber door—
Perched upon a bust of Pallas just above my chamber
door—
     Perched, and sat, and nothing more.

Then this ebony bird beguiling my sad fancy into
smiling,
By the grave and stern decorum of the countenance it
wore,
"Though thy crest be shorn and shaven, thou," I said,
"art sure no craven,
Ghastly grim and ancient Raven wandering from the
Nightly shore—
Tell me what thy lordly name is on the Night's Pluto-
nian shore!"
     Quoth the Raven, "Nevermore."

Much I marvelled this ungainly fowl to hear discourse
so plainly,
Though its answer little meaning—little relevancy bore;
For we cannot help agreeing that no living human
being
Ever yet was blessed with seeing bird above his chamber door—

Bird or beast upon the sculptured bust above his chamber door,
        With such name as "Nevermore."

But the Raven, sitting lonely on the placid bust, spoke
only
That one word, as if his soul in that one word he did
outpour.
Nothing farther then he uttered—not a feather then he
fluttered—
Till I scarcely more than muttered: "Other friends have
flown before—
On the morrow *he* will leave me, as my Hopes have
flown before."
        Then the bird said "Nevermore."

Startled at the stillness broken by reply so aptly spoken,
"Doubtless," said I, "what it utters is its only stock and
store,
Caught from some unhappy master whom unmerciful
Disaster
Followed fast and followed faster till his songs one
burden bore—
Till the dirges of his Hope that melancholy burden bore
        Of 'Never—nevermore.'"

But the Raven still beguiling my sad fancy into smiling,
Straight I wheeled a cushioned seat in front of bird, and
bust and door;

Then, upon the velvet sinking, I betook myself to linking
Fancy unto fancy, thinking what this ominous bird of
yore—
What this grim, ungainly, ghastly, gaunt, and ominous
bird of yore
    Meant in croaking "Nevermore."

This I sat engaged in guessing, but no syllable
expressing
To the fowl whose fiery eyes now burned into my bosom's core;
This and more I sat divining, with my head at ease
reclining
On the cushion's velvet lining that the lamp-light
gloated o'er,
But whose velvet-violet lining with the lamp-light gloat-
ing o'er,
    She shall press, ah, nevermore!

Then, methought, the air grew denser, perfumed from
an unseen censer
Swung by seraphim whose foot-falls tinkled on the
tufted floor.
"Wretch," I cried, "thy God hath lent thee—by these
angels he hath sent thee
Respite—respite and nepenthe, from thy memories of
Lenore;
Quaff, oh quaff this kind nepenthe and forget this lost
Lenore!"
    Quoth the Raven, "Nevermore."

"Prophet!" said I, "thing of evil!—prophet still, if bird or devil!—
Whether Tempter sent, or whether tempest tossed thee here ashore,
Desolate yet all undaunted, on this desert land enchanted—
On this home by Horror haunted—tell me truly, I implore—
Is there—*is* there balm in Gilead?—tell me—tell me, I implore!"
Quoth the Raven, "Nevermore."

"Prophet!" said I, "thing of evil!—prophet still, if bird or devil!
By that Heaven that bends above us—by that God we both adore—
Tell this soul with sorrow laden if, within the distant Aidenn,
It shall clasp a sainted maiden whom the angels name Lenore—
Clasp a rare and radiant maiden whom the angels name Lenore."
Quoth the Raven, "Nevermore."

"Be that word our sign of parting, bird or fiend!" I shrieked, upstarting—
"Get thee back into the tempest and the Night's Plutonian shore!
Leave no black plume as a token of that lie thy soul hath spoken!

Leave my loneliness unbroken!—quit the bust above my
door!
Take thy beak from out my heart, and take thy form
from off my door!"
    Quoth the Raven, "Nevermore."

And the Raven, never flitting, still is sitting, *still* is
sitting
On the pallid bust of Pallas just above my chamber
door;
And his eyes have all the seeming of a demon's that is
dreaming,
And the lamp-light o'er him streaming throws his
shadow on the floor;
And my soul from out that shadow that lies floating on
the floor
    Shall be lifted—nevermore!

Hop-Frog

I never knew anyone so keenly alive to a joke as the king was. He seemed to live only for joking. To tell a good story of the joke kind, and to tell it well, was the surest road to his favor. Thus it happened that his seven ministers were all noted for their accomplishments as jokers. They all took after the king, too, in being large, corpulent, oily men, as well as inimitable jokers. Whether people grow fat by joking, or whether there is something in fat itself which predisposes to a joke, I have never been quite able to determine; but certain it is that a lean joker is a rara avis in terris.

About the refinements, or, as he called them, the 'ghost' of wit, the king troubled himself very little. He had an especial admiration for breadth in a jest, and would often put up with length, for the sake of it. Over-niceties wearied him. He would have preferred Rabelais' 'Gargantua' to the 'Zadig' of Voltaire: and, upon the whole, practical jokes suited his taste far better than verbal ones.

At the date of my narrative, professing jesters had not altogether gone out of fashion at court. Several of the great continental 'powers' still retain their 'fools,' who wore motley, with caps and bells, and who were expected to be always ready with sharp witticisms, at a moment's notice, in consideration of the crumbs that fell from the royal table.

Our king, as a matter of course, retained his 'fool.' The fact is, he required something in the way of folly—if only to counterbalance the heavy wisdom of the seven wise men who were his ministers—not to mention himself.

His fool, or professional jester, was not only a fool, however. His value was trebled in the eyes of the king, by the fact of his being also a dwarf and a cripple. Dwarfs were as common at court, in those days, as fools; and many monarchs would have found it difficult to get through their days (days are rather longer at court than elsewhere) without both a jester to laugh with, and a dwarf to laugh at. But, as I have already observed, your jesters, in ninety-nine cases out of a hundred, are fat, round, and unwieldy—so that it was no small source of self-gratulation with our king that, in Hop-Frog (this was the fool's name), he possessed a triplicate treasure in one person.

I believe the name 'Hop-Frog' was not that given to the dwarf by his sponsors at baptism, but it was conferred upon him, by general consent of the several ministers, on account of his inability to walk as other men do. In fact, Hop-Frog could only get along by a sort of interjectional gait—something between a leap and a wriggle—a movement that afforded illimitable amusement, and of course consolation, to the king, for (notwithstanding the protuberance of his stomach and a constitutional swelling of the head) the king, by his whole court, was accounted a capital figure.

But although Hop-Frog, through the distortion of his legs, could move only with great pain and difficulty along a road or floor, the prodigious muscular power which nature seemed to have bestowed upon his arms, by way of compensation for deficiency in the lower limbs, enabled him to perform many feats of wonderful dexterity, where trees or ropes were in question, or anything else to climb. At such exercises he certainly much more resembled a squirrel, or a small monkey, than a frog.

I am not able to say, with precision, from what country Hop-Frog originally came. It was from some barbarous region, however, that no person ever heard of—a vast distance from the court of our king. Hop-Frog, and a young girl very little less dwarfish than himself (although of exquisite proportions, and a marvellous dancer), had been forcibly carried off from their respective homes in adjoining provinces, and sent as presents to the king, by one of his ever-victorious generals.

Under these circumstances, it is not to be wondered at that a close intimacy arose between the two little captives. Indeed, they soon became sworn friends. Hop-Frog, who, although he made a great deal of sport, was by no means popular, had it not in his power to render Trippetta many services; but she, on account of her grace and exquisite beauty (although a dwarf), was universally admired and petted; so she possessed much influence; and never failed to use it, whenever she could, for the benefit of Hop-Frog.

On some grand state occasion—I forgot what—the king

determined to have a masquerade, and whenever a masquerade or anything of that kind, occurred at our court, then the talents both of Hop-Frog and Trippetta were sure to be called into play. Hop-Frog, in especial, was so inventive in the way of getting up pageants, suggesting novel characters, and arranging costumes, for masked balls, that nothing could be done, it seems, without his assistance.

The night appointed for the fete had arrived. A gorgeous hall had been fitted up, under Trippetta's eye, with every kind of device which could possibly give eclat to a masquerade. The whole court was in a fever of expectation. As for costumes and characters, it might well be supposed that everybody had come to a decision on such points. Many had made up their minds (as to what roles they should assume) a week, or even a month, in advance; and, in fact, there was not a particle of indecision anywhere—except in the case of the king and his seven minsters. Why they hesitated I never could tell, unless they did it by way of a joke. More probably, they found it difficult, on account of being so fat, to make up their minds. At all events, time flew; and, as a last resort they sent for Trippetta and Hop-Frog.

When the two little friends obeyed the summons of the king they found him sitting at his wine with the seven members of his cabinet council; but the monarch appeared to be in a very ill humor. He knew that Hop-Frog was not fond of wine, for it excited the poor cripple almost to madness; and madness is no comfortable feeling. But the king loved his practical jokes, and took pleasure in forcing Hop-Frog to drink and (as the king called it) 'to be merry.'

"Come here, Hop-Frog," said he, as the jester and his friend entered the room; "swallow this bumper to the health of your absent friends, [here Hop-Frog sighed,] and then let us have the benefit of your invention. We want characters—characters, man—something novel—out of the way. We are wearied with this everlasting sameness. Come, drink! the wine will brighten your wits."

Hop-Frog endeavored, as usual, to get up a jest in reply to these advances from the king; but the effort was too much. It happened to be the poor dwarf's birthday, and the command to drink to his 'absent friends' forced the tears to his eyes. Many large, bitter drops fell into the goblet as he took it, humbly, from the hand of the tyrant.

"Ah! ha! ha!" roared the latter, as the dwarf reluctantly drained the beaker.—"See what a glass of good wine can do! Why, your eyes are shining already!"

Poor fellow! his large eyes gleamed, rather than shone; for the effect of wine on his excitable brain was not more powerful than instantaneous. He placed the goblet nervously on the table, and looked round upon the company with a half-insane stare. They all seemed highly amused at the success of the king's 'joke.'

"And now to business," said the prime minister, a very fat man.

"Yes," said the king; "Come lend us your assistance. Characters, my fine fellow; we stand in need of characters—all of us—ha! ha! ha!" and as this was seriously meant for a joke, his laugh was chorused by the seven.

Hop-Frog also laughed although feebly and somewhat vacantly.

"Come, come," said the king, impatiently, "have you nothing to suggest?"

"I am endeavoring to think of something novel," replied the dwarf, abstractedly, for he was quite bewildered by the wine.

"Endeavoring!" cried the tyrant, fiercely; "what do you mean by that? Ah, I perceive. You are Sulky, and want more wine. Here, drink this!" and he poured out another goblet full and offered it to the cripple, who merely gazed at it, gasping for breath.

"Drink, I say!" shouted the monster, "or by the fiends—"

The dwarf hesitated. The king grew purple with rage. The courtiers smirked. Trippetta, pale as a corpse, advanced to the monarch's seat, and, falling on her knees before him, implored him to spare her friend.

The tyrant regarded her, for some moments, in evident wonder at her audacity. He seemed quite at a loss what to do or say—how most becomingly to express his indignation. At last, without uttering a syllable, he pushed her violently from him, and threw the contents of the brimming goblet in her face.

The poor girl got up the best she could, and, not daring even to sigh, resumed her position at the foot of the table.

There was a dead silence for about half a minute, during which the falling of a leaf, or of a feather, might have been heard. It was interrupted by a low, but harsh and protracted grating sound which seemed to come at once from every corner of the room.

"What—what—what are you making that noise for?" demanded the king, turning furiously to the dwarf.

The latter seemed to have recovered, in great measure, from his intoxication, and looking fixedly but quietly into the tyrant's face, merely ejaculated:

"I—I? How could it have been me?"

"The sound appeared to come from without," observed one

of the courtiers. "I fancy it was the parrot at the window, whetting his bill upon his cage-wires."

"True," replied the monarch, as if much relieved by the suggestion; "but, on the honor of a knight, I could have sworn that it was the gritting of this vagabond's teeth."

Hereupon the dwarf laughed (the king was too confirmed a joker to object to any one's laughing), and displayed a set of large, powerful, and very repulsive teeth. Moreover, he avowed his perfect willingness to swallow as much wine as desired. The monarch was pacified; and having drained another bumper with no very perceptible ill effect, Hop-Frog entered at once, and with spirit, into the plans for the masquerade.

"I cannot tell what was the association of idea," observed he, very tranquilly, and as if he had never tasted wine in his life, "but just after your majesty had struck the girl and thrown the wine in her face—just after your majesty had done this, and while the parrot was making that odd noise outside the window, there came into my mind a capital diversion—one of my own country frolics—often enacted among us, at our masquerades: but here it will be new altogether. Unfortunately, however, it requires a company of eight persons and—"

"Here we are!" cried the king, laughing at his acute discovery of the coincidence; "eight to a fraction—I and my seven ministers. Come! what is the diversion?"

"We call it," replied the cripple, "the Eight Chained Ourang-Outangs, and it really is excellent sport if well enacted."

"We will enact it," remarked the king, drawing himself up, and lowering his eyelids.

"The beauty of the game," continued Hop-Frog, "lies in the fright it occasions among the women."

"Capital!" roared in chorus the monarch and his ministry.

"I will equip you as ourang-outangs," proceeded the dwarf; "leave all that to me. The resemblance shall be so striking, that the company of masqueraders will take you for real beasts—and of course, they will be as much terrified as astonished."

"Oh, this is exquisite!" exclaimed the king. "Hop-Frog! I will make a man of you."

"The chains are for the purpose of increasing the confusion by their jangling. You are supposed to have escaped, en masse, from your keepers. Your majesty cannot conceive the effect produced, at a masquerade, by eight chained ourang-outangs, imagined to be real ones by most of the company; and rushing in with savage cries, among the crowd of delicately and gorgeously habited men and women. The contrast is inimitable!"

"It must be," said the king: and the council arose hurriedly (as it was growing late), to put in execution the scheme of Hop-Frog.

His mode of equipping the party as ourang-outangs was very simple, but effective enough for his purposes. The animals in question had, at the epoch of my story, very rarely been seen in any part of the civilized world; and as the imitations made by the dwarf were sufficiently beast-like and more than sufficiently hideous, their truthfulness to nature was thus thought to be secured.

The king and his ministers were first encased in tight-fitting stockinet shirts and drawers. They were then saturated with tar. At this stage of the process, some one of the party suggested feathers; but the suggestion was at once overruled by the dwarf, who soon convinced the eight, by ocular demonstration, that the hair of such a brute as the ourang-outang was much more efficiently represented by flu. A thick coating of the latter was accordingly plastered upon the coating of tar. A long chain was now procured. First, it was passed about the waist of the king, and tied, then about another of the party, and also tied; then about all successively, in the same manner. When this chaining arrangement was complete, and the party stood as far apart from each other as possible, they formed a circle; and to make all things appear natural, Hop-Frog passed the residue of the chain in two diameters, at right angles, across the circle, after the fashion adopted, at the present day, by those who capture Chimpanzees, or other large apes, in Borneo.

The grand saloon in which the masquerade was to take place, was a circular room, very lofty, and receiving the light of the sun only through a single window at top. At night (the season for which the apartment was especially designed) it was illuminated principally by a large chandelier, depending by a chain from the centre of the sky-light, and lowered, or elevated, by means of a counter-balance as usual; but (in order not to look unsightly) this latter passed outside the cupola and over the roof.

The arrangements of the room had been left to Trippetta's superintendence; but, in some particulars, it seems, she had been guided by the calmer judgment of her friend the dwarf. At his suggestion it was that, on this occasion, the chandelier was removed. Its waxen drippings (which, in weather so warm, it was quite impossible to prevent) would have been seriously detrimental to the rich dresses of the guests, who, on account of the crowded state of the saloon, could not all be expected to keep from out its centre; that is to say, from under the chande-lier. Additional sconces were set in various parts of the hall, out of the war, and a flambeau, emitting sweet odor, was placed in the right hand of each of the Caryaides [Caryatides] that stood against the wall—some fifty or sixty altogether.

The eight ourang-outangs, taking Hop-Frog's advice, waited patiently until midnight (when the room was thoroughly filled with masqueraders) before making their appearance. No sooner had the clock ceased striking, however, than they rushed, or rather rolled in, all together—for the impediments of their chains caused most of the party to fall, and all to stumble as they entered.

The excitement among the masqueraders was prodigious, and filled the heart of the king with glee. As had been anticipated, there were not a few of the guests who supposed the ferocious-looking creatures to be beasts of some kind in reality, if not precisely ourang-outangs. Many of the women swooned with affright; and had not the king taken the precaution to exclude all weapons from the saloon, his party might soon have expiated their frolic in their blood. As it was, a general rush was made for the doors; but the king had ordered them to be locked immediately upon his entrance; and, at the dwarf's suggestion, the keys had been deposited with him.

While the tumult was at its height, and each masquerader attentive only to his own safety (for, in fact, there was much real danger from the pressure of the excited crowd), the chain by which the chandelier ordinarily hung, and which had been drawn up on its removal, might have been seen very gradually to descend, until its hooked extremity came within three feet of the floor.

Soon after this, the king and his seven friends having reeled about the hall in all directions, found themselves, at length, in its centre, and, of course, in immediate contact with the chain. While they were thus situated, the dwarf, who had followed noiselessly at their heels, inciting them to keep up the commotion, took hold of their own chain at the intersection of the two portions which crossed the circle diametrically and at right angles. Here, with the rapidity of thought, he inserted the hook from which the chandelier had been wont to depend; and, in an instant, by some unseen agency, the chandelier-chain was drawn so far upward as to take the hook out of reach, and, as an inevitable consequence, to drag the ourang-outangs together in close connection, and face to face.

The masqueraders, by this time, had recovered, in some measure, from their alarm; and, beginning to regard the whole matter as a well-contrived pleasantry, set up a loud shout of laughter at the predicament of the apes.

"Leave them to me!" now screamed Hop-Frog, his shrill voice making itself easily heard through all the din. "Leave them to me. I fancy I know them. If I can only get a good look at them, I can soon tell who they are."

Here, scrambling over the heads of the crowd, he managed to get to the wall; when, seizing a flambeau from one of the Caryatides, he returned, as he went, to the centre of the room—leaping, with the agility of a monkey, upon the king's head, and thence clambered a few feet up the chain; holding down the torch to examine the group of ourang-outangs, and still screaming: "I shall soon find out who they are!"

And now, while the whole assembly (the apes included) were convulsed with laughter, the jester suddenly uttered a shrill whistle; when the chain flew violently up for about thirty feet—dragging with it the dismayed and struggling ourang-outangs, and leaving them suspended in mid-air between the sky-light and the floor. Hop-Frog, clinging to the chain as it rose, still maintained his relative position in respect to the eight maskers, and still (as if nothing were the matter) continued to thrust his torch down toward them, as though endeavoring to discover who they were.

So thoroughly astonished was the whole company at this ascent, that a dead silence, of about a minute's duration, ensued. It was broken by just such a low, harsh, grating sound, as had before attracted the attention of the king and his councillors when the former threw the wine in the face of Trippetta. But, on the present occasion, there could be no question as to whence the sound issued. It came from the fang-like teeth of the dwarf, who ground them and gnashed them as he foamed at the mouth, and glared, with an expression of maniacal rage, into the upturned countenances of the king and his seven companions.

"Ah, ha!" said at length the infuriated jester. "Ah, ha! I begin to see who these people are now!" Here, pretending to scrutinize the king more closely, he held the flambeau to the flaxen coat which enveloped him, and which instantly burst into a sheet of vivid flame. In less than half a minute the whole eight ourang-outangs were blazing fiercely, amid the shrieks of the multitude who gazed at them from below, horror-stricken, and without the power to render them the slightest assistance.

At length the flames, suddenly increasing in virulence, forced the jester to climb higher up the chain, to be out of their reach; and, as he made this movement, the crowd again sank, for a brief instant, into silence. The dwarf seized his opportunity, and once more spoke:

"I now see distinctly," he said, "what manner of people these maskers are. They are a great king and his seven privy-councillors,—a king who does not scruple to strike a defence-less girl, and his seven councillors who abet him in the outrage. As for myself, I am simply Hop-Frog, the jester—and this is my last jest."

Owing to the high combustibility of both the flax and the tar to which it adhered, the dwarf had scarcely made an end of his brief speech before the work of vengeance was complete. The eight corpses swung in their chains, a fetid, blackened, hid-eous, and indistinguishable mass. The cripple hurled his torch at them, clambered leisurely to the ceiling, and disappeared through the sky-light.

It is supposed that Trippetta, stationed on the roof of the saloon, had been the accomplice of her friend in his fiery re-venge, and that, together, they effected their escape to their own country: for neither was seen again.

The Oval Portrait

he chateau into which my valet had ventured to make forcible entrance, rather than permit me, in my desperately wounded condition, to pass a night in the open air, was one of those piles of commingled gloom and grandeur which have so long frowned among the Appennines, not less in fact than in the fancy of Mrs. Radcliffe. To all appearance it had been temporarily and very lately abandoned. We established ourselves in one of the smallest and least sumptuously furnished apartments. It lay in a remote turret of the building. Its decorations were rich, yet tattered and antique. Its walls were hung with tapestry and bedecked with manifold and multiform armorial trophies, together with an unusually great number of very spirited modern paintings in frames of rich golden arabesque. In these paintings, which depended from the walls not only in their main surfaces, but in very many nooks which the bizarre architecture of the chateau rendered necessary—in these paintings my incipient delirium, perhaps, had caused me to take deep interest; so that I bade Pedro to close the heavy shutters of the room—since it was already night—to light the tongues of a tall candelabrum which stood by the head of my bed—and to throw open far and wide the fringed curtains of black velvet which enveloped the bed itself. I wished all this done that I might resign myself, if not to sleep, at least alternately to the contemplation of these pictures, and the perusal of a small volume which had been found upon the pillow, and which purported to criticise and describe them.

Long—long I read—and devoutly, devotedly I gazed. Rapidly and gloriously the hours flew by and the deep midnight came. The position of the candelabrum displeased me, and outreaching my hand with difficulty, rather than disturb my slumbering valet, I placed it so as to throw its rays more fully upon the book.

But the action produced an effect altogether unanticipated. The rays of the numerous candles (for there were many) now fell within a niche of the room which had hitherto been thrown into deep shade by one of the bed-posts. I thus saw in vivid light a picture all unnoticed before. It was the portrait of a young girl just ripening into womanhood. I glanced at the painting hurriedly, and then closed my eyes. Why I did this was not at first apparent even to my own perception. But while my lids remained thus shut, I ran over in my mind my reason for so shutting them. It was an impulsive movement to gain time for thought—to make sure that my vision had not deceived me—to calm and subdue my fancy for a more sober and more certain gaze. In a very few moments I again looked fixedly at the painting.

That I now saw aright I could not and would not doubt; for the first flashing of the candles upon that canvas had seemed to dissipate the dreamy stupor which was stealing over my senses, and to startle me at once into waking life.

The portrait, I have already said, was that of a young girl. It was a mere head and shoulders, done in what is technically termed a vignette manner; much in the style of the favorite heads of Sully. The arms, the bosom, and even the ends of the radiant hair melted imperceptibly into the vague yet deep shadow which formed the back-ground of the whole. The frame was oval, richly gilded and filigreed in Moresque. As a thing of art nothing could be more admirable than the painting itself. But it could have been neither the execution of the work, nor the immortal beauty of the countenance, which had so suddenly and so vehemently moved me. Least of all, could it have been that my fancy, shaken from its half slumber, had mistaken the head for that of a living person. I saw at once that the peculiarities of the design, of the vignetting, and of the frame, must have instantly dispelled such idea—must have prevented even its momentary entertainment. Thinking earnestly upon these points, I remained, for an hour perhaps, half sitting, half reclining, with my vision riveted upon the portrait. At length, satisfied with the true secret of its effect, I fell back within the bed. I had found the spell of the picture in an absolute life-likeliness of expression, which, at first startling, finally confounded, subdued, and appalled me. With deep and reverent awe I replaced the candelabrum in its former position. The cause of my deep agitation being thus shut from view, I sought eagerly the volume which discussed the paintings and their histories. Turning to the number which designated the oval portrait, I there read the vague and quaint words which follow:

"She was a maiden of rarest beauty, and not more lovely than full of glee. And evil was the hour when she saw, and loved, and wedded the painter. He, passionate, studious, austere, and having already a bride in his Art; she a maiden of rarest beauty, and not more lovely than full of glee; all light and smiles, and frolicsome as the young fawn; loving and cherishing all things; hating only the Art which was her rival; dreading only the pallet and brushes and other untoward instruments which deprived her of the countenance of her lover. It was thus a terrible thing for this lady to hear the painter speak of his desire to portray even his young bride. But she was humble and obedient, and sat meekly for many weeks in the dark, high turret-chamber where the light dripped upon the pale canvas only from overhead. But he, the painter, took glory in his work, which went on from hour to hour, and from day to day. And he was a passionate, and wild, and moody man, who became lost in reveries; so that he would not see that the light which fell so ghastly in that lone turret withered the health and the spirits of his bride, who pined visibly to all but him. Yet she smiled on and still on, uncomplainingly, because she saw that the painter (who had high renown) took a fervid and burning pleasure in his task, and wrought day and night to depict her who so loved him, yet who grew daily more dispirited and weak. And in sooth some who beheld the portrait spoke of its resemblance in low words, as of a mighty marvel, and a proof not less of the power of the painter than of his deep love for her whom he depicted so surpassingly well. But at length, as the labor drew

nearer to its conclusion, there were admitted none into the turret; for the painter had grown wild with the ardor of his work,
and turned his eyes from canvas merely, even to regard the
countenance of his wife. And he would not see that the tints
which he spread upon the canvas were drawn from the cheeks
of her who sat beside him. And when many weeks had passed,
and but little remained to do, save one brush upon the mouth
and one tint upon the eye, the spirit of the lady again flickered
up as the flame within the socket of the lamp. And then the
brush was given, and then the tint was placed; and, for one
moment, the painter stood entranced before the work which
he had wrought; but in the next, while he yet gazed, he grew
tremulous and very pallid, and aghast, and crying with a loud
voice, 'This is indeed Life itself!' turned suddenly to regard his
beloved:—She was dead!"

The Masque of the Red Death

The "Red Death" had long devastated the country. No pestilence had ever been so fatal, or so hideous. Blood was its Avatar and its seal—the redness and the horror of blood. There were sharp pains, and sudden dizziness, and then profuse bleeding at the pores, with dissolution. The scarlet stains upon the body and especially upon the face of the victim, were the pest ban which shut him out from the aid and from the sympathy of his fellow-men. And the whole seizure, progress and termination of the disease, were the incidents of half an hour.

But the Prince Prospero was happy and dauntless and sagacious. When his dominions were half depopulated, he summoned to his presence a thousand hale and light-hearted friends from among the knights and dames of his court, and with these retired to the deep seclusion of one of his castellated abbeys. This was an extensive and magnificent structure, the creation of the prince's own eccentric yet august taste. A strong and lofty wall girdled it in. This wall had gates of iron. The courtiers, having entered, brought furnaces and massy hammers and welded the bolts. They resolved to leave means neither of ingress or egress to the sudden impulses of despair or of frenzy from within. The abbey was amply provisioned. With such precautions the courtiers might bid defiance to contagion. The external world could take care of itself. In the meantime it was folly to grieve, or to think. The prince had provided all the appliances of pleasure. There were buffoons, there were improvisatori, there were ballet-dancers, there were musicians, there was Beauty, there was wine. All these and security were within. Without was the "Red Death."

It was toward the close of the fifth or sixth month of his seclusion, and while the pestilence raged most furiously abroad, that the Prince Prospero entertained his thousand friends at a masked ball of the most unusual magnificence.

It was a voluptuous scene, that masquerade. But first let me tell of the rooms in which it was held. There were seven—an imperial suite. In many palaces, however, such suites form a long and straight vista, while the folding doors slide back nearly to the walls on either hand, so that the view of the whole extent is scarcely impeded. Here the case was very different; as might have been expected from the duke's love of the bizarre. The apartments were so irregularly disposed that the vision embraced but little more than one at a time. There was a sharp turn at every twenty or thirty yards, and at each turn a novel effect. To the right and left, in the middle of each wall, a tall and narrow Gothic window looked out upon a closed corridor which pursued the windings of the suite. These windows were of stained glass whose color varied in accordance with the prevailing hue of the decorations of the chamber into which it opened. That at the eastern extremity was hung, for example, in blue—and vividly blue were its windows. The second chamber was purple in its ornaments and tapestries, and here the panes were purple. The third was green throughout, and so were the casements. The fourth was furnished and lighted with orange—the fifth with white—the sixth with violet. The seventh apartment was closely shrouded in black velvet tapestries that hung all over the ceiling and down the walls, falling in heavy folds upon a carpet of the same material and hue. But in this chamber only, the color of the windows failed to correspond with the decorations. The panes here were scarlet—a deep blood color. Now in no one of the seven apartments was there any lamp or candelabrum, amid the profusion of golden ornaments that lay scattered to and fro or depended from the roof. There was no light of any kind emanating from lamp or candle within the suite of chambers. But in the corridors that followed the suite, there stood, opposite to each window, a heavy tripod, bearing a brazier of fire that projected its rays through the tinted glass and so glaringly illumined the room. And thus were produced a multitude of gaudy and fantastic appearances. But in the western or black chamber the effect of the fire-light that streamed upon the dark hangings through the blood-tinted panes, was ghastly in the extreme, and produced so wild a look upon the countenances of those who entered, that there were few of the company bold enough to set foot within its precincts at all.

It was in this apartment, also, that there stood against the western wall, a gigantic clock of ebony. Its pendulum swung to and fro with a dull, heavy, monotonous clang; and when the minute-hand made the circuit of the face, and the hour was to be stricken, there came from the brazen lungs of the clock a sound which was clear and loud and deep and exceedingly musical, but of so peculiar a note and emphasis that, at each lapse of an hour, the musicians of the orchestra were constrained to pause, momentarily, in their performance, to hearken to the sound; and thus the waltzers perforce ceased their evolutions; and there was a brief disconcert of the whole gay company; and, while the chimes of the clock yet rang, it was observed that the giddiest grew pale, and the more aged and sedate passed their hands over their brows as if in confused reverie or meditation. But when the echoes had fully ceased, a light laughter at once pervaded the assembly; the musicians looked at each other and smiled as if at their own nervousness and folly, and made whispering vows, each to the other, that the next chiming of the clock should produce in them no similar emotion; and then, after the lapse of sixty minutes, (which embrace three thousand and six hundred seconds of the Time that flies,) there came yet another chiming of the clock, and then were the same disconcert and tremulousness and meditation as before.

But, in spite of these things, it was a gay and magnificent revel. The tastes of the duke were peculiar. He had a fine eye for colors and effects. He disregarded the decora of mere fashion. His plans were bold and fiery, and his conceptions glowed with barbaric lustre. There are some who would have thought him mad. His followers felt that he was not. It was necessary to hear and see and touch him to be sure that he was not.

He had directed, in great part, the moveable embellishments of the seven chambers, upon occasion of this great fete; and it was his own guiding taste which had given character to the masqueraders. Be sure they were grotesque. There were much glare and glitter and piquancy and phantasm—much of what has been since seen in "Hernani." There were arabesque figures with unsuited limbs and appointments. There were delirious fancies such as the madman fashions. There was much of the beautiful, much of the wanton, much of the bizarre, something of the terrible, and not a little of that which might have excited disgust. To and fro in the seven chambers there stalked, in fact, a multitude of dreams. And these—the dreams—writhed in and about, taking hue from the rooms, and causing the wild music of the orchestra to seem as the echo of their steps. And, anon, there strikes the ebony clock which stands in the hall of the velvet. And then, for a moment, all is still, and all is silent save the voice of the clock. The dreams are stiff-frozen as they stand. But the echoes of the chime die away—they have endured but an instant—and a light, half-subdued laughter floats after them as they depart. And now again the music swells, and the dreams live, and writhe to and fro more merrily than ever, taking hue from the many-tinted windows through which stream the rays from the tripods. But to the chamber which lies most westwardly of the seven, there are now none of the maskers who venture; for the night is waning away; and there flows a ruddier light through the blood-colored panes; and the blackness of the sable drapery appals;

and to him whose foot falls upon the sable carpet, there comes from the near clock of ebony a muffled peal more solemnly emphatic than any which reaches their ears who indulge in the more remote gaieties of the other apartments.

But these other apartments were densely crowded, and in them beat feverishly the heart of life. And the revel went whirlingly on, until at length there commenced the sounding of midnight upon the clock. And then the music ceased, as I have told; and the evolutions of the waltzers were quieted; and there was an uneasy cessation of all things as before. But now there were twelve strokes to be sounded by the bell of the clock; and thus it happened, perhaps, that more of thought crept, with more of time, into the meditations of the thoughtful among those who revelled. And thus, too, it happened, perhaps, that before the last echoes of the last chime had utterly sunk into silence, there were many individuals in the crowd who had found leisure to become aware of the presence of a masked figure which had arrested the attention of no single individual before. And the rumor of this new presence having spread itself whisperingly around, there arose at length from the whole company a buzz, or murmur, expressive of disapprobation and surprise—then, finally, of terror, of horror, and of disgust.

In an assembly of phantasms such as I have painted, it may well be supposed that no ordinary appearance could have excited such sensation. In truth the masquerade license of the night was nearly unlimited; but the figure in question had out-Heroded Herod, and gone beyond the bounds of even the prince's indefinite decorum. There are chords in the hearts of the most reckless which cannot be touched without emotion. Even with the utterly lost, to whom life and death are equally jests, there are matters of which no jest can be made. The whole company, indeed, seemed now deeply to feel that in the costume and bearing of the stranger neither wit nor propriety existed. The figure was tall and gaunt, and shrouded from head to foot in the habiliments of the grave. The mask which concealed the visage was made so nearly to resemble the countenance of a stiffened corpse that the closest scrutiny must have had difficulty in detecting the cheat. And yet all this might have been endured, if not approved, by the mad revellers around. But the mummer had gone so far as to assume the type of the Red Death. His vesture was dabbled in blood—and his broad brow, with all the features of the face, was besprinkled with the scarlet horror.

When the eyes of Prince Prospero fell upon this spectral image (which with a slow and solemn movement, as if more fully to sustain its role, stalked to and fro among the waltzers) he was seen to be convulsed, in the first moment with a strong shudder either of terror or distaste; but, in the next, his brow reddened with rage.

"Who dares?" he demanded hoarsely of the courtiers who stood near him—"who dares insult us with this blasphemous mockery? Seize him and unmask him—that we may know whom we have to hang at sunrise, from the battlements!"

It was in the eastern or blue chamber in which stood the Prince Prospero as he uttered these words. They rang throughout the seven rooms loudly and clearly—for the prince was a bold and robust man, and the music had become hushed at the waving of his hand.

It was in the blue room where stood the prince, with a group of pale courtiers by his side. At first, as he spoke, there was a slight rushing movement of this group in the direction of the intruder, who at the moment was also near at hand, and now, with deliberate and stately step, made closer approach to the speaker. But from a certain nameless awe with which the mad assumptions of the mummer had inspired the whole party, there were found none who put forth hand to seize him; so that, unimpeded, he passed within a yard of the prince's person; and, while the vast assembly, as if with one impulse, shrank from the centres of the rooms to the walls, he made his way uninterruptedly, but with the same solemn and measured step which had distinguished him from the first, through the blue chamber to the purple—through the purple to the green—through the green to the orange—through this again to the white—and even thence to the violet, ere a decided movement had been made to arrest him. It was then, however, that the Prince Prospero, maddening with rage and the shame of his own momentary cowardice, rushed hurriedly through the six chambers, while none followed him on account of a deadly terror that had seized upon all. He bore aloft a drawn dagger, and had approached, in rapid impetuosity, to within three or four feet of the retreating figure, when the latter, having attained the extremity of the velvet apartment, turned suddenly and confronted his pursuer. There was a sharp cry—and the dagger dropped gleaming upon the sable carpet, upon which, instantly afterwards, fell prostrate in death the Prince Prospero. Then, summoning the wild courage of despair, a throng of the revellers at once threw themselves into the black apartment, and, seizing the mummer, whose tall figure stood erect and motionless within the shadow of the ebony clock, gasped in unutterable horror at finding the grave-cerements and corpse-like mask which they handled with so violent a rudeness, untenanted by any tangible form.

And now was acknowledged the presence of the Red Death. He had come like a thief in the night. And one by one dropped the revellers in the blood-bedewed halls of their revel, and died each in the despairing posture of his fall. And the life of the ebony clock went out with that of the last of the gay. And the flames of the tripods expired. And Darkness and Decay and the Red Death held illimitable dominion over all.

Ligeia

And the will therein lieth, which dieth not.
Who knoweth the mysteries of the will, with its vigor?
For God is but a great will pervading all things by
nature of its intentness. Man doth not yield himself
to the angels, nor unto death utterly, save only
through the weakness of his feeble will.

—JOSEPH GLANVILL

I cannot, for my soul, remember how, when, or even precisely where, I first became acquainted with the lady Ligeia. Long years have since elapsed, and my memory is feeble through much suffering. Or, perhaps, I cannot now bring these points to mind, because, in truth, the character of my beloved, her rare learning, her singular yet placid cast of beauty, and the thrilling and enthralling eloquence of her low musical language, made their way into my heart by paces so steadily and stealthily progressive that they have been unnoticed and unknown. Yet I believe that I met her first and most frequently in some large, old, decaying city near the Rhine. Of her family—I have surely heard her speak. That it is of a remotely ancient date cannot be doubted. Ligeia! Ligeia! in studies of a nature more than all else adapted to deaden im-

pressions of the outward world, it is by that sweet word alone—
by Ligeia—that I bring before mine eyes in fancy the image
of her who is no more. And now, while I write, a recollection
flashes upon me that I have never known the paternal name of
her who was my friend and my betrothed, and who became the
partner of my studies, and finally the wife of my bosom. Was
it a playful charge on the part of my Ligeia? or was it a test
of my strength of affection, that I should institute no inquiries
upon this point? or was it rather a caprice of my own—a wildly
romantic offering on the shrine of the most passionate devotion? I but indistinctly recall the fact itself—what wonder that
I have utterly forgotten the circumstances which originated or
attended it? And, indeed, if ever she, the wan and the misty-
winged Ashtophet of idolatrous Egypt, presided, as they tell,
over marriages ill-omened, then most surely she presided over
mine.

There is one dear topic, however, on which my memory
fails me not. It is the person of Ligeia. In stature she was tall,
somewhat slender, and, in her latter days, even emaciated. I
would in vain attempt to portray the majesty, the quiet ease, of
her demeanor, or the incomprehensible lightness and elastic-
ity of her footfall. She came and departed as a shadow. I was
never made aware of her entrance into my closed study save
by the dear music of her low sweet voice, as she placed her
marble hand upon my shoulder. In beauty of face no maiden
ever equalled her. It was the radiance of an opium-dream—an
airy and spirit-lifting vision more wildly divine than the phan-
tasies which hovered vision about the slumbering souls of the
daughters of Delos. Yet her features were not of that regular
mould which we have been falsely taught to worship in the

classical labors of the heathen. "There is no exquisite beauty," says Bacon, Lord Verulam, speaking truly of all the forms and genera of beauty, "without some strangeness in the proportion." Yet, although I saw that the features of Ligeia were not of a classic regularity—although I perceived that her loveliness was indeed "exquisite," and felt that there was much of "strangeness" pervading it, yet I have tried in vain to detect the irregularity and to trace home my own perception of "the strange." I examined the contour of the lofty and pale forehead—it was faultless—how cold indeed that word when applied to a majesty so divine!—the skin rivalling the purest ivory, the commanding extent and repose, the gentle prominence of the regions above the temples; and then the raven-black, the glossy, the luxuriant and naturally-curling tresses, setting forth the full force of the Homeric epithet, "hyacinthine!" I looked at the delicate outlines of the nose—and nowhere but in the graceful medallions of the Hebrews had I beheld a similar perfection. There were the same luxurious smoothness of surface, the same scarcely perceptible tendency to the aquiline, the same harmoniously curved nostrils speaking the free spirit. I regarded the sweet mouth. Here was indeed the triumph of all things heavenly—the magnificent turn of the short upper lip—the soft, voluptuous slumber of the under—the dimples which sported, and the color which spoke—the teeth glancing back, with a brilliancy almost startling, every ray of the holy light which fell upon them in her serene and placid, yet most exultingly radiant of all smiles. I scrutinized the formation of the chin—and here, too, I found the gentleness of breadth, the softness and the majesty, the fullness and the spirituality, of the Greek—the contour which the god Apollo revealed but in a dream, to Cleomenes, the son of the Athenian. And then I peered into the large eyes of Ligeia.

For eyes we have no models in the remotely antique. It might have been, too, that in these eyes of my beloved lay the secret to which Lord Verulam alludes. They were, I must believe, far larger than the ordinary eyes of our own race. They were even fuller than the fullest of the gazelle eyes of the tribe of the valley of Nourjahad. Yet it was only at intervals—in moments of intense excitement—that this peculiarity became more than slightly noticeable in Ligeia. And at such moments was her beauty—in my heated fancy thus it appeared perhaps—the beauty of beings either above or apart from the earth—the beauty of the fabulous Houri of the Turk. The hue of the orbs was the most brilliant of black, and, far over them, hung jetty lashes of great length. The brows, slightly irregular in outline, had the same tint. The "strangeness," however, which I found in the eyes, was of a nature distinct from the formation, or the color, or the brilliancy of the features, and must, after all, be referred to the expression. Ah, word of no meaning! behind whose vast latitude of mere sound we intrench our ignorance of so much of the spiritual. The expression of the eyes of Ligeia! How for long hours have I pondered upon it! How have I, through the whole of a midsummer night, struggled to fathom it! What was it—that something more profound than the well of Democritus—which lay far within the pupils of my beloved? What was it? I was possessed with a passion to discover. Those eyes! those large, those shining, those divine orbs! they became to me twin stars of Leda, and I to them devoutest of astrologers.

There is no point, among the many incomprehensible anomalies of the science of mind, more thrillingly exciting than the fact—never, I believe, noticed in the schools—that, in our endeavors to recall to memory something long forgotten, we often find ourselves upon the very verge of remembrance, without being able, in the end, to remember. And thus how frequently, in my intense scrutiny of Ligeia's eyes, have I felt approaching the full knowledge of their expression—felt it approaching—yet not quite be mine—and so at length entirely depart! And (strange, oh strangest mystery of all!) I found, in the commonest objects of the universe, a circle of analogies to that expression. I mean to say that, subsequently to the period when Ligeia's beauty passed into my spirit, there dwelling as in a shrine, I derived, from many existences in the material world, a sentiment such as I felt always aroused within me by her large and luminous orbs. Yet not the more could I define that sentiment, or analyze, or even steadily view it. I recognized it, let me repeat, sometimes in the survey of a rapidly-growing vine—in the contemplation of a moth, a butterfly, a chrysalis, a stream of running water. I have felt it in the ocean; in the falling of a meteor. I have felt it in the glances of unusually aged people. And there are one or two stars in heaven—(one especially, a star of the sixth magnitude, double and changeable, to be found near the large star in Lyra) in a telescopic scrutiny of which I have been made aware of the feeling. I have been filled with it by certain sounds from stringed instruments, and not unfrequently by passages from books. Among innumerable other instances, I well remember something in a volume of Joseph Glanvill, which (perhaps merely from its quaintness—who shall say?) never failed to inspire me with the sentiment;—"And the will therein lieth, which dieth not. Who knoweth the mysteries of the will, with its vigor? For God is but a great will pervading all things by nature of its intentness. Man doth not yield him to the angels, nor unto death utterly, save only through the weakness of his feeble will."

Length of years, and subsequent reflection, have enabled me to trace, indeed, some remote connection between this passage in the English moralist and a portion of the character of Ligeia. An intensity in thought, action, or speech, was possibly, in her, a result, or at least an index, of that gigantic volition which, during our long intercourse, failed to give other and more immediate evidence of its existence. Of all the women whom I have ever known, she, the outwardly calm, the ever-placid Ligeia, was the most violently a prey to the tumultuous vultures of stern passion. And of such passion I could form no estimate, save by the miraculous expansion of those eyes which at once so delighted and appalled me—by the almost magical melody, modulation, distinctness and placidity of her very low voice—and by the fierce energy (rendered doubly effective by contrast with her manner of utterance) of the wild words which she habitually uttered.

I have spoken of the learning of Ligeia: it was immense—such as I have never known in woman. In the classical tongues was she deeply proficient, and as far as my own acquaintance extended in regard to the modern dialects of Europe, I have never known her at fault. Indeed upon any theme of the most admired, because simply the most abstruse of the boasted erudition of the academy, have I ever found Ligeia at fault? How singularly—how thrillingly, this one point in the nature of my wife has forced itself, at this late period only, upon my attention! I said her knowledge was such as I have never known in woman—but where breathes the man who has traversed, and

successfully, all the wide areas of moral, physical, and mathematical science? I saw not then what I now clearly perceive,
that the acquisitions of Ligeia were gigantic, were astounding;
yet I was sufficiently aware of her infinite supremacy to resign
myself, with a child-like confidence, to her guidance through
the chaotic world of metaphysical investigation at which I was
most busily occupied during the earlier years of our marriage.
With how vast a triumph—with how vivid a delight—with
how much of all that is ethereal in hope—did I feel, as she bent
over me in studies but little sought—but less known—that delicious vista by slow degrees expanding before me, down whose
long, gorgeous, and all untrodden path, I might at length pass
onward to the goal of a wisdom too divinely precious not to be
forbidden!

How poignant, then, must have been the grief with which,
after some years, I beheld my well-grounded expectations take
wings to themselves and fly away! Without Ligeia I was but as
a child groping benighted. Her presence, her readings alone,
rendered vividly luminous the many mysteries of the transcen-
dentalism in which we were immersed. Wanting the radiant
lustre of her eyes, letters, lambent and golden, grew duller
than Saturnian lead. And now those eyes shone less and less
frequently upon the pages over which I pored. Ligeia grew ill.
The wild eyes blazed with a too—too glorious effulgence; the
pale fingers became of the transparent waxen hue of the grave,
and the blue veins upon the lofty forehead swelled and sank
impetuously with the tides of the gentle emotion. I saw that she
must die—and I struggled desperately in spirit with the grim
Azrael. And the struggles of the passionate wife were, to my
astonishment, even more energetic than my own. There had

been much in her stern nature to impress me with the belief
that, to her, death would have come without its terrors;—but
not so. Words are impotent to convey any just idea of the fierce-
ness of resistance with which she wrestled with the Shadow.
I groaned in anguish at the pitiable spectacle. I would have
soothed—I would have reasoned; but, in the intensity of her
wild desire for life,—for life—but for life—solace and reason
were the uttermost folly. Yet not until the last instance, amid
the most convulsive writhings of her fierce spirit, was shaken
the external placidity of her demeanor. Her voice grew more
gentle—grew more low—yet I would not wish to dwell upon
the wild meaning of the quietly uttered words. My brain reeled
as I hearkened entranced, to a melody more than mortal—to
assumptions and aspirations which mortality had never before
known.

That she loved me I should not have doubted; and I might
have been easily aware that, in a bosom such as hers, love
would have reigned no ordinary passion. But in death only,
was I fully impressed with the strength of her affection. For
long hours, detaining my hand, would she pour out before me
the overflowing of a heart whose more than passionate devotion amounted to idolatry. How had I deserved to be so blessed
by such confessions?—how had I deserved to be so cursed with
the removal of my beloved in the hour of her making them?
But upon this subject I cannot bear to dilate. Let me say only,
that in Ligeia's more than womanly abandonment to a love,
alas! all unmerited, all unworthily bestowed, I at length recognized the principle of her longing with so wildly earnest a desire
for the life which was now fleeing so rapidly away. It is this wild
longing—it is this eager vehemence of desire for life—but for

life—that I have no power to portray—no utterance capable of expressing.

At high noon of the night in which she departed, beckoning me, peremptorily, to her side, she bade me repeat certain verses composed by herself not many days before. I obeyed her.— They were these:

Lo! 'tis a gala night
    Within the lonesome latter years!
An angel throng, bewinged, bedight
    In veils, and drowned in tears,
Sit in a theatre, to see
    A play of hopes and fears,
While the orchestra breathes fitfully
    The music of the spheres.

Mimes, in the form of God on high,
    Mutter and mumble low,
And hither and thither fly;
    Mere puppets they, who comes and go
At bidding of vast formless things
    That shift the scenery to and fro,
Flapping from out their Condor wings
    Invisible Wo!

That motley drama!—oh, be sure
    It shall not be forgot!
With its Phantom chased forever more,
    By a crowd that seize it not,
Through a circle that ever returneth in

To the self-same spot,
And much of Madness and more of Sin
        And Horror the soul of the plot.

But see, amid the mimic rout,
        A crawling shape intrude!
A blood-red thing that writhers from out
        The scenic solitude!
It writhes!—it writhes!—with mortal pangs
        The mimes become its food,
And the seraphs sob at vermin fangs
        In human gore imbued.

Out—out are the lights—out all!
        And over each quivering form,
The curtain, a funeral pall,
        Comes down with the rush of a storm,
And the angels, all pallid and wan,
        Uprising, unveiling, affirm
That the play is the tragedy, "Man,"
        And its hero the Conqueror Worm.

"O God!" half shrieked Ligeia, leaping to her feet and ex-tending her arms aloft with a spasmodic movement, as I made an end of these lines—"O God! O Divine Father!—shall these things be undeviatingly so?—shall this Conqueror be not once conquered? Are we not part and parcel in Thee? Who—who knoweth the mysteries of the will with its vigor? Man doth not yield him to the angels, nor unto death utterly, save only through the weakness of his feeble will."

And now, as if exhausted with emotion, she suffered her white arms to fall, and returned solemnly to her bed of death. And as she breathed her last sighs, there came mingled with them a low murmur from her lips. I bent to them my ear and distinguished, again, the concluding words of the passage in Glanvill—"Man doth not yield him to the angels, nor unto death utterly, save only through the weakness of his feeble will."

She died;—and I, crushed into the very dust with sorrow, could no longer endure the lonely desolation of my dwelling in the dim and decaying city by the Rhine. I had no lack of what the world calls wealth. Ligeia had brought me far more, very far more than ordinarily falls to the lot of mortals. After a few months, therefore, of weary and aimless wandering, I purchased, and put in some repair, an abbey, which I shall not name, in one of the wildest and least frequented portions of fair England. The gloomy and dreary grandeur of the building, the almost savage aspect of the domain, the many melancholy and time-honored memories connected with both, had much in unison with the feelings of utter abandonment which had driven me into that remote and unsocial region of the country. Yet although the external abbey, with its verdant decay hanging about it, suffered but little alteration, I gave way, with a child-like perversity, and perchance with a faint hope of alleviating my sorrows, to a display of more than regal magnificence within.—For such follies, even in childhood, I had imbibed a taste and now they came back to me as if in the dotage of grief. Alas, I feel how much even of incipient madness might have been discovered in the gorgeous and fantastic draperies, in the solemn carvings of Egypt, in the wild cornices and furniture, in the Bedlam patterns of the carpets of tufted gold! I had become a bounden slave in the trammels of opium, and my labors and my orders had taken a coloring from my dreams. But these absurdities I must not pause to detail. Let me speak only of that one chamber, ever accursed, whither in a moment of mental alienation, I led from the altar as my bride—as the successor of the unforgotten Ligeia—the fair-haired and blue-eyed Lady Rowena Trevanion, of Tremaine.

There is no individual portion of the architecture and decoration of that bridal chamber which is not now visibly before me. Where were the souls of the haughty family of the bride, when, through thirst of gold, they permitted to pass the threshold of an apartment so bedecked, a maiden and a daughter so beloved? I have said that I minutely remember the details of the chamber—yet I am sadly forgetful on topics of deep moment—and here there was no system, no keeping, in the fantastic display, to take hold upon the memory. The room lay in a high turret of the castellated abbey, was pentagonal in shape, and of capacious size. Occupying the whole southern face of the pentagon was the sole window—an immense sheet of unbroken glass from Venice—a single pane, and tinted of a leaden hue, so that the rays of either the sun or moon, passing through it, fell with a ghastly lustre on the objects within. Over the upper portion of this huge window, extended the trellice-work of an aged vine, which clambered up the massy walls of the turret. The ceiling, of gloomy-looking oak, was excessively lofty, vaulted, and elaborately fretted with the wildest and most grotesque specimens of a semi-Gothic, semi-Druidical device. From out the most central recess of this melancholy vaulting, depended, by a single chain of gold with long links, a huge censer of the same metal, Saracenic in pattern, and with many perforations so contrived that there writhed in and out of them, as if endued with a serpent vitality, a continual succession of parti-colored fires.

Some few ottomans and golden candelabra, of Eastern figure, were in various stations about—and there was the couch, too—bridal couch—of an Indian model, and low, and sculptured of solid ebony, with a pall-like canopy above. In each of the angles of the chamber stood on end a gigantic sarcophagus of black granite, from the tombs of the kings over against Luxor, with their aged lids full of immemorial sculpture. But in the draping of the apartment lay, alas! the chief phantasy of all. The lofty walls, gigantic in height—even unproportionably so—were hung from summit to foot, in vast folds, with a heavy and massive-looking tapestry—tapestry of a material which was found alike as a carpet on the floor, as a covering for the ottomans and the ebony bed, as a canopy for the bed, and as the gorgeous volutes of the curtains which partially shaded the window. The material was the richest cloth of gold. It was spotted all over, at irregular intervals, with arabesque figures, about a foot in diameter, and wrought upon the cloth in patterns of the most jetty black. But these figures partook of the true character of the arabesque only when regarded from a single point of view. By a contrivance now common, and indeed traceable to a very remote period of antiquity, they were made changeable in aspect. To one entering the room, they bore the appearance of simple monstrosities; but upon a farther advance, this appearance gradually departed; and step by step, as the visitor moved his station in the chamber, he saw himself surrounded by an endless succession of the ghastly forms which belong to the superstition of the Norman, or arise in the guilty slumbers of the monk. The phantasmagoric effect was vastly heightened by the artificial introduction of a strong continual current of wind behind the draperies—giving a hideous and uneasy animation to the whole.

In halls such as these—in a bridal chamber such as this—I passed, with the Lady of Tremaine, the unhallowed hours of the first month of our marriage—passed them with but little disquietude. That my wife dreaded the fierce moodiness of my temper—that she shunned me and loved me but little—I could not help perceiving; but it gave me rather pleasure than otherwise. I loathed her with a hatred belonging more to demon than to man. My memory flew back, (oh, with what intensity of regret!) to Ligeia, the beloved, the august, the beautiful, the entombed. I revelled in recollections of her purity, of her wisdom, of her lofty, her ethereal nature, of her passionate, her idolatrous love. Now, then, did my spirit fully and freely burn with more than all the fires of her own. In the excitement of my opium dreams (for I was habitually fettered in the shackles of the drug) I would call aloud upon her name, during the silence of the night, or among the sheltered recesses of the glens by day, as if, through the wild eagerness, the solemn passion, the consuming ardor of my longing for the departed, I could restore her to the pathway she had abandoned—ah, could it be forever?—upon the earth.

About the commencement of the second month of the marriage, the Lady Rowena was attacked with sudden illness, from which her recovery was slow. The fever which consumed her rendered her nights uneasy; and in her perturbed state of half-slumber, she spoke of sounds, and of motions, in and about the chamber of the turret, which I concluded had no origin save in the distemper of her fancy, or perhaps in the phantasmagoric influences of the chamber itself. She became at length convalescent—finally well. Yet but a brief period elapsed, ere a second more violent disorder again threw her upon a bed of suffering; and from this attack her frame, at all times feeble, never altogether recovered. Her illnesses were, after this epoch, of alarming character, and of more alarming recurrence, defying alike the knowledge and the great exertions of her physicians. With the increase of the chronic disease which had thus, apparently, taken too sure hold upon her constitution to be eradicated by human means, I could not fail to observe a similar increase in the nervous irritation of her temperament, and in her excitability by trivial causes of fear. She spoke again, and now more frequently and pertinaciously, of the sounds—of the slight sounds—and of the unusual motions among the tapestries, to which she had formerly alluded.

One night, near the closing in of September, she pressed this distressing subject with more than usual emphasis upon my attention. She had just awakened from an unquiet slumber, and I had been watching, with feelings half of anxiety, half of vague terror, the workings of her emaciated countenance. I sat by the side of her ebony bed, upon one of the ottomans of India. She partly arose, and spoke, in an earnest low whisper, of sounds which she then heard, but which I could not hear—of motions which she then saw, but which I could not perceive. The wind was rushing hurriedly behind the tapestries, and I wished to show her (what, let me confess it, I could not all believe) that those almost inarticulate breathings, and those very gentle variations of the figures upon the wall, were but the natural effects of that customary rushing of the wind. But a deadly pallor, overspreading her face, had proved to me that my exertions to reassure her would be fruitless. She appeared to be fainting, and no attendants were within call. I remembered where was deposited a decanter of light wine which had been ordered by her physicians, and hastened across the chamber to procure it. But, as I stepped beneath the light of the censer, two circumstances of a startling nature attracted my attention. I had felt that some palpable although invisible object had passed lightly by my person; and I saw that there lay upon the golden carpet, in the very middle of the rich lustre thrown from the censer, a shadow—a faint, indefinite shadow of angelic aspect—such as might be fancied for the shadow of a shade. But I was wild with the excitement of an immoderate dose of opium, and heeded these things but little, nor spoke of them to Rowena. Having found the wine, I recrossed the chamber, and poured out a gobletful, which I held to the lips of the fainting lady. She had now partially recovered, however, and took the vessel herself, while I sank upon an ottoman near me, with my eyes fastened upon her person. It was then that I became distinctly aware of a gentle footfall upon the carpet, and near the couch; and in a second thereafter, as Rowena was in the act of raising the wine to her lips, I saw, or may have dreamed that I saw, fall within the goblet, as if from some invisible spring in the atmosphere of the room, three or four large drops of a brilliant and ruby colored fluid. If this I saw—not so Rowena. She swallowed the wine unhesitatingly, and I forbore to speak to her of a circumstance which must, after all, I considered, have been but the suggestion of a vivid imagination, rendered morbidly active by the terror of the lady, by the opium, and by the hour.

Yet I cannot conceal it from my own perception that, immediately subsequent to the fall of the ruby-drops, a rapid change for the worse took place in the disorder of my wife; so that, on the third subsequent night, the hands of her menials prepared her for the tomb, and on the fourth, I sat alone, with her shrouded body, in that fantastic chamber which had received her as my bride.—Wild visions, opium-engendered, flitted, shadow-like, before me. I gazed with unquiet eye upon the sarcophagi in the angles of the room, upon the varying figures of the drapery, and upon the writhing of the parti-colored fires in the censer overhead. My eyes then fell, as I called to mind the circumstances of a former night, to the spot beneath the glare of the censer where I had seen the faint traces of the shadow. It was there, however, no longer; and breathing with greater freedom, I turned my glances to the pallid and rigid figure upon the bed. Then rushed upon me a thousand memories of Ligeia—and then came back upon my heart, with the turbulent violence of a flood, the whole of that unutterable wo with which I had regarded her thus enshrouded. The night waned; and still, with a bosom full of bitter thoughts of the one only and supremely beloved, I remained gazing upon the body of Rowena.

It might have been midnight, or perhaps earlier, or later, for I had taken no note of time, when a sob, low, gentle, but very distinct, startled me from my revery.—I felt that it came from the bed of ebony—the bed of death. I listened in an agony of superstitious terror—but there was no repetition of the sound. I strained my vision to detect any motion in the corpse—but there was not the slightest perceptible. Yet I could not have been deceived. I had heard the noise, however faint, and my soul was awakened within me. I resolutely and per-severingly kept my attention riveted upon the body. Many minutes elapsed before any circumstance occurred tending to throw light upon the mystery. At length it became evident that a slight, a very feeble, and barely noticeable tinge of color had flushed up within the cheeks, and along the sunken small veins of the eyelids. Through a species of unutterable horror and awe, for which the language of mortality has no sufficiently energetic expression, I felt my heart cease to beat, my limbs grow rigid where I sat. Yet a sense of duty finally operated to restore my self-possession. I could no longer doubt that we had been precipitate in our preparations—that Rowena still lived. It was necessary that some immediate exertion be made; yet the turret was altogether apart from the portion of the abbey tenanted by the servants—there were none within call—I had no means of summoning them to my aid without leaving the room for many minutes—and this I could not venture to do. I therefore struggled alone in my endeavors to call back the spirit ill hovering. In a short period it was certain, however, that a relapse had taken place; the color disappeared from both eyelid and cheek, leaving a wanness even more than that of marble; the lips became doubly shrivelled and pinched up in the ghastly expression of death; a repulsive clamminess and coldness overspread rapidly the surface of the body; and all the usual rigorous illness immediately supervened. I fell back with a shudder upon the couch from which I had been so startlingly aroused, and again gave myself up to passionate waking visions of Ligeia.

An hour thus elapsed when (could it be possible?) I was a second time aware of some vague sound issuing from the region of the bed. I listened—in extremity of horror. The sound came again—it was a sigh. Rushing to the corpse, I saw—distinctly saw—a tremor upon the lips. In a minute afterward they relaxed, disclosing a bright line of the pearly teeth. Amazement now struggled in my bosom with the profound awe which had hitherto reigned there alone. I felt that my vision grew dim, that my reason wandered; and it was only by a violent effort that I at length succeeded in nerving myself to the task which duty thus once more had pointed out. There was now a partial glow upon the forehead and upon the cheek and throat; a perceptible warmth pervaded the whole frame; there was even a slight pulsation at the heart. The lady lived; and with redoubled ardor I betook myself to the task of restoration. I chafed and bathed the temples and the hands, and used every exertion which experience, and no little medical reading, could suggest. But in vain. Suddenly, the color fled, the pulsation ceased, the lips resumed the expression of the dead, and, in an instant afterward, the whole body took upon itself the icy chilliness, the livid hue, the intense rigidity, the sunken outline, and all the loathsome peculiarities of that which has been, for many days, a tenant of the tomb.

And again I sunk into visions of Ligeia—and again, (what marvel that I shudder while I write,) again there reached my ears a low sob from the region of the ebony bed. But why shall I minutely detail the unspeakable horrors of that night? Why shall I pause to relate how, time after time, until near the period of the gray dawn, this hideous drama of revivification was repeated; how each terrific relapse was only into a sterner and apparently more irredeemable death; how each agony wore the aspect of a struggle with some invisible foe; and how each struggle was succeeded by I know not what of wild change in the personal appearance of the corpse? Let me hurry to a conclusion.

The greater part of the fearful night had worn away, and she who had been dead, once again stirred—and now more vigorously than hitherto, although arousing from a dissolution more appalling in its utter hopelessness than any. I had long ceased to struggle or to move, and remained sitting rigidly upon the ottoman, a helpless prey to a whirl of violent emotions, of which extreme awe was perhaps the least terrible, the least consuming. The corpse, I repeat, stirred, and now more vigorously than before. The hues of life flushed up with unwonted energy into the countenance—the limbs relaxed—and, save that the eyelids were yet pressed heavily together, and that the bandages and draperies of the grave still imparted their charnel character to the figure, I might have dreamed that Rowena had indeed shaken off, utterly, the fetters of Death. But if this idea was not, even then, altogether adopted, I could at least doubt no longer, when, arising from the bed, tottering, with feeble steps, with closed eyes, and with the manner of one bewildered in a dream, the thing that was enshrouded advanced boldly and palpably into the middle of the apartment.

I trembled not—I stirred not—for a crowd of unutterable fancies connected with the air, the stature, the demeanor of the figure, rushing hurriedly through my brain, had paralyzed—had chilled me into stone. I stirred not—but gazed upon the apparition. There was a mad disorder in my thoughts—a tumult unappeasable. Could it, indeed, be the living Rowena who confronted me? Could it indeed be Rowena at all—the fair-haired, the blue-eyed Lady Rowena Trevanion of Tremaine?

Why, why should I doubt it? The bandage lay heavily about the mouth—but then might it not be the mouth of the breathing Lady of Tremaine? And the cheeks—there were the roses as in her noon of life—yes, these might indeed be the fair cheeks of the living Lady of Tremaine. And the chin, with its dimples, as in health, might it not be hers?—but had she then grown taller since her malady? What inexpressible madness seized me with that thought? One bound, and I had reached her feet! Shrinking from my touch, she let fall from her head, unloosened, the ghastly cerements which had confined it, and there streamed forth, into the rushing atmosphere of the chamber, huge masses of long and dishevelled hair; it was blacker than the raven wings of the midnight! And now slowly opened the eyes of the figure which stood before me. "Here then, at least," I shrieked aloud, "can I never—can I never be mistaken— these are the full, and the black, and the wild eyes—of my lost love—of the lady—of the LADY LIGEIA."

The Fall of the House of Usher

Son cœur est un luth suspend;

Sitôt qu'on le touche il résonne.

DE BÉRANGER

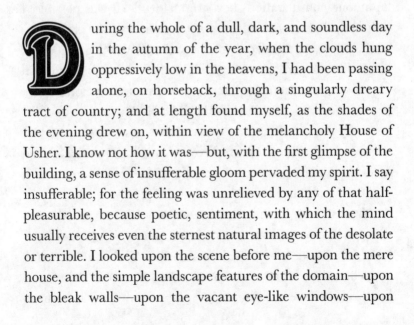

uring the whole of a dull, dark, and soundless day in the autumn of the year, when the clouds hung oppressively low in the heavens, I had been passing alone, on horseback, through a singularly dreary tract of country; and at length found myself, as the shades of the evening drew on, within view of the melancholy House of Usher. I know not how it was—but, with the first glimpse of the building, a sense of insufferable gloom pervaded my spirit. I say insufferable; for the feeling was unrelieved by any of that half-pleasurable, because poetic, sentiment, with which the mind usually receives even the sternest natural images of the desolate or terrible. I looked upon the scene before me—upon the mere house, and the simple landscape features of the domain—upon the bleak walls—upon the vacant eye-like windows—upon a few rank sedges—and upon a few white trunks of decayed trees—with an utter depression of soul which I can compare to no earthly sensation more properly than to the after-dream of the reveller upon opium—the bitter lapse into common life— the hideous dropping off of the veil. There was an iciness, a sinking, a sickening of the heart—an unredeemed dreariness of thought which no goading of the imagination could torture into aught of the sublime. What was it—I paused to think— what was it that so unnerved me in the contemplation of the House of Usher? It was a mystery all insoluble; nor could I grapple with the shadowy fancies that crowded upon me as I pondered. I was forced to fall back upon the unsatisfactory conclusion, that while, beyond doubt, there *are* combinations of very simple natural objects which have the power of thus affecting us, still the reason, and the analysis, of this power, lie among considerations beyond our depth. It was possible, I reflected, that a mere different arrangement of the particulars of the scene, of the details of the picture, would be sufficient to modify, or perhaps to annihilate its capacity for sorrowful impression; and, acting upon this idea, I reined my horse to the precipitous brink of a black and lurid tarn that lay in unruffled lustre by the dwelling, and gazed down—but with a shudder even more thrilling than before—upon the re-modelled and inverted images of the gray sedge, and the ghastly tree-stems, and the vacant and eye-like windows.

Nevertheless, in this mansion of gloom I now proposed to myself a sojourn of some weeks. Its proprietor, Roderick Usher, had been one of my boon companions in boyhood; but many years had elapsed since our last meeting. A letter, however, had lately reached me in a distant part of the country—a letter from him—which, in its wildly importunate nature, had admitted of no other than a personal reply. The MS. gave evidence of nervous agitation. The writer spoke of acute bodily illness—of a pitiable mental idiosyncrasy which oppressed him—and of an earnest desire to see me, as his best, and indeed, his only personal friend, with a view of attempting, by the cheerfulness of my society, some alleviation of his malady. It was the manner in which all this, and much more, was said—it was the apparent *heart* that went with his request—which allowed me no room for hesitation—and I accordingly obeyed, what I still considered a very singular summons, forthwith.

Although, as boys, we had been even intimate associates, yet I really knew little of my friend. His reserve had been always excessive and habitual. I was aware, however, that his very ancient family had been noted, time out of mind, for a peculiar sensibility of temperament, displaying itself, through long ages, in many works of exalted art, and manifested, of late, in repeated deeds of munificent yet unobtrusive charity, as well as in a passionate devotion to the intricacies, perhaps even more than to the orthodox and easily recognisable beauties, of musical science. I had learned, too, the very remarkable fact, that the stem of the Usher race, all time-honored as it was, had put forth, at no period, any enduring branch; in other words, that the entire family lay in the direct line of descent, and had always, with very trifling and very temporary variation, so lain. It was this deficiency, I considered, while running over in thought the perfect keeping of the character of the premises with the accredited character of the people, and while speculating upon the possible influence which the one, in the long lapse of centuries, might have exercised upon the other—it was this deficiency, perhaps, of collateral issue, and the consequent undeviating transmission, from sire to son, of the patrimony with the name, which had, at length, so identified the two as to merge the original title of the estate in the quaint and equivocal appellation of the "House of Usher"—an appellation which seemed to include, in the minds of the peasantry who used it, both the family and the family mansion.

I have said that the sole effect of my somewhat childish experiment, of looking down within the tarn, had been to deepen the first singular impression. There can be no doubt that the consciousness of the rapid increase of my superstition—for why should I not so term it?—served mainly to accelerate the increase itself. Such, I have long known, is the paradoxical law of all sentiments having terror as a basis. And it might have been for this reason only, that, when I again uplifted my eyes to the house itself, from its image in the pool, there grew in my mind a strange fancy—a fancy so ridiculous, indeed, that I but mention it to show the vivid force of the sensations which oppressed me. I had so worked upon my imagination as really to believe that around about the whole mansion and domain there hung an atmosphere peculiar to themselves and their immediate vicinity—an atmosphere which had no affinity with the air of heaven, but which had reeked up from the decayed trees, and the gray wall, and the silent tarn, in the form of an inelastic vapor or gas—dull, sluggish, faintly discernible, and leaden-hued.

Shaking off from my spirit what *must* have been a dream, I scanned more narrowly the real aspect of the building. Its principal feature seemed to be that of an excessive antiquity. The discoloration of ages had been great. Minute fungi overspread the whole exterior, hanging in a fine tangled web-work from the eaves. Yet all this was apart from any extraordinary dilapidation. No portion of the masonry had fallen; and there appeared to be a wild inconsistency between its still perfect adaptation of parts, and the utterly porous, and evidently decayed condition of the individual stones. In this there was much that reminded me of the specious totality of old wood-work which has rotted for long years in some neglected vault, with no disturbance from the breath of the external air. Beyond this indication of extensive decay, however, the fabric gave little token of instability. Perhaps the eye of a scrutinizing observer might have discovered a barely perceptible fissure, which, extending from the roof of the building in front, made its way down the wall in a zig-zag direction, until it became lost in the sullen waters of the tarn.

Noticing these things, I rode over a short causeway to the house. A servant in waiting took my horse, and I entered the Gothic archway of the hall. A valet, of stealthy step, thence conducted me, in silence, through many dark and intricate passages in my progress to the *studio* of his master. Much that I encountered on the way contributed, I know not how, to heighten the vague sentiments of which I have already spoken. While the objects around me—while the carvings of the ceilings, the sombre tapestries of the walls, the ebon blackness of the floors, and the phantasmagoric armorial trophies which rattled as I strode, were but matters to which, or to such as which, I had been accustomed from my infancy—while I hesitated not to acknowledge how familiar was all this—I still wondered to find how unfamiliar were the fancies which ordinary images were stirring up. On one of the staircases, I met the physician of the family. His countenance, I thought, wore a mingled expression of low cunning and perplexity. He accosted me with trepidation and passed on. The valet now threw open a door and ushered me into the presence of his master.

The room in which I found myself was very large and excessively lofty. The windows were long, narrow, and pointed, and at so vast a distance from the black oaken floor as to be altogether inaccessible from within. Feeble gleams of encrimsoned light made their way through the trellissed panes, and served to render sufficiently distinct the more prominent objects around; the eye, however, struggled in vain to reach the remoter angles of the chamber, or the recesses of the vaulted and fretted ceiling. Dark draperies hung upon the walls. The general furniture was profuse, comfortless, antique, and tattered. Many books and musical instruments lay scattered about, but failed to give any vitality to the scene. I felt that I breathed an atmosphere of sorrow. An air of stern, deep, and irredeemable gloom hung over and pervaded all.

Upon my entrance, Usher arose from a sofa upon which he had been lying at full length, and greeted me with a vivacious warmth which had much in it, I at first thought, of an overdone cordiality—of the constrained effort of the *ennuyé* man of the world. A glance, however, at his countenance convinced me of his perfect sincerity. We sat down; and for some moments, while he spoke not, I gazed upon him with a feeling half of pity, half of awe. Surely, man had never before so terribly altered, in so brief a period, as had Roderick Usher! It was with difficulty that I could bring myself to admit the identity of the wan being before me with the companion of my early boyhood. Yet the character of his face had been at all times

remarkable. A cadaverousness of complexion; an eye large, liquid, and luminous beyond comparison; lips somewhat thin and
very pallid, but of a surpassingly beautiful curve; a nose of a
delicate Hebrew model, but with a breadth of nostril unusual
in similar formations; a finely moulded chin, speaking, in its
want of prominence, of a want of moral energy; hair of a more
than web-like softness and tenuity; these features, with an inordinate expansion above the regions of the temple, made up
altogether a countenance not easily to be forgotten. And now
in the mere exaggeration of the prevailing character of these
features, and of the expression they were wont to convey, lay
so much of change that I doubted to whom I spoke. The now
ghastly pallor of the skin, and the now miraculous lustre of the
eye, above all things startled and even awed me. The silken
hair, too, had been suffered to grow all unheeded, and as, in its
wild gossamer texture, it floated rather than fell about the face,
I could not, even with effort, connect its arabesque expression
with any idea of simple humanity.

In the manner of my friend I was at once struck with an
incoherence—an inconsistency; and I soon found this to arise
from a series of feeble and futile struggles to overcome an habitual trepidancy, an excessive nervous agitation. For something of this nature I had indeed been prepared, no less by
his letter, than by reminiscences of certain boyish traits, and
by conclusions deduced from his peculiar physical conforma-
tion and temperament. His action was alternately vivacious
and sullen. His voice varied rapidly from a tremulous indecision (when the animal spirits seemed utterly in abeyance) to
that species of energetic concision—that abrupt, weighty, un-
hurried, and hollow-sounding enunciation—that leaden, self-

balanced and perfectly modulated guttural utterance, which may be observed in the moments of the intensest excitement of the lost drunkard, or the irreclaimable eater of opium, during the periods of his most intense excitement.

It was thus that he spoke of the object of my visit, of his earnest desire to see me, and of the solace he expected me to afford him. He entered, at some length, into what he conceived to be the nature of his malady. It was, he said, a constitutional and a family evil, and one for which he despaired to find a remedy—a mere nervous affection, he immediately added, which would undoubtedly soon pass off. It displayed itself in a host of unnatural sensations. Some of these, as he detailed them, interested and bewildered me—although, perhaps, the terms, and the general manner of the narration had their weight. He suffered much from a morbid acuteness of the senses; the most insipid food was alone endurable; he could wear only garments of certain texture; the odors of all flowers were oppressive; his eyes were tortured by even a faint light; and there were but peculiar sounds, and these from stringed instruments, which did not inspire him with horror.

To an anomalous species of terror I found him a bounden slave. "I shall perish," said he, "I *must* perish in this deplorable folly. Thus, thus, and not otherwise, shall I be lost. I dread the events of the future, not in themselves, but in their results. I shudder at the thought of any, even the most trivial, incident, which may operate upon this intolerable agitation of soul. I have, indeed, no abhorrence of danger, except in its absolute effect—in terror. In this unnerved—in this pitiable condition— I feel that I must inevitably abandon life and reason together in my struggles with some fatal demon of FEAR."

I learned, moreover, at intervals, and through broken and equivocal hints, another singular feature of his mental condition. He was enchained by certain superstitious impressions in regard to the dwelling which he tenanted, and from which, for many years, he had never ventured forth—in regard to an influence whose supposititious force was conveyed in terms too shadowy here to be restated—an influence which some peculiarities in the mere form and substance of his family mansion, had, by dint of long sufferance, he said, obtained over his spirit—an effect which the *physique* of the gray walls and turrets, and of the dim tarn into which they all looked down, had, at length, brought about upon the *morale* of his existence.

He admitted, however, although with hesitation, that much of the peculiar gloom which thus afflicted him could be traced to a more natural and far more palpable origin—to the severe and long-continued illness—indeed to the evidently approaching dissolution—of a tenderly beloved sister; his sole companion for long years—his last and only relative on earth. "Her decease," he said, with a bitterness which I can never forget, "would leave him (him the hopeless and the frail) the last of the ancient race of the Ushers." As he spoke the lady Madeline (for so was she called) passed slowly through a remote portion of the apartment, and, without having noticed my presence, disappeared. I regarded her with an utter astonishment not unmingled with dread. Her figure, her air, her features—all, in their very minutest development were those—were identically, (I can use no other sufficient term,) were identically those of the Roderick Usher who sat beside me. A feeling of stupor oppressed me, as my eyes followed her retreating steps. As a door, at length, closed upon her exit, my glance sought instinctively and eagerly the countenance of the brother—but he had buried his face in his hands, and I could only perceive that a far more than ordinary wanness had overspread the emaciated fingers through which trickled many passionate tears.

The disease of the lady Madeline had long baffled the skill of her physicians. A settled apathy, a gradual wasting away of the person, and frequent although transient affections of a partially cataleptical character, were the unusual diagnosis. Hitherto she had steadily borne up against the pressure of her malady, and had not betaken herself finally to bed; but, on the closing in of the evening of my arrival at the house, she succumbed, as her brother told me at night with inexpressible agitation, to the prostrating power of the destroyer—and I learned that the glimpse I had obtained of her person would thus probably be the last I should obtain—that the lady, at least while living, would be seen by me no more.

For several days ensuing, her name was unmentioned by either Usher or myself; and during this period, I was busied in earnest endeavors to alleviate the melancholy of my friend. We painted and read together—or I listened, as if in a dream, to the wild improvisations of his speaking guitar. And thus, as a closer and still closer intimacy admitted me more unreservedly into the recesses of his spirit, the more bitterly did I perceive the futility of all attempt at cheering a mind from which darkness, as if an inherent positive quality, poured forth upon all objects of the moral and physical universe, in one unceasing radiation of gloom.

I shall ever bear about me a memory of the many solemn hours I thus spent alone with the master of the House of Usher. Yet I should fail in any attempt to convey an idea of the ex-

act character of the studies, or of the occupations, in which
he involved me, or led me the way. An excited and highly dis-
tempered ideality threw a sulphurous lustre over all. His long
improvised dirges will ring forever in my ears. Among other
things, I bear painfully in mind a certain singular perversion
and amplification of the wild air of the last waltz of Von Weber.
From the paintings over which his elaborate fancy brooded,
and which grew, touch by touch, into vaguenesses at which I
shuddered the more thrillingly, because I shuddered knowing
not why, from these paintings (vivid as their images now are before me) I would in vain endeavor to educe more than a small
portion which should lie within the compass of merely written
words. By the utter simplicity, by the nakedness of his designs,
he arrested and overawed attention. If ever mortal painted an
idea, that mortal was Roderick Usher. For me at least—in the
circumstances then surrounding me—there arose out of the
pure abstractions which the hypochondriac contrived to throw
upon his canvas, an intensity of intolerable awe, no shadow of
which felt I ever yet in the contemplation of the certainly glowing yet too concrete reveries of Fuseli.

One of the phantasmagoric conceptions of my friend,
partaking not so rigidly of the spirit of abstraction, may be
shadowed forth, although feebly, in words. A small picture presented the interior of an immensely long and rectangular vault
or tunnel, with low walls, smooth, white, and without interruption or device. Certain accessory points of the design served
well to convey the idea that this excavation lay at an exceeding
depth below the surface of the earth. No outlet was observed
in any portion of its vast extent, and no torch, or other artificial source of light was discernible—yet a flood of intense rays

rolled throughout, and bathed the whole in a ghastly and inappropriate splendor.

I have just spoken of that morbid condition of the auditory nerve which rendered all music intolerable to the sufferer, with the exception of certain effects of stringed instruments. It was, perhaps, the narrow limits to which he thus confined himself upon the guitar, which gave birth, in great measure, to the fantastic character of his performances. But the fervid *facility* of his *impromptus* could not be so accounted for. They must have been, and were, in the notes, as well as in the words of his wild fantasias, (for he not unfrequently accompanied himself with rhymed verbal improvisations,) the result of that intense mental collectedness and concentration to which I have previously alluded as observable only in particular moments of the highest artificial excitement. The words of one of these rhapsodies I have easily borne away in memory. I was, perhaps, the more forcibly impressed with it, as he gave it, because, in the under or mystic current of its meaning, I fancied that I perceived, and for the first time, a full consciousness on the part of Usher, of the tottering of his lofty reason upon her throne. The verses, which were entitled "The Haunted Palace," ran very nearly, if not accurately, thus:

I.

In the greenest of our valleys,
    By good angels tenanted,
Once a fair and stately palace—
    Radiant palace—reared its head.
In the monarch Thought's dominion—
    It stood there!

Never seraph spread a pinion
　　Over fabric half so fair.

II.

Banners yellow, glorious, golden,
　　On its roof did float and flow;
(This—all this—was in the olden
　　Time long ago)
And every gentle air that dallied,
　　In that sweet day,
Along the ramparts plumed and pallid,
　　A winged odor went away.

III.

Wanderers in that happy valley
　　Through two luminous windows saw
Spirits moving musically
　　To a lute's well-tunéd law,
Round about a throne, where sitting
(Porphyrogene!)
In state his glory well befitting,
The ruler of the realm was seen.

IV.

And all with pearl and ruby glowing
　　Was the fair palace door,
Through which came flowing, flowing, flowing,

And sparkling evermore,
A troop of Echoes whose sweet duty
    Was but to sing,
In voices of surpassing beauty,
    The wit and wisdom of their king.

V.

But evil things, in robes of sorrow,
    Assailed the monarch's high estate;
(Ah, let us mourn, for never morrow
    Shall dawn upon him, desolate!)
And, round about his home, the glory
    That blushed and bloomed
Is but a dim-remembered story
    Of the old time entombed.

VI.

And travellers now within that valley,
    Through the red-litten windows, see
Vast forms that move fantastically
    To a discordant melody;
While, like a rapid ghastly river,
    Through the pale door,
A hideous throng rush out forever,
    And laugh—but smile no more.

I well remember that suggestions arising from this ballad led us into a train of thought wherein there became manifest an opinion of Usher's which I mention not so much on account of its novelty, (for other men* have thought thus,) as on account of the pertinacity with which he maintained it. This opinion, in its general form, was that of the sentience of all vegetable things. But, in his disordered fancy, the idea had assumed a more daring character, and trespassed, under certain conditions, upon the kingdom of inorganization. I lack words to express the full extent, or the earnest *abandon* of his persuasion. The belief, however, was connected (as I have previously hinted) with the gray stones of the home of his forefathers. The conditions of the sentience had been here, he imagined, fulfilled in the method of collocation of these stones—in the order of their arrangement, as well as in that of the many fungi which overspread them, and of the decayed trees which stood around—above all, in the long undisturbed endurance of this arrangement, and in its reduplication in the still waters of the tarn. Its evidence—the evidence of the sentience—was to be seen, he said, (and I here started as he spoke,) in the gradual yet certain condensation of an atmosphere of their own about the waters and the walls. The result was discoverable, he added, in that silent, yet importunate and terrible influence which for centuries had moulded the destinies of his family, and which made *him* what I now saw him—what he was. Such opinions need no comment, and I will make none.

Our books—the books which, for years, had formed no small portion of the mental existence of the invalid—were, as might be supposed, in strict keeping with this character of

---

* Watson, Dr. Percival, Spallanzani, and especially the Bishop of Landaff.— See "Chemical Essays," vol v.

phantasm. We pored together over such works as the Ververt et Chartreuse of Gresset; the Belphegor of Machiavelli; the Selenography of Brewster; the Heaven and Hell of Swedenborg; the Subterranean Voyage of Nicholas Klimm de Holberg; the Chiromancy of Robert Flud, of Jean d'Indaginé, and of De la Chambre; the Journey into the Blue Distance of Tieck; and the City of the Sun of Campanella. One favorite volume was a small octavo edition of the Directorium Inquisitorium, by the Dominican Eymeric de Gironne; and there were passages in Pomponius Mela, about the old African Satyrs and œgipans, over which Usher would sit dreaming for hours. His chief delight, however, was found in the earnest and repeated perusal of an exceedingly rare and curious book in quarto Gothic— the manual of a forgotten church—the *Vigilae Mortuorum secundum Chorum Ecclesiae Maguntinae.*

I could not help thinking of the wild ritual of this work, and of its probable influence upon the hypochondriac, when, one evening, having informed me abruptly that the lady Madeline was no more, he stated his intention of preserving her corpse for a fortnight, (previously to its final interment,) in one of the numerous vaults within the main walls of the building. The worldly reason, however, assigned for this singular proceeding, was one which I did not feel at liberty to dispute. The brother had been led to his resolution (so he told me) by considerations of the unusual character of the malady of the deceased, of certain obtrusive and eager inquiries on the part of her medical men, and of the remote and exposed situation of the burial-ground of the family. I will not deny that when I called to mind the sinister countenance of the person whom I met upon the staircase, on the day of my arrival at the house, I had no desire to oppose what I regarded as at best but a harmless, and not by any means an unnatural, precaution.

At the request of Usher, I personally aided him in the arrangements for the temporary entombment. The body having been encoffined, we two alone bore it to its rest. The vault in which we placed it (and which had been so long unopened that our torches, half smothered in its oppressive atmosphere, gave us little opportunity for investigation) was small, damp, and entirely without means of admission for light; lying, at great depth, immediately beneath that portion of the building in which was my own sleeping apartment. It had been used, apparently, in remote feudal times, for the worst purposes of a donjon-keep, and, in later days, as a place of deposit for powder, or other highly combustible substance, as a portion of its floor, and the whole interior of a long archway through which we reached it, were carefully sheathed with copper. The door, of massive iron, had been, also, similarly protected. Its immense weight caused an unusually sharp grating sound, as it moved upon its hinges.

Having deposited our mournful burden upon tressels within this region of horror, we partially turned aside the yet unscrewed lid of the coffin, and looked upon the face of the tenant. The exact similitude between the brother and sister even here again startled and confounded me. Usher, divining, perhaps, my thoughts, murmured out some few words from which I learned that the deceased and himself had been twins, and that sympathies of a scarcely intelligible nature had always existed between them. Our glances, however, rested not long upon the dead—for we could not regard her unawed. The disease which had thus entombed the lady in the maturity of youth, had left, as usual in all maladies of a strictly cataleptical character, the mockery of a faint blush upon the bosom and the face, and that suspiciously lingering smile upon the lip which is so terrible in death. We replaced and screwed down the lid, and, having secured the door of iron, made our way, with toil, into the scarcely less gloomy apartments of the upper portion of the house.

And now, some days of bitter grief having elapsed, an observable change came over the features of the mental disorder of my friend. His ordinary manner had vanished. His ordinary occupations were neglected or forgotten. He roamed from chamber to chamber with hurried, unequal, and objectless step. The pallor of his countenance had assumed, if possible, a more ghastly hue—but the luminousness of his eye had utterly gone out. The once occasional huskiness of his tone was heard no more; and a tremulous quaver, as if of extreme terror, habitually characterized his utterance. There were times, indeed, when I thought his unceasingly agitated mind was laboring with an oppressive secret, to divulge which he struggled for the necessary courage. At times, again, I was obliged to resolve all into the mere inexplicable vagaries of madness, as I beheld him gazing upon vacancy for long hours, in an attitude of the profoundest attention, as if listening to some imaginary sound. It was no wonder that his condition terrified—that it infected me. I felt creeping upon me, by slow yet certain degrees, the wild influences of his own fantastic yet impressive superstitions.

It was, most especially, upon retiring to bed late in the night of the seventh or eighth day after the placing of the lady Madeline within the donjon, that I experienced the full power of such feelings. Sleep came not near my couch—while the hours waned and waned away. I struggled to reason off the nervousness which had dominion over me. I endeavored to believe that much, if not all of what I felt, was due to the phantasmagoric influence of the gloomy furniture of the room—of the dark and tattered draperies, which, tortured into motion by the breath of a rising tempest, swayed fitfully to and fro upon the walls, and rustled uneasily about the decorations of the bed. But my efforts were fruitless. An irrepressible tremor gradually pervaded my frame; and, at length, there sat upon my very heart an incubus of utterly causeless alarm. Shaking this off with a gasp and a struggle, I uplifted myself upon the pillows, and, peering earnestly within the intense darkness of the chamber, harkened—I know not why, except that an instinctive spirit prompted me—to certain low and indefinite sounds which came, through the pauses of the storm, at long intervals, I knew not whence. Overpowered by an intense sentiment of horror, unaccountable yet unendurable, I threw on my clothes with haste, for I felt that I should sleep no more during the night, and endeavored to arouse myself from the pitiable condition into which I had fallen, by pacing rapidly to and fro through the apartment.

I had taken but few turns in this manner, when a light step on an adjoining staircase arrested my attention. I presently recognised it as that of Usher. In an instant afterwards he rapped, with a gentle touch, at my door, and entered, bearing a lamp. His countenance was, as usual, cadaverously wan—but there was a species of mad hilarity in his eyes—an evidently restrained *hysteria* in his whole demeanor. His air appalled me—but anything was preferable to the solitude which I had so long endured, and I even welcomed his presence as a relief.

"And you have not seen it?" he said abruptly, after having stared about him for some moments in silence—"you have not then seen it?—but, stay! you shall." Thus speaking, and having carefully shaded his lamp, he hurried to one of the gigantic casements, and threw it freely open to the storm.

The impetuous fury of the entering gust nearly lifted us from our feet. It was, indeed, a tempestuous yet sternly beautiful night, and one wildly singular in its terror and its beauty. A whirlwind had apparently collected its force in our vicinity; for there were frequent and violent alterations in the direction of the wind; and the exceeding density of the clouds (which hung so low as to press upon the turrets of the house) did not prevent our perceiving the life-like velocity with which they flew careering from all points against each other, without passing away into the distance. I say that even their exceeding density did not prevent our perceiving this—yet we had no glimpse of the moon or stars—nor was there any flashing forth of the lightning. But the under surfaces of the huge masses of agitated vapor, as well as all terrestrial objects immediately around us, were glowing in the unnatural light of a faintly luminous and distinctly visible gaseous exhalation which hung about and enshrouded the mansion.

"You must not—you shall not behold this!" said I, shudderingly, to Usher, as I led him, with a gentle violence, from the window to a seat. "These appearances, which bewilder you, are merely electrical phenomena not uncommon—or it may be that they have their ghastly origin in the rank miasma of the tarn. Let us close this casement—the air is chilling and dangerous to your frame. Here is one of your favorite romances.

I will read, and you shall listen—and so we will pass away this terrible night together."

The antique volume which I had taken up was the "Mad Trist" of Sir Launcelot Canning—but I had called it a favorite of Usher's more in sad jest than in earnest; for, in truth, there is little in its uncouth and unimaginative prolixity which could have had interest for the lofty and spiritual ideality of my friend. It was, however, the only book immediately at hand; and I indulged a vague hope that the excitement which now agitated the hypochondriac might find relief (for the history of mental disorder is full of similar anomalies) even in the extremeness of the folly which I should read. Could I have judged, indeed by the wild overstrained air of vivacity with which he hearkened, or apparently hearkened, to the words of the tale, I might have well congratulated myself upon the success of my design.

I had arrived at that well-known portion of the story where Ethelred, the hero of the Trist, having sought in vain for peaceable admission into the dwelling of the hermit, proceeds to make good an entrance by force. Here, it will be remembered, the words of the narrative run thus:—

"And Ethelred, who was by nature of a doughty heart, and who was now mighty withal, on account of the powerfulness of the wine which he had drunken, waited no longer to hold parley with the hermit, who, in sooth, was of an obstinate and maliceful turn, but, feeling the rain upon his shoulders, and fearing the rising of the tempest, uplifted his mace outright, and, with blows, made quickly room in the plankings of the door for his gauntleted hand, and now pulling therewith sturdily, he so cracked, and ripped, and tore all asunder, that the noise of the dry and hollow-sounding wood alarummed and reverberated throughout the forest."

At the termination of this sentence I started, and for a moment, paused; for it appeared to me (although I at once concluded that my excited fancy had deceived me)—it appeared to me that, from some very remote portion of the mansion or of its vicinity, there came, indistinctly, to my ears, what might have been, in its exact similarity of character, the echo (but a stifled and dull one certainly) of the very cracking and ripping sound which Sir Launcelot had so particularly described. It was, beyond doubt, the coincidence alone which had arrested my attention; for, amid the rattling of the sashes of the casements, and the ordinary commingled noises of the still increasing storm, the sound, in itself, had nothing, surely, which should have interested or disturbed me. I continued the story.

"But the good champion Ethelred, now entering within the door, was sore enraged and amazed to perceive no signal of the maliceful hermit; but, in the stead thereof, a dragon of a scaly and prodigious demeanor, and of a fiery tongue, which sate in guard before a palace of gold, with a floor of silver; and upon the wall there hung a shield of shining brass with this legend enwritten—

Who entereth herein, a conqueror hath bin,
Who slayeth the dragon the shield he shall win.

And Ethelred uplifted his mace, and struck upon the head of the dragon, which fell before him, and gave up his pesty breath, with a shriek so horrid and harsh, and withal so piercing, that Ethelred had fain to close his ears with his hands

against the dreadful noise of it, the like whereof was never before heard."

Here again I paused abruptly, and now with a feeling of wild
amazement—for there could be no doubt whatever that, in this
instance, I did actually hear (although from what direction it
proceeded I found it impossible to say) a low and apparently
distant, but harsh, protracted, and most unusual screaming or
grating sound—the exact counterpart of what my fancy had
already conjured up as the sound of the dragon's unnatural
shriek as described by the romancer.

Oppressed, as I certainly was, upon the occurrence of this
second and most extraordinary coincidence, by a thousand
conflicting sensations, in which wonder and extreme terror
were predominant, I still retained sufficient presence of mind
to avoid exciting, by any observation, the sensitive nervousness of my companion. I was by no means certain that he had
noticed the sounds in question; although, assuredly, a strange
alteration had, during the last few minutes, taken place in his
demeanor. From a position fronting my own, he had gradually
brought round his chair, so as to sit with his face to the door
of the chamber, and thus I could but partially perceive his features, although I saw that his lips trembled as if he were mur-
muring inaudibly. His head had dropped upon his breast—yet
I knew that he was not asleep, from the wide and rigid opening
of the eye as I caught a glance of it in profile. The motion of his
body, too, was at variance with this idea—for he rocked from
side to side with a gentle yet constant and uniform sway. Having rapidly taken notice of all this, I resumed the narrative of
Sir Launcelot, which thus proceeded:—

"And now, the champion, having escaped from the terrible

fury of the dragon, bethinking himself of the brazen shield, and of the breaking up of the enchantment which was upon it, removed the carcass from out of the way before him, and approached valorously over the silver pavement of the castle to where the shield was upon the wall; which in sooth tarried not for his full coming, but fell down at his feet upon the silver floor, with a mighty great and terrible ringing sound."

No sooner had these syllables passed my lips, than—as if a shield of brass had indeed, at the moment, fallen heavily upon a floor of silver—I became aware of a distinct, hollow, metallic, and clangorous, yet apparently muffled reverberation. Completely unnerved, I started convulsively to my feet; but the measured rocking movement of Usher was undisturbed. I rushed to the chair in which he sat. His eyes were bent fixedly before him, and throughout his whole countenance there reigned a more than stony rigidity. But, as I laid my hand upon his shoulder, there came a strong shudder over his frame; a sickly smile quivered about his lips; and I saw that he spoke in a low, hurried, and gibbering murmur, as if unconscious of my presence. Bending closely over his person, I at length drank in the hideous import of his words.

"Not hear it?—yes, I hear it, and *have* heard it. Long—long—long—many minutes, many hours, many days, have I heard it—yet I dared not—oh, pity me, miserable wretch that I am!—I dared not—I *dared* not speak! *We have put her living in the tomb!* Said I not that my senses were acute? I *now* tell you that I heard her first feeble movements in the hollow coffin. I heard them—many, many days ago—yet I dared not—*I dared not speak!* And now—to-night—Ethelred—ha! ha!—the breaking of the hermit's door, and the death-cry of the dragon, and the clangor of the shield—say, rather, the rending of the coffin, and the grating of the iron hinges, and her struggles within the coppered archway of the vault! Oh whither shall I fly? Will she not be here anon? Is she not hurrying to upbraid me for my haste? Have I not heard her footsteps on the stair? Do I not distinguish that heavy and horrible beating of her heart? Madman!"—here he sprung violently to his feet, and shrieked out his syllables, as if in the effort he were giving up his soul— *"Madman! I tell you that she now stands without the door!"*

As if in the superhuman energy of his utterance there had been found the potency of a spell—the huge antique panels to which the speaker pointed, threw slowly back, upon the instant, their ponderous and ebony jaws. It was the work of the rushing gust—but then without those doors there *did* stand the lofty and enshrouded figure of the lady Madeline of Usher. There was blood upon her white robes, and the evidence of some bitter struggle upon every portion of her emaciated frame. For a moment she remained trembling and reeling to and fro upon the threshold—then, with a low moaning cry, fell heavily inward upon the person of her brother, and in her horrible and now final death-agonies, bore him to the floor a corpse, and a victim to the terrors he had dreaded.

From that chamber, and from that mansion, I fled aghast. The storm was still abroad in all its wrath as I found myself crossing the old causeway. Suddenly there shot along the path a wild light, and I turned to see whence a gleam so unusual could have issued—for the vast house and its shadows were alone behind me. The radiance was that of the full, setting, and blood-red moon, which now shone vividly through that once barely-discernible fissure, of which I have before spoken, as extending from the roof of the building, in a zigzag direction to the base. While I gazed, this fissure rapidly widened—there came a fierce breath of the whirlwind—the entire orb of the satellite burst at once upon my sight—my brain reeled as I saw the mighty walls rushing asunder—there was a long tumultuous shouting sound like the voice of a thousand waters—and the deep and dank tarn at my feet closed sullenly and silently over the fragments of the "*House of Usher.*"

The Murders in the Rue Morgue

What song the Syrens sang, or what name Achilles
assumed when he hid

himself among women, although puzzling questions,
are not beyond all conjecture.

—Sir Thomas Browne

The mental features discoursed of as the analytical, are, in themselves, but little susceptible of analysis. We appreciate them only in their effects. We know of them, among other things, that they are always to their possessor, when inordinately possessed, a source of the liveliest enjoyment. As the strong man exults in his physical ability, delighting in such exercises as call his muscles into action, so glories the analyst in that moral activity which *disentangles*. He derives pleasure from even the most trivial occupations bringing his talent into play. He is fond of enigmas, of conundrums, of hieroglyphics; exhibiting in his solutions of each a degree of *acumen* which appears to the ordinary apprehension præternatural. His results, brought about by the very soul and essence of method, have, in truth, the whole air of intuition.

The faculty of re-solution is possibly much invigorated by mathematical study, and especially by that highest branch of it which, unjustly, and merely on account of its retrograde operations, has been called, as if *par excellence,* analysis. Yet to calculate is not in itself to analyse. A chess-player, for example, does the one without effort at the other. It follows that the game of chess, in its effects upon mental character, is greatly misunderstood. I am not now writing a treatise, but simply prefacing a somewhat peculiar narrative by observations very much at random; I will, therefore, take occasion to assert that the higher powers of the reflective intellect are more decidedly and more usefully tasked by the unostentatious game of draughts than by all the elaborate frivolity of chess. In this latter, where the pieces have different and *bizarre* motions, with various and variable values, what is only complex is mistaken (a not unusual error) for what is profound. The *attention* is here called powerfully into play. If it flag for an instant, an oversight is committed resulting in injury or defeat. The possible moves being not only manifold but involute, the chances of such oversights are multiplied; and in nine cases out of ten it is the more concentrative rather than the more acute player who conquers. In draughts, on the contrary, where the moves are *unique* and have but little variation, the probabilities of inadvertence are diminished, and the mere attention being left comparatively unemployed, what advantages are obtained by either party are obtained by superior *acumen.* To be less abstract—Let us suppose a game of draughts where the pieces are reduced to four kings, and where, of course, no oversight is to be expected. It is obvious that here the victory can be decided (the players being at all equal) only by some *recherché* movement, the result of some strong exertion of the intellect. Deprived of ordinary resources, the analyst throws himself into the spirit of his opponent, identifies himself therewith, and not unfrequently sees thus, at a glance, the sole methods (sometime indeed absurdly simple ones) by which he may seduce into error or hurry into miscalculation.

Whist has long been noted for its influence upon what is termed the calculating power; and men of the highest order of intellect have been known to take an apparently unaccountable delight in it, while eschewing chess as frivolous. Beyond doubt there is nothing of a similar nature so greatly tasking the faculty of analysis. The best chess-player in Christendom *may* be little more than the best player of chess; but proficiency in whist implies capacity for success in all those more important undertakings where mind struggles with mind. When I say proficiency, I mean that perfection in the game which includes a comprehension of *all* the sources whence legitimate advantage may be derived. These are not only manifold but multiform, and lie frequently among recesses of thought altogether inaccessible to the ordinary understanding. To observe attentively is to remember distinctly; and, so far, the concentrative chess-player will do very well at whist; while the rules of Hoyle (themselves based upon the mere mechanism of the game) are sufficiently and generally comprehensible. Thus to have a retentive memory, and to proceed by "the book," are points commonly regarded as the sum total of good playing. But it is in matters beyond the limits of mere rule that the skill of the analyst is evinced. He makes, in silence, a host of observations and inferences. So, perhaps, do his companions; and the difference in the extent of the information obtained, lies not so much in the validity of the inference as in the quality of the observation. The necessary knowledge is that of *what* to observe. Our player confines himself not at all; nor, because the game is the object, does he reject deductions from things external to the game. He examines the countenance of his partner, comparing it carefully with that of each of his opponents. He considers the mode of assorting the cards in each hand; often counting trump by trump, and honor by honor, through the glances bestowed by their holders upon each. He notes every variation of face as the play progresses, gathering a fund of thought from the differences in the expression of certainty, of surprise, of triumph, or of chagrin. From the manner of gathering up a trick he judges whether the person taking it can make another in the suit. He recognises what is played through feint, by the air with which it is thrown upon the table. A casual or inadvertent word; the accidental dropping or turning of a card, with the accompanying anxiety or carelessness in regard to its concealment; the counting of the tricks, with the order of their arrangement; embarrassment, hesitation, eagerness or trepidation—all afford, to his apparently intuitive perception, indications of the true state of affairs. The first two or three rounds having been played, he is in full possession of the contents of each hand, and thenceforward puts down his cards with as absolute a precision of purpose as if the rest of the party had turned outward the faces of their own.

The analytical power should not be confounded with ample ingenuity; for while the analyst is necessarily ingenious, the ingenious man is often remarkably incapable of analysis. The constructive or combining power, by which ingenuity is usually manifested, and to which the phrenologists (I believe erroneously) have assigned a separate organ, supposing it a primitive faculty, has been so frequently seen in those whose intellect bordered otherwise upon idiocy, as to have attracted general observation among writers on morals. Between ingenuity and the analytic ability there exists a difference far greater, indeed, than that between the fancy and the imagination, but of a character very strictly analogous. It will be found, in fact, that the ingenious are always fanciful, and the *truly* imaginative never otherwise than analytic.

The narrative which follows will appear to the reader somewhat in the light of a commentary upon the propositions just advanced.

Residing in Paris during the spring and part of the summer of 18—, I there became acquainted with a Monsieur C. Auguste Dupin. This young gentleman was of an excellent—indeed of an illustrious family, but, by a variety of untoward events, had been reduced to such poverty that the energy of his character succumbed beneath it, and he ceased to bestir himself in the world, or to care for the retrieval of his fortunes. By courtesy of his creditors, there still remained in his possession a small remnant of his patrimony; and, upon the income arising from this, he managed, by means of a rigorous economy, to procure the necessaries of life, without troubling himself about its superfluities. Books, indeed, were his sole luxuries, and in Paris these are easily obtained.

Our first meeting was at an obscure library in the Rue Montmartre, where the accident of our both being in search of the same very rare and very remarkable volume, brought us into closer communion. We saw each other again and again. I was deeply interested in the little family history which he detailed to me with all that candor which a Frenchman indulges whenever mere self is his theme. I was astonished, too, at the vast extent of his reading; and, above all, I felt my soul enkindled within me by the wild fervor, and the vivid freshness of his imagination. Seeking in Paris the objects I then sought, I felt that the society of such a man would be to me a treasure beyond price; and this feeling I frankly confided to him. It was at length arranged that we should live together during my stay in the city; and as my worldly circumstances were somewhat less embarrassed than his own, I was permitted to be at the expense of renting, and furnishing in a style which suited the rather fantastic gloom of our common temper, a time-eaten and grotesque mansion, long deserted through superstitions into which we did not inquire, and tottering to its fall in a retired and desolate portion of the Faubourg St. Germain.

Had the routine of our life at this place been known to the world, we should have been regarded as madmen—although, perhaps, as madmen of a harmless nature. Our seclusion was perfect. We admitted no visitors. Indeed the locality of our retirement had been carefully kept a secret from my own former associates; and it had been many years since Dupin had ceased to know or be known in Paris. We existed within ourselves alone.

It was a freak of fancy in my friend (for what else shall I call it?) to be enamored of the Night for her own sake; and into this *bizarrerie*, as into all his others, I quietly fell; giving myself up to his wild whims with a perfect *abandon*. The sable divinity would not herself dwell with us always; but we could counterfeit her presence. At the first dawn of the morning we closed all the messy shutters of our old building; lighting a couple of tapers which, strongly perfumed, threw out only the ghastliest and feeblest of rays. By the aid of these we then busied our souls in dreams—reading, writing, or conversing, until warned by the clock of the advent of the true Darkness. Then we sallied forth into the streets arm in arm, continuing the topics of the day, or roaming far and wide until a late hour, seeking, amid the wild lights and shadows of the populous city, that infinity of mental excitement which quiet observation can afford.

At such times I could not help remarking and admiring (although from his rich ideality I had been prepared to expect it) a peculiar analytic ability in Dupin. He seemed, too, to take an eager delight in its exercise—if not exactly in its display—and did not hesitate to confess the pleasure thus derived. He boasted to me, with a low chuckling laugh, that most men, in respect to himself, wore windows in their bosoms, and was wont to follow up such assertions by direct and very startling proofs of his intimate knowledge of my own. His manner at these moments was frigid and abstract; his eyes were vacant in expression; while his voice, usually a rich tenor, rose into a treble which would have sounded petulantly but for the deliberateness and entire distinctness of the enunciation. Observing him in these moods, I often dwelt meditatively upon the old philosophy of the Bi-Part Soul, and amused myself with the fancy of a double Dupin—the creative and the resolvent.

Let it not be supposed, from what I have just said, that I am detailing any mystery, or penning any romance. What I have described in the Frenchman, was merely the result of an excited, or perhaps of a diseased intelligence. But of the character of his remarks at the periods in question an example will best convey the idea.

We were strolling one night down a long dirty street in the vicinity of the Palais Royal. Being both, apparently, occupied with thought, neither of us had spoken a syllable for fifteen minutes at least. All at once Dupin broke forth with these words:

"He is a very little fellow, that's true, and would do better for the *Théâtre des Variétés.*"

"There can be no doubt of that," I replied unwittingly, and not at first observing (so much had I been absorbed in reflection) the extraordinary manner in which the speaker had chimed in with my meditations. In an instant afterward I recollected myself, and my astonishment was profound.

"Dupin," said I, gravely, "this is beyond my comprehension. I do not hesitate to say that I am amazed, and can scarcely credit my senses. How was it possible you should know I was thinking of——?" Here I paused, to ascertain beyond a doubt whether he really knew of whom I thought.

——"of Chantilly," said he, "why do you pause? You were remarking to yourself that his diminutive figure unfitted him for tragedy."

This was precisely what had formed the subject of my reflections. Chantilly was a *quondam* cobbler of the Rue St. Denis, who, becoming stage-mad, had attempted the *rôle* of Xerxes, in Crébillon's tragedy so called, and been notoriously Pasquinaded for his pains.

"Tell me, for Heaven's sake," I exclaimed, "the method—if method there is—by which you have been enabled to fathom my soul in this matter." In fact I was even more startled than I would have been willing to express.

"It was the fruiterer," replied my friend, "who brought you

to the conclusion that the mender of soles was not of sufficient height for Xerxes *et id genus omne.*"

"The fruiterer!—you astonish me—I know no fruiterer whomsoever."

"The man who ran up against you as we entered the street—it may have been fifteen minutes ago."

I now remembered that, in fact, a fruiterer, carrying upon his head a large basket of apples, had nearly thrown me down, by accident, as we passed from the Rue C——into the thoroughfare where we stood; but what this had to do with Chantilly I could not possibly understand.

There was not a particle of *charlatanerie* about Dupin. "I will explain," he said, "and that you may comprehend all clearly, we will first retrace the course of your meditations, from the moment in which I spoke to you until that of the *rencontre* with the fruiterer in question. The larger links of the chain run thus—Chantilly, Orion, Dr. Nichols, Epicurus, Stereotomy, the street stones, the fruiterer."

There are few persons who have not, at some period of their lives, amused themselves in retracing the steps by which particular conclusions of their own minds have been attained. The occupation is often full of interest and he who attempts it for the first time is astonished by the apparently illimitable distance and incoherence between the starting-point and the goal. What, then, must have been my amazement when I heard the Frenchman speak what he had just spoken, and when I could not help acknowledging that he had spoken the truth. He continued:

"We had been talking of horses, if I remember aright, just before leaving the Rue C——. This was the last subject we discussed. As we crossed into this street, a fruiterer, with a large basket upon his head, brushing quickly past us, thrust you upon a pile of paving stones collected at a spot where the causeway is undergoing repair. You stepped upon one of the loose fragments, slipped, slightly strained your ankle, appeared vexed or sulky, muttered a few words, turned to look at the pile, and then proceeded in silence. I was not particularly attentive to what you did; but observation has become with me, of late, a species of necessity.

"You kept your eyes upon the ground—glancing, with a petulant expression, at the holes and ruts in the pavement, (so that I saw you were still thinking of the stones,) until we reached the little alley called Lamartine, which has been paved, by way of experiment, with the overlapping and riveted blocks. Here your countenance brightened up, and, perceiving your lips move, I could not doubt that you murmured the word 'stereotomy,' a term very affectedly applied to this species of pavement. I knew that you could not say to yourself 'stereotomy' without being brought to think of atomies, and thus of the theories of Epicurus; and since, when we discussed this subject not very long ago, I mentioned to you how singularly, yet with how little notice, the vague guesses of that noble Greek had met with confirmation in the late nebular cosmogony, I felt that you could not avoid casting your eyes upward to the great *nebula* in Orion, and I certainly expected that you would do so. You did look up; and I was now assured that I had correctly followed your steps. But in that bitter *tirade* upon Chantilly, which appeared in yesterday's '*Musée,*' the satirist, making some disgraceful allusions to the cobbler's change of name upon assuming the buskin, quoted a Latin line about which we have often conversed. I mean the line

Perdidit antiquum litera sonum.

"I had told you that this was in reference to Orion, formerly written Urion; and, from certain pungencies connected with this explanation, I was aware that you could not have forgotten it. It was clear, therefore, that you would not fail to combine the two ideas of Orion and Chantilly. That you did combine them I saw by the character of the smile which passed over your lips. You thought of the poor cobbler's immolation. So far, you had been stooping in your gait; but now I saw you draw yourself up to your full height. I was then sure that you reflected upon the diminutive figure of Chantilly. At this point I interrupted your meditations to remark that as, in fact, he was a very little fellow—that Chantilly—he would do better at the *Théâtre des Variétés*."

Not long after this, we were looking over an evening edition of the "Gazette des Tribunaux," when the following paragraphs arrested our attention.

"EXTRAORDINARY MURDERS.—This morning, about three o'clock, the inhabitants of the Quartier St. Roch were aroused from sleep by a succession of terrific shrieks, issuing, apparently, from the fourth story of a house in the Rue Morgue, known to be in the sole occupancy of one Madame L'Espanaye, and her daughter Mademoiselle Camille L'Espanaye. After some delay, occasioned by a fruitless attempt to procure admission in the usual manner, the gateway was broken in with a crowbar, and eight or ten of the neighbors entered accompanied by two *gendarmes*. By this time the cries had ceased; but, as the party rushed up the first flight of stairs, two or more rough voices in angry contention were distinguished and seemed to proceed from the upper part of the house. As the second landing was reached, these sounds, also, had ceased and everything remained perfectly quiet. The party spread themselves and hurried from room to room. Upon arriving at a large back chamber in the fourth story, (the door of which, being found locked, with the key inside, was forced open,) a spectacle presented itself which struck every one present not less with horror than with astonishment.

"The apartment was in the wildest disorder—the furniture broken and thrown about in all directions. There was only one bedstead; and from this the bed had been removed, and thrown into the middle of the floor. On a chair lay a razor, besmeared with blood. On the hearth were two or three long and thick tresses of grey human hair, also dabbled in blood, and seeming to have been pulled out by the roots. Upon the floor were found four Napoleons, an ear-ring of topaz, three large silver spoons, three smaller of *métal d'Alger,* and two bags, containing nearly four thousand francs in gold. The drawers of a *bureau,* which stood in one corner were open, and had been, apparently, rifled, although many articles still remained in them. A small iron safe was discovered under the *bed* (not under the bedstead). It was open, with the key still in the door. It had no contents beyond a few old letters, and other papers of little consequence.

"Of Madame L'Espanaye no traces were here seen; but an unusual quantity of soot being observed in the fire-place, a search was made in the chimney, and (horrible to relate!) the corpse of the daughter, head downward, was dragged therefrom; it having been thus forced up the narrow aperture for a considerable distance. The body was quite warm. Upon examining it, many excoriations were perceived, no doubt occasioned by the violence with which it had been thrust up and disengaged. Upon the face were many severe scratches, and, upon the throat, dark bruises, and deep indentations of finger nails, as if the deceased had been throttled to death.

"After a thorough investigation of every portion of the house, without farther discovery, the party made its way into a small paved yard in the rear of the building, where lay the corpse of the old lady, with her throat so entirely cut that, upon an attempt to raise her, the head fell off. The body, as well as the head, was fearfully mutilated—the former so much so as scarcely to retain any semblance of humanity.

"To this horrible mystery there is not as yet, we believe, the slightest clew."

The next day's paper had these additional particulars.

"*The Tragedy in the Rue Morgue.* Many individuals have been examined in relation to this most extraordinary and frightful affair. [The word 'affaire' has not yet, in France, that levity of import which it conveys with us,] "but nothing whatever has transpired to throw light upon it. We give below all the material testimony elicited.

"*Pauline Dubourg,* laundress, deposes that she has known both the deceased for three years, having washed for them during that period. The old lady and her daughter seemed on good terms—

very affectionate towards each other. They were excellent pay. Could not speak in regard to their mode or means of living. Believed that Madame L. told fortunes for a living. Was reputed to have money put by. Never met any persons in the house when she called for the clothes or took them home. Was sure that they had no servant in employ. There appeared to be no furniture in any part of the building except in the fourth story.

"*Pierre Moreau,* tobacconist, deposes that he has been in the habit of selling small quantities of tobacco and snuff to Madame L'Espanaye for nearly four years. Was born in the neighborhood, and has always resided there. The deceased and her daughter had occupied the house in which the corpses were found, for more than six years. It was formerly occupied by a jeweller, who under-let the upper rooms to various persons. The house was the property of Madame L. She became dissatisfied with the abuse of the premises by her tenant, and moved into them herself, refusing to let any portion. The old lady was childish. Witness had seen the daughter some five or six times during the six years. The two lived an exceedingly retired life—were reputed to have money. Had heard it said among the neighbors that Madame L. told fortunes—did not believe it. Had never seen any person enter the door except the old lady and her daughter, a porter once or twice, and a physician some eight or ten times.

"Many other persons, neighbors, gave evidence to the same effect. No one was spoken of as frequenting the house. It was not known whether there were any living connexions of Madame L. and her daughter. The shutters of the front windows were seldom opened. Those in the rear were always closed, with the exception of the large back room, fourth story. The house was a good house—not very old.

"*Isidore Muset, gendarme,* deposes that he was called to the house about three o'clock in the morning, and found some twenty or thirty persons at the gateway, endeavoring to gain admittance. Forced it open, at length, with a bayonet—not with a crowbar. Had but little difficulty in getting it open, on account of its being a double or folding gate, and bolted neither at bottom not top. The shrieks were continued until the gate was forced—and then suddenly ceased. They seemed to be screams of some person (or persons) in great agony—were loud and drawn out, not short and quick. Witness led the way up stairs. Upon reaching the first landing, heard two voices in loud and angry contention—the one a gruff voice, the other much shriller—a very strange voice. Could distinguish some words of the former, which was that of a Frenchman. Was positive that it was not a woman's voice. Could distinguish the words '*sacré*' and '*diable.*' The shrill voice was that of a foreigner. Could not be sure whether it was the voice of a man or of a woman. Could not make out what was said, but believed the language to be Spanish. The state of the room and of the bodies was described by this witness as we described them yesterday.

"*Henri Duval,* a neighbor, and by trade a silver-smith, deposes that he was one of the party who first entered the house. Corroborates the testimony of Muset in general. As soon as they forced an entrance, they reclosed the door, to keep out the crowd, which collected very fast, notwithstanding the lateness of the hour. The shrill voice, this witness thinks, was that of an Italian. Was certain it was not French. Could not be sure that it was a man's voice. It might have been a woman's. Was not acquainted with the Italian language. Could not distinguish the words, but was convinced by the intonation that the speaker was an Italian. Knew Madame L. and her daughter. Had conversed with both frequently. Was sure that the shrill voice was not that of either of the deceased.

"——*Odenheimer, restaurateur.* This witness volunteered his testimony. Not speaking French, was examined through an interpreter. Is a native of Amsterdam. Was passing the house at the time of the shrieks. They lasted for several minutes—probably ten. They were long and loud—very awful and distressing. Was one of those who entered the building. Corroborated the previous evidence in every respect but one. Was sure that the shrill voice was that of a man—of a Frenchman. Could not distinguish the words uttered. They were loud and quick—unequal—spoken apparently in fear as well as in anger. The voice was harsh—not so much shrill as harsh. Could not call it a shrill voice. The gruff voice said repeatedly '*sacré*,' '*diable*,' and once '*mon Dieu*.'

"*Jules Mignaud*, banker, of the firm of Mignaud et Fils, Rue Deloraine. Is the elder Mignaud. Madame L'Espanaye had some property. Had opened an account with his banking house in the spring of the year—(eight years previously). Made frequent deposits in small sums. Had checked for nothing until the third day before her death, when she took out in person the sum of 4000 francs. This sum was paid in gold, and a clerk went home with the money.

"*Adolphe Le Bon*, clerk to Mignaud et Fils, deposes that on the day in question, about noon, he accompanied Madame L'Espanaye to her residence with the 4000 francs, put up in two bags. Upon the door being opened, Mademoiselle L. appeared and took from his hands one of the bags, while the old lady relieved him of the other. He then bowed and departed. Did not see any person in the street at the time. It is a bye-street—very lonely.

"*William Bird*, tailor, deposes that he was one of the party who entered the house. Is an Englishman. Has lived in Paris two years. Was one of the first to ascend the stairs. Heard the voices in contention. The gruff voice was that of a Frenchman. Could make out several words, but cannot now remember all. Heard distinctly '*sacré*' and '*mon Dieu.*' There was a sound at the moment as if of several persons struggling—a scraping and scuffling sound. The shrill voice was very loud—louder than the gruff one. Is sure that it was not the voice of an Englishman. Appeared to be that of a German. Might have been a woman's voice. Does not understand German.

"Four of the above-named witnesses, being recalled, deposed that the door of the chamber in which was found the body of Mademoiselle L. was locked on the inside when the party reached it. Every thing was perfectly silent—no groans or noises of any kind. Upon forcing the door no person was seen. The windows, both of the back and front room, were down and firmly fastened from within. A door between the two rooms was closed, but not locked. The door leading from the front room into the passage was locked, with the key on the inside. A small room in the front of the house, on the fourth story, at the head of the passage was open, the door being ajar. This room was crowded with old beds, boxes, and so forth. These were carefully removed and searched. There was not an inch of any portion of the house which was not carefully searched. Sweeps were sent up and down the chimneys. The house was a four story one, with garrets (*mansardes.*) A trap-door on the roof was nailed down very securely—did not appear to have been opened for years. The time elapsing between the hearing of the voices in contention and the breaking open of the room door, was variously stated by the witnesses. Some made it as short as three minutes—some as long as five. The door was opened with difficulty.

"*Alfonzo Garcio*, undertaker, deposes that he resides in the Rue Morgue. Is a native of Spain. Was one of the party who entered the house. Did not proceed up stairs. Is nervous, and was apprehensive of the consequences of agitation. Heard the voices in contention. The gruff voice was that of a Frenchman. Could not distinguish what was said. The shrill voice was that of an Englishman—is sure of this. Does not understand the English language, but judges by the intonation.

"*Alberto Montani*, confectioner, deposes that he was among the first to ascend the stairs. Heard the voices in question. The gruff voice was that of a Frenchman. Distinguished several words. The speaker appeared to be expostulating. Could not make out the words of the shrill voice. Spoke quick and unevenly. Thinks it the voice of a Russian. Corroborates the general testimony. Is an Italian. Never conversed with a native of Russia.

"Several witnesses, recalled, here testified that the chimneys of all the rooms on the fourth story were too narrow to admit the passage of a human being. By 'sweeps' were meant cylindrical sweeping brushes, such as are employed by those who clean chimneys. These brushes were passed up and down every flue in the house. There is no back passage by which any one could have descended while the party proceeded up stairs. The body of Mademoiselle L'Espanaye was so firmly wedged in the chimney that it could not be got down until four or five of the party united their strength.

"*Paul Dumas*, physician, deposes that he was called to view the bodies about day-break. They were both then lying on the sacking of the bedstead in the chamber where Mademoiselle L. was found. The corpse of the young lady was much bruised and excoriated. The fact that it had been thrust up the chimney would sufficiently account for these appearances. The throat was greatly chafed. There were several deep scratches just below the chin, together with a series of livid spots which were evidently the impression of fingers. The face was fearfully discolored, and the eye-balls protruded. The tongue had been partially bitten through. A large bruise was discovered upon the pit of the stomach, produced, apparently, by the pressure of a knee. In the opinion of M. Dumas, Mademoiselle L'Espanaye had been throttled to death by some person or persons unknown. The corpse of the mother was horribly mutilated. All the bones of the right leg and arm were more or less shattered. The left *tibia* much splintered, as well as all the ribs of the left side. Whole body dreadfully bruised and discolored. It was not possible to say how the injuries had been inflicted. A heavy club of wood, or a broad bar of iron—a chair—any large, heavy, and obtuse weapon would have produced such results, if wielded by the hands of a very powerful man. No woman could have inflicted the blows with any weapon. The head of the deceased, when seen by witness, was entirely separated from the body, and was also greatly shattered. The throat had evidently been cut with some very sharp instrument—probably with a razor.

"*Alexandre Etienne*, surgeon, was called with M. Dumas to view the bodies. Corroborated the testimony, and the opinions of M. Dumas.

"Nothing farther of importance was elicited, although several other persons were examined. A murder so mysterious, and so perplexing in all its particulars, was never before committed in Paris—if indeed a murder has been committed at all. The police are entirely at fault—an unusual occurrence in affairs of this nature. There is not, however, the shadow of a clew apparent."

The evening edition of the paper stated that the greatest excitement still continued in the Quartier St. Roch—that the premises in question had been carefully re-searched, and fresh examinations of witnesses instituted, but all to no purpose. A postscript, however, mentioned that Adolphe Le Bon had been arrested and imprisoned—although nothing appeared to crim-inate him, beyond the facts already detailed.

Dupin seemed singularly interested in the progress of this affair—at least so I judged from his manner, for he made no comments. It was only after the announcement that Le Bon had been imprisoned, that he asked me my opinion respecting the murders.

I could merely agree with all Paris in considering them an insoluble mystery. I saw no means by which it would be possi-ble to trace the murderer.

"We must not judge of the means," said Dupin, "by this shell of an examination. The Parisian police, so much extolled for *acumen*, are cunning, but no more. There is no method in their proceedings, beyond the method of the moment. They make a vast parade of measures; but, not unfrequently, these are so ill adapted to the objects proposed, as to put us in mind of Monsieur Jourdain's calling for his *robe-de-chambre—pour mieux entendre la musique*. The results attained by them are not unfrequently surprising, but, for the most part, are brought about by simple diligence and activity. When these qualities are unavailing, their schemes fail. Vidocq, for example, was a good guesser and a persevering man. But, without educated thought, he erred continually by the very intensity of his investigations. He impaired his vision by holding the object too close. He might see, perhaps, one or two points with unusual clearness, but in so doing he, necessarily, lost sight of the matter as a whole. Thus there is such a thing as being too profound. Truth is not always in a well. In fact, as regards the more important knowledge, I do believe that she is invariably superficial. The depth lies in the valleys where we seek her, and not upon the mountain-tops where she is found. The modes and sources of this kind of error are well typified in the contemplation of the heavenly bodies. To look at a star by glances—to view it in a side-long way, by turning toward it the exterior portions of the *retina* (more susceptible of feeble impressions of light than the interior), is to behold the star distinctly—is to have the best appreciation of its lustre—a lustre which grows dim just in proportion as we turn our vision *fully* upon it. A greater number of rays actually fall upon the eye in the latter case, but, in the former, there is the more refined capacity for comprehension. By undue profundity we perplex and enfeeble thought; and it is possible to make even Venus herself vanish from the firmament by a scrutiny too sustained, too concentrated, or too direct.

"As for these murders, let us enter into some examinations for ourselves, before we make up an opinion respecting them. An inquiry will afford us amusement," [I thought this an odd term, so applied, but said nothing] "and, besides, Le Bon once rendered me a service for which I am not ungrateful. We will go and see the premises with our own eyes. I know G——, the Prefect of Police, and shall have no difficulty in obtaining the necessary permission."

The permission was obtained, and we proceeded at once to the Rue Morgue. This is one of those miserable thorough-fares which intervene between the Rue Richelieu and the Rue St. Roch. It was late in the afternoon when we reached it; as this quarter is at a great distance from that in which we re-sided. The house was readily found; for there were still many persons gazing up at the closed shutters, with an objectless curiosity, from the opposite side of the way. It was an ordinary Parisian house, with a gateway, on one side of which was a glazed watch-box, with a sliding panel in the window, indicating a *loge de concierge*. Before going in we walked up the street, turned down an alley, and then, again turning, passed in the rear of the building—Dupin, meanwhile examining the whole neighborhood, as well as the house, with a minuteness of attention for which I could see no possible object.

Retracing our steps, we came again to the front of the dwelling, rang, and, having shown our credentials, were admitted by the agents in charge. We went up stairs—into the chamber where the body of Mademoiselle L'Espanaye had been found, and where both the deceased still lay. The disorders of the room had, as usual, been suffered to exist. I saw nothing beyond what had been stated in the "Gazette des Tribunaux." Dupin scrutinized every thing—not excepting the bodies of the victims. We then went into the other rooms, and into the yard; a *gendarme* accompanying us throughout. The examination occupied us until dark, when we took our departure. On our way home my companion stepped in for a moment at the office of one of the daily papers.

I have said that the whims of my friend were manifold, and that *Je les ménageais*:—for this phrase there is no English equivalent. It was his humor, now, to decline all conversation on the subject of the murder, until about noon the next day. He then asked me, suddenly, if I had observed any thing *peculiar* at the scene of the atrocity.

There was something in his manner of emphasizing the word "peculiar," which caused me to shudder, without knowing why.

"No, nothing *peculiar*," I said; "nothing more, at least, than we both saw stated in the paper."

"The 'Gazette,'" he replied, "has not entered, I fear, into the unusual horror of the thing. But dismiss the idle opinions of this print. It appears to me that this mystery is considered insoluble, for the very reason which should cause it to be regarded as easy of solution—I mean for the *outré* character of its features. The police are confounded by the seeming absence of motive—not for the murder itself—but for the atrocity of the murder. They are puzzled, too, by the seeming impossibility of reconciling the voices heard in contention, with the facts that no one was discovered up stairs but the assassinated Mademoiselle L'Espanaye, and that there were no means of egress without the notice of the party ascending. The wild disorder of the room; the corpse thrust, with the head downward, up the chimney; the frightful mutilation of the body of the old lady; these considerations, with those just mentioned, and others which I need not mention, have sufficed to paralyze the powers, by putting completely at fault the boasted *acumen*, of the government agents. They have fallen into the gross but common error of confounding the unusual with the abstruse. But it is by these deviations from the plane of the ordinary, that reason feels its way, if at all, in its search for the true. In investigations such as we are now pursuing, it should not be so much asked 'what has occurred,' as 'what has occurred that has never occurred before.' In fact, the facility with which I shall arrive, or have arrived, at the solution of this mystery, is in the direct ratio of its apparent insolubility in the eyes of the police."

I stared at the speaker in mute astonishment.

"I am now awaiting," continued he, looking toward the door of our apartment—"I am now awaiting a person who, although perhaps not the perpetrator of these butcheries, must have been in some measure implicated in their perpetration. Of the worst portion of the crimes committed, it is probable that he is innocent. I hope that I am right in this supposition; for upon it I build my expectation of reading the entire riddle. I look for the man here—in this room—every moment. It is true that he may not arrive; but the probability is that he will. Should he come, it will be necessary to detain him. Here are pistols; and we both know how to use them when occasion demands their use."

I took the pistols, scarcely knowing what I did, or believing what I heard, while Dupin went on, very much as if in a soliloquy. I have already spoken of his abstract manner at such times. His discourse was addressed to myself; but his voice, although by no means loud, had that intonation which is commonly employed in speaking to some one at a great distance. His eyes, vacant in expression, regarded only the wall.

"That the voices heard in contention," he said, "by the party upon the stairs, were not the voices of the women themselves, was fully proved by the evidence. This relieves us of all doubt upon the question whether the old lady could have first destroyed the daughter and afterward have committed suicide. I speak of this point chiefly for the sake of method; for the strength of Madame L'Espanaye would have been utterly unequal to the task of thrusting her daughter's corpse up the chimney as it was found; and the nature of the wounds upon her own person entirely preclude the idea of self-destruction. Murder, then, has been committed by some third party; and the voices of this third party were those heard in contention. Let me now advert—not to the whole testimony respecting these voices—but to what was *peculiar* in that testimony. Did you observe any thing peculiar about it?"

I remarked that, while all the witnesses agreed in supposing the gruff voice to be that of a Frenchman, there was much disagreement in regard to the shrill, or, as one individual termed it, the harsh voice.

"That was the evidence itself," said Dupin, "but it was not the peculiarity of the evidence. You have observed nothing distinctive. Yet there *was* something to be observed. The witnesses, as you remark, agreed about the gruff voice; they were here unanimous. But in regard to the shrill voice, the peculiarity is—not that they disagreed—but that, while an Italian, an Englishman, a Spaniard, a Hollander, and a Frenchman attempted to describe it, each one spoke of it as that *of a foreigner.* Each is sure that it was not the voice of one of his own countrymen. Each likens it—not to the voice of an individual of any nation with whose language he is conversant—but the converse. The Frenchman supposes it the voice of a Spaniard, and 'might have distinguished some words *had he been acquainted with the Spanish.*' The Dutchman maintains it to have been that of a Frenchman; but we find it stated that '*not understanding French this witness was examined through an interpreter.*' The Englishman thinks it the voice of a German, and '*does not understand German.*' The Spaniard 'is sure' that it was that of an Englishman, but 'judges by the intonation' altogether, '*as he has no knowledge of the English.*' The Italian believes it the voice of a Russian, but '*has never conversed with a native of Russia.*' A second Frenchman differs, moreover, with the first, and is positive that the voice was that of an Italian; but, *not being cognizant of that tongue,* is, like the Spaniard, 'convinced by the intonation.' Now, how strangely unusual must that voice have really been, about which such testimony as this *could* have been elicited!—in whose *tones,* even, denizens of the five great divisions of Europe could recognise nothing familiar! You will say that it might have been the voice of an Asiatic—of an African. Neither Asiatics nor Africans abound in Paris; but, without denying the inference, I will now merely call your attention to three points. The voice is termed by one witness 'harsh rather than shrill.' It is represented by two others to have been 'quick and *unequal.*' No words—no sounds resembling words—were by any witness mentioned as distinguishable.

"I know not," continued Dupin, "what impression I may have made, so far, upon your own understanding; but I do not hesitate to say that legitimate deductions even from this portion of the testimony—the portion respecting the gruff and shrill voices—are in themselves sufficient to engender a suspicion which should give direction to all farther progress in the investigation of the mystery. I said 'legitimate deductions;' but my meaning is not thus fully expressed. I designed to imply that the deductions are the *sole* proper ones, and that the suspicion arises *inevitably* from them as the single result. What the suspicion is, however, I will not say just yet. I merely wish you to bear in mind that, with myself, it was sufficiently forcible to give a definite form—a certain tendency—to my inquiries in the chamber.

"Let us now transport ourselves, in fancy, to this chamber. What shall we first seek here? The means of egress employed by the murderers. It is not too much to say that neither of us believe in præternatural events. Madame and Mademoiselle L'Espanaye were not destroyed by spirits. The doers of the deed were material, and escaped materially. Then how? Fortunately, there is but one mode of reasoning upon the point, and that mode *must* lead us to a definite decision.—Let us examine, each by each, the possible means of egress. It is clear that the assassins were in the room where Mademoiselle L'Espanaye was found, or at least in the room adjoining, when the party ascended the stairs. It is then only from these two apartments that we have to seek issues. The police have laid bare the floors, the ceilings, and the masonry of the walls, in every direction. No *secret* issues could have escaped their vigilance. But, not trusting to *their* eyes, I examined with my own. There were, then, no secret issues. Both doors leading from the rooms into the passage were securely locked, with the keys inside. Let us turn to the chimneys. These, although of ordinary width for some eight or ten feet above the hearths, will not admit, throughout their extent, the body of a large cat. The impossibility of egress, by means already stated, being thus absolute, we are reduced to the windows. Through those of the front room no one could have escaped without notice from the crowd in the street. The murderers *must* have passed, then, through those of the back room. Now, brought to this conclusion in so unequivocal a manner as we are, it is not our part, as reasoners, to reject it on account of apparent impossibilities. It is only left for us to prove that these apparent 'impossibilities' are, in reality, not such.

"There are two windows in the chamber. One of them is unobstructed by furniture, and is wholly visible. The lower portion of the other is hidden from view by the head of the un-wieldy bedstead which is thrust close up against it. The former was found securely fastened from within. It resisted the utmost force of those who endeavored to raise it. A large gimlet-hole had been pierced in its frame to the left, and a very stout nail was found fitted therein, nearly to the head. Upon examining the other window, a similar nail was seen similarly fitted in it; and a vigorous attempt to raise this sash, failed also. The police were now entirely satisfied that egress had not been in these directions. And, *therefore*, it was thought a matter of supereroga-tion to withdraw the nails and open the windows.

"My own examination was somewhat more particular, and was so for the reason I have just given—because here it was, I knew, that all apparent impossibilities *must* be proved to be not such in reality.

"I proceeded to think thus—*a posteriori*. The murderers did escape from one of these windows. This being so, they could not have refastened the sashes from the inside, as they were found fastened;—the consideration which put a stop, through its obviousness, to the scrutiny of the police in this quarter. Yet the sashes *were* fastened. They *must*, then, have the power of fastening themselves. There was no escape from this conclusion. I stepped to the unobstructed casement, withdrew the nail with some difficulty and attempted to raise the sash. It resisted all my efforts, as I had anticipated. A concealed spring must, I now know, exist; and this corroboration of my idea convinced me that my premises at least, were correct, however mysterious still appeared the circumstances attending the nails. A careful search soon brought to light the hidden spring. I pressed it, and, satisfied with the discovery, forbore to upraise the sash.

"I now replaced the nail and regarded it attentively. A person passing out through this window might have reclosed it, and the spring would have caught—but the nail could not have been replaced. The conclusion was plain, and again narrowed in the field of my investigations. The assassins *must* have escaped through the other window. Supposing, then, the springs upon each sash to be the same, as was probable, there *must* be found a difference between the nails, or at least between the modes of their fixture. Getting upon the sacking of the bedstead, I looked over the headboard minutely at the second casement. Passing my hand down behind the board, I readily discovered and pressed the spring, which was, as I had supposed, identical in character with its neighbor. I now looked at the nail. It was as stout as the other, and apparently fitted in the same manner—driven in nearly up to the head.

"You will say that I was puzzled; but, if you think so, you must have misunderstood the nature of the inductions. To use a sporting phrase, I had not been once 'at fault.' The scent had never for an instant been lost. There was no flaw in any link of the chain. I had traced the secret to its ultimate result,—and that result was *the nail*. It had, I say, in every respect, the appearance of its fellow in the other window; but this fact was an absolute nullity (conclusive as it might seem to be) when compared with the consideration that here, at this point, terminated the clew. 'There *must* be something wrong,' I said, 'about the nail.' I touched it; and the head, with about a quarter of an inch of the shank, came off in my fingers. The rest of the shank was in the gimlet-hole where it had been broken off. The fracture was an old one (for its edges were incrusted with rust), and had apparently been accomplished by the blow of a hammer, which had partially imbedded, in the top of the bottom sash, the head portion of the nail. I now carefully replaced this head portion in the indentation whence I had taken it, and the resemblance to a perfect nail was complete—the fissure was invisible. Pressing the spring, I gently raised the sash for a few inches; the head went up with it, remaining firm in its bed. I closed the window, and the semblance of the whole nail was again perfect.

"The riddle, so far, was now unriddled. The assassin had escaped through the window which looked upon the bed. Dropping of its own accord upon his exit (or perhaps purposely closed), it had become fastened by the spring; and it was the retention of this spring which had been mistaken by the police for that of the nail,—farther inquiry being thus considered unnecessary.

"The next question is that of the mode of descent. Upon this point I had been satisfied in my walk with you around the building. About five feet and a half from the casement in question there runs a lightning-rod. From this rod it would have been impossible for any one to reach the window itself, to say nothing of entering it. I observed, however, that the shutters of the fourth story were of the peculiar kind called by Parisian carpenters *ferrades*—a kind rarely employed at the present day, but frequently seen upon very old mansions at Lyons and Bordeaux. They are in the form of an ordinary door, (a single, not a folding door) except that the lower half is latticed or worked in open trellis—thus affording an excellent hold for the hands. In the present instance these shutters are fully three feet and a half broad. When we saw them from the rear of the house, they were both about half open—that is to say, they stood off at right angles from the wall. It is probable that the police, as well as myself, examined the back of the tenement; but, if so, in looking at these *ferrades* in the line of their breadth (as they must have done), they did not perceive this great breadth itself, or, at all events, failed to take it into due consideration. In fact, having once satisfied themselves that no egress could have been made in this quarter, they would naturally bestow here a very cursory examination. It was clear to me, however, that the shutter belonging to the window at the head of the bed, would, if swung fully back to the wall, reach to within two feet of the lightning-rod. It was also evident that, by exertion of a very unusual degree of activity and courage, an entrance into the window, from the rod, might have been thus effected.—By reaching to the distance of two feet and a half (we now suppose the shutter open to its whole extent) a robber might have taken a firm grasp upon the trellis-work. Letting go, then, his hold upon the rod, placing his feet securely against the wall, and springing boldly from it, he might have swung the shutter so as to close it, and, if we imagine the window open at the time, might even have swung himself into the room.

"I wish you to bear especially in mind that I have spoken of a *very* unusual degree of activity as requisite to success in so hazardous and so difficult a feat. It is my design to show you, first, that the thing might possibly have been accomplished:—but, secondly and *chiefly,* I wish to impress upon your understanding the *very extraordinary*—the almost præternatural character of that agility which could have accomplished it.

"You will say, no doubt, using the language of the law, that 'to make out my case,' I should rather undervalue, than insist upon a full estimation of the activity required in this matter. This may be the practice in law, but it is not the usage of reason. My ultimate object is only the truth. My immediate purpose is to lead you to place in juxtaposition, that *very unusual* activity of which I have just spoken with that *very peculiar* shrill (or harsh) and *unequal* voice, about whose nationality no two persons could be found to agree, and in whose utterance no syllabification could be detected."

At these words a vague and half-formed conception of the meaning of Dupin flitted over my mind. I seemed to be upon the verge of comprehension without power to comprehend— men, at times, find themselves upon the brink of remembrance without being able, in the end, to remember. My friend went on with his discourse.

"You will see," he said, "that I have shifted the question from the mode of egress to that of ingress. It was my design to convey the idea that both were effected in the same manner, at the same point. Let us now revert to the interior of the room. Let us survey the appearances here. The drawers of the bureau, it is said, had been rifled, although many articles of apparel still remained within them. The conclusion here is absurd. It is a mere guess—a very silly one—and no more. How are we to know that the articles found in the drawers were not all these drawers had originally contained? Madame L'Espanaye and her daughter lived an exceedingly retired life—saw no company—seldom went out—had little use for numerous changes of habiliment. Those found were at least of as good quality as any likely to be possessed by these ladies. If a thief had taken any, why did he not take the best—why did he not take all? In a word, why did he abandon four thousand francs in gold to encumber himself with a bundle of linen? The gold *was* abandoned. Nearly the whole sum mentioned by Monsieur Mignaud, the banker, was discovered, in bags, upon the floor. I wish you, therefore, to discard from your thoughts the blundering idea of *motive*, engendered in the brains of the police by that portion of the evidence which speaks of money delivered at the door of the house. Coincidences ten times as remarkable as this (the delivery of the money, and murder committed within three days upon the party receiving it), happen to all of us every hour of our lives, without attracting even momentary notice. Coincidences, in general, are great stumbling-blocks in the way of that class of thinkers who have been educated to know nothing of the theory of probabilities—that theory to which the most glorious objects of human research are indebted for the most glorious of illustration. In the present instance, had the gold been gone, the fact of its delivery three days before would have formed something more than a coincidence. It would have been corroborative of this idea of motive. But, under the real circumstances of the case, if we are to suppose gold the motive of this outrage, we must also imagine the perpetrator so vacillating an idiot as to have abandoned his gold and his motive together.

"Keeping now steadily in mind the points to which I have

drawn your attention—that peculiar voice, that unusual agility, and that startling absence of motive in a murder so singularly atrocious as this—let us glance at the butchery itself. Here is a woman strangled to death by manual strength, and thrust up a chimney, head downward. Ordinary assassins employ no such modes of murder as this. Least of all, do they thus dispose of the murdered. In the manner of thrusting the corpse up the chimney, you will admit that there was something *excessively outré*—something altogether irreconcilable with our common notions of human action, even when we suppose the actors the most depraved of men. Think, too, how great must have been that strength which could have thrust the body *up* such an aperture so forcibly that the united vigor of several persons was found barely sufficient to drag it *down!*

"Turn, now, to other indications of the employment of a vigor most marvellous. On the hearth were thick tresses—very thick tresses—of grey human hair. These had been torn out by the roots. You are aware of the great force necessary in tearing thus from the head even twenty or thirty hairs together. You saw the locks in question as well as myself. Their roots (a hideous sight!) were clotted with fragments of the flesh of the scalp—sure token of the prodigious power which had been exerted in uprooting perhaps half a million of hairs at a time. The throat of the old lady was not merely cut, but the head absolutely severed from the body: the instrument was a mere razor. I wish you also to look at the *brutal* ferocity of these deeds. Of the bruises upon the body of Madame L'Espanaye I do not speak. Monsieur Dumas, and his worthy coadjutor Monsieur Etienne, have pronounced that they were inflicted by some obtuse instrument; and so far these gentlemen are very correct.

The obtuse instrument was clearly the stone pavement in the yard, upon which the victim had fallen from the window which looked in upon the bed. This idea, however simple it may now seem, escaped the police for the same reason that the breadth of the shutters escaped them—because, by the affair of the nails, their perceptions had been hermetically sealed against the possibility of the windows having ever been opened at all.

"If now, in addition to all these things, you have properly reflected upon the odd disorder of the chamber, we have gone so far as to combine the ideas of an agility astounding, a strength superhuman, a ferocity brutal, a butchery without motive, a *grotesquerie* in horror absolutely alien from humanity, and a voice foreign in tone to the ears of men of many nations, and devoid of all distinct or intelligible syllabification. What result, then, has ensued? What impression have I made upon your fancy?"

I felt a creeping of the flesh as Dupin asked me the question. "A madman," I said, "has done this deed—some raving maniac, escaped from a neighboring *Maison de Santé.*"

"In some respects," he replied, "your idea is not irrelevant. But the voices of madmen, even in their wildest paroxysms, are never found to tally with that peculiar voice heard upon the stairs. Madmen are of some nation, and their language, however incoherent in its words, has always the coherence of syllabification. Besides, the hair of a madman is not such as I now hold in my hand. I disentangled this little tuft from the rigidly clutched fingers of Madame L'Espanaye. Tell me what you can make of it."

"Dupin!" I said, completely unnerved; "this hair is most unusual—this is no *human* hair."

"I have not asserted that it is," said he; "but, before we decide this point, I wish you to glance at the little sketch I have here traced upon this paper. It is a *fac-simile* drawing of what has been described in one portion of the testimony as 'dark bruises, and deep indentations of finger nails,' upon the throat of Mademoiselle L'Espanaye, and in another, (by Messrs. Dumas and Etienne,) as a 'series of livid spots, evidently the impression of fingers.'

"You will perceive," continued my friend, spreading out the paper upon the table before us, "that this drawing gives the idea of a firm and fixed hold. There is no *slipping* apparent. Each finger has retained—possibly until the death of the victim—the fearful grasp by which it originally imbedded itself. Attempt, now, to place all your fingers, at the same time, in the respective impressions as you see them."

I made the attempt in vain.

"We are possibly not giving this matter a fair trial," he said. "The paper is spread out upon a plane surface; but the human throat is cylindrical. Here is a billet of wood, the circumference of which is about that of the throat. Wrap the drawing around it, and try the experiment again."

I did so; but the difficulty was even more obvious than before. "This," I said, "is the mark of no human hand."

"Read now," replied Dupin, "this passage from Cuvier."

It was a minute anatomical and generally descriptive account of the large fulvous Ourang-Outang of the East Indian Islands. The gigantic stature, the prodigious strength and activity, the wild ferocity, and the imitative propensities of these mammalia are sufficiently well known to all. I understood the full horrors of the murder at once.

"The description of the digits," said I, as I made an end of reading, "is in exact accordance with this drawing. I see that no animal but an Ourang-Outang, of the species here mentioned, could have impressed the indentations as you have traced them. This tuft of tawny hair, too, is identical in character with that of the beast of Cuvier. But I cannot possibly comprehend the particulars of this frightful mystery. Besides, there were *two* voices heard in contention, and one of them was unquestionably the voice of a Frenchman."

"True; and you will remember an expression attributed almost unanimously, by the evidence, to this voice,—the expression, '*mon Dieu!*' This, under the circumstances, has been justly characterized by one of the witnesses (Montani, the confectioner,) as an expression of remonstrance or expostulation. Upon these two words, therefore, I have mainly built my hopes of a full solution of the riddle. A Frenchman was cognizant of the murder. It is possible—indeed it is far more than probable—that he was innocent of all participation in the bloody transactions which took place. The Ourang-Outang may have escaped from him. He may have traced it to the chamber; but, under the agitating circumstances which ensued, he could never have re-captured it. It is still at large. I will not pursue these guesses—for I have no right to call them more— since the shades of reflection upon which they are based are scarcely of sufficient depth to be appreciable by my own intellect, and since I could not pretend to make them intelligible to the understanding of another. We will call them guesses then, and speak of them as such. If the Frenchman in question is indeed, as I suppose, innocent of this atrocity, this advertisement which I left last night, upon our return home, at the office of 'Le Monde,' (a paper devoted to the shipping interest, and much sought by sailors,) will bring him to our residence."

He handed me a paper, and I read thus:

CAUGHT—*In the Bois de Boulogne, early in the morning of the—inst., (the morning of the murder,) a very large, tawny Ourang-Outang of the Bornese species. The owner, (who is ascertained to be a sailor, belonging to a Maltese vessel,) may have the animal again, upon identifying it satisfactorily, and paying a few charges arising from its capture and keeping. Call at No.——, Rue——, Faubourg St. Germain—au troisième.*

"How was it possible," I asked, "that you should know the man to be a sailor, and belonging to a Maltese vessel?"

"I do *not* know it," said Dupin. "I am not *sure* of it. Here, however, is a small piece of ribbon, which from its form, and from its greasy appearance, has evidently been used in tying the hair in one of those long *queues* of which sailors are so fond. Moreover, this knot is one which few besides sailors can tie, and is peculiar to the Maltese. I picked the ribbon up at the foot of the lightning-rod. It could not have belonged to either of the deceased. Now if, after all, I am wrong in my induction from this ribbon, that the Frenchman was a sailor belonging to a Maltese vessel, still I can have done no harm in saying what I did in the advertisement. If I am in error, he will merely suppose that I have been misled by some circumstance into which he will not take the trouble to inquire. But if I am right, a great point is gained. Cognizant although innocent of the murder, the Frenchman will naturally hesitate about replying to the advertisement—about demanding the Ourang-Outang. He will reason thus:—'I am innocent; I am poor; my Ourang-Outang is of great value—to one in my circumstances a fortune of itself—why should I lose it through idle apprehensions of danger? Here it is, within my grasp. It was found in the Bois de Boulogne—at a vast distance from the scene of that butchery. How can it ever be suspected that a brute beast should have done the deed? The police are at fault—they have failed to procure the slightest clew. Should they even trace the animal, it would be impossible to prove me cognizant of the murder, or to implicate me in guilt on account of that cognizance. Above all, *I am known.* The advertiser designates me as the possessor of the beast. I am not sure to what limit his knowledge may extend. Should I avoid claiming a property of so great value, which it is known that I possess, I will render the animal at least, liable to suspicion. It is not my policy to attract attention either to myself or to the beast. I will answer the advertisement, get the Ourang-Outang, and keep it close until this matter has blown over.'"

At this moment we heard a step upon the stairs.

"Be ready," said Dupin, "with your pistols, but neither use them nor show them until at a signal from myself."

The front door of the house had been left open, and the visitor had entered, without ringing, and advanced several steps upon the staircase. Now, however, he seemed to hesitate. Presently we heard him descending. Dupin was moving quickly to the door, when we again heard him coming up. He did not turn back a second time, but stepped up with decision, and rapped at the door of our chamber.

"Come in," said Dupin, in a cheerful and hearty tone.

A man entered. He was a sailor, evidently,—a tall, stout, and muscular-looking person, with a certain dare-devil expression of countenance, not altogether unprepossessing. His face, greatly sunburnt, was more than half hidden by whisker and *mustachio*. He had with him a huge oaken cudgel, but appeared to be otherwise unarmed. He bowed awkwardly, and bade us "good evening," in French accents, which, although somewhat Neufchatelish, were still sufficiently indicative of a Parisian origin.

"Sit down, my friend," said Dupin. "I suppose you have called about the Ourang-Outang. Upon my word, I almost envy you the possession of him; a remarkably fine, and no doubt a very valuable animal. How old do you suppose him to be?"

The sailor drew a long breath, with the air of a man relieved of some intolerable burden, and then replied, in an assured tone:

"I have no way of telling—but he can't be more than four or five years old. Have you got him here?"

"Oh no, we had no conveniences for keeping him here. He is at a livery stable in the Rue Dubourg, just by. You can get him in the morning. Of course you are prepared to identify the property?"

"To be sure I am, sir."

"I shall be sorry to part with him," said Dupin.

"I don't mean that you should be at all this trouble for nothing, sir," said the man. "Couldn't expect it. Am very willing to pay a reward for the finding of the animal—that is to say, any thing in reason."

"Well," replied my friend, "that is all very fair, to be sure. Let me think!—what should I have? Oh! I will tell you. My reward shall be this. You shall give me all the information in your power about these murders in the Rue Morgue."

Dupin said the last words in a very low tone, and very quietly. Just as quietly, too, he walked toward the door, locked it and put the key in his pocket. He then drew a pistol from his bosom and placed it, without the least flurry, upon the table.

The sailor's face flushed up as if he were struggling with suffocation. He started to his feet and grasped his cudgel, but the next moment he fell back into his seat, trembling violently, and with the countenance of death itself. He spoke not a word. I pitied him from the bottom of my heart.

"My friend," said Dupin, in a kind tone, "you are alarming yourself unnecessarily—you are indeed. We mean you no harm whatever. I pledge you the honor of a gentleman, and of a Frenchman, that we intend you no injury. I perfectly well know that you are innocent of the atrocities in the Rue Morgue. It will not do, however, to deny that you are in some measure implicated in them. From what I have already said, you must know that I have had means of information about this matter—means of which you could never have dreamed. Now the thing stands thus. You have done nothing which you could have avoided—nothing, certainly, which renders you culpable. You were not even guilty of robbery, when you might have robbed with impunity. You have nothing to conceal. You have no reason for concealment. On the other hand, you are bound by every principle of honor to confess all you know. An innocent man is now imprisoned, charged with that crime of which you can point out the perpetrator."

The sailor had recovered his presence of mind, in a great measure, while Dupin uttered these words; but his original boldness of bearing was all gone.

"So help me God," said he, after a brief pause, "I will tell

you all I know about this affair;—but I do not expect you to
believe one half I say—I would be a fool indeed if I did. Still, I
am innocent, and I will make a clean breast if I die for it."

What he stated was, in substance, this. He had lately made
a voyage to the Indian Archipelago. A party, of which he
formed one, landed at Borneo, and passed into the interior on
an excursion of pleasure. Himself and a companion had captured the Ourang-Outang. This companion dying, the animal
fell into his own exclusive possession. After great trouble, occasioned by the intractable ferocity of his captive during the
home voyage, he at length succeeded in lodging it safely at his
own residence in Paris, where, not to attract toward himself
the unpleasant curiosity of his neighbors, he kept it carefully
secluded, until such time as it should recover from a wound in
the foot, received from a splinter on board ship. His ultimate
design was to sell it.

Returning home from some sailors' frolic the night, or
rather in the morning of the murder, he found the beast occupying his own bed-room, into which it had broken from a
closet adjoining, where it had been, as was thought, securely
confined. Razor in hand, and fully lathered, it was sitting before a looking-glass, attempting the operation of shaving, in
which it had no doubt previously watched its master through
the key-hole of the closet. Terrified at the sight of so dangerous
a weapon in the possession of an animal so ferocious, and so
well able to use it, the man, for some moments, was at a loss
what to do. He had been accustomed, however, to quiet the
creature, even in its fiercest moods, by the use of a whip, and
to this he now resorted. Upon sight of it, the Ourang-Outang
sprang at once through the door of the chamber, down the

stairs, and thence, through a window, unfortunately open, into the street.

The Frenchman followed in despair; the ape, razor still in hand, occasionally stopping to look back and gesticulate at its pursuer, until the latter had nearly come up with it. It then again made off. In this manner the chase continued for a long time. The streets were profoundly quiet, as it was nearly three o'clock in the morning. In passing down an alley in the rear of the Rue Morgue, the fugitive's attention was arrested by a light gleaming from the open window of Madame L'Espanaye's chamber, in the fourth story of her house. Rushing to the building, it perceived the lightning rod, clambered up with inconceivable agility, grasped the shutter, which was thrown fully back against the wall, and, by its means, swung itself directly upon the headboard of the bed. The whole feat did not occupy a minute. The shutter was kicked open again by the Ourang-Outang as it entered the room.

The sailor, in the meantime, was both rejoiced and perplexed. He had strong hopes of now recapturing the brute, as it could scarcely escape from the trap into which it had ventured, except by the rod, where it might be intercepted as it came down. On the other hand, there was much cause for anxiety as to what it might do in the house. This latter reflection urged the man still to follow the fugitive. A lightning rod is ascended without difficulty, especially by a sailor; but, when he had arrived as high as the window, which lay far to his left, his career was stopped; the most that he could accomplish was to reach over so as to obtain a glimpse of the interior of the room. At this glimpse he nearly fell from his hold through excess of horror. Now it was that those hideous shrieks arose upon the night, which had startled from slumber the inmates of the Rue Morgue. Madame L'Espanaye and her daughter, habited in their night clothes, had apparently been occupied in arranging some papers in the iron chest already mentioned, which had been wheeled into the middle of the room. It was open, and its contents lay beside it on the floor. The victims must have been sitting with their backs toward the window; and, from the time elapsing between the ingress of the beast and the screams, it seems probable that it was not immediately perceived. The flapping-to of the shutter would naturally have been attributed to the wind.

As the sailor looked in, the gigantic animal had seized Madame L'Espanaye by the hair, (which was loose, as she had been combing it,) and was flourishing the razor about her face, in imitation of the motions of a barber. The daughter lay prostrate and motionless; she had swooned. The screams and struggles of the old lady (during which the hair was torn from her head) had the effect of changing the probably pacific purposes of the Ourang-Outang into those of wrath. With one determined sweep of its muscular arm it nearly severed her head from her body. The sight of blood inflamed its anger into phrenzy. Gnashing its teeth, and flashing fire from its eyes, it flew upon the body of the girl, and imbedded its fearful talons in her throat, retaining its grasp until she expired. Its wandering and wild glances fell at this moment upon the head of the bed, over which the face of its master, rigid with horror, was just discernible. The fury of the beast, who no doubt bore still in mind the dreaded whip, was instantly converted into fear. Conscious of having deserved punishment, it seemed desirous of concealing its bloody deeds, and skipped about the chamber in an agony of nervous agitation; throwing down and breaking the furniture as it moved, and dragging the bed from the bedstead. In conclusion, it seized first the corpse of the daughter, and thrust it up the chimney, as it was found; then that of the old lady, which it immediately hurled through the window headlong.

As the ape approached the casement with its mutilated burden, the sailor shrank aghast to the rod, and, rather gliding than clambering down it, hurried at once home—dreading the consequences of the butchery, and gladly abandoning, in his terror, all solicitude about the fate of the Ourang-Outang. The words heard by the party upon the staircase were the Frenchman's exclamations of horror and affright, commingled with the fiendish jabberings of the brute.

I have scarcely anything to add. The Ourang-Outang must have escaped from the chamber, by the rod, just before the break of the door. It must have closed the window as it passed through it. It was subsequently caught by the owner himself, who obtained for it a very large sum at the *Jardin des Plantes*. Le Don was instantly released, upon our narration of the circumstances (with some comments from Dupin) at the bureau of the Prefect of Police. This functionary, however well disposed to my friend, could not altogether conceal his chagrin at the turn which affairs had taken, and was fain to indulge in a sarcasm or two, about the propriety of every person minding his own business.

"Let him talk," said Dupin, who had not thought it necessary to reply. "Let him discourse; it will ease his conscience, I am satisfied with having defeated him in his own castle. Nevertheless, that he failed in the solution of this mystery, is by no means that matter for wonder which he supposes it; for, in truth, our friend the Prefect is somewhat too cunning to be profound. In his wisdom is no *stamen*. It is all head and no body, like the pictures of the Goddess Laverna,—or, at best, all head and shoulders, like a codfish. But he is a good creature after all. I like him especially for one master stroke of cant, by which he has attained his reputation for ingenuity. I mean the way he has '*de nier ce qui est, et d'expliquer ce qui n'est pas.*'" (†)

---

† Rousseau—Nouvelle Heloise.

About Edgar Allan Poe

EDGAR ALLAN POE was born on January 19, 1809, in Boston, Massachusetts, to traveling stage actors David and Elizabeth "Eliza" Arnold Hopkins Poe. Following his father's abandonment and his mother's death, Poe was taken into the wealthy household of John and Frances Allan, and christened Edgar Allan Poe in 1812. He attended boarding schools in England during his family's temporary move, and enrolled in the University of Virginia in 1826. However, after only a year, he was forced to leave due to lack of funds, and he moved to Boston and enlisted in the army under the name Edgar A. Perry. It was then that his publishing career began with his poetry collection *Tamerlane and Other Poems*, published in 1827 and credited to an anonymous Bostonian.

Poe was promoted and eventually released from the army in 1829, after which he attended and thrived at West Point, until he once again fell short on funds and was dishonorably discharged. He continued to publish more poetry, and then ultimately found story publication as well via a variety of periodicals. After a stint as an assistant editor at a periodical in Richmond, Poe moved back to Baltimore, where he had been living with his widowed aunt, and married her daughter, Virginia Clemm, who was a young teenager at the time.

In 1842, Virginia began to show signs of tuberculosis, and in 1847, she succumbed to the disease. Two years later, in October, Poe was found delirious and close to unconsciousness in the streets of Baltimore. He died on October 7, 1849, without a certain cause of death.

Don't miss

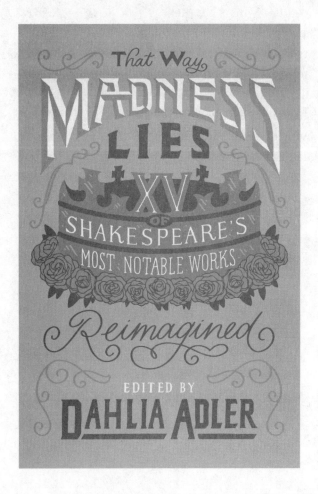

"From comedy to tragedy to sonnet, from texts to storms to prom,
this collection is a knockout."   —*BuzzFeed*

DAHLIA ADLER is an editor of mathematics by day, a book blogger by night, and a young adult author at every spare moment in between. She is the editor of the anthologies *His Hideous Heart* and *That Way Madness Lies* and the author of, most recently, *Cool for the Summer*. Dahlia lives in New York with her family and an obscene number of books.

www.dahliaadler.com

 @MissDahlELama